1624

The year everything changed. An alternate pirate story.

SAUL BEN

Copyright © 2022 Saul Ben

All rights reserved. No part of this publication may be reproduced, distributed, or transmitted in any form or by any means, without prior written permission.

This is a work of fiction. Names, characters, places, and incidents are a product of the author's imagination. Places and public names are sometimes used for atmospheric purposes. Any resemblance to anyone, living or dead, or to businesses, companies, events, institutions, or localities is completely coincidental.

ISBN: 9798362003739

To all those who have suffered under the Inquisition.
May you be revenged.

To Dawn Knox for her unstinting inspiration and advice and without whom writing this book would have been half as much fun.

1624

ONE — *that wasn't so bad*

A strand of smoke slunk skywards. Rows of fire-ravaged corpses hung in chains from charred stakes. The soldier's knees cracked as he stooped for a smouldering twig. Blowing, he kindled a tiny flame. He was in the act of lighting his pipe when the blackened figure looming above him stirred and gasped. The soldier leapt back, dropping his weapon. The clay pipe flew from his grasp and shattered on the flagstones. His shriek echoed off the surrounding buildings. He recovered his spontoon, if not his dignity, and ran the victim through. Piercing the flaking crust sent a cloud of ash drifting on the breeze, and foul-smelling liquid spurting from the wound. Mouth dry, voice cracking, the trembling soldier yelled to his mate across the square.

'Devil take them. It's hard work killing these bastards.'

Joseph Amsalem hobbled into the Jewish whorehouse. He ordered a fine bottle of Burgundy and the most expensive girl in the establishment. Replete with alcohol and spent of seed, he made his way home unsteadily through the dark rainy streets. Arriving at the less affluent end of Jodenbreestraat, he stood swaying for a moment fumbling for keys.

His young wife Rachael didn't look up from her embroidery. Her face fixed in her permanent scowl as he shambled past and shut himself in his study. His hands, crippled as they were, opened the razor with difficulty. He paused for a while staring at his lamplit reflection in the gleaming steel. Then he took a breath and drew the blade across his throat. It was his earnest intention to go from ear-to-ear; to do a thorough job like a shochet, a kosher slaughterer. But the razor jolted from his weak grasp when the blade bit into the hard cartilage of his trachea.

His last thoughts: 'Well, that wasn't so bad —'

Rachael was never an early riser. The servants took advantage. This day they had yet to clean the grates. Joseph's son Isaac left early, attending his uncle Abraham's yeshiva. It was Esther, Joseph's daughter, discovered him. His poor gentle face reflected in the glistening crimson surface of congealing blood, overspilling his desk and pooling on the floor. She reported to her stepmother that father was still sleeping. This lie shielded her young mind for the subsequent decade. Then one morning, aged fourteen, she woke screaming.

The protective plug of self-delusion had dissolved; the truth flooded in. If the fates had judged she was ready for this, they were wrong.

As time passed Esther outwardly absorbed the trauma. But it left an indelible scar in that secret place she allowed no one to penetrate. She grew into a strange child. Thinking wider and deeper than her peers. Obsessed with peering beneath the cloak of the least consequential of everyday events. She'd noticed people in general put inordinate store in 'truth.' Her stepmother clung to a narrow bourgeois consensus reality, as though to release her grip on bigotry would tempt a tide of free-thinking insanity. Not that her stepmother owned the monopoly on unquestioning acceptance of implausible truths. Esther despised closed-mindedness. Nothing, she concluded, was more elastic, malleable or deceptive than truth.

She even came to suspect it may not exist. Certainly not as an empirical, monolithic unchanging fact. Truth, in her young opinion, was simply an unreliable recollection, coloured with self-interest and wishful thinking. Nothing she asserted, to the horror of her religiously fixated elders, was absolute. The jot of a pen, or an unfounded rumour can upset the accepted version of reality or deny it entirely. That being so, why couldn't she change *her* truth? Why couldn't she rewrite the events of *her* past? Scrub out the blood-saturated visions haunting her sleep. The images bubbling up whenever her concentration drifted.

It surfaced in inconvenient ways. Awake, she couldn't bear to be in the presence of red. She's seen too much of the colour, every shade and tonal variation. Her father's face, eyes open, sightless staring at her across an endless plain of scarlet. Why couldn't she erase the horror carved so wickedly deep and so piteously early into her memory? Like words gouged into the bark of a living tree, her nightmares grew with each passing year. Less distinct, but incrementally larger.

Joseph, her suicide father, had been a prosperous spice trader in Lisbon. His wife was proud of this success, she took no steps to conceal his wealth — servants, carriages, houses. Not flaunting, she'd have protested, but hardly discrete either. The Inquisition arrived in the city.

1624

Envious competitors accused Joseph of being a *crypto* Jew. Plotting against Mother Church — the blood libel revisited.

The Amsalems were Jewish converts to Catholicism. They assiduously took the sacraments; supported the cathedral with lavish gifts. Nevertheless, they were *conversos*. As such Joseph fell under the authority of the Roman Church. Hauled before the Inquisition. Put to the question. Shoulders dislocated by strappado. Arms and fingers broken. Feet crushed. Water forced down his throat, belly bursting. He held out longer than most men. Finally, resistance collapsed in a delirium of agony. He admitted the sin of which he was innocent. Implicated his extended family. Gave up members of the converso community. He expected death. Indeed, earnestly prayed for the blessing of oblivion.

Without explanation they released him. Cast him into the street. A pariah now to Jew and Catholic alike. A few weeks earlier he'd been a respected member of Lisbon society. A generous employer, an honest trader, a confidante of the mighty. Now he was a shunned and penniless cripple. Small consolation, his agonising fortitude saved others. His wife Rachael had escaped from Portugal. She'd taken seven-year-old Isaac, Joseph's concubine Inga and her two-year-old daughter Esther. They travelled to Morocco and thence Amsterdam. With them, as much family wealth as they could liquidate at such short notice. But not all those who Joseph had implicated were so fortunate. Many close to him suffered the *Auto-da-Fé*, robbed and put to the flames.

Through the charity of a Muslim trading partner Joseph followed his family to the Protestant Low Countries. His older brother Abraham Amsalem had foreseen this calamity two decades earlier. He was a ship broker and merchant, a Rabbi and pillar of the thriving Sephardic *expulso* community. He hurried to the docks when word arrived his younger brother's ship was in the Zuyder Zee. As the broken and lonely figure of Joseph shambled down the gangplank, he wept.

Abraham found light work for him in his counting rooms. Joseph's body recovered to a limited degree, but his guilt-addled spirit seemed beyond redemption. Reuniting with his family brought brief but scant relief. Over the years his existence fell into a predictable, if aimless, pattern. A remote figure of awe to Isaac and Esther, but a lost cause to his increasingly razor-tongued wife. What little solace he found was with Inga, his Swedish concubine, Esther's birth mother. But cholera swept Amsterdam and Inga died nursing Abraham's infected wife. Robbed of Inga's support, Joseph fell into a dark morass of despair. Whatever money he earned he drank, gambled, or whored away. Perhaps seeking the oblivion, the Inquisition so cruelly denied him.

1624

When Joseph took his own life, Abraham shouldered the full burden of the family. Eventually, as was Jewish custom, he married his brother's widow. Rachael was young, still comely and twenty years his junior — this arrangement wasn't such an imposition. Accustomed to haranguing poor broken Joseph without consequence, Rachael soon learned no one raised their voice to her new husband. Thereafter the children bore the entire brunt of her caustic venting.

Abraham's marriage to his deceased wife had been childless. Within a year Rachael became pregnant, delivering Benjamin. Abraham determined Benjamin would follow him into the Rabbinate. But Benjamin, outwardly compliant, harboured a radically different ambition. The sea whispered to him in his sleep, as it had his notorious seafaring great grandfather. Isaac worked in his stepfather's shipyard, proving an able and imaginative administrator and something of a savant ship designer.

For all Esther's precocious rationality, the nightmares persisted. Esther the problem child. Stubborn. Spiteful. Uncompliant. Unmarriageable. Quite possibly mad — Isaac and Benjamin adored her; she could make them do anything. And she did.

1624

TWO — *the new Yerushaláyim*

Amsterdam's docks were as all docks are, noisy, confusing, and crowded, both on and off the water. Masts, like a vast forest blasted leafless, mediated restlessly between sky and sea. The air was dense with the everyday astringency of pitch and hemp, competing with pungent aromas leaking from rows of cheek-by-jowl warehouses — cinnamon, nutmeg, pepper, sumac, sandalwood.

Gaggles of Portuguese Jews were disembarking, in their strange Eastern robes. Shambling, shivering but joyous from ships newly arrived from sun-scorched Morocco. Relatives and friends greeted the few fortunate, dancing and jabbering in their mysterious Ladino tongue. For the first time in generations, they were free to reclaim their religious heritage. To practice the age-old religion of their ancestors. Some fell to their knees, kissing the dockside grime of this potential new *Yerusháláyim*. Others shuffled trancelike; their gait unsteady from weeks at sea. Protestants passed by, black-clad, white collared, straight-backed, doing their best to ignore this undignified, all too familiar spectacle.

Couple of loiterers, seafaring gents (or would be, should any quartermaster be foolish enough to sign them onboard his ship), were observing the scene from their perch on a stack of leaky herring barrels. They went by the names of Roelant and Rinus. Benjamin Amsalem sat with them. His concentration fixed on the fore topmasts of the vessels moored at the harbour wall. He had set himself a daunting task. Memorising each of what landsmen called ropes and what seamen called something else. Shifting backstays, standing backstays, breast backstays, shrouds. He sniggered, distracted by his shiftless companions' antics. Then he got on with the serious business of studying for his fantasy career. Outhaul, downhaul, tackline...

'Hope the Rabbi's sharpened his blade,' chuckled Roelant, the tall skinny rat-faced one. 'He's going to be in for a busy week.'

'How much d'ya reckon he charges?' said short fat 'Piggy' Rinus.

1624

'How should I know?'

'Just thinking. What about setting ourselves up in competition?'

Rinus looked to his companion, flashing his eyebrows and drawing a rusty seaman's knife from his boot.

'Hey friend,' he bawled at a new arrival, dragging his baggage down the crowded gangplank. The man turned, looking blank. 'Oi, you. Yes, you. D'you fancy a half-price circumcision?'

The man shrugged and continued his trudge to freedom.

'Not sure he understood you,' said Roelant.

'His loss. The offer won't last forever,' said his mate, replacing his boot knife.

Benjamin followed their inane banter with undisguised glee. Older men, acting like children. He was more accustomed to children acting like older men. He was a good-looking lad at that awkward age — half-boy, half-man. Gave the impression of poised for a growth spurt in both body and soul. Today he'd cut classes at the *yeshiva*, destined as he was for the life of a scholar, a rabbi. Potentially, his teachers declaimed, a great one. But his heart wasn't in books. The dockyard layabouts had adopted him. If not as one of them, as a curiosity, a mascot, allowing him to dip in and out of their simple slovenly world.

The studio was purposefully dark. Sunlight, which attempted entry through rippled multi-paned leaded windows, arrested by heavy brocade hangings. In the centre was an easel supporting a huge half-finished canvas. Completed paintings covered the walls and every other available surface. Stacks of them turned the tessellated floor into an obstacle course; the air was redolent with the pine-rich reek of turpentine and refined linseed oil.

Illumination came from a cluster of candles melted into a flickering, formless multi-flamed mass. Mirrors directed their warm glow towards an heroic tableau dominating the cramped space. A young woman, goose-pimpled, naked and undernourished, clutched a rusty sword. Before her, an oval shield offered a modicum of modesty. A male warrior-companion, sporting a skimpy stained loincloth, was positioned behind her, spear in hand, from which depended an elaborately embroidered banner. In the corner a lamb nibbled contentedly on a bale of hay. An allegory today — a feast come Sunday. Gerrit Dou, the great master's pupil was pacing, absently cleaning brushes with an old rag, fiddling with his cuticles, chewing the occasional fingernail. Every so often he parted the drapes, squinting out impatiently into the crowded street. There was the unmistakable sound of a fart, in the higher register.

The female model reddened, soundlessly giggling; the male tutted and shook his head; the painter hesitated momentarily and continued his agitated pacing.

The door burst open flooding the room with light, and the stench of effluent-clogged canals. Benjamin staggered in, weighed down by an armful of awkwardly shaped packages. He grunted, unloading his burden on a long paint-smeared trestle table. Gerrit's little white dog followed him in. It ambled over to the lamb, sniffing its arse suspiciously.

'Shut that bloody door,' yelled the woman, dropping her shield with a clatter and reaching for a shawl.

Benjamin ignored her, addressing himself to the painter. 'Think I've got everything Gerrit. But v-van Velde wasn't happy. Says he n-needs his account s-settled.'

'Trust you told him to sod right off.' Dou sniffed and pointed to the gap in his composition. 'Now shut up and take your place you little tyke whilst I immortalise your grubby *Jood* soul.'

'And I'll want p-paying too,' said Benjamin. He shrugged off his doublet and breeches to resume his pose at the feet of the shivering woman. 'I'm s-serious Gerrit,' he said, sternly creasing his brow.

'Little turd,' said Gerrit. 'Lucky, I don't charge you for the pleasure of gawping at Francine's tits.'

Too late. The damage had been done. The other two models turned to the artist-in-training, hands out. Gerrit reached for his purse without taking his fierce gaze off Benjamin.

'Now see what you've started?'

Benjamin climbed the creaking stairs to a room on the third floor of the 'Monkey House,' a lively hostelry cum brothel.

Retired Captain Hannes Terbrugghen was snoozing in a chair by a cobwebbed window. Small bubbles of saliva inflated and deflated at the corners of his stubble circumscribed lips. Jerking awake at the sound of Benjamin's knock, he stared wildly about his chamber like a victim of abduction. Recovering, he donned his threadbare horsehair wig, then adjusted its angle in the small area of mirror which still retained its silvering. Shuffling to the door in a cloud of chalk dust, he straightened himself painfully. He rolled his neck, bones popping, before peering through a crack in the door.

'Ah, it's you.'

'Who did you expect?'

Guiding Benjamin inside, he accepted a proffered bottle with the air of a Caesar receiving tribute from a subjugated nation.

'Now where were we up to young man?' said the captain, in a tone appropriately professorial. Milky, cataract-dimmed eyes scanned the wine. Tutting as though the vintage was beneath him, he shuffled into an adjoining room, returning with two grubby, green-tinged glasses.

'Astrolabe,' said Benjamin. 'And, and, and I've still s-some questions regarding the long staff and back s-staff, and taking soundings, and, and ...'

So today they were working their way through the arcane complexities of astral navigation. An essential qualification when Benjamin finally plucked up courage to announce to his Rabbi father his intention to make his way at sea. As the evening wore on, the level in the bottle diminished. They were down to dregs by the time the captain touched on the thorny issue of the traverse board. The session rounded off with an exercise based on the classic trigonometric conundrum, 'The Pyrate Question.'

'An honest merchant falls into the hands of pyrates. They dispossess him of the wherewithal to navigate. Escaping, the merchant sails away in a straight line. After two days he crosses paths with a man-of-war. What course should the man-of-war shape to intercept the pyrates?'

The old navigator had returned to his chair by the window. Unkind comparisons with a plucked crow floated through Benjamin's mind, as he struggled manfully to reconcile speed-over-ground, tidal drift and leeway.

His eyes began glazing, enough for one day. He passed his calculations over to the old captain, who gave them a cursory glance and sniffed. This being an improvement on his previous reaction, Benjamin took it as a minor victory. The wine had taken its toll on his instructor, his voice was slurring. Conversation deviated, as it invariably did, to his glory days. The light flickered back into his eyes. He was young again, dodging French corsairs, outfoxing marauding Barbary galleys, taking prizes. Living it large in the disreputable and dangerous pirate republic of Salé.

Benjamin's nightly dreams of seaborne adventures had lately overtopped the dykes of boyish fantasy; he was now deeply into the realms of planning. Proficiency at such sought-after skills was essential to his future as a sailor. Loathe as he was to admit it, never had the old navigator taught such an eager and accomplished pupil. Learning was serious business for Benjamin Amsalem — the yeshiva had taught him that much at least.

1624

This was always the period he enjoyed most, adding fuel to his secret high seas fantasies. Yes, he simply needed to await his chance. And when chance called, be certain he'd be ready. |He was the natural grandson of the Moroccan pirate Rabbi Samuel Pallache. So he knew it was possible to live two lives — the sacred and the profane. Leaving his family would be a wrench, especially his halfsiblings. But he'd be back, with riches, stories, and glory.

His teacher was barely awake when Benjamin said his good nights. On his way out of the dingy chamber he dropped the few gilders he'd prised from Gerrit Dou into the clutter of the captain's desk. Shutting the door quietly, he descended the shadowy footworn staircase, emerging into the brightness and noise and stink of the inn. Taking a breath, he braced himself, then began weaving his way through the dense crowd. Running the usual barroom gauntlet, he arrived at the exit suffering nothing worse than an arse pinch from the chattering whores.

On the way home to Jodenbreestraat in the gathering dusk he began practicing his lie. Old Rabbi Yossi kept him late studying scripture. Hadn't used that one for a while.

Outside the Churchyard, Amsterdam was awakening to its noisy, frenetic business. Benjamin's hands were sore; a blister was on the way. He let the long-handled scythe rest in the crook of his elbow and took a breath. His mouth was dry from chanting a navigation mnemonic.

'You first see Andromeda's belt rising in the sky, pursued by Cetus the Whale, followed by the ear of Aries the ram — da de da, de da ...'

The sweet smell of newly cut grass almost mitigated the stench drifting in from the streets. It wasn't particularly hot, but he was sweating. He loosened his garters and allowed his amber coloured hose to drop to his ancles. Had he done yet, was the grass short enough? The church door creaked. Captain Terbrugghen's son Erasmus, the unlikely District Pastor, materialised — darkness from darkness, squinting against the sunlight. He approached, navigating a passage between memorial stones as crooked as his old father's teeth. Benjamin's palms tingled. Was his first combat lesson about to commence? Was this ruddy-faced preacher really the most apt of tutors?

'So, young man,' said the Pastor, 'My father tells me he's never had such an able student. Astral navigation, eh.'

Benjamin glowed with pride. 'The captain is an excellent teacher,' he said. But then his morning took a turn for the unexpected.

'Tell me, are you a righteous man?' said the Pastor.

1624

Benjamin was unsure how he should respond. Buying thinking time, he carefully leant the scythe against a much-eroded gravestone. Not waiting for an answer, the Pastor took his elbow and led him into the shade of an old apple tree. In its dappled shadow was a wooden bench on which a haphazard collection of edged weapons glinted in the watery sunlight. Benjamin was immediately entranced. Was it the artistry of form and decoration that snagged his imagination? Or was it the sheer variety of implements by which man could do lethal injury to his fellow? We had come a long way from the jawbone of an ass. A quiet voice, from that small part of him yet unaffected by this steely glamour, questioned this assumption.

'Is that true?' the Pastor insisted, his sharp tone jolting Benjamin back to the moment.

'S-sorry. Don't understand Pastor.'

'You being a fellow man of God, albeit in training, perhaps you think it goes without saying.'

Benjamin looked blank. 'Goes without saying?'

'Let me put it another way,' said the Pastor. 'Would you kill a man for a shilling? Would you cut a man's throat for the joy of watching his lifeblood splash at your feet? Would you rape women and children at the point of a sword merely for the pleasure of getting your dick wet?'

Benjamin's jaw dropped — *children?*

'Well, would you?' insisted the Pastor, slipping off his long black clerical coat.

'No. Certainly not. And I observe the other three-hundred and t-twelve mitzvot as well as I c-can,' he said indignantly. He reddened. How pompous, how naive that outburst must have sounded.

'Detail,' said the Pastor, dismissively. 'Far as I'm concerned, they all lead back to a single principle — "Don't do to others what is hateful to you".'

He rolled up his right shirtsleeve revealing a forearm stringy and knotted as an old ships hawser. Grasping the shagreen hilt of a basket-hilted rapier, he casually flicked off its crisp leather scabbard.

'You're facing a fellow and for whatever reason he's got it in his head to murder you.' He twirled the glittering blade with a surprisingly supple wrist. 'It's you or him. Right?'

The Pastor struck the pose of a practiced duelist, at odds with his austere clerical persona.

'Yes, I s-suppose.'

'Wrong.' The pastor's auger eyes drilled into him. 'Haven't we just established you're a righteous man? This person poised to launch an attack on you is intent on taking your life. By this action we know he is not a righteous man. So, now it's not just you and he involved in this life-or-death contest. Numerous other lives are at stake. You must consider all those he'll go on to kill and maim and riddle with the pox if you allow him to overcome you.

'Reach out with your mind. Feel his past and future victims jostling around you, whispering encouragement in your ear. Lending strength to your arm, courage to your heart. Rid the world of this devil and you cut off his branch of evil forever. Do this and you'll be redeeming countless unseen innocent souls. Those born and those yet to be born. And those who may never be born if you allow this miscreant to slaughter you. Overcome him, and the heavens will ring with your praise.'

Benjamin stood; mouth open, unsure how he should react. Receiving no response the Pastor's blade flashed, snicking the boy's cheek with the tip. He ignored Benjamin's yelp, looming over him, locking eyes with the boy. His voice rumbled like distant thunder. 'I want this lesson driven so deep you'll never need to think of it again. Never question your actions — never, ever hesitate. To hesitate is to invite your destruction.'

A trickle of blood ran down Benjamin's face. Pastor Terbrugghen handed him a kerchief. He sniffed and looked away, scanning the rooftops of the city, the tips of the masts in the harbour beyond.

'May that be your worst wound,' he said, guiding the trembling Benjamin back to the array of exotic weapons. 'So, on board ship, this thing's no use.' He tossed the rapier aside. 'Gentleman's sword. Facing a single opponent, the exaggerated length can provide a decisive advantage. But get closer, get beyond that sharp point. And it's not difficult. I'll be showing you how later. The length of the thing becomes its weakness.

'On a ship. Boarding or boarded. Enemy will be at you from every quarter. You'll be engaging two, three at a time. Can't prance around sticking folk with a long darning needle. One crack with something solid, the blade'll shatter. Wave it around on a crowded deck, it's bound to snag on something. Then where'll you be?' He picked up a simple, short-bladed sword. 'Cleaved in half with one of these. That's where you'll be.'

'Did you sail with y-your father?' said Benjamin, seeking relief from this gore-soaked sermon.

'Sorry?'

'Your father, Captain Hannes, did you sail with him?'

'Yes, old bastard. Many years. What the hell d'you think drove me to the church?' He chuckled, briefly.

He noticed Benjamin's eyes straying to the assorted weapons.

'So, over here we have the dussack, what you'd think of as a classic naval weapon. Hand well protected by a steel basket and a scallop guard. Not so long, nice and manageable but heavy. And here we have the falchion, lighter, big pommel, better balanced. But limited hand protection. With your build, I'd be looking on the lighter side ideally. Something fast and manoeuvrable.'

'Pastor, have you s-s-sailed on the Rabbi's ships?'

'Sorry?' His student's deviations from his didactic theme were clearly beginning to irritate.

'Served on any of m-m-my father's ships?'

'Occasionally. Didn't know they were his at the time. Far as North Africa. Mediterranean. Most of my travelling's been with United East India Company ships. Round the Cape. Malacca, Batavia, Ambolina, Guinea. Trading spices and rare timber...'

Benjamin's inner picture gallery spontaneously activated at these glamorous place names. Images of the Orient, or what he imagined 'the Orient' to be, flooded his mind, augmented by the misinformed and sexually charged exaggerations of his itinerant dock mates. Vast bejewelled palaces cast their shadows over him. Pleasure domes of all-powerful Emperors and Moguls and Khans. Beautiful bare-breasted women — full, pert, hollow-backed and flesh-arsed — overlaid his vision. Variants of Francine but painted in a more colourful pallet on less troubled dermis. Whole harems of satin-skinned sirens crowded in. The heady aroma of sandalwood, ambergris, and musk. Fantastical beasts of myth and legend competed unsuccessfully for his attention. Man apes and sea serpents, unicorn, giraffe, elephant, and rhinoceros. But nothing overrode his vision of a pigeon egg ruby, mounted in the fragrant navel of a Persian princess.

The Pastor, noticing his absence, clapped him on the back. Benjamin's fantasies reluctantly dissipated. Visions, like sea mist, swirled back into the nether regions of his mind. He shuddered, taking a deep breath, the sour smell and jangle of the city signalling his return to everyday reality. Once more his life stretched before him in all its monotonal, bourgeois predictability. Was his restless soul truly doomed to hover over dusty worn-out texts, in shadowy seats of learning? The Lord's words were all very well. But what's so wrong with yearning to experience the Lord's works as well?

'You can have too much of that world, you know.' It was as though the Pastor had accessed his inner thoughts. 'No matter how many horizons you cross, you still have to come home to this.' He tapped his temple with a stubby index finger, releasing a long sigh. He shivered — dispelling their shared vision like a dog shaking off water.

He pointed to a range of unfamiliar blades.

'That's where these originate. This one's from Sarawak. Primitive warriors, no bigger than half-grown girls. Head-hunters. Grass huts. Yet they produce the sharpest blades on Earth. Mystery how they work the steel. Edge bevelled one side only, hollow ground like a razor. That handle's a human thighbone. And, yes,' he ran the long black pommel-tassel through his fingers, 'this is the scalp of an enemy. And these little tools tucked in the scabbard are for scooping out the brains of their "trophies."

'Now that double-edged wavy piece over there, that's a Moro Keris, picked it up trading *nootmusckaat*, nutmeg. Wicked weapon. Balance may not suit you though. Doesn't suit many Europeans. And this is a Javanese version, made from iron folded with layers of meteoric nickel. Magical weapons. Said to warn the owner of an approaching enemy by rattling in their scabbards. Wear them at their backs, tucked in a sash. See the way the blade has eroded with cleaning, could be a thousand years old. Not very sturdy, but you wouldn't want one between your ribs.'

He took hold of a crude axe. Rust-pitted blade one side, spike the other. There was a blur of movement. Benjamin started as the weapon whistled over his shoulder. It embedded in the trunk of an apple tree, shaking down the last of the crop. Retrieving the weapon, the Pastor stooped for a rosy apple, tossing it to Benjamin.

'Now these handy little fellows may suit you,' the Pastor offered the axe shaft to Benjamin. The boy hefted it, the smooth age-darkened wood felt good in his hand. Taking a couple of experimental swings, he stumbled as the weight pulled him off balance. The Pastor tutted, releasing a theatrical sigh of despair.

'You could do worse than carrying a pair of these,' said the Pastor. 'Hand-to-hand combat at sea invariably takes the form of a melee. No room for subtlety. Pair of boarding axes are as good as anything. Some of us must learn our lessons the hard way,' he held up the stump which once extended to his left hand, smiling wryly.

'Don't swing wildly. You'll open yourself to a counter. Now, come on, try to attack me ...'

Deflecting Benjamin's axe hand, he thumped him hard under the armpit, causing him to cough up a chunk of apple. 'Close quarters hold the axe right up by the head, punch like a prize-fighter. For now let's begin with the classics — dussack and parrying dagger.

Benjamin took up the weapons indicated. 'Now strike at me,' said the Pastor. 'Go on, like you mean it this time. Like your very life depended on it.'

His student loosed a looping swing with the short stout sword. The Pastor sidestepped, easily evading. Benjamin staggered a couple of steps, colliding painfully with a gravestone.

'No, look you've over balanced, don't commit so, always think ahead to your next move, and the one after that. Now try again my *kleine piratenkapitein...*'

On the third month after this first lesson the Pastor said: 'I'm going away. Preaching to the poor benighted heathen in North Africa. You won't see me for a while.'

Months later he returned with more items of exotic weaponry, a deep tan, and a few more scars. And thus the pattern of their relationship became established. Intensive training, followed by prolonged absences, coinciding, strangely, with those of Benjamin's father.

1624

THREE — *the shadchanit*

A maid had slept in Esther's room since the nightmares began. Mother sent her Fat Mariss. She wanted Pretty Neeltje. So Fat Mariss took a tumble down the stairs and Esther got pretty Neeltje, after all. It had been two years now. The arrangement had begun with Neeltje sleeping on a straw mattress in a draughty corner of the room. It didn't remain that way. They became close. Shared secrets. Shared beds. Shared bodies. Like sisters, incestuous sisters. They even had their own maid. A maid with a maid, what a thing.

'So, is it just girls you like kissing?'

Neeltje brushed Esther's lips with her own, pulling away teasingly as her young mistress reached for her.

'I don't know, I've only ever kissed you.' Esther's eyes fluttered shut. She sighed and then said: 'What's it like with your boyfriend?'

'Different.'

'How?'

'Want to find out?'

The Rabbi was at his shipbroking business, doing whatever shipbrokers do. Her stepmother, the Rebbetzin, was chairing a Jewish women's meeting, doing whatever chairpersons do. The servants were in their attic quarters, asleep or drunk on brandy provided by Neeltje. And Neeltje was whispering and chivvying her clumsy boyfriend up the back stairs. Esther waited in her chambers on the third floor, her heart doing a little dance.

Neeltje shoved the boy through the door. A big lad, dressed like a common trooper.

'Mistress, this is my Luuk,' Neeltje giggled.

There was a man in Esther's bed chamber. A stranger to her. This was the very definition of impropriety, regardless her maidservant was present. Her body tingled with excitement. She couldn't conceive of any plausible excuse were this liaison discovered. Her pulse raced; her cheeks flushed. She bit her lip until it bled. Sexual curiosity is a powerful thing. She offered wine. There were no chairs, she and Luuk sat on the bed, Neeltje on the floor looking up at them, face aglow, expectant. Luuk gulped his wine. Esther heard herself launch into a series of inconsequential ramblings. She interrogated him about the progress of the eternal war with the Spanish Empire. About the readiness of the regiment, his embryonic army career. His answers were monosyllabic, eyes rigidly fixed on her breasts. After a while they lapsed into a febrile silence. It was Neeltje took the initiative:

'Go on mistress, no harm.'

Esther hesitated. Clearly pleasure was the objective. But beyond that so wasn't sure what to do. Neeltje joined them on the bed, Luuk uneasy between them.

'Well go on Luuk, kiss my pretty mistress.' She nudged him. 'It's not like you to be shy.'

Esther blushed and submitted passively to Luuk's hesitant advances. When Luuk kissed her, she knew she'd been kissed. When Luuk touched her, she knew she'd been touched. When Neeltje kissed her worlds collided. When Neeltje touched her, she burst into flames.

Neeltje lifted her skirt, opening her legs for her boyfriend's caresses. Esther found herself ravaged by jealousy and throbbing with desire. But not for him. He was pretty enough with his lean, angular body, golden hair and blunt features.

Neeltje's hand disappeared into his breaches emerging clutching his fleshy member.

'Go on. Touch it mistress, it won't bite,' she giggled.

So, Esther did. Luuk gasped, his hips tensing at her cool touch. Neeltje took Esther's hand and together they worked him to climax. Those grunty breathy sounds, like an animal out of control. The sour leathery smell of his body, the tobacco-laden breath. His wispy goatee chafed her soft lips. Her mouth opened, allowing entry of his tongue. He spasmed, crushing her to him. The sudden effusion of hot pearlescent liquid both fascinated and disgusted her. She pushed him away, wiping her hand on the coverlet — a lesson well learnt.

That night Esther frigged Neeltje raw and sobbed herself to sleep. In the morning she woke, her head a rat's nest of confused and maldigested feelings. She raged incoherently at Neeltje and beat her. Not because Neeltje had done anything wrong. Just she couldn't release these unfamiliar and all-consuming emotions other than through violence. Neeltje defiantly provoked her to ever greater ferocity. Then they wept uncontrollably for the rest of the day. Confused servants whispered in

1624

the corridors. That evening they were alone again in the soft flickering candlelight. Esther coaxed poor bruised Neeltje back into her bed. She sobbed for Neeltje's forgiveness holding her desperately tight. When the first rays of dawn entered the room, her trembling finally subsided, and she drifted to sleep.

Esther was uneasy when Fat Mariss brought the message that her stepmother required her in the withdrawing room — her worse nightmare. And, sure enough, there was Frau Niedermeyer, the shadchanit, in full flow. Esther knew this day would come. Unease ossified into dread. Her stepmother nodded imperiously to a ladder-back chair. When Esther sat, the Rebbetzin returned her attention to the matchmaker.

'So, Frau Amsalem,' said Frau Niedermeyer, 'I understand Rabbi Abraham is your second husband?' Sipping tea, her gaze danced about the room's contents, like a pawnbroker valuing pledges.

'Yes, my first husband, Joseph Amsalem, may his name be for a blessing, passed away before his time.'

'Would it be indelicate to enquire as to what caused this sad event?'

'A haemorrhage, very sudden.'

'Terrible, terrible thing...'

'And your current husband, you met him how...?'

'He's my Joseph's elder brother, as is fit.'

'As is fit, of course.'

'Rabbi Abraham anticipated the troubles, removing his family to Amsterdam. My Joseph couldn't bear to leave everything we'd built, and we stayed on. Catholics, you know. The priests. Broke his hands, tore his arms. Tortured him for our every schelling. We ourselves barely escaped with our...'

A tear trickled down her face; Frau Niedermeyer, flapping her hands like she was drying tears, changed the subject.

'And aside from his Rabbinical duties I understand Rabbi Abraham is involved in commerce...?'

'That is true.'

'In what line of business, may I enquire?'

'Shipping.'

'Ah, what an enterprise. No wonder you have such a fine house. So many beautiful things. And you have just three children I'm led to believe?'

'Yes, my daughter,' she glanced at Esther, 'and two sons.'

'Boys, boys, such a mitzvah.'

'The oldest, Isaac, he's twenty-two, by my first husband Joseph. And Benjamin my youngest is just fourteen, from Rabbi Abraham.'

'Now the girl...?'

'Esther?'

'Yes, Esther. She's from your first husband or your second?'

'My first.'

'And how many years has she seen?'

'Nineteen.'

'Wonderful age. But we must face it, a little late for marriage.'

Frau Niedermeyer rotated her plump body towards Esther as though her neck wasn't capable of articulation. She squinted with misaligned eyes giving the impression she didn't entirely approve of what she saw. Esther shuddered, visualising this crone inspecting her maidenhead. Did they do that?

'And so this is young Esther? Such a pretty thing. A little on the tall side, maybe? But fair hair, blue eyes, daughter of a Rabbi. A generous dowry, I presume. Yes, of course. Goes without saying. Allow me a month. I'll have suiters queuing down the street, see if I don't.

'Now let's talk about the boys...? Why don't we begin with your Isaac. Why isn't he married yet? He should be busy giving you lots of grandchildren.'

As events unfolded the avaricious Frau Niedermeyer was in for a disappointment. Rabbi Abraham had plans for Esther which didn't involve the expense of a shadchanit. And, unbeknownst to both parties, Esther was making plans for herself. And they didn't involve either the offices of Frau Niedermeyer or the Rabbi.

Surprisingly, especially to her, Esther had become involved with another soldier. The brother of her only friend outside the insular Jewish community. Noémie was a Huguenot girl of the aristocratic Delacherois family. They had fled France, escaping the terrors of the St. Bartholomew's Day massacre. Her father had profitably backed several of the Rabbi's shipping enterprises and, although not coreligionists, they had become close friends.

Noémie was the only person outside the family who knew the secret of her fair complexion. Who knew her mother had been a freed Swedish slave and her natural father's concubine. And that she'd died when Esther was only two, nursing the Rabbi's first wife in the cholera epidemic. In Jewish tradition Esther was of equal status to her siblings.

1624

But to circumvent Dutch Calvinist bigotry the Rabbi's wife was nominally accepted as Esther's mother.

Marc-René Delacherois was a junior officer, a cornet in a distinguished cavalry regiment. Eight years her senior he was confident, sophisticated and refined of movement and feature, almost feminine. Very much the opposite of Luuk. As this clandestine relationship deepened, poor Neeltje went from bed mate to go-between.

Esther was recovering from Frau Niedermeyer's visit when, to her abject horror, the Rabbi announced he'd found her an excellent match. The recently widowed son of a business partner. A pinched little fellow, at least twice her age. Faced with this drear prospect Esther took drastic action. Her Huguenot suitor's unit was deploying to relieve the besieged city fortress of Breda. She determined to run away with him to join his regiment.

She kissed Neeltje's forehead as she slept. At her bedside she left a beaded purse containing twenty guilders, an affectionate note and instructions.

At six a.m. the Rabbi left for their makeshift synagogue for morning prayers. Her mother and the rest of the household were yet to stir. Marc-René stood in the service alley outside the servants' entrance leading two horses. He helped Esther mount and together they rode through the awakening city thoroughfares.

The Haarlem gatehouse echoed to the clatter of their horse's hooves as they passed under its tower. Early though it was, the drawbridge was already down. Once through they picked up pace, trotting down the long causeway crossing the moat. Esther released a loud whoop, urging her mount to a wild canter. Turf flying from its hooves, city to her back, she raced into the breaking dawn. Taken by surprise, Marc-René spurred his horse to catch up, held back by their pack horse.

1624

FOUR — *no one need know*

Massive timbers curved skywards like the ribs of some vast leviathan cast up on a beach — carcass picked clean by scavenging birds. Vessels in various stages of completion ranged as far as the eye could see. A swarming army of craftsmen laboured over their genesis. Shaping, bending, hammering. Torturing trees into shape and utility other than the Creator had intended.

Great windmill-powered sawblades hissed through fragrant oak logs. Forges blazed like the nightmare mindscapes of mad Jheronimus van Aken. Scrawny apprentices sweated over bellows. Blacksmiths with the ardent expressions of murderers hammered the scale from huge iron fittings.

Directing this extravagant industrial theatre was Isaac Amsalem, ancle deep in wood shavings. His stepfather's latest commission, the Rachael was taking final shape. With a fair wind in a month or so she'd be ready for launching. Providing shelter for his long workbench was a retired ship's mainsail, flapping as though restless to return to its former employment.

Benjamin peered into Isaac's world. The drizzle disguising his tears. His older brother was employing huge bronze dividers over a set of ship's plans, concentrating fiercely. An oasis of calm amidst choreographed mayhem. Isaac seemed unaware of his brother at first. But then he heard the words:

'Esther's gone missing.'

Isaac pinned Neeltje against the wall, red marks on her cheeks, blood on her lips. Her eyes darted about the shabby attic room. Anywhere but meet his fierce gaze.

'You can tell me. I won't let on it came from you.' His tone softer now. Tears streamed down the girl's cheeks. Her tiny hand squeezed into her bodice, emerging with a creased envelope.

'Miss Esther made me promise to leave this for the mistress to find tomorrow,' she sobbed.

Isaac broke the seal, reading with growing incredulity. His sister had eloped with a cavalry officer. How the hell was he going to break this to mother? Perhaps he wouldn't bother.

Neeltje retreated to the opposite side of the bed. She cowered as he approached. But he'd got what he came for. No need for spite. He took a handful of coins, slipping them into her pinafore pocket and kissing the top of her head. She backhanded the blood from her lip with a sniff and a shy smile. Isaac wondered why he hadn't noticed before, Neeltje wasn't unattractive.

'There, there, Neeltje, your secret's safe with me. No one need know.'

The Amsalem household was in turmoil. The Rebbetzin paced the checkerboard scullery floor. Keeping herself busy, she said. Poor her. More likely this location provided the heaviest concentration of servants to berate, and time-honoured procedures with which to interfere.

Her eyes, her finest feature, were red and swollen, her cheeks tear streaked. Her black mourning dress was rent ragged at the neck. Mirrors throughout the house wore black shrouds. The Rabbi, consumed with rage and hurt, pronounced his adoptive daughter dead. Declared he would sit shiva for her ungrateful soul. The Rebbetzin had begged him not to announce it from the bimah. What would people say? And how should she respond? Such shame. Too much shame in one lifetime. First Joseph and now this.

The cook was glowering at her mistress from the shadows. Hissing contradictory instructions to the scullery maids. The Rebbetzin pronounced herself unhappy at the organisation of the kitchens. The shelves could be cleaner. The cutlery should shine brighter. Raging, smashing plates she declared inadequately washed. Biting her nails to the quick. Chewing her lip. A picture of madness. Meat might spoil, bread might burn, cream might curdle. The Rabbi might fall into one of his rages. Stony-faced, the cook removed her apron, good cooks were in demand, she didn't need this.

Into this steam-filled vortex of misdirected recrimination stumbled Isaac. All eyes save the Rebbetzin's turned to him. Maybe he'd prove the lightning rod for their mistress's ire. He froze, taking in the scene. Then, erring on the side of discretion, began to back away. The Rebbetzin spun round. Her eyes impaling him like an entomological specimen. Isaac braced himself for the now customary torrent of abuse. And she didn't disappoint.

'Ever since your father, may his name be for a curse...'

He let her run on. Heard it all before. Her nerves. Shredded. Can't cope. An endless list of woes. The mountain of blame heaped on his dead, defenceless father. How her children took after him. Feckless, indolent dreamers. Esther may be the cause, but at that moment Joseph became the prime focus of her bitterness.

'Esther has been difficult ever since...'

When she got like this, communication was wasted effort. She was simply making sounds. It was almost coincidental they formed words. Benjamin appeared in the doorway, partially obscured by Isaac. He had yet to develop his brother's reticence. Maybe never would.

'And my father,' he said, 'forcing Esther to marry that straggle bearded idiot. That, of course, has no bearing on this situation.'

'Respect,' shrieked the Rebbetzin, 'have some respect. If it hadn't been for the Rabbi, we'd all be in the poor house. And you, you little wretch, wouldn't even have been born...'

Benjamin shrugged. Yes, thanks so much for the biology lesson. He carried on down the corridor, he'd also heard it all before. Isaac shook his head, watching him go. Another of his mother's evergreen favourites. Saved from penury by the Rabbi discharging his fraternal duty. The man was far from a saint. He could be as bigoted and inflexible as the Catholics they'd escaped. Give him his due though, he was big on rebuking, but he'd yet to torture anyone, let alone burn them.

His natural father, the 'haemorrhage' sufferer, may his name be for a euphemism, always re-entered the picture when mother was stressed. So easy to blame. The deceased weren't there to defend themselves. Not that Joseph would have bothered. In life forgiveness had eluded him. Slim chance he'd find it in death. But he'd seen it as a chance worth taking. Isaac earnestly hoped his father had found peace. Hoped, but by no means confident.

The Rabbi had recently returned from abroad. One of his periodic diplomatic missions. Sponsored by the Office of the Stadtholder, he would frequently travel to the Iberian peninsula to ransom Dutch subjects, and *conversos* or *moriscos* from the Spanish and Portuguese Authorities. As was usually the case, he looked tired and somewhat battered. Were the circumstances more normal, he would take time off from Rabbinical and business duties to recover his strength.

But circumstances were far from normal.

1624

FIVE — *oyl of man*

Marc-René and Esther cantered through the crisp frosty morning, their horses' breath billowing before them. Each rider inhabiting crazy new worlds, effervescing with romance and adventure. He was bubbling with excitement at the prospect of joining the regiment and potentially engaging the Catholic foe. And she at escaping her bottled-up existence in that monolithic house on Jodenbreestraat. Certainly, neither were unhappy to be leaving the city. The stench from rubbish-clogged canals, excrement littering the crowded streets. And were another incentive required, there were rumours the plague was returning.

The Jewish community had a low incidence of disease. Christians often accused them of enjoying satanic protection. Marc-René had once questioned Esther as to their secret.

'Simple,' she'd said, 'We don't eat *traif.* We don't mix with Christians, and we wash.'

A slim patchwork of fields took the eye to a low horizon broken only by the occasional windmill. The heavens dominated these flatlands. Esther's attention fixed on the sky and the mountainous clouds piled high above them. Shafts of low sunlight teased the earth beneath. Small wonder the population was so righteous. Compared with such grandeur humanity appeared embarrassingly sordid and inconsequential.

As for her family, her stepfather would calm down eventually. And her stepmother, how could things have got worse between them? She was confident this parting from her brothers wouldn't be for long.

On the fifth night of their journey the couple lodged at the Magpie Inn. At supper they sat in a crowded hall at a table constructed of repurposed oak casks. Esther stood out from the other female clientele. Strikingly tall, blond, feminine, elegantly costumed. That, and her breasts were covered. In the harsh lamplight the difference in their ages appeared more marked. Marc-René's fashionable goatee beard and high-cheekboned, aristocratic demeanour reinforced the impression. As usual he wore the heavy buff leather jerkin and gorget of a junior cavalry officer. His big downturned riding boots jangling as he walked. Within easy reach, his basket-hilted sword rested against the wall. His cuirass was under the table with the precious baggage they dare not leave in their insecure room.

A whole roast chicken graced their table. Beside it an earthenware flagon and thick green wine glasses. Marc-René relished the novelty of these earthy, proletarian surroundings, despite his privileged background. Esther, with an equally comfortable upbringing, had a contrary impression. Marc-René attacked the fowl with gusto. Honest, wholesome, unpretentious, he declared. Esther refrained from comment, contenting herself with wine and dry bread.

She studied the fast-diminishing carcass as would an anatomist. Fascinated by the bone structure, the musculature, the connective tissue. But as for eating it? Famished though she was, nothing could be further from her mind. Her companion didn't appear to notice her lack of appetite. Perhaps caught up with the romance of their situation. Esther frowned, feeling her enthusiasm curdling to regret. But shuddering she remembered the stinking streets, suffocating parents, forced betrothal, and her resolve hardened.

In the far corner some musicians began plying their cacophonous trade. There was a one-legged ex-soldier wheezing life into a set of patched bagpipes. A blind Methuselah grinding a hurdy-gurdy. A dwarf mercilessly torturing a two-string fiddle. A walleyed imbecile beating out the rhythm on a three-legged stool. And a woman of faded glamour belting out the verses and exhorting the room to join in the chorus.

Each age grows riper, love does still prevail
And maidenheads at sixteen now are stale
Young Girls to Mothers will be turn'd e'er they
Knows what it means, slie Cupid does betray
Fires them with love, and then there's nothing can
Cure their distemper, unless oyl of man.

'Come on, everybody...'

Cure their distemper, unless oyl of man.
Cure their distemper, unless oyl of —

The inn was at capacity, perhaps beyond capacity. Sappy wood crackled and spat in a hearth tall enough for a man to stand within, and some did. The military were the main source of trade that night. In the corner a big drum emblazoned with regimental insignia perched atop a stack of armour. Hard by, a stand of spontoons and muskets stood like drunks providing their mates with mutual support.

Soldiers and camp followers exemplified every classic stage of inebriation. The hugger, the shover, the blind totterer. Raucous they were at their cards and their backgammon. Drinking, eating, smoking, petting their hired women. Whores of every age, shape, size and gender were hard at work plying their insanitary trade. Taking men upstairs, or to the stables, or doing them at the table, dependent on purse or preference.

Some of the more far-gone patrons snored, curled on benches, or in the arms of their ladies of easy virtue. Others collapsed on the dirt floor amidst oyster shells, broken clay pipes and horse dung. Dogs hunted scraps. Children sold flowers. Paupers begged coin. The landlord's wife and daughter took orders on chalk boards strung round their necks. Chicken stew, dumplings, smoked eel and flatfish emerged from the kitchen. Wine, beer, and gin came in battered pewter jugs.

Esther slipped outside to relieve herself. The night was bitterly cold. But it was good to be in fresh air. And away from all those people, the stench of their bodies, the relentless noise. A slim crescent moon afforded scant light as she sought a place of privacy. Eyeing the shadows warily, she lifted her skirt and crouched by a stand of trees set back from the roadway. Her piss steamed as it drained away from her on the frosty soil. A rat scampered up and hovered on her foot, sniffing the air, attracted by the unfamiliar aroma. She stifled a yell, in no haste to draw attention to her position.

Once back inside, she shivered (with the cold and something else). This place may be hell on earth but at least the devil kept a warm house. On the way back to Marc-René she paused before a roaring fire and rubbed her hands. By the time she re-joined him he'd finished his food and pushed his plate away. A mongrel terrier mutt and a lop-eared spaniel sidled up and begged at their table. Marc-René tossed them the hen's carcass, laughing as they fought over it. Then lost a wager with the next table when the little Spaniel was victorious. Esther viewed the scene as through the eyes of a stranger. Was this to be her future? To fight for scraps whilst drunkards bet on the outcome.

1624

The evening arrived at that point when petty squabbles escalated into full-blown vendettas. Although not taken with drink Esther too was in a belligerent mood. Marc-René yelled for another bottle of wine.

'So, how much will you have to fork out tonight,' she said. 'Keep on drinking like this and we'll have no money left.'

Her eyes swept the room. Was that resignation or desperation in her voice? A reveller brushed past their table and emptied his bladder into the fireplace. A cloud of foul-smelling steam billowed up. A howl of jovial disapproval went about the room. The perpetrator turned smiling with an expression of mock innocence. Esther glared. Marc-René seemed not to notice the tang of ammonia in the air.

'I've two month's pay coming. Get it soon as I catch up with the lads, find the quartermaster.' He stretched as he spoke, like a man beset by tedious detail, like the topic of money was beneath him. 'Until then...? Well, let's just get there quickly shall we?'

'Can't your father...?' said Esther, hating herself for bringing this up. But one of them had to be practical.

'What, help us? Can hardly expect that. What with me running off with a...'

He reached across smiling his handsome smile. Patted her pale cheek with a slim, chicken grease hand. He didn't say Jewess — he didn't have to.

'...with you,' he finished.

She looked away.

'What about the Rabbi then?' he countered.

She couldn't resist. 'Hardly, what with me running away with a...?'

The door burst open. A captain of cavalry barged his way through the crowd. Big man with a pronounced belly and a swaggering gait. Ruddy faced, goatee bearded, flamboyantly and expensively dressed. Ordering beer and gin, he enquired of the landlord as to the availability of whores. He was disappointed to discover all were currently engaged. Then he caught sight of the golden-haired Esther sitting with a lowly Cornet. He blundered his way to their table. Taking hold of her arm, he yanked her to her feet.

'Won't mind if I jump her first old chap.' He tossed a few guilders before Marc-René, 'that be enough for the trollop?'

Marc-René's response was immediate. He jumped up and knocked the brute to the ground with a looping hook. Rising red-faced and bloody nosed, the captain scrambled to unsheathe his sword. The quick-thinking landlord threw himself between them.

The ensuing commotion drew the attention of other officers, who attempted to mediate. Regardless she was the subject of the quarrel, Esther found herself side-lined. There followed an argument amongst the growing crowd of bystanders as to who was the injured party. Was it the man who had insulted the woman, or the man who had assaulted the man who had insulted the woman.

Either way, neither party was prepared to apologise. The debate drifted onto which of them had choice of weapons. But then someone pointed out that the matter was academic. It was raining outside. No one was in a hurry to get wet, and in any event the damp would make pistols problematic. That they'd finally agree on swords was inevitable. Esther pushed through the crowd, gasping when she discovered arrangements for a duel were under discussion. And it was more for the patrons' entertainment, she suspected, than any scrupulous dedication to her honour. This was a journey of discovery indeed. Why wasn't her heart in her mouth, why wasn't she hysterical? As with the onlookers, was she simply seeking a break from monotony. Like, something's happening. It's not good. But something's happening. And that's good.

What followed was typical of these affairs she learned. The challenge offered and accepted. Now all was depersonalised ritual. Not that heat went out of it, but there were rules, a code, procedures. It was no longer a sordid scrap in a grubby drinking house over a boorish insult to a woman. Etiquette elevated the dispute to heroic status. Esther might have been Helen of Troy, the combatants Hector and Achilles.

As to when? Why wait till morning. As to where? The stables had ample room. Floor space, ceiling height, all good. As to weapons? Marc-René would have preferred a small-sword. His fencing instructor had trained him with an épée. Something light, agile suited to his athleticism and build. A heavy mortuary-hilted straight-bladed cavalry sword was so clumsy. Well balanced, no question. But designed for use in the saddle, for reach and durability. Certainly not suited to fine exhibitions of swordsmanship.

Marc-René selected one of the least inebriated, hopefully non-partisan soldiers as his second. Both combatants surrendered their gorgets and submitted to searches for other items of armour. Despite the cold Marc-René stripped down to his shirt. The captain, embarrassed by his paunch, retained his doublet.

'No point in butchering a fellow and dying of the ague,' he quipped.

The captain was by far the larger man, heavily set, muscular under all that flab. The weight of these heavy military swords imparted him an immediate advantage. And judging from his age and his scars, he was more experienced in these matters than his opponent. Strength, yes. But stamina? We'd see.

The horses were restless in their stalls. More lanterns were lit, shadows retreated.

A grizzled and grey-bearded cavalier officiated, ritualistically intoning the obligatory plea for reconciliation. His tone leaving the strong impression he'd be disappointed if they were. Looking from one to the other, their expressions told him all he needed to know. There being no physician he doused a kerchief in gin and carefully wiped the length of their blades. Each took a pace back. And it began.

The captain proved to have the aggression and raw power of a hippopotamus, but none of its fabled grace. First blood went to Marc-René with a darting jab to the forearm. The captain flinched yet kept pressing forwards. And this proved to be the pattern of the confrontation. Marc-René backing away, jabbing at targets of opportunity with surgical precision. His opponent pressing forward with wild slashing cuts. Three more times Marc-René connected. Tiny punctures, never quite finding the opportunity for a decisive thrust.

One connecting cut from the captain could end this matter in a spectacular bloodbath. Marc-René remembered the surgeon's maxim. Eighty percent of thrusts prove fatal; eighty percent of cuts prove survivable. But, given the weight of these blades, little comfort there.

Finally, the captain's persistence bore fruit and his weapon connected. Marc-René's blouse parted. His chest unfolded like a scarlet curtain as he stumbled backwards The captain charged on, pressing the advantage.

Marc-René clutched his chest with his free arm. Stepping back, he successfully countered. The now over-confident Captain received a stinging peck on the wrist, deeper this time, spouting scarlet. Marc-René drew back his shoulders and took a breath, pressing on despite the pain and loss of blood. He rolled his head, eyeing his panting opponent defiantly. He'd have to do better than that.

The Captain caught his breath and rushed again. Marc-René changed tactics. Instead of backing off, he stepped forward and met his opponent halfway. Their swords clashed and locked at the cross-guard. They stood eyeball-to-eyeball, panting, the blades now pressing into their cheeks. Marc-René found himself losing ground to the heavier man.

Without breaking eye contact, he stamped on the Captain's booted toe. His opponent yelped and reflexively reached for his foot. Marc-René broke away and inverted his sword. Gripping it by the end of the blade, he spun round clubbing the weighted pommel into the back of the captain's head. The big man stood for a while with a puzzled expression. Then, eyes fluttering, he collapsed on his face in a pile of fresh horse dung.

Marc-René dropped his sword with a clatter, bending double, hands on knees. He retained this position chest heaving, as he regained his breath. Blood poured from his wound, pooling on the straw. Esther yelled to him. Hearing her voice Marc-René straightened. He staggered, reaching out for a crooked roof beam to steady himself as his legs began to fail. The Old Cavalier rushed to help, easing Marc-René to the ground as he slipped from consciousness. He parted the blood-soaked blouse and examined the wound.

'That'll need stitches, lots of them,' he said turning to Esther. 'There's a fellow staying at the inn can do that. Trouble being, he's passed out drunk.'

'And in the meantime...?' Esther sniffed, fighting back tears.

'Chance he'll bleed to death.'

She swallowed.

'I'll do it myself then.'

'Needles?'

She nodded, yes, she had needles.

'Sooner we get started then.'

Knees cracking, the Old Cavalier hoisted himself up, pushing through the throng to one of the horse stalls. Returning he held up a dozen long strands of white tail hair.

'Yarn won't do, you'll want this. And you'll be needing me to hold him.'

There was a commotion behind them.

They span round.

The captain had regained his feet.

With a great roar he rushed towards them, swinging his sword at Marc-René's unprotected neck. Esther grabbed a rusty pitchfork, impaling him through the thigh. The stout Captain tumbled forwards, his momentum forcing the tines deeper. Blood spurted from the wound as he crashed down eyes bulging, shivering with shock.

Opinion divided as to the legitimacy of Esther's intervention. Despite vociferous protest from the Captain's supporters, the consensus agreed to reserve judgement. They'd decide in the sobriety of the morning. If either of the combatants survived.

1624

SIX — *flounder and potatoes*

Isaac was city born. His stepfather, the Rabbi, had wealth enough to own carriages. Horseback for Isaac was an infrequent inconvenience. He never developed the enthusiasm his siblings had for riding. Water was his preferred mode of transport. In Amsterdam that wasn't a problem. And he was even less enthusiastic after five days in the saddle. He'd left it to Benjamin to break the news he'd defied the Rabbi's edict.

Eloping was horror enough. But with goyim? Marrying out of the faith? The Rabbi accused Esther of doing the Pope's filthy work for him. Of annihilating future generations of Jews. From the moment he learned of her departure she was dead to him. He forbade the brothers to enquire after her. Never should they mention her name henceforth. He raged when they sought to defend her or pleaded for forgiveness on her behalf.

'It's a father's duty to find a good match for his daughter.'

'Good for whom?' Isaac had countered, bitterly.

'I'll hear nothing more,' hissed the Rabbi. 'That child is dead to us.'

'How can you say that Papa?' Tears welled in Benjamin's eyes. 'If you won't go after her, please let me.'

'You'll stay here and sit shiva with the rest of us,' screamed his mother. White faced; she slammed her hands on the table with a crash like twin musket shots.

'But she isn't dead,' persisted Benjamin. 'How can you say that about your own daughter?' He got that look. His mother didn't have to say it. 'She was never a daughter of mine,' went unspoken. But its stink hovered over the household like a corrupting corpse. The Rabbi stormed out and locked himself in his office. Through the door they could hear prayers for the dead.

And thus the matter of Esther concluded. The brothers no longer had a sister. Benjamin looked to Isaac for support. Isaac avoided his younger brother's eyes, lest he betray his intentions. Whilst the battle raged, Isaac was making his plans. You either talk, or you act. That morsel of wisdom he'd gleaned from his natural father. Joseph never burdened others with his black moods. He simply acted when he could bear them no longer. Isaac too had chosen action. More talk would be a hurtful exercise in futility.

Isaac strapped the bulging leather saddlebags over his mount's rump. Benjamin kept watch, glancing this way and that.

'D'you know where they're heading?' he said, lip trembling.

'South.'

'Why south?'

'Spoken with Marc-René's parents. Awkward conversation. Believe me they're not happy either. The Rabbi has accused their son of abduction. Marc-René will be looking to join up with his regiment. They've a good head start, but if I ride hard I'll overtake them before they arrive. If I don't, then I'll just have to appeal to his commanding officer and hope he's a reasonable man.'

He checked the priming pans of his pistols, gingerly lowering the cocks onto the frizzens. Never know who you'll meet on the road. That done he slid them into the well-worn leather holsters slung one each side of the saddle.

'Don't worry, I'll fetch her back,' he said, surprising himself with his confidence. Spurring his mount, he clattered out of the yard. Benjamin stood, tear in his eye. Now he was without both siblings. He determined to delay as long as possible before admitting knowledge of his brother's departure.

Isaac had been on the runaway's trail for five days. The Magpie was the seventh hostelry at which he'd made enquiries. At two of them he'd encountered patrons who recognised the couple's description. His information had been good, they were heading south.

Sleeping little, on the road at first light, he must overtake them soon. He'd departed in a blaze of optimism, unthinking of what action he'd take when he located them. And this hadn't altered after his days in the saddle. Save his optimism was as depleted and his thighs were sore. Esther left home willingly. The Rabbi was wrong, she was not the victim of abduction. She was merely avoiding an unsuitable marriage. This was playing out like a typical storybook romance. And suspiciously so. Did an elder half-brother even have the legal or moral authority to compel her to return. Albeit she was two years under her majority. Would he force her at gunpoint. The thought was ridiculous. What if they'd found someone to marry them? What if Mark Rene had dishonoured her, what then? He finally admitted the truth of it. He didn't have any idea of how he'd react, or what he'd do. As he rode the rutted track, he boiled with anger at the participants of this drama. What had he done to get caught up in this emotional hairball.

Isaac dismounted with a groan, stretching his cramped muscles. He absently stroked his horse's long neck. It had been a day since his last meal. Bread and cheese and some thin wine picked up at his last stop. A flaking sign creaked in the wind proclaimed this the Magpie Inn. There was a split in it, as though subjected to a sword strike. The last rays of the sun were disappearing behind the broken ridge of a stable block. He led his horse clattering across the cobbled forecourt. The place stunk of horse shit and stale beer; then again didn't they all. A groom slouched out from the stables scratching his arse through patched breeches.

'You stayin' the night?'

'Maybe. What's the food like?'

The boy shrugged.

Isaac removed the pistols from their saddle pouches. Tucking them into his waist sash, he concealed their bulk under his cloak. He was by no means an expert pistoleer. But footpads wouldn't know that. And these were mighty weapons which commanded respect. Could be he'd need a little respect along the way, who could tell? He slipped the boy a coin and passed over his mount's reins.

'Give her a good rub down, there's a lad.'

The Magpie Inn smelled worse inside than out, but at least it was warm. The interior was smoky from a combination of a damp peat fire and inadequate ventilation. Watery eyes turned to him as he entered. He pulled off his gloves and warmed his back by a big open fire. The landlord shuffled up, pear shaped and ruddy faced, with a nose like an over-ripe strawberry. Unafraid to pull a cork with his patrons, evidently. He greeted this new arrival with a crooked smile. Two women, who could have been a mother and daughter, were serving table.

'First things first,' said the landlord. 'What does the young gentleman want to drink?

Behind the bar was like an alchemist's laboratory. Barrels and copper casks and bottles of all shapes and sizes. What, Isaac calculated, was less likely to poison him?

'Ale,' he said, then thought, why not? 'And fetch me a mug of Genievre.'

The landlord waddled off across a stamped earth floor, scattered with oyster shells and broken clay pipes. Isaac followed him to the bar.

'I'm looking for a couple. A woman blond and young. Man's a little older. But still young, military, he'd have looked like a cavalryman.'

'Will you want to be eatin?' said the landlord. Was the man deaf?

'We've got goose on today, roast or cold. A few eels. Some smoked, some still wrigglin,' do 'em however you want 'em, go nice fried they would. Lamb's all gone though. Ain't it Ma?'

'What?'

'Lamb's all gone, right?'

'Right.'

Isaac spread ten guilders on the bar.

'Oh that couple,' said the landlord. He slapped the side of his head, like he was rectifying a faulty clock mechanism.

'Right. That couple, why didn't you say? Oo could forget 'em, must be gettin' old. Caused a real bleedin' ruckus those two did. Half-killed a poor captain of 'orse. Proper poorly he was for a while. Didn't 'arf howl when ee got it. Made us all laugh ee did.'

'What? When was that?'

'Two days ago, wasn't it Ma?'

'Wasn't what?'

'I'm sayin' that couple Ma,' he shouted. 'Proper mess that was, wasn't it?'

'Oh yes mate, proper mess.'

'Least they did it in the stables,' said the landlord.

'Did what in the stables?'

'Their bleedin.' Over an insult to the young lady it was.'

'Which way?'

'Over there across the yard.'

'No, not the stables. Which way did they go when they left here?'

'Which way did who go? There were so many of 'em coming and going. Gets confusin.' I say, gets confusin' don't it Ma?'

'I'm talking about the couple,' said Isaac, trying hard and failing to hide his impatience.

'Which way? Well we only got two ways,' retorted the landlord. 'That way, and the other way. You come in one way, work it out for your damned self.'

An ear-piercing shriek split the air, followed by a gurgling, spluttering splashy sound.

'Oops, forgot about that. Pork's back on the menu,' he yelled above the hubbub of the room. And to Isaac, 'Nice and fresh. No? Oh well. Anyway, Like I was saying, three days ago. The Captain, van Zoon was his name, went after 'em. That's when they could get 'is fat arse on a 'orse, that is. Wasn't 'appy, was 'e Ma? I said, "he wasn't 'appy".'

'Don't know wasn't 'appy,' said his wife. 'Wasn't walkin' straight, that's for sure.'

She chuckled toothlessly, saliva dribbling down her chin. The younger woman joined in the cackle, setting her tits ajiggling.

'So what happened? Give me some detail,' said Isaac, taking a seat on an upturned half-barrel by the fire.

At a coin an episode, came a bloated, imaginatively embellished retelling of events. Best as they could recall that is, they said, not having seen it all. From time to time they called on the occasional patron to fill in the gaps.

'It was the lady what stuck 'im. Stuck the Captain of 'orse,' said the younger crone, 'you was there wasn't you Jurjen?'

'Oh, yes.' An aged face appeared from the fast-gathering audience. 'She did 'im up like a smoked 'erring with a rusty pitchfork.'

'They sent to the city for a surgeon,' said the landlord. 'Must have cost 'em a fortune. Came all the way in his bleedin' carriage.'

Isaac hadn't eaten since the night before. He took a meal of grilled flounder and boiled potatoes by the open fire. Fish being the lesser of the many menu evils. It was surprisingly good. He'd never tasted flat fish before. The creature's lack of scales forbidding them to Jewish tables. Adding to his mounting dietary transgressions he took a pair of eels for the road. Smoked stiff as walking sticks, wrapped in oily paper. A half round of cheese and gritty bread stuffed in a flour sack completed his supplies. Rabbis conceded it was permissible to break Kashrūt to preserve life. Yours or that of someone else. Surely saving Esther from her reckless choices was such a matter.

With mixed results, he tried not to enjoy this forbidden repast. The landlord sidled over enquiring how the food had gone down. He seemed keen to revisit the profitable conversation. A huddle of soldiers had been giving Isaac looks of disapproval. Grumbling he should be doing his bit defending the Provinces like them. He hurriedly finished his meal and settled with the landlord. Regardless of the temperature outside he felt no temptation to lodge therein. Isaac had gleaned enough. He paid the bill and reclaimed his cloak drying by the fire.

'Where you going?' said the landlord. 'There's ne'er do wells out at night. Got this nice cosy room. One of those nice young gents,' he nodded towards the troopers, 'won't mind sharin'.'

Abandoning the warmth of the Inn, Isaac snatched some sleep in the stables. His horse providing warmth and infinitely superior company. He hadn't liked the way those soldiers had been eyeing him. Last thing he needed was pressing into service. His horse's oaty breath was a relief from the inn's malodorous denizens. He had recompensed he groom generously. The boy loaded an extra supply of oats into Isaac's saddlebags. No need to carry water in this saturated landscape. Thus horse and rider rode provisioned for the next two or three days.

Isaac replaced his pistols in their saddle holsters. Turning to lead his horse out he clattered into the old cavalier, swapping apologies. On impulse Isaac enquired whether he'd seen the couple.

'And why do you seek them?' came the suspicious reply.

'She's my sister. I'm here to fetch her home.'

'Oh to be young,' said the Old Cavalier, addressing the canopy of fading stars above them. He fixed Isaac with a steely gaze.

'You seek no revenge?'

'Just my sister's safety and a peaceful resolution.'

'Strikberg,' said the Old Cavalier. 'They're bound for Strikberg. That's where his regiment will be massing before joining Fredrick Henry. Just you keep going south. River Mark to your right, you'll get there soon enough. Take my warning there's others looking for them.'

'So I was told.'

'You heard about the scrap then. If van Zoon's men find them I wouldn't give a schilling for their chances. He's offered a promotion and a hundred guilders for their apprehension. I fear some terrible mischief might befall them.'

Isaac's imagination conjured up a picture of two figures hanging from a wayside tree. Back on the trail Isaac's head was reeling. The complexion of his mission was now completely unambiguous. This was a rescue. Esther attack a grown man? Surely not. But there was something in the back of his mind thought otherwise.

Spring was late that year. The green stalks of wild daffodils had yet to reveal their trumpets. Traces of frost still crisped the ground. Isaac rode slumped in the saddle, blowing on his fingers in their thin leather gloves. He was following the meandering track south. He'd misjudged the climate outside the city. When dusk fell he dismounted and led his horse. On these unfamiliar unlit trackways, injuring his mount was a very real danger. Adding to his misery, rain began to fall in icy waves. Encountering a derelict barn he took shelter. He rubbed down the horse with handfuls of straw. Then slept curled up and shivering, wrapped in a horse blanket on mildewed hay. He woke up early stretching painfully. The rain had ceased, and the first rays of dawn were piercing a stand of misty poplars. He stamped the life back into his feet, fed and re-saddled his horse, their breath merging in cloudy billows.

At midday Isaac came across a signpost for Terheijden. Soon the rooftops of the hamlet came into sight. He abandoned the track, taking to the fields, not wishing to draw unwelcome attention. Strikberg and Marc-René's regiment would be a few more miles south. That's if they hadn't moved on. He re-joined the track. It was wider now, earth and undergrowth newly trampled. A thousand horses would do that; an army would do that. On the Banks of the River Mark he came across a scene of carnage, warming in the noonday sun. Far as he could see corpses of men and horses littered the boggy fields. Women hunched over the fallen, squabbling over their clothing. Stripping away dignity along with their clothes. Mud caked orange and blue sashes spoke of a Dutch defeat. Ravens massing in a nearby copse, expressed their collective impatience.

Isaac was aware of the sequence of events. The generals took the glory. Their troops looted the corpses to supplement their pay. Finally came the women to glean the field of death. They looked up but paid scant attention at Isaac's arrival. What threat was an animated scarecrow astride an exhausted mud-spattered mount. They returned to squabbling over a battered snuff box. In the far distance men were herding hundreds of unsaddled horses towards the south.

Something familiar attracted Isaac's attention. Could that be Esther's white horse? Could that be her 'Africa,' the mare with the single black patch on its rump the shape of the dark continent. Guts blown open, entrails scattered, ribcage splayed, tongue lolling in the mud. Women were tearing garments from the saddlebags strapped to its back. Was that Esther's white and blue striped dress. The scavengers ignored his yells of protest. He drew his pistol, firing in the air. A cloud of dark birds took to the sky and whirled overhead. The women scattered, dispersing across the field. A gust caught the dress, and it snagged on the branches of a stunted tree. The women settled in another area and continued working like a swarm of flies. Heart pounding, he dismounted to examine the horse.

Hooves came thundering through the mud. Isaac turned, reflexively ducking. The rider's boot had him reeling to his knees. He reached up for his saddle pistol. But his startled horse tore the reins from his grip. Now he had only a discharged pistol with which to defend himself. The attacker reigned back, slithering to a halt fifty yards hence. Another cavalryman trotted up to join the first. They wore red sashes. The insignia of the Spanish Army of Flanders. By their chatter, Italian mercenaries. Isaac heard, or imagined he heard, the steely scrape of a sword drawn from its scabbard. Spurs dug into the horses flank. It cantered at first and then broke into a pounding gallop towards him. The rider hung low in the saddle; a gleaming sword blade levelled at Isaac.

The blade skimmed across his forehead. Grazing his hairline and opening a bloody parting. He stood swaying, dazed, wiping away the blood threatening to obscure his vision.

He almost missed what happened next. The rider hauled his mount's head to one side. Snorting, nostrils flaring, eyes bulging it wheeled about in the mud. Rearing up, pawing the air, the rider dug his spurs deep. The horse screamed and took off towards Isaac again. He counted himself a dead man. But instead of finishing him off the rider pounded on past. Isaac whipped round, following the horse. Another horseman came thundering towards Isaac's aggressor. They met with a clash of swords. Isaac recognised Marc-René as his saviour. But then Marc-René's horse stumbled, and he tumbled from the saddle.

The Italian horseman carried on to the edge of the woods, slowly slid from his mount and lay still. The horse trotted off until lost to sight in the mist. Marc-René, struggled to remount, but his horse slid in the mud. The other Italian spurred his horse towards Marc-René. As he cantered past, Isaac leapt up and dragged him from the saddle. Scrambling to his feet the unseated rider swung his sword at Isaac. Esther leapt from hiding behind a dead horse, firing Isaac's other pistol. The ball ricocheted off the officer's breastplate knocking him from his feet. Isaac and Esther fell on him pinning him down. Marc-René struggled to them through the mud, driving his blade into the man's throat.

They retreated to the north of Terheijden, finding a deserted farmstead. With their horses out of sight they collapsed on straw bales. Were it not that her flaxen hair had tumbled loose from her cap, Esther would have passed for a scrawny lad. It is likely all three were thinking the same thing. But it was Esther who voiced it. She was tending to Isaac's head wound.

'So?' she said. Looking to Isaac and then to Marc-René. Isaac understood what she was asking but wasn't yet ready to meet the issue full on.

'So, what?' he said.

She looked away and shook her head, her gaze returned to him with an affectionate smile.

'What happens now you've found us?'

'Come back?' Isaac said. It sounded so lame.

Marc-René ducked down from where he was gazing out of a shattered window. He beckoned, signalling to them to keep low. A dozen Dutch troopers were trotting along the trackway. One reined in his mount, turned and stared straight at them, shielding his eyes against the low sun. He paused; they held their breaths. But then he turned and cantered off to join his platoon. They released a collective gasp of relief. They turned and slid down the barn wall, collapsing breathless and boneless in the soft straw.

'Well, I can't go back. I must join my regiment,' said Marc-René. 'If I delay I'll be a deserter and end up swinging from a tree. Jesu, I'm late already.'

'He *can't* go back. And I *won't* go back,' said Esther.

'They're sitting shiva, saying Kaddish for you, you have to come home.'

'How can the dead return home?' she fixed him with steely blue eyes.

This was the Esther of which he'd only ever caught the occasional glimpse. Who'd existed beneath the suffocating shell of orthodoxy and compliance. The shell had broken, that both protects and constrains, the shards scattered. Things would never be the same. He knew that any promise, any trick, any threat, any pleading would meet with a similar response.

'Esther, is there nothing I can say to make you come home?'

'This family is disintegrating. You may not see it. It's happening slowly, in God's time. A fuse lit a long time ago by our enemies. Though we have travelled to another land our family cannot escape the effects.

'I'm not a confused little female needing man's guidance and protection. I'm just the first of the fragments to break away in the explosion. What did you think you'd achieve by following me? Face it, my departure was a convenient excuse. The same way an arranged marriage was an excuse for me. You needed to get away.'

'But we miss you.'

'Of course you do. And we'll be together again one day. But for now we have to part.'

'Will you keep in contact?'

'When I can.'

She reached to her neck, removing a chain from which hung a pendant in the shape of an inverted hammer. This was all she had from her Swedish birth mother, who in turn had received it from her mother. It would be recognisable to anyone in her family. She'd fought hard to retain this pagan artifact.

'Tell them you found this.'

1624

SEVEN — *good business*

The strangled cry of a dog fox echoed outside in the unlit street. A vixen answered on the far side of the canal. Abraham Amsalem opened his eyes and blinked himself awake. He wiped saliva from his beard, yawned slowly raising his head from the desk. To his right a much-worn terrestrial globe pinned down a set of plans. To his left a large bottle of wine and a wedge of cheese were likewise employed. The detailed schematic of a ship came into focus, open like a Torah scroll.

The Rabbi removed his thick spectacles. Squeezing the bridge of his nose, he refocused on the specifications of the Rachael. A new merchantman commissioned by a prosperous trading syndicate. As was his preferred practice he was also investing in the project. This on the understanding the vessel took shape at his shipyard. That's the way he liked to do business. Three slices of the cake: broker, investor, shipbuilder. Good business for him was good business for everyone. Such was his reputation.

He reached for the wine bottle. As he was refilling his glass, the rebellious plans made a break for freedom. He let them go. They instantly curled into a cylinder. Enough for one day. He turned his attention to the globe. His stubby fingers revolved the continents in the sparse light of the oil lamp. A light fuelled by fat rendered from creatures living beneath those fathomless oceans. Oceans which the Rachael would soon be bestriding. Closing his heavily lidded eyes, he imagined the sights she would see. The bounty she would return to him, like a good and faithful daughter. And unlike the one who had so recently deserted him.

The Rachael was a fluyt, the most numerous of Dutch merchantman. This class of vessel had enabled the Free Provinces to dominate international trade, establishing Amsterdam as the most prosperous port in Europe. Which in turn funded their war for independence against their former Spanish oppressors. She would be a fast, three masted, high-capacity three hundred tonner. Eighty feet on the waterline, with the narrow deck and the pear-shaped profile of her kind. The keel laid, the timbers fastened. Employing the Dutch 'plank on first' technique, it wouldn't be long before she kissed the water.

Other European nations legislated the construction of hybrid vessels — part merchantmen, part warships, pressed into service at times of war. Thus saving the expense of a standing navy. But in common with most compromises, they weren't ideal for either purpose. By contrast the Dutch fluyt was a specialist. Lightly armed, if armed at all. Sleek-hulled dedicated bulk carriers. And, given the productivity and economy of Dutch shipyards, verging on disposable.

The Rachael was slightly heavier than most of her type. But still light compared to heavily armed foreign merchantman. They intended her for the Americas trade. Specifically New Amsterdam, where privateering and piracy was rife. Overseeing the build was the Rabbi's older son Isaac. He had added cunningly disguised gun ports, ten per side, bow and stern chasers. Pull along side the Rachael expecting an easy prize, and you'd be in for a very upsetting day. Carrying weighty armament would cut the hold capacity by ten percent and double the crew. But they'd still need only half the seamen of a typical hybrid merchantman of equivalent tonnage and carry half again their cargo.

Abraham Amsalem looked every inch a prosperous Dutch businessman. Only his full beard might speak to his Jewish heritage. As well as a shipbroker, he served as Rabbi to a growing Sephardic community. He was strict in his observance. Some might say harsh. He wasn't a demagogue just typical of his generation. A product of hard circumstances and treatment, influenced by austere Protestant values. He was fiercely protective of Jewish identity and customs, and grateful to his host country for the freedom they allowed. His nation, cast out from Judea to the Iberian Peninsula by the Romans. Then a thousand years later Roman Catholics, kicked them out of there.

Openly Jewish, Rabbi Abraham's family escaped Portugal a generation back. Few foresaw the persecution. The Rabbi's father did. He underwent this latest exodus early, leaving unhindered with his wealth intact. In the decades that followed, thousands weren't so fortunate. He relocated his family to the Low Countries. Others chose the Ottoman Empire, which greeted Jews with open arms. Even sent their fleet to protect them. Sultan Bajazet famously saying:

'How can you call Ferdinand of Aragon a wise king. The same Ferdinand who impoverished his own land and enriched ours?'

The Dutch took a similar attitude. They welcomed this influx of skilled craftsmen, merchants, bankers and entrepreneurs. Jews and

Protestants alike found haven in the embryonic Dutch Republic. The Free Provinces. This was the only country in Europe to do so and prospered directly as a result. The proof came two years later. Admiral Hein, supported by Moses Cohen Henriques captured a Spanish treasure fleet. Enough silver to pay off the Dutch national debt, near bankrupting the Spanish empire.

Starting from the bottom, Abraham's father Geršom, may his name be for a blessing, clawed his way from able seaman to ship owner. From a penniless immigrant to prosperity. From an immigrant to a position of respect in the embryonic Hebrew community. His eldest son, Rabbi Abraham continued his mission. He did what he could for expulsos flooding in from the Iberian Peninsular. Both converso Jews and Muslim moriscos should the opportunity arise. Catholic convert Jews were eager to return to their former faith. When he could he met their ships. And yes, as the community's mohel he did, indeed, keep a very sharp blade.

A rap on the door. The Rabbi turned slowly, leaning back in his chair.

'Come,' he shouted.

A hooded figure entered, from absolute darkness into lamplit gloom. The midnight visitor gasped and took an involuntarily step back. There was a pistol in each of the Rabbi's hands, lamplight glinting off gold-chased steel barrels.

'And you would be?' said the Rabbi.

'Navarro your Worship. Rodrigo Navarro.'

'And do you have a word?'

The visitor cleared his throat. 'Isaiah.'

'Which Isaiah?'

'The third, may the Lord praise him.'

The Rabbi took a deep breath and dropped his shoulders. Easing the cocks back on his pistols he tucked the guns back under a fold in the heavy tapestry table covering. Despite the chill of the evening Navarro wiped a bead of sweat from his brow.

'Come in,' said the Rabbi, 'Navarro is it? Come in. I'd been told to expect you. Take a seat. Wine?' He poured another glass. 'So, what news from Spain?'

Navarro's hands were shaking as he accepted the glass. He drew up a stool. The Rabbi leaned across and slapped his shoulder, chuckling at the man's discomposure.

Rabbi Abraham developed an international network of 'intelligencers.' Open Jews and secret Jews, Muslims and secret Muslims, and bribed

Catholics. It was beneficial for business. Certainly for his relationship with his trading partners near and far. But also for the conduct of the Spanish war. These free and independent Protestant provinces were essential to Jewish interests. Indeed for their survival in Europe. The Spanish were eager to reconquer these rebellious possessions. And with them would come the Inquisition, as was happening throughout the New World. Disastrous for Jew, Muslim and Protestant alike. Three peoples bonded by fear, and a common respect for each others' cherished freedoms.

The Stadtholder would need to have this news immediately. The House of Orange-Nassau welcomed rabbi's counsel any time, day or night. He was pulling on his boots when he felt a breeze.

Benjamin, accustomed to his father's caution, didn't flinch finding himself staring down the business end of twin flintlocks:

'Isaac's gone after her,' he said.

1624

EIGHT — *cross stitch*

Marc-René was awake early. That is, if he'd slept at all. His ashen face creased with pain as he raised himself on one elbow. Peering down at his chest, he lifted the dressing and inhaled sharply.

'What no flowers?' he groaned.

'Sorry, *lieveling*, flowers?' said Esther.

'Flowers, don't you ladies always add a few flowers to your embroidery?'

'Very funny. Keep it covered.'

'Christ woman, I'm going to have one tit higher than the other.'

'I'd have done better work if you hadn't been wriggling so. And not to mention squealing like a little piglet.'

He glanced down again, shaking his head in disbelief.

'Cross stitch? Bloody cross stitch?'

'Hey, it's all I know. You want we should leave you hanging open?'

No witty comeback this time. He swung his feet off the bed. She helped him on with this tall riding boots. He sat with gritted teeth, breath pumping. Though he was staring through the window, all his concentration inward.

There came a knock at the door. Esther was using the chamber pot. 'Hang on,' she hissed, 'hang on,' toeing the pot under the bed and slopping the steaming contents on the wooden floor. Rearranging her skirts, she tutted in disgust, these damned things will have to go.

She opened the door. The old Cavalier didn't wait for an invitation; he just nodded and brushed past her, dumping a basket on the table. It smelled of freshly baked bread. Despite her agitation, Esther felt her appetite returning.

'You two need to make yourselves scarce, the Captain's men are starting to come round. And you two aren't going to be popular.'

Marc-René struggled unsteadily to his feet. He flexed his shoulder, grimacing at the resistance of the crude stitches.

'How is the idiot?' he said.

1624

'Who, Van Zoon? Looks like the valiant Captain may not survive. If he does he'll not walk straight again, thanks to your young…'

The blood had drained from Marc-René's face, he dropped back down on the bed with a jolt, staring blankly ahead of him.

'Sorry,' said Esther, 'did you say Van Zoon, Cornelius van Zoon?'

'You know him?' said the Cavalier, glancing from one the other.

'No. I mean yes,' said Esther, 'He's the…' She looked to Marc-René.

He finished the sentence: 'He commands Sixty Third Brabant. The troop I'm commissioned to join. Never met the man before… Well, before last night.'

The Cavalier checked the window. Troopers were milling in the in the courtyard.

'Can you ride?' he hissed urgently.

1624

NINE — *Roman insanity*

Marc-René rode silently, hunched under a damp cloak, Esther beside him. Early morning mist swirled about their horses' feet. By the time it had begun to dissipate Esther was confident they were not being pursued. Standing high in the stirrups she scanned the flatlands once more. Dropping back to the saddle, she snapped the telescope shut. She was riding Marc-René's stallion, sixteen hands at least. He was on her smaller, more docile chestnut mare. The pain had taken him somewhere deep inside himself; he rode as if asleep. They would have to stop soon; she'd need to check his wound.

Astride the creaking saddle Esther contemplated the potential consequences of her reckless impetuosity. She had abandoned the security of her wealthy family. Cast herself adrift in this rain-sodden wasteland. The man she'd so recently been convinced she adored now relegated to the lesser of two evils. She shuddered as images of wedding nights flashed before her. Naked and trembling before her stepfather's choice for husband. His thin lips touching hers through a straggling beard, his touch hesitant, respectful. Then there was Marc-René. Respectful, anything but hesitant. Was this what Joseph, her father, would wish for her the lesser of two evils.

Esther had only fond memories of her natural father. Such vague memories as a traumatised four-year-old could store away. A general impression of a gentle kind but troubled soul. Her mother gave every impression of despising him. Of hatred whilst he lived. And now hatred of his memory.

Conversos, crypto Jews, secret Jews — they go by many names. Hebrews forcibly converted to Catholicism. The motivation rarely pure. Threat of violence and death on one extreme. Social, business and political advancement on the other. A community caught between furnace and finance. The Iberian peninsula cleansed of its Jewish population. But it hadn't been such a thorough cleansing. Jews simply went underground. Took the sacraments. Integrated into Spanish and

Portuguese society. Decades later the inquisition began tormenting these 'New Christians.'

This, she understood, led to the family's downfall. Her poor father. Hung by his wrists, shoulders dislocated, fingers broken. In the delirium of agony he's provided evidence that consigned his wife's family, her parents her brothers, to the flames. Or so the Inquisitors had said. How could a wife live with such a husband.

Joseph the man was gone. Joseph the shell remained. Esther was too young to remember him as any other. She never knew the Joseph who'd kept a wife and concubines in such fine style. The man who was fêted by the highest in society. Who lent money freely to the mighty. The man about whom a wife could boast from the comfort of a perfumed palace, with servants beyond count. The inner armature which gave a man stature had corroded, leaving him a shuffling shadow of his former self. All Esther knew was Joseph the walking ghost. She remembered his wan intoxicated smile. And it was a memory she treasured.

Catholics filled Esther with loathing. Their bizarre beliefs a bloated monster leaching on Jewish sacred beliefs. Like a son torturing his father for his inheritance. And not content with butchering her people, Romans had hacked the Hebrew God into three. Insane people, infected by grotesque Roman values. She'd even heard rumour they venerated Yĕhôshúa ben Joseph's foreskin. Yet they eschewed circumcision, whilst persecuting his co-religionists. She longed to emulate her namesake the Hebrew wife of the Persian King Xerxes who defeated a plot to annihilate the Jewish population. She burned with a desire too wreak vengeance on those who extorted, tortured, and exiled her people. Who were attacking the Protestant States which gave her nation shelter. Who had destroyed her father, and her family. That, if nothing else, she had in common with Marc-René. Frenzied French Catholics had obliterated half his family. She straightened herself in the saddle, squaring her shoulders. The world was crying out for another Esther.

She was wearing some of Marc-René's spare clothes, the better to ride in. Also a disguise. 'Zoon's men would be seeking, if seeking at all, a man and a woman, not a Cavalry officer and his boy servant. And there was something else. These clothes, this masculine identity, felt surprisingly natural to her.

'All I wanted to do was serve my homeland,' hissed Marc-René: 'for all that, I'm a wanted man.'

Esther brushed rain droplets from her newly acquired leather breeches: 'Don't you mean *we* are wanted *men*,' she said, liking the sound.

1624

TEN — *cheese and tobacco*

The landscape underwent dramatic changes. For the last ten miles, crops were increasingly untended, fields overgrown, fences broken, farmhouse chimneys bereft of smoke. The fleeing couple had entered the zone of alienation. That disputed area of borderland, trampled over successively by the foraging mercenary armies of both sides. So picked clean, the Protestant population had long since joined the exodus to the cities.

Towards dusk on the second day, exhausted and saddle sore, they arrived at a deserted farmhouse. There was fresh water in a rain-swollen stream, and ample grazing for the horses in an enclosed meadow. The place stank of ammonia. Esther chased away invading pigeons and cleared a space amongst the detritus for Marc-René to rest. Up stream was a derelict windmill, arms rotted and useless, groaning as they moved. Esther explored its dark recesses for remnants of grain, but the rats had picked the floor clean.

Scrawny hens roamed through the farm buildings. Esther managed to snatch one, tempting it with their last crust, trying to remember how the scullery maids dealt with fowl. She gathered wood, and as night fell, they had their first decent meal in two days. She made Marc-René comfortable with what of their clothing was least saturated, arranging the rest to dry around the fire.

They sheltered in the farmhouse for three days whilst Marc-René regained his strength. When they had consumed the last chicken they moved on to another deserted homestead. This time it was pigeons which sustained them. Esther joked it would be sparrows next, and then what? Marc-René attempted to convince Esther to return home to the protection of her family. She refused, as he knew she would. Furniture had been smashed wherever they went, as though to deny comfort to the enemy. But the previous tenants had stopped short of torching the properties. Could be, they harboured hope, however vain, of return. Broken tables and chairs became fuel for their fires. In smoke filled rooms fragments of wishful fantasies coalesced into a rudimentary plan.

1624

Reporting to Van Zoon's regiment was out of the question. But, what if they penetrated enemy lines and joined the Dutch defenders in Breda? Was that an option? Having attended the Breda Military Academy, Marc-René knew the city well. Sneaking in and out of the defences had been a rite of passage for students. And a Protestant city encircled by a hostile Catholic army could, ironically, be the only place in the Free Provinces where they might be safe. And should Marc-René find the opportunity to sufficiently distinguish himself it might go some way towards mitigating their grievous offence.

The next day found them in a misty waterlogged wood to the north of Breda. The defenders had recently breached the dikes, flooding the fields creating a massive moat.

Marc-René thought back to his time in Breda. Ambrogio Spinola, the besieging general, was the stuff of legend — a Genoese military genius commissioned by the Spanish — his tactics required reading at the academy. Spinola's engineers had encircled the city in the classic manner which centuries before had brought Caesar victory in the Gallic wars. Three months had seen the construction of twenty-five miles of double-trenched fortifications defending the besiegers from both the aggression of the Breda garrison and the relieving Dutch army.

Despite pounding by cannon and Spanish attempts at undermining the fortifications, the Dutch still regularly sallied out to wreak havoc amongst the enemy lines. Both commanders knew this was a waiting game. Which side would first succumb to starvation? The defenders comprised highly motivated Protestant Dutch and English troops. Their leader was the charismatic Justine of Nassau, William the Silent's only illegitimate son, supported by the citizens of Breda who had chosen to remain.

All Esther and Marc-René needed to do now was to overcome the double encirclement of Spain's leading military strategist and penetrate the most sophisticated city defences in Europe.

Mice go where cats can't. Spinoza's mighty army couldn't smash through the fortifications. Could runaway lovers find a way in?

Clouds were blanketing the moon. From a low hill Esther and Marc-René shadowed Spanish soldiers patrolling the desolate stretch of no man's land between the Spanish trenches and the city walls. They were attempting to discern a pattern, something of which they could take advantage. Esther passed the telescope back to Marc-René.

'Over there. Base of the city wall,' she whispered.

He sighted along her arm.

'Corner. Bottom of that turret, there's movement.'

And, yes, dark figures were appearing, from nowhere. Before the Spanish knew it, they fell under attack. First aquabusiers belched out a volley. Then pistoleers rushed through their ranks firing at closer range. Those Spanish soldiers who'd survived the initial onslaught cast away their spades and picks and took to their heels. But before they could reach their weapons, the Dutch raiders fell on them. From what Esther could tell it was a devastating attack. At least a score of Spanish lay dead or dying. The rest, fleeing to their trenches, were cut down in the confusion by their own troops. Injured Dutch soldiers hobbled back to the safety of the walls. Spanish cannons fired blindly. Round shot bounced over the turf, smashing harmlessly into the city wall. Cannon fire erupted from the ramparts. Soon the whole area was thick with smoke.

'Can you see it, a sally port,' said Marc-René, passing Esther the telescope. 'So,' he sniffed dismissively, 'the Spanish lost a couple of dozen men. That only leaves Spinola eighty thousand more.'

'So why —?' said Esther.

'Morale's everything in a siege. In the city the troops will be living in houses with warm fires. Outside, the Spanish will be shivering in sodden bivouacs. Now they'd suffered a defeat. A tiny one, but that'll get exaggerated. Spinola men are fighting for wages. One day when their mates are dying of cholera, when food's rationed to starvation levels, and when their feet are rotting in their boots, they might decide they've had enough. Our people are fighting for their freedom, for their religion. Because they don't want to see their families massacred, their priests tortured and burned in the streets. And, most importantly, because the second the first volley of round shot passed over Breda's walls the city's population became exempt from Dutch taxes.' He chuckled.

They returned to their horses, wading knee deep through the flooded forest. Morale is everything, theirs was ebbing away.

'We need to dry off,' said Esther.

The next evening they were observing from a concealed position five or so miles to the east. The moon was but a slither periodically appearing through the clouds. The once lush forest now consisted only of stumps and saplings and low bushes. The mature trees now fortified the Spanish trenches or warmed Spanish feet. This area would afford scant cover for a daylight reconnoitre. Leaving their horses in one of the less flooded fields, they darkened their faces with mud and sneaked towards where the Spanish lines appeared at their narrowest and least defended.

There was no specific plan. Desperation and empty bellies were their driving forces now. As far as they knew a hangman's rope awaited them and closer by the minute. They arrived at the edge of the flooded Vucht Polder. Flickering lights by the shore aroused their curiosity. Moving closer, they could make out figures with lanterns under the causeway constructed by the besiegers. Two boats, men loading packages from one to the other. By their identifying sashes and scarves, orange and blue for the Free Provinces and red for the Spanish, they consisted of both forces. Taking his life in his hands Marc-René broke cover and approached a Dutch officer.

'Cornet Delacherois Sir, we urgently require passage to the city.'

The officer spun round, reaching for his pistols. Seeing the bedraggled pair he appeared relieved. Marc-René took his arm and whispered:

'Urgent message from Prince Mauritz.'

'Give it to me lad.' The officer held out his hand.

'It's in here sir,' said Marc-René tapping his temple. 'Forgive me. Been told it's for Commander Justinus ears only. With respect, if I entrust it to anyone else, Prince Mauritz will have mine.'

The officer gave him a long hard look: 'Very well, in the boat. Be quick. This little arrangement won't go unnoticed forever.'

Esther stared past them to where Spanish and Dutch troops were busy exchanging loads.

'Bread for them, cheese and tobacco for us and a bit of profit along the way,' said the officer, 'makes life a little more bearable for us all.'

The Dutch officer waved his Spanish counterpart farewell. Halfway across the dark lake, hostilities recommenced. Was this unofficial trading mission misinterpreted as hostility? Cannon fire erupted from both sides; one boat erupted into matchwood, the other capsized. Marc-René and Esther struggled to the opposite bank. A door in the wall burst open and a dozen musketeers charged out. They began laying down covering fire as the rest of the Dutchmen struggled to shore. Boxes of cheese and tobacco bobbed to the surface and the musketeers, having discharged their pieces, waded in to retrieve them.

In the confusion Marc-René and Esther, clutching bundles of cheese, found themselves hustled through the impregnable fortifications.

Once past the inner walls they emerged wet and exhausted into a courtyard, lit by half-a-dozen braziers.

'Come,' said the Captain, 'let's see if Nassau has time to see you.'

1624

ELEVEN — *beyond the veil*

In the warmth of a shadowy lamp-lit hall, two dozen gaudily dressed officers gathered around a table, tucking into a feast. For a city in the seventh month of a siege they seemed remarkably well provisioned. On entering, Marc-René instantly recognised Justinus Van Nassau, the city governor — though seated, the chamber's occupants seemed to swirl about him like dancers round a maypole. The least flamboyantly costumed, which distinguished him the more. All in black velvet, his gold engraved gorget glinted in the lamplight. A broad-brimmed hat with a single white plume, rested on his knee. His riding boots fashionably turned back revealing their red leather lining, and his vivid yellow hose.

Nassau turned when he heard them enter.

'Well? Did you get it?'

'Yes, your honour,' said the captain delivering the packages. 'Tobacco's a little damp, but I'm sure it'll light —. eventually.'

'How was it?' said Nassau.

'They appreciated the bread.' said the captain.

'Would have thought so too. We burned every wheat field and bakery for a twenty-mile radius. Anything else?'

The officer passed across another package.

'Good Dutch cheese your lordship.'

'Damnit, I was hoping for French. Still, beggars can't be choosers.'

The party was in remarkably good cheer. All save a gaudily dressed individual next to Nassau, absently spinning the rowel on one of his spurs, and silently sobbing.

'So whom have we here?' said Nassau, looking past the officer.

'Delacherois, your honour,' said Marc-René, sweeping off his hat and executing a low bow. 'A humble Huguenot begging the privilege of joining your company.'

'Come. Sit down. Bring your boy. What news?'

'I'm a soldier not a spy your honour,' said Marc-René. 'The Prince is massing a relief force, that's all I know.'

This clearly wasn't news to Nassau. He changed the subject. 'So, I hear you want work. We'll find work for them, won't we, eh?'

His companion sniffed, nodding through his tears.

'So, what do you do? What can you offer us?'

'I'm a cornet in the Brabant. Trained here at the Academy.'

'That'd be cavalry if I'm not mistaken,' said Nassau. 'Unfortunately, we have only one use for horses around here. Don't we, eh?'

He nodded at a huge pie in the centre of the table. The crying man erupted into further floods of tears.

'Alternatively,' said Nassau, 'we have some delicious dog stew, and the rat pasties, I'm reliably informed, are quite piquant.'

After the incident with Captain Van Zoon, Marc-René was convinced the day would come when he'd need every good report and was determined to impress his superiors. He made sure he was the first to volunteer for every mission outside the city walls, gaining a reputation for bravery and ingenuity. After six months he gained a promotion to Captain and given charge of a hundred men. His new responsibilities drove the affair of the duel from his mind.

This was to be the fifth sortie with his command, and he had selected his twenty best men. He was lucky in his sergeant, Wopke Vondel. Stout man, reliable, if a little loquacious. He had mustered his chosen men in a disused tavern. They were blacking their faces with soot and goose grease, passing round the pot. Old Vondel was sharpening his dagger on an oiled stone, going on at great length as always.

'What's it all for? A cause, a sodding religion? The right to worship as you bastard well please. What do most of those pricks outside care. It's just another earner to them. The only secure employment for a chap nowadays. Butchering your brother. It's come to that. Army of Flanders bedamned. Call themselves Spanish. South Dutch they are most of them. Germans, Italians, a sprinkling of English and Irish. Not even a quarter of 'em's Spanish. No work at home so they come up here to make mischief and take home a bit of coin. Chance of some plunder, no doubt. An' look where they've ended up.

'You've got to feel sorry for 'em out there. Muddy flooded trenches. Saturated bivouacs, foot rot, arse rot, cock rot. Far from home. Far from the dubious comforts of their fat titted wives. Not to mention the kids and their dear old mums. Didn't know what they were in for did they. Here's us, snug and sheltered in here, more houses than we can occupy. Nice warm peat fires. Not such bad grub. A few shortages. Gotta expect that, it's a Christ damned siege. But we're not starving. And they are.

Four-thousand wagons they've got, lugging provisions all the way from buggerin' Antwerp. Harried by our brave Prince's gallopers. And it's still not enough for 'em. So there they are. Starving us out. And here's us with full bellies.

'They signed up as soldiers and they've become ditch diggers. No amount of extra pay would have me doin' labouring. I'm a soldier. So was me dad. Got me pride. Won't get the likes of me picking up a bastard shovel. Cutting us off, stopping us getting relief. That's what they're trying to do. Relief from what? This place is impregnable. You've seen it, five or six thousand of us keeping eighty thousand 'Spanish' soldiers well occupied. Breaking poor old lop-jawed Philip's purse. There's even rumours he's making nice old General Spinola pay for his own troops. You've got to wonder who's besieging who. Can't help feeling sorry for the poor pricks. Half-rations, half-pay, digging ditches in a land below sea level. Up to their arses in mud, sleeping in sodden blankets. Diseased, shivering with bleeding cold, miserable as sin, far from hearth and home. Anyway, we hold the physic for alls as ails 'em, eh boys.' He felt the edge of his dagger and returned it to its sheath.

'Come on lads,' added Marc-René, finishing his beer and getting to his feet, 'time to cut some Papist throats.'

It was a successful raid. They only lost one man, another wounded, nothing serious. They had come across a working party in the trenches building a stake wall. The bastards had no chance to get to their weapons. Slaughtered them all, lost count at eleven. Not a bad night's work. He was in bed just before dawn and slept until noon. Walking across the city square to hand in his report to the adjutant he collided with Van Zoon, walking painfully with the aid of a stick. Words exchanged, blows struck.

Another duel. Pistols this time. And Justinus, far from forbidding it, had decided this is just what they needed to relieve the stultifying boredom of the siege.

They faced each other in the chill morning air, pistols raised. The crowd hushed. Even the bird noise appeared to fade. Someone sneezed. Esther started, heart pounding, mouth dry, her view constrained by the crush of the crowd. And for this she was grateful.

Marc-René had explained to her the duellist's dilemma. Fire first, risk snatching the shot. Delay, and the other party may kill you before you'd had your chance to fire. But the longer you held the pistol, the more unsteady became your aim, after a while your arm would begin to shake uncontrollably.

1624

And then it happened. One shot. Van Zoon had discharged his piece. His opponent dropped to his knees, his weapon unfired.

Marc-René fancied he'd seen the ball coming, blasting a vortex through a cloud of white smoke. Half an ounce of crudely moulded lead. Tumbling through space, bowling towards him like a planet through the heavens, whining like an angry hornet. Music of the spheres. He reeled as it clipped his left orbit, pivoting his head, passing down his temple, snicking off the top of his ear. A thousand church bells pealed as one, reverberating through the ages. Mountainous waves pounded into rocky shores. Hosts of celestial trumpets blared discordantly.

All was sky, then cobbled pavement. Blinking, seeing nothing, feeling nothing, dropping as though hamstrung. He swayed backwards and forwards on his knees, like an infidel at prayer. Staring sightlessly ahead, it was like he was enjoying a brief glimpse of the undifferentiated world beyond the veil.

Voices. Screams. He stared in numbed silence at the pistol hanging from his right hand, cocked, unfired. Resting his free hand on his knee, he heaved himself back to his feet, shivering like the wind-blown leaves of a poplar. Shaking his head, heart of oak; he steadied his mind. Something was wrong with his eyesight. Footsteps approached. Esther's voice, saying something. He flinched as her cool hand took hold of the nape of his neck. Rough cloth cleared blood from his eyes. And there it was, her face riven with horror. Carefully, she tied a scarf about his head.

An officer took Esther by the arm, pulling her from the line of fire. The smoke cleared as did Marc-René's vision, his corpulent opponent visible once more.

Fierce quarrels broke out amongst the onlookers. Most accusing Van Zoon of discharging his weapon prematurely. Whatever argument would win the day, one matter was beyond dispute – Van Zoon must stand fire.

Blood trickled from beneath the grubby improvised bandage. Marc-René wiped it away with the back of his arm. Calm your breathing, slow your heart, steady your damned shaking hands. He snatched quick breaths, saturating his blood with oxygen. Then emptied his lungs and inflated them slowly, simultaneously raising the heavy pistol.

Marc-René was considering that other grim duellist's dilemma. Receiving fire, sideways, or square on? Sideways, smaller target, but a ball could pierce both lungs, take out both kidneys. The alternative was square on. Bigger target, greater chance of ball strike, but only one of each organ was vulnerable. So, what option would Van Zoon adopt? Square on. Probably square on. *His build, what's the difference?* Marc-René chuckled inwardly, couldn't help himself, despite the sting of his wounds. His heart pumped hard in anticipation; his pistol hand began shaking even before he'd lifted it. He flexed his shoulders, rotated his head, stared into the Captain's face. There was a twitch to the man's waxed moustache, his eyes blinking rapidly. In all other respects impassive. He'd guessed right. Square on, pistol against his chest, protecting his heart.

He sighted above Van Zoon's head. Directly behind his target was the stables' weathervane. It would be a difficult shot, but not impossible. He could do it. The ball would pass high over the Captain's head, striking the cockerel's tail, sending it spinning. What a gallant gesture that would be. Unfortunately for Van Zoon he wasn't in a gallant mood. He lowered his arm, waited until the pistol was a blur and his target had come into sharp focus. He swallowed and slowly squeezed the trigger.

The cock snapped into the frizzen, the flint ignited the primer, the charge erupted in the barrel. With a brutal jolt the heavy calibre weapon leapt in his hand releasing a cloud of white smoke. He'd aimed low, judging the barrel would lift and he'd catch Van Zoon in the chest. But the recoil moved the shot higher than anticipated. Instead of hitting centre mass, the ball passed through the Captain's throat, severing his spine. His head flopped loose, blood jetted from the wound, and he dropped backwards with a surprised expression on his face.

Marc-René tossed the pistol to the ground, took a step forward and staggered. Esther rushed to embrace him. His wound seemed superficial, he refused attention and died nine days later with Esther holding his hand. It was speculated that a bullet fragment might have penetrated his brain.

1624

TWELVE — *that cannon's had it*

She could have left. She could have returned home. No one in Breda would have thought the less of her. One fewer unproductive mouth to feed, which would have been her own harsh reaction. The garrison was more charitable.

Choosing to stay hadn't been a difficult decision. Leaving would have represented a massive personal defeat. She missed her brothers like a physical pain. But she'd suffer that if she had to. There'd be no retreating into the closeted life of comfort and constraint. No giant step backwards in her evolution. It had been but a brief time since leaving home, but she'd undergone irrevocable and profound changes. She'd made the break, and some breaks don't mend. She was miserable, but not broken. She felt alive and authentic for the first time in her short existence. Like a butterfly contemplating its chrysalis, pumping blood into untested wings. No going back. Something must die for something to grow — life was sacrifice. Hadn't the Rabbi said that? She didn't feel better or worse, simply different. Pointless to mourn the natural order of things. It wasn't that she was unwilling (which she was) to plunge back into that sea of social entropy — she couldn't, she would no longer fit.

The women of the garrison treated her widowhood with a respect, even reverence. But Marc-René, she admitted, if only to herself, was not the love of her life. They were not romantic echoes of Abelard and Heloise. Their brief story was not the libretto to some tragic opera. Marc-René had been a convenience. One of which she'd grown fond. Nevertheless the relationship was a means to an end. A lesser of two evils. As for love, that was complicated and a future ideal. She decided that if she was going to mourn Marc-René she'd do so actively, purposefully. She might play the role of the tragic heroine. But she wouldn't be consumed by the character. Marc-René's had been a useless death. Unproductive of any advantage, a life squandered, a gift to the enemy. The Free Provinces had suffered the loss of two frontline combatants. And it had all been her fault. Rather, she'd been the cause, or more accurately, the excuse. And not of glorious deaths. Just a testosterone-fuelled squabble, hurt pride, hubris. But what were wars anyway, but men's bickering played out on the world stage. Injured pride on a global scale.

So, she did what women do in sieges. Cooked, cleaned, comforted, lit a few fires and scrambled to extinguish others, tended the wounded, buried the dead. She threw herself into these tasks, but soon became painfully bored with a woman's limitations. The new Esther Amsalem was bigger than this. In frustration she sought opportunity to approach Justinus. Beg for a more active, a more significant role. On one day the bombardment was particularly half-hearted. Just a few lightly injured casualties had straggled into the church doubling as a hospital. The women were scrubbing blood from the floor with vinegar, about to shut up shop when Dyrcx Van Oosterhout, Justinus' deputy, staggered through the door looking deeply sorry for himself.

'Leave this one to me,' said Esther, sensing potential opportunity.

She beckoned Dyrcx to her station. 'Now Your Honour, what's the problem.'

'Pain,' he said, tapping the right upper quadrant of his cuirass with a metalic clatter. Realising he was still wearing steel gauntlets, he prised them off.

'Right, let's get this thing out of the way,' said Esther, tapping his armoured chest.

He winced as she unbuckled the belt holding the front and back plate in place. As she unhooked the shoulder straps the back dropped to the floor with a hollow clatter. He wasn't a slim man, she repressed a smile, this was like peeling a turtle. There was a patch of blood on his buff jerkin. She unlaced the front and eased the heavy leather over his shoulders. Beneath his linen shirt she discovered a six-inch splinter, four inches of which embedded along his breastbone. Dyrcx squinted at it with a look of puzzlement.

'Cannon?' she said.

'Just missed me.'

'And splintered the town hall door?'

'How did you...?'

'Paint colour. Just a guess.'

Esther passed him a stone gin bottle. Taking two big gulps, he stared up at her like a frightened puppy. His big eyes widened in his ruddy face as she retrieved the bottle and doused a large set of pincers.

'Look at me,' she said, gripping his shoulder. Without warning she tugged the splinter out. His fleshy backside levitated from the wooden stool, landing back down with a well upholstered thump.

'That's it, worst over with,' she said.

He hissed as she irrigated the wound with alcohol. 'Must have gone through the arm hole,' he said, eyes watering, examining a scratch on his breastplate.

She passed him the bottle and he took two more big gulps. She waited for him to settle, then put her big blue eyes to work.

'I need a favour,' she said, tenderly brushing the curls from his eyes.

'Name it.'

François Kellerman ran the courier section of Justinus van Nassau's team of intelligencers. He accepted Esther on Dyrcx's recommendation, without hesitation. Soon he had Esther, disguised as a local urchin, sneaking through enemy lines carrying messages between the garrison and the forces of the Free Provinces. She was quick to memorise the complicated arrangement of fortifications, the curtain wall, the *faussebraye*, the ditch, revetments and horn works. The enemy's parallel earthworks — the curcumvallation and contravallation — were surprisingly easy to negotiate. Smugglers did it all the time, carrying inflated priced contraband to the Dutch garrison. She'd slip out of a sally port whilst the defenders were harrying the startled Spanish forces, melting into the night in the confusion.

One rain-sodden evening, returning from a similar mission, she stumbled upon a broad path churned by hooves. Deep wagon tracks triggered her interest. Dark clouds obscured the moon as she trailed them through sparse pine forests. After an hour, the trees gave way to heathland. As she mounted a low ridge, the clouds parted, and she saw the cause of the tracks. Twenty or so horses, still steaming from their exertions, corralled close by the carriage of a gigantic bronze cannon. She recognised this as a *kartouwe*. She knew to look out for these. Siege ordinance capable of hurling massively destructive fifty-six pound shot two-thousand yards.

There it sat, proud and menacing in the moonlight, a gleaming newborn monster, fresh cast from the foundry, with not a trace yet of patina. She stood frozen in awe of its elegance of purpose. A Catholic cannon primed to impregnate poor Protestant Breda with the seed of death. She wondered at the foundry's paradoxically feminine urge to decorate. At the swirls and curlicues and swags covering its gleaming surface, the massive barrel tapering elegantly from a cascabel resembling a pinecone to the foreskin-flare of the muzzle. The lips of the vent hole protruded from an intricate representation of the arms of Burgundy. All this baroque extravagance sat on trunions atop an iron bound carriage of brutal proportions like an overfed prince on a palanquin. Esther stepped cautiously from the cover of the undergrowth to examine it further.

Beside the cannon was a sledge on which rested neatly stacked iron shot and barrels of powder. Her trance broke when she caught sight of a gunner's stiletto resting on the carriage. Its slim triangular-section blade engraved with Roman numerals. An aid to calculation, doubling as a weapon of last resort. She grabbed it by its turned steel hilt and jammed it into the cannon's vent hole. Hefting an eight-pound ball she hammered it down on the pommel. On her third strike the blade had penetrated deep into the vent. Arms aching, she raised the ball for the fourth time when rough hands grabbed her, lifting her struggling from her feet. She kicked out, connecting with the dagger's hilt, snapping off the blade. Her last thoughts before fists pummelled her into unconsciousness — *that cannon's fucked.*

An icy torrent drenched her face, shocking her to consciousness. There was no liminal hiatus. No slow transition from one state to the next. Fully awake, she shook her head, blinking away the water, taking in her new surroundings.

To call this a tent would be to describe Noordeinde Palace as a shed. This was a pavilion of extraordinary proportion: fine Oriental carpets beneath her feet, baroque gilded furniture, tapestry wall hangings depicting classical heroes. A diagonal saw-toothed Burgundian cross, draped behind a long, intricately carved table, brought forth a reflexive shudder. Men in courtly costume clustered around. Far away the screams of souls in extremis rent the air, the crack of lash on flesh. Through the pavilion entrance, past the liveried guards and their ceremonial halberds, Esther made out four bodies, backs a bloody pulp, cut raw, roped to stakes, twitching as whips cut to the bone.

An effete Spanish voice brought her attention back to her situation. The crowd of gentlemen parted. She saw the speaker.

'Young man, I don't blame you. You were doing your duty. As for those wretches,' he nodded to the carnage outside, 'they should have been doing theirs, guarding my bastard cannon. You, my friend, don't deserve to suffer.'

Esther met his eyes. 'Thank you, your worship,' she croaked.

'No thanks required,' he said, turning to the sergeant at arms. 'Hang him with the rest in the morning.'

1624

THIRTEEN — *cut her down*

Hessel Gerritsen, drunk from the night before. Not tottering drunk, but certainly a little unsteady. By lunchtime he'd be developing a headache. Plenty of time for a top up 'tween now and then. This was profitable work. And none too taxing. Damned wars had been raging all his life. The butchery business had collapsed. Founded by his grandfather. Crying shame. This work he was at today was now the family's only source of income. Demands for his services were frequent of late. His purse had been swelling, his family were feeding well, the excess he pissed away at the inn.

So why couldn't just anyone do this? Ask yourself, would you want the job? And there's more to it than you'd think. This was execution not simple butchery. Although to the condemned the result would be the same. A judicial execution requires a certain finesse. A theatrical ritual enacted. A sense of pageantry demanded. Hessel Gerritsen saw himself as an artist. Today it was tawdry rainy, muddy, cloudy pageantry. Important, none-the-less.

Take the black mask. Truth was he didn't give a wet fart who saw his face. Everyone knew what he did for a living. There was no shame as far as he was concerned. Putting bread on the family's table, that's noble work however it's achieved. No one else involved in this business wore a mask. As for fear of reprisals, hardly. No, the mask was pure theatre; it instilled awe and dread. The faceless executioner, his part in this play. Hangings were judicial, there were set procedures. And his, he prided himself, was the principal role in this theatre of dread.

There were eleven of them. He hated uneven numbers. Something about them, he didn't know what. How or when it had started, he'd no idea. But he could only execute those they sent him. And, of course, in the manner prescribed. Who was he to argue about numbers? Still, he wasn't happy. Ever the professional, he pushed his foreboding to the back of his mind.

So, eleven of them, bound hand and ankle. Standing on stools. Ropes round their necks strung tight to the long beam of the gallows. There was room for three more, at least. Eleven, would one more really have hurt? The priest was moving down the line, getting a mixed reaction. His boy stood by with a bowl and cloth. Sometimes the protestants spat at the priest. Most simply ignored him. One began a speech, as was his right. But was it his right? He was never sure on that point. Anyway, Maybe. But this one was abusing the privilege. Going on for far too long, rambling inconsequential nonsense. He nodded to his son who tightened the rope, cutting him off short.

Pity on that skinny kid in the middle. He could dangle up there for hours. A crowd was gathering, muttering for him to get on with it. They weren't here for this event. It'd be strappado next; a few mutilations were scheduled and a couple of fellas to break on the wheel. That always made for lively entertainment.

Three horsemen from the Ginneken Compartment office pressed through the crowd.

'Everything ready?'

'Yes, Your Honour,' replied the hangman. *Christ in heaven, what the hell does it look like?*

Another of the riders read out the names of the condemned. 'Everyone present, yes?' he said, counting them off with a kid-gloved hand. Satisfied the number agreed with his list, he droned on with the usual. 'By order of His Worship Francisco Medina, Comandante General of...' Gerritsen had heard it all before, *blah, buggering, blah, blah, blah.*

'By the authority invested in me ...'

Gerritsen nodded to his youngster who proceeded down the line kicking out the stools. Halfway down, there was a flash of yellow. That skinny one, the cap had fallen off. Waist length hair the colour of ripe wheat tumbled out, waving in the wind as the body thrashed on the rope. Bulging tear-filled cornflower blue eyes bulged, a delicate pink tongue protruded.

Another rider drew up, shared a softly spoken word with the Ginneken officers and then rode away.

One of the horsemen yelled at Gerritsen:

'My man, that one, stop it.'

'Stop what sir? You've just pronounced sentence. Can't interrupt the doings of justice can we now? I've me job to do. Me civic responsibilities.'

'Take that one down, now,' yelled the official.

He pointed to the youth. The beam of the gallows was bending under the weight of the victims. Vibrating with their struggles, their soundless gasps.

'But sir,' Gerritsen protested.

The rider nudged his horse a couple of paces forward and thrust an ornate saddle pistol into the hangman's face.

'Let me do my job.' said Gerritsen, affronted. Then in a lower voice. 'For a couple of silver pieces you can have the body for your personal pleasure whilst its still warm.'

'Cut her down you insolent moron. Says here you're to hang a boy, not a girl.'

'I'll still get paid for the full eleven, right?'

'By the order of Comandante General Francisco Medina cut that person the hell down.' By way of emphasis he pulled back the cock on his pistol. The hangman shrugged, least he had his even number.

'Yes, Your Worship, of course.'

The crust gluing her lids parted and her eyes flashed open to an inverted world. Her throat was desert dry; she went to swallow, felt her face contorting in agony. She took a breath feeling her lungs bubbling with fluid. When she coughed it felt like her ribcage would explode.

Shouldn't she be dead. Shouldn't she be beyond all this. Her head was spinning. That unmistakable musky equine smell. The ponderous clop of its hooves. She found herself slung like a rolled-up carpet across the back of a mule. Her head lolled like a damaged puppet. Opening her mouth to say something and harp strings of saliva stretched between her teeth. She retched. Watery vomit splashed down the creature's flank, blood and bile dribbled from her nose. Then she began tumbling down a long dark corridor to a temporary oblivion.

Surfacing, however much later, she was shocked to discover herself still not quite dead. Breath was coming in wheezing gasps as her lungs fought to suck breath passed a swollen windpipe. Something caught in her throat propelling her into a series of wracking coughs. Constellations exploded behind her eyes. Darkness closed in once more.

Her eyes fluttered open, the movement was at an end, the donkey stink gone. She was laying on a straw-filled mattress, shivering, mind scrambled. What had her last meal been, molten lead? Her head locked to one side by spasming muscles. Tentatively, she touched her throat, rewarded by an avalanche of searing pain. Her fingers came away bloody. Agony like a burning necklace circumscribed her throat. She panted hard against the constriction of her airways. Tentatively she sat up, her movement slow, gentle, balancing her head like a fishwife with an overladen basket.

Was she truly saved? Or was the sentence merely postponed. God

1624

knows, she couldn't go through that again. She laughed, choked and spat blood. There was someone else in the room. A woman offered her a ladle of rusty water. Attempts to swallow resulted in violent coughs and sprays of mucus. She attempted to speak and failed. A cool dampened cloth draped about her neck. Her eyes were swollen, tears, blurring her vision. More shallow breaths. More darkness. Dreams of happier times. Of the caresses of pretty Neeltje that she'd abandoned.

She awoke flooded with sensory impressions. Perhaps rebounding from the insults to her body, her senses took flight. The shock of the drop. The greater shock of survival. Suffocation taking her to the very edge of oblivion. Could it be if you approach so close to death, you bring back some Heavenly Grace. Like a bee returning with pollen to the hive. She could smell every blade of the sun-warmed grass outside. Taste its sweetness as it swayed in the wind. She imagined a farm, and a family wresting a living from honest soil. Animals in the fields, children playing under a blue canopy.

Then they came for her. Rough hands stripped off her soiled clothing. Ice-cold water cascaded over her. They scrubbed her until she bled. There were chattering voices; she barely registered the content, or even the language. When she was half-dried they forced her into a dress, dragged a comb through her hair. That done, the hidden hands dragged her into a warm room. Her eyes had continued to swell, her vision was now almost non-existent. Her world reduced to simple moving shapes and vague ill-defined colours, bleeding one into the other, overlapping, intersecting. These shapes had male voices. Spanish. Yes, they were Spanish, she could tell that now. Hands began pulling at her. Feeling under her dress, touching her, squeezing her.

She spat bloody phlegm. Screamed obscenities, oblivious of the agony, lashing out blindly. A fist knocked her to the ground. Boots kicked her. Dragged backwards, cold granite cobbles chilling her bare feet. Hands trussed above her. Knees collapsing, hanging from rope once more. The first stroke overpowered her senses. Those that followed took her to a world beyond imagination. But deep inside, behind the layers of pain and humiliation, a voice reminded her she had just survived a judicial execution. How hard could an informal whipping be to endure?

She should call this her lucky day.

1624

FOURTEEN — *Truly and Well-beloved*

Isaac had promised Esther. A promise is a sacred thing. But sacred things, he was soon to discover, were heavy burdens indeed. Especially when they involve lies.

Sagging in the saddle, he passed under the archway of the Amsalem's stable yard. It was hard to see which was the most road-weary, the rider or his mount. Indeed, it was almost impossible to tell where horse ended and man began, so complete was the accretion of mud. Isaac dismounted like an equestrian statue come to life. His feet touched ground as though unprepared for the rigor of gravity. Snorting vaporous plumes of relief, the horse stamped its approval on the cobbles. A groom rushed from his stable fiefdom to eject this dirt-caked interloper.

'Hello Hendrik,' said Isaac, brushing past him, and stumbling to the horse trough. Cracking the thin crust of ice, he dunked his face, and splashed the back of his neck.

'Is that you sir?' said Hendrik, flashing a tentative smile.

'Certainly hope so. Let's get me cleaned up, and then we can be sure.'

Fat Marris, observing the unfolding drama from the bready warmth of the scullery, rushed to inform the Rebbetzin of Isaac's return. She in turn dispatched a runner to the docks in search of the Rabbi. Isaac glimpsed her staring down from an upper window, breaking out a thin, muddy smile. Her face retreated into darkness, like a moon behind a midnight cloud.

'Can't possibly enter the house like this,' said Isaac, a rasp in his voice, 'not with me looking like a half-drowned golem.' A soft chuckle ended in a wracking cough.

Whilst Hendrik took charge of his horse, Isaac emptied the tin trough and dragged it into the straw-sweet warmth of the stables. A yell into the scullery put Mariss and Neeltje to heating water. Soon they were transporting steaming pans across the yard. Neeltje gathered fresh clothes from Isaac's chamber. The two girls hung around for morsels of information. Mariss for gossip's sake, pretty Neeltje for heart's sake.

1624

'Out,' Isaac commanded.

Marris, gathering her skirts in plump fingers, waddled back to the house. Neeltje hesitated: 'Mister Isaac,' she said, 'my mistress, what news?'

Promises are easy in the making, difficult in the keeping. Isaac took this opportunity to practice his lie. Soon there would be a more stringent test.

'Sorry, it's not good news,' he said.

'*No* Sir.' Neeltje's pleading eyes met his, her pretty lips trembling.

'I'm afraid so.' Isaac confirmed, stony faced.

'*No* sir, please not.' Neeltje took a step backwards, and then another, as though distance might somehow reverse the outcome. Her pretty expression collapsed. Covering her face with her apron, she whirled round and ran from the stables, shoulders heaving with silent misery. A shiver ran through Isaac. There was no going back now. The pebble had broken the surface, and the first ripple had begun.

His clothes felt loose. Not as much of him as had left, had returned. He entered the kitchen with its homely aromas: smouldering peat, poultry, bread and women. Cook was sitting in a shadowy corner, face haloed in the glow of the stove. Her plump arms wrapped around Neeltje, collapsed on her knees on the cold tiled floor, head buried in cook's aproned lap. Cook nodded towards the scrubbed pine table. A plate of beef and bread and a mug of ale awaited him. But the lie had left a bitter taste, and he wasn't hungry. Regardless his proximity to the oven, he shivered still and every so often a saddle-sore shudder ran through him.

'Where's my brother?'

'At his studies Sir,' whispered cook, absently rocking the sobbing Neeltje, 'won't be back for quite a while yet. Shall you send for him?'

Isaac dreaded imparting this news to Benjamin. He forced himself to eat, if only to delay the moment of confrontation with his parents. Dressed, fed and fragrant, word came that the Master had returned.

The Rabbi and the Rebbetzin received him in the withdrawing room, side by side, as though sitting for a family portrait, his mother still in her black weeds. Isaac had departed in defiance of their wishes. What sort of welcome should he expect? Not that of a returning hero, of that much he was certain. Should he begin by apologising? This would have been his inclination before he'd left, but not now, he'd changed.

'Dare we guess where you've been,' said the Rabbi, stonily.

'You know where I've been.'

The Rebbetzin turned on him, eyes flaring. The Rabbi held up his hand, silencing her before a bitter flood erupted. 'What news?' he said.

1624

Isaac heard himself mouthing the story he'd rehearsed. The narrative, he noted, took a spear-like form. A long shaft of truths tipped at the very last by a lie.

'Terheijden, followed them to a town called Terheijden, just north of Breda.'

'Yes, I know Terheijden,' snapped the Rabbi, impatiently.

'There'd been a great battle. Fields strewn with the bodies of English allies. Spanish patrols were everywhere. Italian mercenaries rode me down. For their amusement. Protestant soldiers came to my aid. I was fortunate to escape with my life.' His hand touched the wound at his brow. 'At a local inn, someone tended to me. Said the English had been on a mission to relieve Breda. There was a commotion in the bar. The innkeeper was haggling with customers over a bag of trinkets. That's when I caught sight of this...'

Isaac dropped Esther's necklace onto the table.

'It's how soldiers pay their bills,' he said. 'Plundered loot. In this case stolen from still-warm bodies on the field of Terheijden.'

Esther would never willingly part with this remembrance of her birthmother. The family's proxy grief had suddenly become all too real. Hard to believe, but the Rebbetzin's mood seemed to lighten. No more pretending, no more public stigma, dead really did mean dead now.

The Rabbi let out a long sigh. Despite the dimly lit interior, Isaac thought he glimpsed moisture in his stepfather's eyes.

'The *Rachael* is coming on well,' he said, shuffling to the window, to gaze distractedly towards the harbour. 'Her launch should be on schedule. Spars are completing soon. You might want to talk to the sailmaker, Old Groot, you know him of course.'

Isaac went to stand. Was it the abrupt change of subject, or fatigue that sent his head spinning so? He reached out grabbing a chairback for support.

Benjamin arrived home shortly after Isaac fell into bed. He stood over his sleeping brother, candle in hand: 'You promised,' he said, wiping a tear from his cheek, 'You promised you'd bring her home.'

Isaac dreamed of Esther. Her prophesy of the family disintegrating, he saw them tearing apart, spinning away from each other through endless space. He awoke the following morning no less fatigued, teeth chattering, despite the warmth of the room. That day he kept to his bed, his mind whirling with bizarre otherworldly abstractions.

There was a sound. Shivering uncontrollably, he forced his weighted eyelids open. Benjamin was at his bedside, dressed to leave for the

1624

yeshiva. Through chattering teeth Isaac repeated the story he'd spun for their parents. The lance of truth tipped with a lie. After the retelling Isaac felt less guilty. This untruth had taken on a slick quality, like reciting a memorised passage of scripture. Was repetition transmuting his lie into a tainted truth. The secret of the philosopher's stone. Everything becomes something else under pressure of will. Esther was making an alchemist of him. Or simply tarnishing his soul. After Benjamin had left, the servants stoked the fire.

He remained in bed all day sweating and shivering, refusing food. That night Fat Marris slipped between his sheets holding him in a musky embrace until the fever broke. She was back in her own bed by sunrise. Shortly afterwards, Benjamin paid Isaac another visit. Isaac had no fresh platitudes to comfort his brother. Instead he reached under his pillow with trembling fingers.

'Keep this for her,' he said, handing Benjamin Esther's amulet. 'Perhaps one day, you never know...'

The moon was full. But darkly bruised clouds negated its illumination. The Rabbi took a light from the Rattle Watch when his lantern blew out. Along the canal, candles flickered in doorways. He walked distractedly, head bowed, despite the ever-present danger of tripping into the watery depths or falling foul cutpurses. The cantillation of a familiar prayer calmed his turbulent thoughts. Shadows crossed the bridge behind him, keeping pace. In this moment, personal safety was not paramount in his consciousness. As though to contradict this feeling of relaxed confidence, he found his free hand loosening his dagger in it's sheath.

He was returning from a congregant's house which substituted for a formal synagogue. There was a fund to establish a permanent bet ha-kneset. There were two fiercely debated options – repurpose an existing building or build anew. He was in favour of building anew. But that was just another matter he couldn't generate the enthusiasm to care about. Since the news of Esther, his normally lively mind had dulled. Goyim partners were taking adequate care of the business interests he was shamefully neglecting. Similarly, the charitable fund for the city poor. Mokum had been kind to his community. He hadn't been demonstrating much gratitude of late.

The shadows were keeping pace. No lantern, breaching local ordinance, he could feel them, nevertheless. Once in Jodenbreestraat the Rabbi continued past his front door. An alleyway led to a separate entrance to his personal quarters. He watched the street as he fumbled the heavy key into the lock. Once inside, he slid the bolt across with more vigour than strictly necessary. Shrugging, he questioned this small sign of anxiety. Lighting an oil lamp from his lantern candle, the chamber brightened. He nudged the smoking turf in the grate with the toe of his boot, embers sparked and glowed brighter — fire, such a primitive comfort.

There came a gentle tapping. He raised his tired shoulders. Releasing a deep sigh, he slid the bolt quietly aside. His instincts had been correct. Never doubt them. Taking a seat at a table facing the door, he said:

'It's not locked, come in why don't you.'

The door creaked open. A slim figure stepped from the watery moon into a halo of amber lamplight. Upon hearing the sharp mechanical clicks of pistol cocks drawn back, the visitor froze.

'Hands where I can see them,' said the Rabbi.

In the act of sweeping off a feathered cap, the visitor wisely slowed his movements.

'And you are?' said the Rabbi.

'My name is not important Worship. Do I have the honour of addressing Nathaniel Amsalem?' The Rabbi grunted; his visitor continued. 'My regrets for disturbing you at this hour Your Worship. I'm bearing urgent news from a certain Royal Personage of your acquaintance. We understand you offered a reward for the return of a certain relative's remains.'

'You have news? Are you claiming the reward?'

'Yes and no, your Worship. There may be better news to offer — *your daughter lives.*'

The Rabbi gasped, rising to his feet. Then swaying he reached to the table for support. The brocade table-covering began to slide. A beaten brass fruit bowl fell to the floor, its contents rolling into the shadows.

The nameless visitor supported the Rabbi to a fireside chair. Removing the pistols from his hands, he eased the cocks back down, taking the seat opposite him.

'My master has received intelligence from Breda. Your relative did not meet her end in that skirmish near Terheijden, as we believe you suspected. Her companion did not survive, but she did. How this came about is unknown. Thereafter she entered employment with Justinus Nassau, serving with distinction as a courier. Captured, she was about to hang as a spy, but the Duke of Medina reprieved her. Now she's enslaved and bound for his colonial estates. Currently she's en route from Antwerp to Cadiz. From there she will take ship to the West Indies.'

'The Royal Personage charged me to impart this news verbally, and to leave you with this.'

The Rabbi's visitor placed a sealed paper on the table. The Rabbi cracked the wax open, eyes glazed, like an opium eater.

My Truly and Well-beloved subject Nathaniel. Next to Popery there is no Debasement lower than Slavery, save to be a Slave to a Papist. Present this token to any Office in my lands and they will know to Facilitate any action necessary for your Deliverance from these present miseries. May Almighty God look with Favour on any such enterprise you Undertake.

At the foot was the seal of Orange-Nassau and His Highness's signature.

The Rabbi walked his midnight visitor to the door and into the dark street, where his escort waited. As their voices drifted out of hearing, Benjamin slipped away, replacing the borrowed book as he went. His first reaction was joy at Esther's survival. But then the full weight of his sister's plight fell on him. He was horrified at his father's indifference. Unseen, he stumbled back to his room. Collapsing onto his bed he fell off a precipice and into a void so dark he might never find his way out. And there in this dark oblivion he found numbing comfort. Out in the street, the Rabbi caught the messenger's arm:

'We must contact this Medina immediately. Negotiate a ransom.'

'We've tried. Medina is obdurate. When the money mounts up he may comply. But even now it would be too late to intercept your ward before her ship leaves for the Americas. And should he accept your offer it could be months before word arrives with Medina's agents in Cuba.'

Tears rimmed the Rabbi's eyes, blurring his focus. Esther's death, he could deal with. Indeed, had dealt with. He'd already grieved for a living Esther; and he'd grieved for an ambiguously deceased Esther. Now there was the captive Esther to deal with. Esther alive, but in the limbo of slavery. The pain he had so stoically borne, so successfully hidden, hit him like a Biblical flood. He wiped his eyes and shook the messenger's hand, wordlessly expressing his gratitude. He returned to his study, shoulders shaking.

Benjamin awoke full of purpose, clutching Esther's amulet. He didn't even make a pretence of attending yeshiva. Instead, he marched round to the Monkey House and awoke his navigation tutor. If his father was indifferent to Esther's fate, he certainly was not.

His first words: 'Cuba. Tell me what you know about Cuba.'

1624

FIFTEEN — *warring ghosts*

Harsh and immoderate words had spilled between Benjamin and the Rabbi his father. Life had lost its savour without his sister – his closest confidante and friend. Colours dulled, sounds became muted and discordant. The sister who was not a sister. Gone.

But now, this news. News that was not news, because it remained unshared. Esther alive. Esther alive, not dead. He wanted to proclaim it from the rooftops. Esther lives. His father would surely make the announcement the following morning. But he said nothing. Esther remained dead. It had been two weeks now. He began to believe he'd dreamed the mysterious visitor. Two weeks doubting his sanity.

But now on this fine fresh day it all became clear. Opening his sleepy eyes, he overheard an intense inner dialogue. A plan was in progress. Forming, but not yet formed. It began gaining structure as he strolled towards the docks. Life, he decided, felt better with a plan. Plans to a Jew were what a sword is to a heathen. Not all plans are successful, of course. But you always feel purposeful in the planning. Purposeful and powerful. Untested swords are never blunt. Untested plans never fail. This plan, when it emerged, would indeed be tested. And tested potentially to destruction.

Tendrils of mist haunted the harbour despite the predations of the sun. The Zeider Zee sparkled as it swelled its proud breast. Ships rose higher on the wharf. Regardless of the hour, the waterside was busy. Once past the dock gates he merged with the crowd. A minnow blending with the shoal. Passengers and crew embarking and disembarking. Dockers loading and unloading. Vessels berthing and casting off. Capstans creaking. Cranes lifting. Seagulls screeching. Over-burdened wagons rumbled by. Iron-shod wheels striking a rhythm on the cobbles. The tightly choreographed mayhem of the world's busiest port. Cultures of land and sea enjoying tumultuous and profitable collision. Building an empire; fighting a war; feeding a nation. Lethargy was an alien concept within these portals. Vigour and purpose imbued everyone and everything.

Well, not everyone. It had been a while since he'd seen his mates, Roelant and Rinus, the would-be mohels.

'So how's business,' he said, with forced cheer, 'cut off any good dicks recently.'

'Not recently,' said one, 'not professionally, leastwise.'

'But ever hopeful,' said the other.

Benjamin climbed up next to them on bales of cotton. They talked of this and that. Asked after the miser Gerrit Dou and his model Justine. He'd always teased them with hope of an introduction. Conversation drifted as they watched the world whirl noisily by. After a while he enquired, as casually as he could make it appear:

'Any vessels leaving for the West Indies?'

'Sorry?'

'Caribbean, West Indies, maybe Cuba?'

'Cuba, never. We're at war with the bastards, need I remind you.'

'The only place would be a flyspeck called Sint Maarten. There's naff-all there.'

'And not from here,' said the other. 'Maybe Rotterdam for that.'

Somewhere inside, the plan was absorbing this fresh information. Making the appropriate corrections in light of new knowledge.

'Must be plenty bound for North Africa, Morocco?'

'East Indies, different matter entirely. Loading supplies before the Horn.'

Morocco with the chances of unallied shipping heading to the Caribbean. The theatre of Captain Terbrugghen's past glories. A tingle travelled down his spine. Privateers or pirates, allied to no nation. Plunder and profit and adventure.

'That one, that pretty picture over there. The one with an aft castle tarted up like a Catholic cathedral. Ninety-gun two decker ship-of-war. Escorting a flotilla of merchantmen down to Salé. That's Morocco son. Zeelander, she's called. Leaving on the morning tide.'

'How can I get aboard her,' said Benjamin.

'You're not seriously thinking about...'

'What, that? No, just like a closer look at her.'

The plan was rapidly gaining flesh. Benjamin desperately needed this to stabilise his life. One minute buoyed by the thermals of limitless possibility. Next, diving dizzy, dragged down by the vertigo of despair. Intoxicated by the momentousness of this undertaking. Images of Esther enslaved sent him plummeting into the bubbling lava floes of hell. Esther alive and freed sent him soaring to the heavens. Sometimes these notions so close they appeared to coincide. Up or down, up and down, his head a swirling dice-toss of confusion. His companions not as easily fooled.

'You want our help to stow away, it'll cost you.'

Benjamin rifled through the satchel he'd slung over his shoulder. They settled for two half-guilder silver pieces.

'How much more scratch you got?' said Roelant. 'Got an idea, but we gonna need bribe money.'

Up and down the gangplank, Benjamin panted and sweated, his future a swirl of possibilities. Mind engaged in reconnoitring potential hiding places, he clattered into a body as unyielding as a temple pillar. Towering above him was a creature from the most extravagant of nightmares. Tattoos he'd seen before. But never anything like these. A stubbled face and shaven head delineated in intricate baroque patterns. Tattoos. But not just tattoos, carved. Incised into living flesh like the leatherwork on Spanish boots. The vision smiled as Benjamin imagined a crocodile might smile. With this change in expression the scarifications moved like they had independent life. Dancing to a rhythm of their own choosing. Benjamin struggle round this heathen who clearly wasn't in the mood to move himself. Wide, red-rimmed eyes followed this manoeuvre. With a grunt the man moved on. Crewmen tugged their forelocks respectfully, making room for him to pass.

The best of plans are simple plans. Benjamin had heard that often. His plan was simply to get close as he could to Esther's location, be those ten or a hundred miles. Improvise from there. It was hardly a plan at all. And this gave him a great degree of confidence. What could go wrong with such a simple plan, which was hardly a plan at all?

Sacks of grain swung through the sky, craned into the hold. This gang's task was loading man-haulable supplies into the galley stores. Money changed hands between his pals and the foreman docker. Benjamin found himself recruited to the victualling gang, loading last minute perishables. No skin off the foreman's arse, free labour and a silver piece. Up and down the gangplank he struggled. His friends returned to practicing strenuous lounging. He'd expected a ship to move with so many feet tramping up and down, so many loaded backs. Maybe it was this expectation gave him the impression the deck was more solid than the dockside.

The cook fussed around the storeroom examining the contents of barrels and sacks, directing the disposition of deliveries. Salt pork here, barley there, live chickens in the coop outside if you please young man.

Sides of beef, sacks of flour and beans, boxes of apples and pears, dried salt fish. Aromas mounted layer-upon-layer until melded into an indistinguishable mélange.

Eight times Benjamin had been up and down that gangplank with a bone crushing load. His back developed a vicious ache, his knees shook, and his legs felt like they might buckle at any minute. Despite the chill in the air, his young brow beaded with sweat. His fellow labourers carried twice his load like they were bags of feathers. By the ninth, or tenth trip he'd decided on his next move. He couldn't handle much more of this.

He'd noticed a door swinging ajar. The shadowed space beyond piled high with coils of rope and great bulks of fresh clean canvas. Sail locker, as good a place as any. Things were falling nicely into place. Now when to make his move? When opportunity presented itself, of course, have faith.

'We've stuffed your satchel in that sack of rolled oats,' Rinus had told him. 'Make sure you can get to it when you need.'

His precious books, his money, a few clothes, some dry rations. When eyes no one was looking he tossed the heavy oat sack in the sail locker. On the next trip to the stores he slipped in with them.

'Where's that boy?' the foreman grunted.

'Looked like he'd had enough,' sniggered one of the gang. 'Sloped off, weak back probably.'

'Hope he doesn't expect payment. That's going in my pocket,' said the foreman. 'Little snip.'

'Oi, hurry up and get this loaded,' yelled the cook, barging between them. 'Crew'll be back soon, pissed as dockside rats and expecting some solid grub to line their bastard guts.'

With that he brushed flour from his face and went back to rolling dumplings. In the light of a flaming range a boy stood on a box stirring a vast pot with a wooden spoon as tall as himself. The dumpling took to the air, landing with a plop amidst the beef and carrots and beans.

The flotilla was due to make way on the next morning's tide. The crew straggled back in raucous drunken groups. Preparations were already underway to warp it from its birth. Leave on the dawn ebb, be in the Zeider Zee deep water channel before the flood returned. Drop anchor if the wind wasn't favourable. Excitement temporarily blunted Benjamin's appetite. But the sounds and smells of eating had him reaching into his satchel — no cheese, no bread, no clothes, no books, no money — *those bastards.* He finally drifted off to sleep hidden under a bolt of canvas, a curse on his lips. He hadn't planned for this.

Roelant and Rinus whiled away the afternoon converting Benjamin's cash into gin and then into hangovers. And no consciences pricked in the doing. With each glass they raised, they wished their departed friend good luck. And luck, they knew, to a stowaway would be a currency of infinitely more value than money. When the pilfered silver ran out, they attempted a similar transmutation with Benjamin's books. But Hebrew-literate dockside drunks proved remarkably rare that night. The early evening found them sitting in the gutter polishing off the last of Benjamin's rations. It was then Rinus remembered the message with which Benjamin had entrusted them. And trust to them was a sacred thing. As was the potential of reward from the recipient.

There came a knock on the street door. It was Friday night. The second day since Benjamin's disappearance. Isaac and the Rabbi had people out combing the streets. The light was fading, soon it would be Sabbath. Mariss was upstairs enduring the Rebbetzin's hysterics. Neeltje passed the door on her way to the kitchen to assist cook. Under the circumstances they weren't expecting guests. Not since young Benjamin had gone God knows where. She removed her kitchen apron and smoothed the front of her dress. Tucking a stray hank of hair behind her ear, she opened the door a crack. Roelant and Rinus were at the bottom of the steps. None too steady, it appeared, on their feet. They looked up at her, saying nothing.

'What?' she said, testily.

Their bloodshot eyes glanced at each other and then back to her. The fat one pursed his lips. Christ, was he going to whistle her a tune? It dawned on Neeltje, in the ensuing silence, each thought the other would do the talking. They stood there for a while longer, metronomically swaying, each to separate tempi. Then both rushed to speak in a collision of garbled words. Another shared look. They lapsed back into silence, baffled. Like this was a problem quite beyond their experience or capacity to comprehend.

Neeltje became nervous, what if the Rebbetzin thought she was entertaining gentleman callers?

'Whatever you're after you ain't getting it here, be off with you.'

She went to close the door. But something about them made her hesitate. The skinny one nudged the calf of the stout one, with the worn-through toe of his boot. He grunted encouragement and flicked his matted hair in Neeltje's direction. His companion took this as his cue for a solo performance and cleared his throat.

'You don't know us missus.' *That's for damned sure.* 'But is this where a Master Benjamin lives?'

Neeltje, almost regretting she was not in a playful mood, snapped back: 'Who wants to know?'

They snatched off their caps. 'Names not important missus. Got a message from Master Benjamin.'

Just then Isaac rounded the corner and grabbed the skinny one by the scruff of his neck.

'Where did you get that scarf?'

The stout one turned to flee and crashed into the Rabbi. A note penned in Benjamin's hand fluttered to the ground.

Isaac loaded a bundle of provisions aboard the Pride of Brabant. Big name for a small ship. Not even a ship, a *kaag*, the yard's working boat. Thirty-five feet over deck, with a ten-foot bowsprit. Flat bottomed, it would float in a duckpond. And, being broad of beam, stood her canvas well. She was his wooden pet; he called her the Braba.

It was blowing from the west. Ideal wind direction, pity it was so light. Likely it would pick up when they made open water. The tide was mid-way through the ebb. Out in the harbour it would be in their favour, pulling them out to sea. Full moon — the tide would be at its strongest. They'd pop into the outer harbour like a cork from a bottle. That is, if they made it that far. When he stepped aboard, the Braba didn't move. Her keel was touching bottom. Their departure now far from certain. Isaac handed one of the long sweeps, jammed it into the mud and levered hard against the gunnel. To his relief she broke away and drifted into the creek. Ten minutes later it would have been a problem. Another six hour wait and forced to leave on an incoming tide. And there'd be awkward questions from that idiot yard manager.

He punted hard against the soft mud until the hull was completely free. Then, taking up the other sweep, he bent his back to rowing. Approaching the creek entrance, he shipped oars. Scrambling to the mast he hauled on the topsail halyard. The triangular red sail rose to the mast peak, flogged and fluttered and finally filled. With a sound of a rippling mountain stream the bows began parting the water. Soon the reedy creek was a memory, and they were passing wharves crowded with ships beyond count. Isaac steered towards the twinkling entrance lights, feeling the tide taking hold. Leaving the tiller, he unbrailed the main. The wind snatched at the sail and the sprit swung away to larboard. Isaac dropped the leeboard and yanked the foresail halyard good and tight. By the time he'd recovered the tiller he could smell the mud of the opposite bank. Not so good on a falling spring tide. He rushed to correct course and tripped on a thwart. Was he wasting his time chasing a fleet of merchantmen in this tiny boat? The very thought was ridiculous. He should be hunting for his missing sister. But he was too busy to curse his little brother, time enough for that later.

The wind strengthened. Isaac steered through the ships anchored outside the harbour walls. Braba's planking creaked as she heeled. Water hissed under her bows, and she picked up speed. She and her sisters were fast. With flat bottoms there was minimal keel drag. Their breath of beam providing ample righting moment. It'd take a much stronger wind for Isaac to consider shortening sail. Driving her hard on a broad reach she could make seven or eight knots, the flotilla, six or less. The Braba could keep going on a zephyr. Light winds would leave the heavier merchantmen drifting on the tide. On that basis, he'd be looking to overtake way before Cherbourg. Could be as early as Dunkirk.

Once through the entrance he kept the lights to his back. The coast was dark, the shallows treacherous. Harbour lights, fast retreating behind him, and the moon were all he had for guides. Wrapping his cloak about him, he settled in for a tense night.

He hadn't slept, at least he didn't think so. But he couldn't remember much of the night. The blanket of stars stretching into infinity, the moon reflecting on the surface of the sea, beauty beyond description. But too much of anything was monotonous. Even glory of creation. The tide, which had turned against them at midnight, was now shifting in their favour. The sun crept over his shoulder, warming his bones. He flapped the feeling back into his arms. Progress had been better than hoped. The wind had swung further north. He'd gybed and eased the canvas as he left the Zuiderzee with Texel to starboard. Hooking south he headed towards the channel, keeping the coast in sight. The light of a fresh dawn saw him sailing at a decent clip. He weaved through a fleet of herring boats hauling their bulging nets, seabirds swooping to pilfer what they could from this bounty. He waved at the fisherman, exchanging bellowed greetings. The featureless coast passed by all that day, as he sailed on a comfortable broad run. He snatched fragments of sleep slumped over the tiller. Flogging sails telling him when he'd strayed off the wind.

As the sun broke over the horizon on the second day he tightened the sheets, heeling the Braba as far as he dared. Her windward stays hummed like over-tightened harp strings; her leeward stays flapped loose. Isaac felt her enthusiasm as she picked up another half knot, chasing the bow wave like a dog on a bone. Acting according to her design, fulfilling her purpose. What more could any of God's creatures demand of their Creator, or He them? Further out to sea waves kicked up, showering Isaac with a refreshing salt spray. His jaw ached from an idiot grin; he forced his face to relax. Regardless of its solemn purpose, this was so much fun. With the sun once more warming his back he powered on. Breakfast consisted of smoked herring and dry bread washed down with flat beer. Lunch was to be bread and cheese.

He calculated they'd be approaching the gut of the channel early next morning. The wind picked up towards evening. He eased the sheets but didn't shorten sail. Being the vessel's only ballast he sat on the windward rail, bracing his feet on the tiny cuddy, stomach muscles straining. The notorious Dunkirkers, marauding French privateers, patrolled this coast. His pulse increased at the thought. Catch me if you can, he'd relish a chase, confident in his vessel and his skills. He'd raced her against other yacht's; few could match her for speed.

The Braba could maintain this pace forever and a day, but not so him. His eyelids were becoming heavy. He'd slumped forwards over the tiller once too often, recovering just before he'd hit the deck. With great reluctance he turned into the wind and backed the jib, lashing the tiller to leeward. Hove to, it was like the wind had ceased entirely. All urgency dissipated, the hull rose and fell lazily on the swell. It was his intention to doze for an hour or so, but inevitably it was longer. Rumblings from the west jolted him awake. Thunder, but no lightning. What made thunder without lightning? Guns. He lowered the Dutch ensign. No point in looking for trouble; the Spanish were occupying Antwerp.

The horizon softened. Soon the distant land dissolved, and the air took on a tangible cloying quality. He eased the tiller to leeward, away from the coast, aiming for relative safety mid-channel. As the mist thickened into dense fog, he steered by compass alone. There were gusts coming. Braba heeled harder. Unlike him, the wind didn't need to see; it knew where it was bound. Isaac cursed; the words hung reproachfully in the air before him, as if reluctant to accept their freedom. He wouldn't show a light; no point in attracting attention.

He eased the sheets, the Braba came upright, slowed to four knots. Isaac stood at the helm, straining his senses. Mist, like giant floating cobwebs, swirled about the mast, teasing the sails. He could hear his heartbeat, the rasping of his lungs sucking in the chill, briny, vapour-rich air. There was something ahead. He sensed it before he saw it. Could it be some vast spectral galleon or a product of his over-stimulated imagination? More shadowy vessels intruded into the grey flat seascape. To his left came a muted pulse of yellow light, a crack of thunder, a rumbling echo. To his right more eruptions of light, more thunder. With a sound like a bosun's whistle the sea erupted ahead of him, an iron ball skipped over the water like a stone on a pond. Another explosion and the sea plumed behind him. He spun about finding himself encircled by huge warring ghost ships.

Pulse racing, he hardened the sails. The Braba picked up speed and they raced on through the fog. Only when the cannon-fire faded in his wake did he relax. A ship's bell rang twice. Second bell of the forenoon watch he was thinking absently, when the massive bows of a merchantman smashed the Braba to matchwood.

1624

SIXTEEN — *thoughts of pie*

Benjamin hadn't planned well. He thought he had. But he hadn't. Impulse is never the best strategist. Since Isaac returned from Breda Benjamin had retreated into himself. His big brother had failed; he never failed. Why choose now, of all times, to become fallible? Esther a slave. Enslaved to a Spaniard, a Catholic. Images of abject suffering and humiliation flooded his mind. He shook his head. This didn't dispel them. But they did at least soften, blur at the edges.

His stepfather retreated into prayer and scripture. He said Kaddish for Esther, the prayer for the dead. Running off with the Goyim, nothing worse could befall the family. He could conceive of no greater insult, such unimaginable ingratitude. She was dead to him. Dead like she'd never existed.

You can't enslave the dead. The dead don't suffer except in Roman Catholic hell. And the hell the Christians visited upon the earth in the name of a murdered Jew. He forbade the mention of her name. He would storm out or rage at the mere mention of her. Their mother was inconsolable. Near madness. So fragile. So strong in her fragility. A mountain of shattered expectations. She devoted herself entirely to her victimhood. She wore black. She rent her clothing to signify deep mourning. Women of the community shuttled in and out in clucking consolation.

Isaac alone stood tall. Frustratingly stoic, amidst this swirling, blasted landscape of morbidity and the madness of grief.

Even under the most propitious of circumstances Benjamin would have been bereft. Esther leaving home. Even happily married to a suitable Jew. Would still have been Esther leaving home. But he'd get over it. He'd miss mischievous, irreverent, sparkling Esther. But he could console himself with her happiness.

Under current circumstances her felt her absence like missing an organ. Something without which he'd continue to live, but rot away inside. There was no shortage of people upon whom he could vent his silent vitriol. Esther, driven to escape an unwanted marriage. It seemed to him, in the eyes of her socially ambitious mother and commercially voracious stepfather, she was a commodity. An asset traded for spurious advantage. No one considered Esther's feelings; it was like she had no soul.

But there was something else. Something deeper, fundamental. Benjamin shared his sister's disruptive impulse. That ember of adventure he barely suppressed, was taunting him, daring him to nurture it to flame. Like Esther, he too needed to escape the monotony of this constrained existence, of the insular ultra-conservative community, reeling from millennia of persecution. The oppressive burden of his parents' expectations was crushing him. He envied Esther her unsuitable liaison with this Huguenot soldier. His own unsuitable liaison would be with the sea. All he lacked was an excuse to break away. A clarion blast of courage — a trigger. And that Esther had now provided. But in seeking freedom, Esther had become enslaved. Was that an omen, a warning?

His intention had been to come out of hiding when there was no possibility of banishment ashore. That moment approached and passed. And yet he hesitated. His fantasy scenario had crashed headlong into a wall of prevarication and inhibition. A cascade of negative potential flooded his mind. The master of the Zeelander swelled in his mind to Godlike proportions. He pictured himself looking up at a huge imposing Abrahamic figure, peeing himself with fear.

In his short unnoticed passage he'd caused endless trouble. His midnight forays into the galley. The fights between the cook and his assistant. The stolen pie. The Quartermaster interrogating the crew. Threats of floggings or worse. Whenever he heard footsteps approaching he hid in a coil of rope. This early in the voyage there'd be little need to renew or replace rigging. That much of his planning he'd got right. He slept in a pile of soft hemp and canvas, only daring to emerge at night. In idle hours, the many of them, he amused himself feeding piecrust to a resident rat.

The second day passed. He braced himself, trembling on the verge of making himself known, rehearsing how to do it. Practicing his tone. *Excuse me my man I wish to speak with your captain.* Or ever so humble, splutter out: *Please sir...*

Unmasking as the pie thief was inevitable. What's the penalty for stealing victuals on board a warship on active duty. Strapped to a grating, lashed to within an inch of his life, keel hauling? Thrashing in the grip of this nightmare, he was shocked awake. The ship was beating to quarters. Exploding into activity. Gun masters barking orders. Feet pounding the between-decks companionways. The trundle of gun carriages run out so close above his head. The roar of the cannons running sequentially along the gundecks. Massive bronze barrels leaping in their mounts. The rumble of wheels as gun crews hauled them inboard for reloading. A distant crackle of musketry. Smoke drifted into his cramped space; he fought a coughing fit. More orders, more firing. Ears ringing. And then silence. He was aware once more of the rippling cadence of the hull parting the waves. Of the comfortable motion of the ship. The smoke dissipated; the sharp stench of gunpowder faded.

Benjamin shivered. Shock or exhilaration? In the end what's the difference? A tinge of disappointment, he'd missed his first gun battle. Now was not the best time to present himself as a stowaway. He set to wondering what to do next — that pie wouldn't last forever.

He was still debating the timing when the hatch burst open, and someone shone a lamp on his face.

What remained of Braba buffeted off the side of the ship, rotating round-and-round in a self-generating maelstrom. Like a leaf sucked down a drain, the shattered hull flipped over, dragging the stunned Isaac down with it. Isaac found himself reflexively clinging to the mainsheet, spinning like a fishing lure. One second all was dark emerald light above, next black depths below. He surfaced gasping, lungs bursting, his world a confusion of sounds and sensations: the rushing of the water over his head, the tearing of sailcloth, the groaning and snapping of tortured timber.

A cry went up from the watch high above on the quarter deck. Boots clattered as the crew rushed to the rail. And then it was over. The ship was gone. The stern light fading into the fog, disappearing like it had never existed. Isaac was alone again clinging with cold-numbed fingers to the upturned hull. Around him the tangled confusion which had once been the Braba. Floating in the rise and fall of the waves, forty fathoms of ocean below. Was this it, the end of a short life. The appearance of another vessel ghosting towards him through the mist reawakened the possibility of survival. He yelled at the top of his voice. No reaction. What did he expect. It ploughed through the wreckage, snagged rigging, flipping the Braba over. Isaac plunged under to the full depth of the mast, ears bursting, eyes bulging, lungs crushed. With a rush, the shattered hull righted itself, scooping Isaac up in the topsail and delivering him gasping to the surface.

Yet another vast shape materialised through the grey blanket of fog.

Yet another ship bearing down on him with an awful unstoppable purpose. This time he laughed. It wasn't a pleasant laugh. It was a laugh full of despair and irony. The oncoming hull missed him, passing within yards.

Isaac was and icy cold and half-drowned, but he'd recovered from the initial shock. In the space of a few minutes the fates had failed to crush and drown him at least twice. What did they have in store next. He shook his fist and yelled at the stern of the retreating ship's ornate aftcastle. They shouldn't get away with wrecking his boat with impunity. Now he'd never find his brother. And if he drowned, then what about his sister? Coughing and spluttering he howled obscenities.

There was a jerk. The Braba, Isaac attached, began racing through the sea like he'd harpooned a mighty whale.

Aboard the galleon the whip staff jumped. Crashed across the cabin, knocking the helmsman over. Scrambling to his feet, he attempted to correct course. The rudder jammed solid. The ship was turning to windward. The helmsman called for assistance. Even with five big men hauling, the tiller didn't budge.

Several tons of dew-drenched canvas began cracking flogging overhead. Yards crashed across to the opposite tack and back again. Officers rushed to the quarterdeck. The sailing master bellowed orders. Deckhands tensioned the braces. Topmen raced up ratlines to reef the sails before they split their seams. The boatswain peered down at the rudder from a stern chaser gun port, identifying the problem. They lowered a longboat.

Wreckage from the Braba's mast had caught on the ship's rudder towering above. Her shrouds were towing the wreckage of the Braba. It was acting as a giant sea anchor, slowing the ship's progress and locking her rudder, dragging her into the wind. Muffled voices floated on the mist. With a dull thud the Braba jerked and dropped back a yard. Isaac yelled till he thought his lungs would burst, till he tasted blood in his throat. He realised now they were cutting the wreckage away. Another axeman joined in, hacking at the obstruction. Isaac abandoned the comforting buoyancy of the wrecked hull, pulling himself hand over hand up the shrouds. He saw the longboat through the fog. Yelled again and waved — this time they noticed him.

Distracted by thoughts of pie, stomach grumbling, Benjamin found himself frogmarched into the Admiral's stateroom. To his shock he found Isaac, slumped in a chair. His hair was wet, his face bloody. He wore ragged, oversized seamen's clothes, a blanket draped round him.

'So you'd be Benjamin.' The admiral was every bit as imposing as Benjamin's most extreme nightmare: skeletally lean, deep-set eyes, brows like a pair of inverted cockroaches, legs wriggling to right themselves. A long mane of white hair tumbled onto the shoulders of his heavy black coat; the collar decorated with elaborate silver braiding. He rose to his feet, towering over the tallest in the room. 'Now tell me *your* story, young man.' He strode to the galleried stateroom window and absently stared into the dense wall of fog.

Benjamin glanced at Isaac, staring vacantly unblinking ahead of him.

'Well sir, I was hungry,' he whispered to the Admiral's back.

He received a cuff from the officer behind him. 'Speak up.'

'Sir, I was hungry.' Louder this time, voice breaking.

The Admiral whirled round, 'Hungry?' he bellowed.

'The pie, sir.'

'Pie?'

'I was hungry,' said Benjamin, retreating to the whisper.

'Hungry?' The Admiral resumed his seat, closed his eyes and sighed. 'Do you know this man?' He nodded towards Isaac.

'My brother Isaac. Isaac Amsalem.'

'And who would you be?'

'Benjamin, sir.'

'And your stepfather is?'

'Rabbi Abraham Amsalem... the ship broker.'

'Christ boy, I know who he is.'

'So, why...?'

'It's only out of respect for your father, I haven't tossed you over the side. So, what to do with ye?' He turned to Isaac. 'And as for you. Damned nearly ripping the rudder off m' ship in the middle of an engagement. And now ye'll no doubt want feeding.' Then pivoting back to the cowering Benjamin, he said: 'And there's the matter of m' pie. Mister Schoenmaecker, put them to work. They can start by swabbing the gun decks. And if they want any hope of getting back home, they'd better start earning their passage.'

Isaac caught Benjamin's eye. 'Sir, if I could...'

'Could what?'

'Make a suggestion, sir.'

The boatswain grabbed Isaac's arm, pulling him to the door.

'A moment Mister Schoenmaecker,' the Admiral turned to Isaac. 'This had better be good young man.'

1624

The wind was increasing, blowing the suds of the waves. The Zeelander took it in her stride, shouldering her way through the rising seas, picking up speed. But the heavier merchantmen were diving into the waves. Topmen were aloft reducing canvas, slowing their progress. The Zeelander followed suit, matching the pace of her charges. Mother goose. Goslings.

Benjamin had never been aloft. He followed unprompted and unnoticed behind the topmen as they clambered skyward to reef the drenched canvas. Perched on the crosstrees he watched them shimmy along the foot ropes. Grasping the canvas, almost inverted, feet above their heads. They hauled in unison on the thrashing sails, subduing them with stout gaskets. Below, another gang was doing the same to the huge main course. The vessel heeled and lurched, falling off a towering wave and into a deep trough. The men aloft clung on; arms wrapped round their spar. Then, as the ship righted itself, pounding through the wave tops. And the topmen continued their work as if nothing had happened.

Benjamin slipped, lost his footing, lost his grip. Hands clawing at saturated canvas; a hundred feet above the deck he fell.

One man glimpsed the moment; they all heard his horrified scream. 'Man overboard,' they bellowed, as one.

The ship was heaving to. Bringing her into the wind. Seas swept the deck as she lost way, sliding side on to the wave train. Canvas flogging above them. Sheets snapped against shrouds. Men tumbled on deck for a roll call — all accounted for, save Benjamin. Isaac scanned the sea, salt spray, stinging his eyes, blurring his vision.

The fleet overtook them like ghosts. Lookouts scanned the seas. Matamata the second mate wrapped a massively muscled arm around Isaac. Shoenmaeker broke the news. Can't launch a longboat in those seas. Your brother has gone. No point in sending other good men to die. Isaac clung to the weather side gunwale, eyes bugging, scanning the waves. He could see it was hopeless and collapsed on the deck.

Orders bellowed, he barely heard. The mighty vessel got underway, slowly at first, like she too was reluctant to give up hope. But soon she caught up with the fleet. The off watch assembled in the fo'c'sle for impromptu prayers. Isaac stood with them mind vacant, limbs trembling like an old man with ague, silently numb, wondering distractedly what the world would be like without his brother.

By morning, the wind began to ease. The topmen went aloft to shake out the courses. And there they found Benjamin. Rolled up tight in the canvas, tied neatly with a gasket, frozen and wet and barely sensible.

1624

Three days later, when he'd partially recovered, rough hands hauled him before Shoenmaeker and the engraved pagan giant, Matamata.

'Lucky the Admiral slept through,' said Shoenmaeker, 'or we'd be keelhauling your arse right now. Making us look like fools in front of the fleet. Risking his precious Zeelander. Losing us time. Prayers. We said bastard prayers for your God-damned soul.' He turned to Matamata. 'Take him outside and strap him to a grating. He'll have twenty, commuted to ten. One more screw-up and he gets the rest.'

Benjamin looked stunned, turning to his brother, silently pleading. Isaac begged Shoenmaeker to have mercy – he was just a boy. Even offered to take the lashing in his brother's stead.

'That would be difficult,' said Shoenmaeker, 'seeing as you'll be the one carrying out the punishment. And you go gentle on him mind, we'll start over. And he'll get the full twenty, and so will you. And it'll be Mister Matamata here'll be laying 'em on.' He shoved Isaac, causing him to stumble towards to where deckhands were strapping up his brother. A stone-faced Matamata forced the lash into Isaac's unwilling hand. Shoenmaeker, strands of wet hair plastering his face, bellowed through the wind. 'Now go about your work my lad. Sooner you start, sooner you'll finish.'

A thousand miles to the east, and a month earlier the lash had cut just as deep.

1624

SEVENTEEN — *fake Christians*

'Lay down my love. That's it, let me see that back.'

Kind hands peeled back the coarse fabric of the dress. Kind hands can hurt just as much as those that are less well intentioned. Congealed blood stuck the wounds to the fabric. The warp and the weft. Water went some way towards breaking the adhesion.

'So how did you come to be here my love?'

Esther pointed to the livid circle around her throat. The woman chattered softly on; the sound of her voice was soothing.

'I'm Aal. You can tell me your name later.'

Esther shot Aal a perplexed look, shaking her head, like she'd just woken up. A pained croak, her throat was getting worse.

'You be quiet now, let me. They call me Aal de Dragonder, case you're interested.'

Her dress pealed back revealing the soft curve of Ester's back. Raised white and purple weals rose above a smudged sea of maroon encrusted from her shoulders to the backs of her thighs. She jumped as her fellow passenger dabbed the wounds until the congealed blood dissolved and ran off, absorbed by the dry planking of the cart.

'So do you want me to tell you what's happening? Esther nodded. 'Don't be too sure about that. We're off to the New World. To the colonies. To Havana, wherever the hell that is. We'll be comforting the poor lonely Conquistadores, sick of humping savages, homesick for some good white pussy.' Horror flashed across Esther's face. 'Well I did warn you.'

They stopped for the night in a fortified encampment. Not safe to travel at night, too many Dutch raiding parties. They relieved themselves in view of the contingent of soldiers that rode with them.

'Don't kid yourself they're here to protect us. They're there to protect the provisions on the way back. From what I can tell the Dutch garrison in Breda are eating a damned site better than the Spanish at its walls.'

The evening meal was stale bread and boiled swede, and little of it.

1624

There was a knock on the side of the wagon. The woman pulled aside the rough canvas canopy; a soldier helped her out. There were giggles, grunts, rhythmic thudding against the wagon side, seemed to go on for an age. Aal clambered back in, out of breath.

'Lively one, that was. Young 'ens the worst.'

She opened a cloth bag.

'Cheese, fucking cheese. "Fucking-cheese" get it?' She broke off a chunk and gave it to Esther with an embarrassed smile, 'Excuse fingers, if you'll forgive an expression.'

The next night it was three soldiers, for which she earned half a chicken carcass, two apples and a pear.

Scabs were forming on Esther's back; the cloth no longer pained her by its touch. They were travelling through forest. It wasn't raining for a change, sunlight rippled through the forest canopy. The soldiers seemed on high alert, galloping up and down the endless line of carts.

Low hanging trees brushed against the wagon canopy.

Esther woke to the crackle of Musket fire, a scream, the wagon bucked forward. Horses whinnied, galloping now. The driver slumped backwards eyes rolled back in the sockets, blood bubbling from his mouth. The cart took off. More shots, cavalrymen went galloping past, swords drawn. The stampeding horses pulled off into a field of blackened stubble. Orders barked, the clash of steel. More musketry. Hooves thundered; the waggon was out of control; soldiers were galloping to catch them up. Horses shrieked as their bridles jerked back. The wagon came to a slithering sliding halt on loose soil. They dumped another soldier in the back. The driver groaned. They looked to the officer. Like what are we supposed to do with him.

'You two bitches, take care of him.'

Aal winked at Esther.

When the cart was back in the convoy, Aal checked the driver's purse, taking some coin. Esther found a slim dagger in his belt. She was removing it when a hand grabbed her wrist. The driver made as though to raise the alarm. Esther clamped her hand over his mouth. Aal swung her weight on him, nodding encouragement to Esther. With her other hand Esther pinched his nose. He ceased to struggle after a couple of minutes, they maintained the pressure much longer to make sure. Esther sat back breathless. Aal crawled forward and informed the driver of his predecessor's passing. He crossed himself, but otherwise seemed unmoved.

Aal put her arm round Esther, 'Didn't like it, eh love?'

'No,' said Esther, face aglow, 'I think I liked it a little too much.'

Dangling on that rope, had she been close to heaven, or to hell. And what might that foraging bee have brought back from there?

The screaming of seagulls replaced the cawing of crows. The sweet air of the countryside replaced by the smell of peat smoke and human excrement, the whistle of the wind by a mélange of noisy human interaction. The horses clattered to a halt on granite cobbles.

The wagon canopy drew back, soldiers dragged the two stiffening corpses out. Esther and Aal followed awkwardly in chains. Retainers wearing the Medina's livery loitered at the city gates. Everywhere civilians were busy. Warehouse doors clattered open, empty wagons loaded for the return journey. Exhausted horses and exhausted soldiers replaced with fresh. No such respite for Esther and Aal. An obese official in a grubby buff leather jerkin arrived and examined a document, then took a step back and scanned them. Two soldiers shuffled up and stood behind him.

'Right, you two. Property of the Duke of Medina. Escort these ladies to the port. *Nuestra Señora de la Visitación*, she's anchored off dock six.'

As the cart progressed through the crowded streets the iodine rich smell of half-tide seaweed increased in pungency. The sun disappeared behind crowded overhanging buildings. Children jeered at them from dark alleys, pelted them with horse manure, until the soldiers saw them off. The streets narrowed as they got closer to their destination. A crush of people blocked their way. Men women and children, weighed down with baggage. The horses came to a halt, rearing, frightened. A soldier got down and calmed them with sweet words and a stroke of their manes. He took a bridle and attempted to encourage them forward. But even were they willing to move, the people before them were not. No amount of bullying and threats could force a passage. They dragged Esther and Aal off the back of the cart and shoved them into the throng.

'This must be the last of them,' said a soldier.

'Last of what?' said the other.

'The *Moriscos*.'

'Sorry?'

'Musselmen, fake Christians.'

'Oh, them. Good riddance.'

'Buggering off to Morocco, piss-hole that is.'

Esther and Aal stumbled ahead of them, bare feet on cold cobbles, they'd have tripped on their ankle chains, but the crush of bodies made it impossible to fall. The canyon of whitewashed buildings gave way to the open blue skies, and saline bustle of the harbour. The scene exploded into a different world. A world of light and frenetic activity.

The sea was no less crowded than the town, endless lines of *expulsados* waiting for transport out to galleons and galleys crowding the seaway. Spanish soldiers were going through their possessions, taking anything of value. On the hills above the city Esther could make out a shanty of tents where the better off Moriscos awaited the arrival of their ships. The poor were getting into anything that floated.

Esther and Aal tumbled aboard a longboat. Before them the *Florencia*, riding at anchor.

'Where bound?' said a soldier.

'Havana.' said a sailor.

The soldier handed the sailor the leg irons. 'See you get these on them. Don't be taking any chances.'

As they reached *Florencia*, the wind strengthened and veered. The galleon turned and presented her rear like a bitch in oestrus. The stern towered above them, a galleried, glittering gilded baroque masterwork of religious iconography, the Virgin Mary forever offering an open-armed benediction above the shield of the House of Medina.

Esther and Aal climbed the ladder with no little loss of dignity. Once on deck Aal adjusted her bodice and inspected the slouching soldiers as though they were her personal honour guard, receiving a slap for her wit.

Two weeks into the voyage Aal fell into her old ways. Returning from an evening's exertions she produced a couple of oranges from under her skirt and tossed one to Esther.

'You do that for oranges?' said Esther.

'Got to do something,' said Aal, 'can't just sit around moping.'

Enough oranges thus earned saw them relocated from the hot airless hold to a cabin, no less cramped, above deck, with the twin benefits of light and ventilation.

1624

EIGHTEEN — *mongrel bitches*

Isaac screwed another ring into the bulkhead of the carpenter's workshop. He slung Benjamin's hammock next to his. Feet sounded on the companionway, Benjamin returning from another watch assisting the navigator.

'They didn't believe me at first. Alone at sea, no fishing nets, no cargo. Hunting for my stowaway brother, who in turn was hunting for our enslaved sister? Who'd believe nonsense like that. If you'd found a better hiding place they'd have hanged me for a spy. Anyway, forgot to ask, how was the pie?'

'Not bad.'

The ship's carpenter had sorely needed an assistant. At the peak of his skills, the Admiral had him working on elaborate cabinet making and marquetery in his stateroom. But he was too old, in truth, for the heavy work of replacing and mending spars. Isaac had been taking this work off his hands for the last two days.

He wasn't accustomed to artisan labour, but he could do it, and it was better that swabbing the gundeck.

Benjamin's hammock swung to the steady motion of the ship.

'Some of the old hands were talking,' he said, contemplating the knotty grain of the planking above his head. 'They reckon something's on the way. Mackerel sky, aching in their bones, that sort of thing...'

Isaac thought his brother had drifted off. But then Benjamin completed the thought. 'Anyway, Mister Shoenmaeker says the Admiral's ordered him to give Biscay a wide berth. It'll add a few days to the passage. But out in the Atlantic the weather turns to shite, won't be pleasant, but less chance of becoming embayed.'

Isaac struggled to pull off his boots. 'Also less likelihood of running foul of Catholic navies. The Zeelander's a beast of a two-decker, but there's still only one of her.'

The next day, they turned out to stand their watch. The steady north-westerly was strengthening. On the poop deck De Fries, the sailing master, was looking to the sky.

Isaac scanned down to the white-capped waves. Favourable wind, but boring. The Amsalem brothers had discussed this, they both yearned to experience heavy weather. Mister De Fries barked across to the First Mate:

'Mister Schoenmaecker. Reefing the courses, what d'you think?'

Schoenmaecker glanced at Matamata, launching a jet of tobacco juice leeward. 'What d'you think?'

The big man nodded to the heavens: 'Topgallants,' he grunted.

'Mister Matamata advises to shorten the uppers first.'

De Fries had no time for the Boatswain. He did the opposite, to snub the man. Ordered the lower courses half-reefed; the topgallants and skysails ignored. Expressionless, Matamata shook his head and plodded off to see about some extra breakfast. Few knew the cause of their animosity. Those that didn't know, didn't dare ask.

At the second noon bell the wind stilled, the sea turned sluggishly oily. The canvas slapped like they'd passed into the doldrums. The ship ceased making way. De Fries strutted the upper deck, a man vindicated. He ordered the courses unreefed.

All hands stopped their doings. A silence descended, made more potent by the creaking of timbers and the lonely frapping of the ropes.

'Now we're in for it lads; now we're in for a blow...'

Isaac turned to find himself facing a cabal of grizzled old hands. He couldn't tell which he should attribute the prediction. Whomever it was spoke for all.

The whole watch was staring in the same direction, like so many compass needles. Each face bore a similar expression. Isaac's eyes widened; his jaw dropped. He reached out and took Benjamin's arm. They joined the rest of the crew in awestruck silence.

As far away as his eyes could focus, the sky assumed the complexion of a drunk-whipped whore. A livid bruise was spreading from the southwest. Impenetrable black in the distance, streaked with sickly shades of amber and green. The contusion was spreading fast. Soon it was overhead, obscuring the sun, robbing their shadows of substance. Through this premature darkness a squall-line came thundering towards them. A wall of white foam from horizon-to-horizon. Deck hands braced themselves like infantrymen facing a cavalry charge.

Storm winds slammed into the ship like a forty-gun broadside, howling across the deck. Horizontal sleet scoured faces and blinded eyes. Every sail was aback. The Zeelander heeled on the brink of capsize.

Cannons strained at their carriages, water poured through gaps in shuttered gunports and cascaded through open hatches.

The leeward scuppers pitched below the churning sea. Crewmen and officers alike slid across the near vertical decks to thud into the gunwale like a pile of discarded dolls. The sailing master dragged himself to his feet, bareheaded now, water tumbling from his clothes.

'Get aloft,' he bellowed at the tangle of humanity, voice breaking. 'Christ, get that Christ-damned canvas in. Topsails, all hands, all hands. Get aloft you motherless sons of mongrel bitches.'

Men scrambled to their feet, swarmed up the ratlines, hauling themselves along the yards. Hand-over-hand they shuffled along the footropes. Their mission to tame acres of leaden rain-saturated canvas until their fingers bled.

The monstrous fist that had so brutalised the sky directed its furious spite towards the Zeelander. The vessel shuddered, hesitated, stunned by the ferocity of the assault. Then, gathering her courage, she fought back to reassert her dignity, proud lady that she was. With a massive effort she righted herself, water cascading from her deck. But then another blow, harder than before, had her reeling again. Wind like a vast hand was forcing her face into the water.

Topmen froze, clinging to the canvas-covered spars for their very lives, prehensile toes gripping the foot ropes. Again a wave swept deckhands along the scuppers. The vessel pitched forward. The naked gilded breasts of the figurehead plunged under the waves. She clawed to the surface battered but defiant, only to plunge once more.

The upper sails — the main topsail and the topgallants — pressed the hull hard over. Half-a-dozen men on the middle deck wrestled with the whip staff, but the force of this onslaught rendered the rudder useless. The staff splintered in their hands, and they rushed to fit a replacement. Running before the wind had its virtues, as did facing the wind and riding to a sea anchor. What had no future was laying broadside on.

The heavy yards of the leeward courses dragged through the churning waves. A sail unfurled, filled with water, and ripped the sixty-foot yard from the main mast. Three hands went with it, one into the sea tangled in the ropes, two broken on the deck. The surgeon arrived, pronounced one dead, the other dying. Hanging by a tangle of rope, the yard pounded the hull like a medieval siege engine. As the ship rolled the rope-entangled man went from submerged to dancing heavenwards and back.

'Cut that damned thing lose,' screamed Schoenmaecker.

The crew didn't need telling. They attacked the bar-taut lines with axes. There was haste, but also reverence in their work. Condemning a crew mate to death was not an easy thing. Eventually the spar carried away and the man's screaming ceased.

The ship shuddered, braced herself and fought back once more, refusing to die. The helmsmen persisted in their battle to turn the bows to leeward. But the press of the storm kept her broadside on, forcing her deeper into the sea. Lightning lanced through the churning darkness. Brilliant flashes burned the terrified faces of the crew deep into Isaac's retina. Off to the starboard he saw a waterspout reaching down from the angry heavens.

'And the Lord went before them by day in a pillar of a cloud, to lead them the way; and by night in a pillar of fire.'

Did He also deal in pillars of water?

The line of merchant ships was not having such a tough time of it. They'd less top-hamper, and no cannon to raise their centre of gravity dangerously high. All their weight was deep in their holds, and they didn't have the idiot De Fries as a sailing master. Soon Isaac lost sight of them behind curtains of rain and wind-driven spray.

Even with the courses reefed and the lanteen mizzen loose sheeted, they had far too much sail aloft. The main mast topsail ripped; a panel came loose. All eyes followed it, flying in the wind like a tattered battle pennant. It was then Isaac noticed the lower main mast bending like a greenstick fracture. With the crack of a cannonade, a split ran along its length. Topmen felt the shudder and scrambled down the ratlines leaving their job undone. As their feet touched deck each man must have counted themselves lucky to be alive.

De Fries called for Janssen. The old carpenter clambered out looking none to pleased to be on deck. He scanned the mast, grimaced and shook his head.

'The main topmast's going,' bellowed De Fries over the roar of the wind.

'Let it go. It'll reduce hamper,' was all Janssen would say.

'And cripple my ship,' said Schoenmaecker. 'Why don't we cut the rest of the masts down and have done with it?' he scoffed.

'May come to that,' said Janssen.

The shrouds supported the middle section of the main mast. But not for much longer. The wind-blasted sails were doing their best to tear it down. And if it went, the back stays might bring down the foremast and mizzen.

'Right,' said De Fries, turning to Schoenmaecker: 'Can't have that thing hanging over our heads. Clear the decks. Organise a party to get up there. Cut the stays and chop the bastard down.'

Schoenmaecker hesitated, as though waiting for De Fries to finish his sentence. De Fries added: 'Silver piece for every man.' Still the hesitation: 'Gold, gold then,' he screamed.

Isaac overheard the exchange: 'Wait, there's a way to save the mast.'

'Sorry?' said De Fries, whirling about.

'Save the mast,' said Isaac. 'It hasn't gone yet. We could splint it, yes?' He looked to the carpenter. 'Splint it, yes?'

'Possible,' said Janssen, with no great enthusiasm. 'Or I could fix it when it's on the deck. And from what I can see, it'll be down here soon enough.'

'Would that be before or after it's smashed a hole in the hull,' snapped Schoenmaecker.

'Four ten-foot beams are all it'd take,' Isaac insisted: 'Strapped over the crack. Pull 'em tight top and bottom. Spanish windlasses. Then bind 'em in place. Stronger than new. My life on it.'

'Could work,' said Janssen, 'in theory. If all that shit doesn't drop down and kill you first. I'm an old man. You're not getting me up there. Don't care how much sodding gold you're offering.'

Isaac recognised opportunity in disaster. What do the military call it, the forlorn hope? Overwhelming probability of death, slim chance of glory. But you can leverage glory if you survive.

'Release the sheets,' he said, 'reduce the stresses. Two men's all I need.'

De Fries looked to Schoenmaecker. Isaac could imagine what they were thinking. What had they to lose? Just the stowaway's know-it-all brother.

Benjamin was desperate to go aloft with Isaac. 'No, I'll need you to organise things down here,' Isaac yelled above the wind.

'We should start by getting a block rigged up there,' said Janssen, 'Then we can begin sending up timbers.'

Schoenmaecker beckoned to a young sailor crouching in the lee of the poop deck. He put an arm round his shoulder and pointed skywards.

'Jan, they're betting me you can't get a block rigged on the first crosstrees. He put a coin in the man's hand. 'And when you've done that, might as well stay there and give us a hand.'

Too late, Benjamin, block in hand, was already halfway to the crosstrees. With a look of resignation Jan discarded his saturated jacket and kicked off his shoes. Then Schoenmaecker followed suit, revealing the well-tuned mechanism that was his tattooed torso.

1624

The crack opened and shut as the mast flexed and relaxed to the onslaught of the gusts. One minute it was invisible. Next it yawned wide revealing the splintering bright resinous pine at its core. Benjamin passed a line through the block and dropped the coil of rope to Janssen below. As he descended Schoenmaecker, and Smitt were on their way up. His foot slipped, he lost his grip, and toppled backwards. Isaac reached out and clasped his wrist, but it slipped through his cold wet fingers. Benjamin fell backwards into the watery void, arms windmilling, mouth agape. Jan reached out. Caught him by the collar and swung him back to the ratlines. Benjamin clung there a while, shivering and then made his way slowly to the deck.

Isaac was waiting in the cross trees. All three roped themselves to the mast. If it went down, they'd go down with it. Isaac feared heights. But he wasn't a great enthusiast of drowning either. He set his mind to neutral, to working in an abbreviated, closed-off world. He didn't see the huge wave trains rolling in from the west. Or the deck ninety feet below, awash with water. Or the mast swaying and creaking overhead. His world was tight focused on a single point of concentration; his peripheral vision relegated to irrelevance.

The mighty bosun hauled on the line and the timbers came aloft. Isaac and Schoenmaecker held them in place. Jan nailed them into position with huge iron spikes. Then they assembled Spanish windlasses top and bottom. Tightening the ropes, drawing together the split when the ship's movement caused its maw to close. Finally it shut and opened no more. They lashed rope round-and-round the mast holding the splints in place. And Isaac was right. Like new, stronger than new. The mast ceased to sway, flexing in time with its siblings fore and aft.

Danger past. Topmen swarmed up the ratlines, clambering over them, bare feet on their shoulders, like so many mischievous monkeys. Soon they had the top sails and topgallants stowed. Isaac clambered down eyes sore, muscles racked, sinews fit to pop, fingers stiff with cold. Pressure off, the helm regained control. Zeelander turned her back on her attacker. Under a lanteen mizzen and reefed lower foresail she was soon running before the wind, her course set diagonal to the waves.

Isaac collapsed into his hammock, the rhythmic clunking gush of the pumps lulling him to sleep. Benjamin remained on deck, enjoying the ride.

The Admiral had awoken irritated from a poor night's sleep. He was sitting at a dressing table as Sheng, his manservant, brushed his long white hair. There came a knock on the adjacent stateroom door. Sheng answered.

'It's Mister Crips, Sir,' he announced.

The Admiral let out a long sigh. Nightshirt dragging on the deck like a bridal train, he entered the stateroom. Two small terriers and a marmalade cat followed behind.

Crips looked weary. His breeches and shirt stained, his hands swollen, his scuffed shoes saturated. But he wore his best canvas jacket. As the Admiral entered Crips removed his woollen cap and tugged an invisible forelock. His receded hair resembled the tonsure of a Chinese Mandarin. A long pigtail draped down his back.

The Admiral took his place behind a lavish baroque desk and waved Crips to a seat. He lay back, the very picture of exhaustion. Crips went to speak, but the Admiral languidly raised his hand. The wind gusted; the angle of heel increased. Sheng tottered in with a bottle of Amontillado and two heavy glasses. They drank quietly, then the Admiral said:

'Tell me. What the bloody hell happened yesterday. I couldn't bear it and took to me bed. Mister Sheng had to lash me down, fear I'd fall out and hurt m'self. It terrified my babies.'

Both terriers jumped on the Admiral's lap. The white one with the impressive beard placed its front paws on the desk and stared at Crips as though it was about to speak. The cat rubbed its face on Crips bare shin and hopped onto his lap. Crips coarse hand stroked gently behind its ears. It looked up gratefully its purr lost in the roar of the ocean.

'Sorry to say your worship, but the men aren't happy, and you said...'

His hoarse Dutch came with a thick Bristol accent. He spoke haltingly, as though repeating the words of an internal translator. The Admiral leaned forwards, elbows on the leather-bound surface of his gilded desk:

'When I first made your acquaintance Mister Crips what did I ask of you?'

'To speak for the men sir.'

'The officers can speak for themselves,' said the Admiral, 'the men need you.'

The wind was strong but steady. Crewmembers crowded the Admiral's stateroom. Those in attendance were on their feet facing the Admiral's desk. Everyone on watch during the near capsize were present. They all had their right knee bent, to counteract the heel of the ship.

'You call me Admiral. But I'm not an admiral. I'm a general. A general of the sea. Barely know what moves this blasted thing. Something to do with the wind, I'm reliably Informed. Or the grace of

God. Doesn't matter. All I demand is that it goes in the general direction I point. Within certain natural limits, there are always limits. Except, that is, for my loyalty to the house of Orange and my dedication to the Protestant cause.

'So, I trust others to transport me and m' guns to where I need to be to fulfil m' duty. In this respect the ship and its crew are a machine. Cogs and wheels. Some bigger some smaller. If one of the small cogs fails it's a concern. If one of the big cogs fails it's a potential disaster. One such cog failed catastrophically yesterday, resulting in three deaths and the damned near sinking of m' ship. To our great good fortune lesser mechanisms heroically averted the ultimate tragedy.'

De fries stepped forward beaming to accept the accolade; the Admiral looked past him.

'Mister **Schoenmaecker**, you're promoted to Sailing Master. You men at the back, take Mister De Fries outside and hang him.'

1624

NINETEEN — *skysails*

It was dawn on the third day after the storm. The wind strength remained high, having veered nor' northwest, but the wave train was regular and predictable. On the Admiral's orders the ship carried all the canvas it possessed. Every so often they hit a big wave. The bow would rise and fall with a jolt; salt spray flying into the air to mist down on the deck.

The ship's boy, clutching a bucket and cloth, followed the terriers as they sniffed and peed their regular circuit of the ship. When the wind gusted causing the vessel to heel especially hard, the dogs would slide like china ornaments. He'd overheard Mister Schoenmaecker saying that this was the fastest way to break a ship. And, as if by way of confirmation, they lost a water sail overnight. But even he, the lowest of the ship's company, understood the need for haste. Having fulfilled the necessities of nature, the little dogs retreated to where the marmalade cat was watching by the stateroom door. The lad ushered them inside and shuffled off to dispose of their leavings over the leeward rail.

The animals waited expectantly by their bowls in the gloom. The door opened flooding the room with light. Mister Sheng bustled in carrying a can of hot water. His master had been restless since they'd lost contact with the merchantmen. Talking in his sleep, muttering honour and reputation, over and over again.

And, indeed, the ship exuded a certain melancholy, like a mother goose mourning the loss of her goslings.

Above, in the swaying rigging, Mister Janssen inspected Isaac's handywork. They sat across from each other in the lower crosstrees. The jury-rigged splints were holding well, the crack hadn't opened appreciably. Working together they added more bindings. Janssen decided to solidify the repair with a heavy layer of pine-tar. Janssen returned to the deck, and his boy prepared a bucket of bubbling pitch. Isaac was concentrating on painting it over the splint when a lookout

1624

above called, *'Sail hoy.'*

Matamata appeared as if from nowhere. He nodded to Isaac like he was surprised to see him. Then continued his climb to the crow's nest, and onward into the skysails. Fifty feet above Isaac, arm and leg wrapped around a stay, he hung over the void scanning the horizon with the aid of a spyglass. Then he sprung down from the skysail yard, handing the glass to the lookout, issuing instructions. Shinning past Isaac, he rolled his eyes. What the hell did that mean? Sixty feet later he was on the deck in a huddle with his friend, the newly appointed sailing master.

Schoenmaecker tapped on the Admiral's door. Sheng opened it a crack.

'I need to speak with the Admiral.'

'He's at his prayers, you come back later.'

'Well, his prayers have just been answered.' Schoenmaecker said, barging past: 'Admiral Sir, it's urgent,' he yelled.

The white-bearded terrier attacked his ankle. The tawny one guarded the threshold to the Admiral's chamber, teeth bared. Schoenmaecker opened the door to the Admiral's inner sanctum, suffering more nips. Sheng burst into tears behind him. The Admiral curled up in his nightshirt cuddling his marmalade cat, snoring gently. Schoenmaecker coughed loudly. The Admiral stirred and snorted.

'What?'

'Sir, masthead lookout spotted our merchant fleet.'

'That's good, now could you just…'

'Captured by the Spanish.'

'Oh dear.'

'Need orders sir.'

The Admiral opened a sleepy eye.

'Where away?' he croaked.

'Twelve miles, sou' southwest.'

'How long?'

'Two and a half hours if the wind holds.'

'The Spanish, how many?'

'Two sir, ships of the line, three-decker, ninety gunners.'

'Wind?'

'Nor' nor' west and steady,'

The Admiral sat bolt upright, displacing the cat.

'Oh, no. What if they see us? We must bear away, bear away. '

'But our flotilla…'

'Leave me now,' the Admiral's eyes began to close like the exertion had taxed him. He collapsed back onto the bed, followed by the cat and one of the terriers; the other growled Schoenmaecker out of the room.

'But sir...' To the sound of the Admiral's snores, Schoenmaecker backed quietly from the room.

'Oh and Mister Schoenmaecker,' came a sleepy voice.

'Sir?'

'Tell Mister Sheng, I'll take m' breakfast presently.'

Schoenmaecker stared into his porridge like he was interrogating an oracle. He tossed his spoon to one side.

'Admiral's probably right,' he sighed. 'Anyway, right or wrong, he's still the bastard Admiral.' He looked to the door, checking for unwelcome ears. 'Well, there are two of 'em, I suppose. Three decker ships of the line. And each one of them has us outgunned. Engaging them would be reckless. So no shame in it. But surely there must be something we could do. Breaks my heart leaving our poor merchantmen in the hands of the Dons.'

Schoenmaecker absently brought the spoon to his lips. The porridge was cold; he spat it out. Matamata raised his tattooed eyebrows. Schoenmaecker wasting food, things must be bad.

Sheng entered the cabin: 'Admiral's compliments. Officers to the stateroom, fifteen minutes, gentlemen please.'

They bumped into Crips on the upper deck. 'So you've been summoned too' he said. 'Any idea what it's about?'

They found the Admiral silhouetted against the long galleried window. Sunlight was taking excessive delight in the illumination of a set of fine court armour. Intricate gilt chasing gleamed jet black beneath his wide ruff. The Admiral's long white hair cascaded over articulated steel shoulder plates, where gilded goddesses frolicked with satyrs engraved on a midnight ground. He turned to face them, haloed against the light: long of limb, hollow of cheek, coal black eyes in a skeletal mask — the angel of death in its Sunday best.

A matching basket-hilted rapier rested on pine boards, protecting his fine mahogany table. Scribbled charcoal calculations and diagrams covered the bleached surface — cardinal points, hull speed, weather gage, windage, elevation. Sheng fussed about with a damp cloth, wiping black smudges from the Admiral's elegant fingers.

Model ships clustered on the table's centre; the two largest painted red. The Admiral unsheathed his sword, pointing to a smaller ship, away to the left.

'This, gentlemen, is us...'

1624

Juan Martínez de Bertendona had somewhat of a reputation. And it was not for his sunny disposition. Yet he found himself leaning on the taffrail of his flagship, the *Grace de Deus*, battling to suppress a grin. Behind him the vessel was all bustle, and in front of him the ocean was no less crowded and frenetic. Across the choppy seaway was his other command, the *San Medel y Celedón*. At eight-hundred tons she was the greater ship. But de Bertendona preferred the more lavish accommodation and seakindly motion of this marginally smaller vessel.

All around them, rising and falling on the heavy swell, captured enemy merchantmen, sails similarly furled. Dozens of longboats plied back and forth between them like the *Virgen del Carmen* regatta. Yes, there was a carefree, fiesta atmosphere; they were all soon to be rich men. And he, Juan Martínez de Bertendona, would be insuperably the richest. The chill wind tugged at his cloak and threatened to carry off his feathered hat. But he paid little heed. With his lion's share of the prize he'd give up the sea. His imagination soared on hot thermals of possibility. He would buy an estate in Cordoba, a title, a governorship. Dare he even dream of a place at court? And all this good fortune had simply dropped in his lap, like he was the appointed of God. An unprotected Dutch flotilla, its holds bulging like gravid sardines. Early reports from his quartermaster suggested they carried enough fine bronze cannon and muskets to equip an army.

Cargo aside, these vessels alone were worth several fortunes. The latest purpose-built merchant ships fresh from the shipyards of Rotterdam. You could still smell the fresh paint. But unprotected? At first none of the captives were willing to provide answers. But a few hangings always loosen tongues. So, they were bound for Morocco, doing business with the damned Corsairs. Protestants equipping Arabs and Turks. Shameful. But what could you expect from the Godless? Lost their escort in the storm, they'd said. And, yes, hadn't it been a beauty. Doubly beautiful for the windfall it had dropped into his lap. What was the fashion for nobility nowadays? He'd need to rethink his tailor.

Lieutenant Gomez, his deputy, interrupted his thoughts. Pointing to a smudge on the western horizon, he offered a spyglass. The smudge resolved into a ship. De Bertendona immediately ordered Gomez to beat to quarters. But the urgent rattle of drums went unanswered. Most of his men were busy ferrying prize crews to the captured merchants and fantasising how to spend their newfound riches.

'Fire off a signal cannon Gomez; get everyone back to stations.'

If this was the Dutch fleet's escort catching up, did he have enough men on deck to ready even a dozen of their ninety guns?

'Fuego,' yelled Gomez.

The signal cannon roared. Smoke billowed from the gun port. Three hundred yards away the elaborate gilded figuring of the *San Medel y Celedón's* quarter gallery erupted into splinters. De Bertendona's shoulders slumped, he shook his head and sighed. He and Gomez would shortly have words.

The Admiral leant over the table. 'Mister Schoenmaecker, I trust that you will inform me if anything I suggest proves unrealistic.'

'Tell me what you want Your Grace.'

'It is my intention to engage those Spanish war ships. We will sink one and take the other as a prize. We will then reclaim our fleet and continue to Morocco as planned. There we will sell the galleon and distribute the prize money as per our articles.'

There was a hushed silence. Gone was the foppish septuagenarian, this man was terrifying. 'Reports from aloft gentlemen, any change?'

'They're bigger than previously estimated, Your Grace.' said Schoenmaecker. 'Three deckers, at least ninety gunner ships of the line.'

'Have they seen us d'ye think?' Said the Admiral.

'They're sails are stowed,' said Schoenmaecker: 'Two ships that powerful, two hundred guns between them, must feel invulnerable. They'll be busy putting prize crews aboard our ships. Estimating the value of the cargo. Thinking about how they'll spend their prize money. Lots for them to organise. May not even have lookouts aloft.'

'Anyone speak Portuguese?' said the Admiral. Isaac and Benjamin shared a glance and stepped forward. 'See me afterwards. Gunnery sergeant, prepare all cannon, both sides, bow chasers, stern chasers, the blasted lot. But, all goes as planned, we'll only be requiring the starboard batteries. Master-at-arms I'll be requiring men in the rigging, muskets out of sight.

'Everybody else to the armoury, draw weapons, you've a prize to earn. Everybody not otherwise engaged in the management of the ship standing by to board, out of sight, below the hatches. Now, break out the Portuguese ensign.'

The Admiral moved the gold ship's model in an erratic course towards the two red ships. 'We are now a Portuguese vessel, out for a pleasure cruise. Some aristocratic dandy showing off to his lady. No threat to anyone except by dint of bad seamanship. So let's see some sloppy sailing shall we gentlemen.'

1624

Benjamin clambered up from the crow's nest into the skysails. He attached a long white Portuguese pennant and set it flying. Halfway to the horizon he spotted the Dutch convoy corralled as if by two sheepdogs. Eight-hundred-ton sheepdogs, towering three decker sheepdogs, each with massive batteries of cannon.

The only sails set on the Spanish warships were lanteen mizzens, holding their bows to windward like weathercocks. About as vulnerable as warships could get, short of anchored or beached. Longboats were in the water, plying between the merchant ships and their captors. For an act of piracy this all appeared very relaxed. And then he saw the Dutch bodies hanging in the rigging, and it brought him up short. Bubbling with fury, he descended the ratlines and joined his brother at the base of the main topmast.

Isaac supervised the rigging of extra stays from the mainmast to the foremast and mizzen.

'All hands below,' he ordered. 'That includes you Benjamin.'

With everyone safely below, he took a deep breath and swallowed a dry lump in his throat. Then he swung the two-handed axe, hacking through the tarred rope which held the splints in place. The crack didn't open at first, like somehow it had miraculously healed. Then, with a jolt, it yawned wide and snaked higher. The topmast began to sway precariously, like a felled tree.

The topmen were having fun, sailing like they as though drunk. Flying a huge Spanish courtesy flag, the Zeelander steered an erratic unseamanlike course, canvas backing and drawing by turn.

The drummer struck up a lively beat and trumpets and horns knocked out a carefree, tuneless melody. Isaac had stationed himself on the fo'c'sle, wearing a garish jacket and a broad-brimmed, excessively feathered hat. He held his 'lady' by the hand. Poor Benjamin wore a fashionably voluminous skirt, surmounted by a pinched-in bodice displaying a newly shaved chest. As to why the Admiral carried a comprehensive collection of women's clothing, and accessories no one felt emboldened to ask.

Crew members not otherwise engaged in the play-acted subterfuge rushed to the rail and waved vigorously to the Spanish crews. Isaac and Benjamin shrieked raucous greetings in impeccable Portuguese.

The Zeelander wove an erratic course through the merchant ships and long boats. Occasionally they came off the wind, simulating a helmsman's incompetence. Spanish officers at first waving pleasantly to their ally, began bellowing and warning them off.

Hearing the recall cannon, Spanish longboats collided in their desperation to return to their ships. Gun ports opened; cannons rolled out. Gun captains yelled their readiness. Sailors swarmed aloft. Sails unfurled. But, facing the wind, their canvas backed uselessly. De Bertendona scanned the approaching ship with growing incredulity. Its main topmast was swaying. Surely it was about to drop. Sails were bagging, the sheets and halyards tangled, yards hung at uneven angles. It was remarkable she was even making way. Then he spied the white of the Portuguese colours at the masthead, which explained much.

One moment the approaching vessel was hard on a beam reach, the next luffing up, sails flapping, then coming back on the wind again. De Bertendona was mesmerised by the worst exhibition of seamanship he'd ever witnessed. A random selection of signal flags decorated the ship's rigging. Closer, he made out a gaudily dressed couple on the fo'c'sle. Jesu, were they dancing? Closer still, was that music? He looked about him for confirmation he wasn't dreaming. His men were falling about laughing. He couldn't help but join in. Five minutes on, it was no longer funny. The damned fools weren't bearing away. They were coming straight for them.

A Portuguese voice amplified by a speaking trumpet wafted over the waves. Something about borrowing a carpenter. Something about theirs being in Porto, too drunk to board the ship. And Christ in heaven, it looked like they were about to lose a mast.

The blaring of the band increased in volume, as the ship ploughed towards them. Sailors were hanging over the rail, cheering. Had the world gone mad? He frantically waved them off. Surely even the Portuguese couldn't be that stupid.

At the last minute, the Zeelander's crew gave every appearance of regaining control. To be bearing away to a safe distance from the Spanish. Then, as though caught out by the wind, it suddenly pulled to larboard, tearing into the bows of the *Grace de Deus*. The vessels collided with a splintering of wood, and a roar like mighty trees crashing to the forest floor. The ships' rigging became entangled as momentum drove the Zeelander down the side of the Grace de Deus. Grapnels hurtled across, locking the ships together.

Exploding grenades scattered the Spaniards fighting to fend off the aggressor. The Admiral in his midnight armour led the boarding party. The Zeelander's men burst through the smoke, swarming across the gunwales, screaming like devils, blasting off pistols, charging the unprepared Spanish with boarding pikes and cutlasses. Carried forward by the surge, Isaac and Benjamin enthusiastically joined in the melee.

The boatswain locked the bows in tight. Then they worked the ropes linking the two vessels so that the Zeelander swung forty-five degrees to the San Medel y Celedón attached only by their aftcastles. The master of guns rolled out both decks of cannons and let rip. Even were the Spaniards able to return fire their cannon batteries were now pointing away from the Zeelander. There was an attempt to manoeuvre into a more favourable position. But that would have required a fuller crew.

The upper row of the Zeelander's cannon aimed high. Chain and ball shot ripped through the rigging, the Spaniard's main and mizzen masts severed. The Zeelander's lower row of guns pounded round shot into the hull. The gap between the ships filled with smoke. There was no return fire and the Zeelander stopped firing. When the smoke drifted away on the wind they were looking at a mastless, smouldering hulk with a deck covered in the blood and bodies of the dead and dying. The Spaniards in the longboats looked confused. Some pulled pistols and the Zeelander's masthead marksmen cut them down with withering fire.

A short-lived hand-to-hand battle raged across the deck. The Spanish forces, though more numerous, were disorganised. The Dutch merchant ships' crews turned on their captors, enacting savage reprisals. Remarkably, there were no Dutch fatalities and few serious casualties. Despite, or maybe because of their early capitulation the Spanish suffered terribly. The survivors flung themselves overboard swimming for the crippled San Medel y Celedón. If they could save the ship they could save themselves. Trembling, tearful, Juan Martínez de Bertendona surrendered his sword. The Dutchmen were all for stringing him up. But the Admiral's adherence to the chivalric code forbade him from giving vent to his basest of instincts. Instead he set De Bertendona adrift in a crowded longboat; let his own men deal with him as they may. He wasn't optimistic for his chances.

On board the Zeelander, Sheng eased the Admiral from his black steel carapace and tutted at the dents on his spectacular armour. The Admiral flexed his shoulder, the steel plates grated.

'Ask me why I hate the sea Mister Sheng. I'll give it to you in one word. Rust, Mister Sheng, rust.'

The prize taker had become the prize. Forty of the Grace de Deus crew petitioned to sail with the Admiral. There were some Spanish, but most were French and German mercenaries with a few English pressed prisoners. Better food, kinder masters, more pay, better prospects for prizes — why not? The most experienced merchant ship captain took command of the Grace de Deus. The newly recruited sailors distributed across the fleet.

The engagement had taken place a hundred or so miles west of Vigo. As a wise precaution, Schoenmaecker plotted a course further out to sea, to avoid the busy shipping lanes around Lisbon. As a further precaution they hoisted Spanish colours. If they need resort to another ruse de guerre, they'd be two Spanish warships escorting their prizes to Cadiz.

In his hammock that night Benjamin nursed his bruises. When he did eventually make it home, he could boast to Captain Terbrugghen of his first piratical adventure. He might omit the bit about the dress. With pride he noted that in a mere month at sea he had acquired not one but two nicknames: *Pie Boy*, and *Chica de la Muerte*. Neither of which he approved, but was that necessarily his choice to make?

1624

TWENTY — *ship of ghosts*

It was still dark. The sea rose and fell steeply as the long Atlantic swell met the shallowing waters of the Bay of Cadiz. The sun's first rays were silhouetting the golden spires of the Cathedral. The pilot had just begun his breakfast. Sardines and fresh bread. His mate pointed out a ship on the horizon. They raised sail to meet her.

The ship appeared lost. Sailing this way and that in the stiffening westerly breeze. Slaver by the look of her, and the smell. Three tacks, he reckoned, they'd be along side her negotiating a big fat fee. It paid to get up early. He wiped sardine grease from his face and rinsed his mouth with the last of the wine. Hawked. Spat. Closer he could make up objects dangling from the yards. Seabirds following in frantic white clouds like they do fishing boats. On the next tack the objects resolved into bodies, strung up by the neck like decorations. At least fifty, must be the whole damned crew. Seagulls pecking at their rotting faces. Arms loosely waving, as though beckoning them to follow. A body dropped, neck rotted through, passing them like driftwood, they let it go.

His gorge rose. He vomited noisily and painfully over the stern. No wine left to wash the bile from his mouth. He let go the mainsheet. The mate let go the rudder. Their tan sails flapped ineffectually. He stared open mouthed as the vessel continued past them at a stately pace. He took off his woollen cap, the mate followed suit, crossing himself vigorously, muttering a prayer. They followed at an awed distance.

The ship of ghosts ran aground at the mouth of the Rio de San Pedro. She twisted, driven broadside on to the sands. The new day's sun blazed through the rigging, silhouetting the swaying bodies of the crew. Out to sea the stern of a great ship making into the Atlantic, yellow and blue ensign fluttering in the breeze.

TWENTY-ONE — *perfumed prophet*

The fleet beat its way south, picking up the first of the trades; the weather remained fair. Westerly winds set them on a comfortable beam reach. The temperature increased. The sailors had little to do save swab the decks to prevent them from drying out. The winds periodically strengthened; gritty red dust coated exposed surfaces. You could taste it in the air. The Sahara, someone said, we're getting close.

On board the Zeelander, eyes stinging, Benjamin had taken his last sunsight. The coast would be soon invisible. The pilot recognised the landmarks. Dolphins played in the bow wave; the sun glistened on the gilded breasts of the figurehead. The sea — Benjamin thought its colour was merely a reflection of the sky. But this sea and sky bore no relation to each other. It was like they came from entirely different spectra. What would Gerard Dou have called the colour of this water, azurite? Colour of Esther's eyes. Biting his lip, he forced back a sob. He climbed high in the rigging best to hide his feelings. And it was he who first glimpsed the Tower of Hassān.

They passed downwind of a galleass, sails set, oars rhythmically dipping in and out of the jewelled water. The wind eddied bringing the rancid smell of human waste. Slaves, someone said, working the oars. He shuddered at the thought of the horror which propelled this elegant craft.

The fleet moored at the mouth of the Bou Regreg River, just out of range of the fort. As the anchors bit, the ships turned as one to face the wind, bringing them at forty-five degrees to the river entrance. To the north were the walls and towers of Old Salé to the south the fortifications of New Salé. They fired an unloaded cannon. A rumble and a distant puff of smoke answered from the battlements. Soon a galley pulled out to meet them. Dark-skinned *Hornacheros* in flowing robes boarded, checking their identity and intentions. Schoenmaecker greeted him. He left with a gap-toothed grin, a gold piece and a letter to Reis Mourad, Grand Admiral and President of the Corsair Republic of Salé, home port of the Sallee Rovers, the most dreaded of the Barbary Pirates. Matamata tossed down some copper for the oarsmen.

The Admiral was on the quarter deck, the lanteen mizzen shading him from the heat of the noonday sun, breeze teasing his long hair. They were waiting for the pilot to become free. Navigate them through the complex of sandbars. Isaac approached him:

'Your Grace, may I beg a moment of your time?' The Admiral nodded, absently: 'Do you know of my father, Your Grace? The Rabbi Abraham Amsalem of Amsterdam.'

'Never had the pleasure. Aware of his reputation. His work for the Protestant cause. Why...?'

'Until recent events I acted as senior architect in his shipyard. I feel compelled to offer advice, Your Grace.'

'Go on,' he said, brushing a strand of silver hair from his face.

'With respect, the Zeelander performed poorly in that storm. Yes, the sail trim was at fault. But there were other factors. Too much top hamper catching the cross wind. Centre of gravity far too high. Miracle she didn't capsize.'

'Can I take it you have recommendations, young man?'

'I do. Few but the Spanish would design a vessel like this anymore. Things have moved on. Ships are no longer fortresses from which soldiers board enemy vessels and fight it out. Nowadays they're primarily mobile artillery platforms.'

Isaac expected a reaction — but it didn't materialise. He continued:

'Get rid of the castles. Trim the superstructure to the barest minimum. There's a French term, *razde* — shaved. Cut her down. She'll ride smoother, point higher, stand more canvas. Be safer to sail, more manoeuvrable and appreciably faster. It would be my honour to prepare plans. That is, if you'll countenance such a procedure.'

The Admiral looked horrified: 'But, but my stateroom?'

Li Sheng opened the great cabin door. He was wearing a plain white robe buttoned high at the neck. It suited him better than European clothing. His long cue hung loose, almost brushing the floor. An unfamiliar fragrance. The background smell of oak and tar overlaid by subtle notes of rose and jasmine.

Isaac proceeded Benjamin into the Admiral's stateroom. There he discovered two men in Arab costume. It took a second for him to realise one was the Admiral, his distinctive white hair hidden beneath a plumed, shimmering silk turban, his lean frame draped in voluminous robes threaded with gold. And instead of his rapier, his manicured hand rested on a curved mameluke sword, ivory hilt, gilded scabbard encrusted with gems. Across the table was a man whose equally exotic attire eclipsed by the haloed face of a lost prophet. A face that'd seen too much of the doings of man and yearned for the doings of God.

'Isaac and Benjamin Amsalem, may I present Jan Janszoon, better known as Grand Admiral Reis Mourad. Do sit.' Mr Sheng showed them to stools. 'We have been discussing your dilemma.'

The perfumed prophet nodded.

'Act first and think later. Not good. But sometimes it's the only way. Describe your sister to me.'

'She's tall, slim, long blonde hair, eyes the colour of the sea. Coming up to twenty.'

'Leave this with me,' said Mourad. We've people all over Spain. If she's passed through one of their ports, I'll know someone who'll know. Keep yourself busy for a couple of weeks, we'll be in touch.'

The brothers squinted as they stumbled down the gangplank. The transition from ship to shore was as much psychological and symbolic as it was physical. Onboard they still inhabited the sombre pallet of rain-drenched Brabant. Shoreside the kaleidoscopic spectrum of subtropical Morocco awaited them.

They'd received warnings. Advice. But no words could have prepared them. The very air appeared to effervesce. Wherever they looked colours exploded, dazzling the eyes, confounding the mind. Such minds accustomed to the ambiguous shadowy shades of Northern Europe. Soft grey days. Nights of infinite tones of peaty drabness. Now everywhere was stark contrast. Abrupt leaps from black, impenetrable shadow to blinding mind-melting colour.

This couldn't be the same sun. Not the mean miser sun they'd left behind. That shy sun, forever peering from behind a veil of mist or rain, ashamed to show its face. A sun scattering light begrudgingly upon a flat monotonous landscape. No, this was a wild, generous, spendthrift sun, blazing an extravagant trail through the sky, naked and unashamed. This was a prodigal sun.

Halfway to the dockside the pair paused as one, blinking. Like newborns opening their eyes to the light of their first day. Like this was their second birth. They'd grown acclimatised to the increasing temperature on the passage south. But, away from the cooling sea breeze, it was like standing before a blast furnace. Touching the chain railing was like a branding.

1624

The captain advised them to avoid the hashish and opium. To treat the Jewish spirit *Mahia* with profound respect. But do try the tea, it's like nothing you've ever experienced. The first mate told them to keep out of the sun till their skin became brown. Always to wear a hat to protect their vision. The boatswain said if they needed a woman or boy (or both, he winked), to stick to the Jewish brothels. The master-at-arms cautioned to look to their weapons. Tutored them in the secrets of street fighting. (Always stab, cut, shoot, bludgeon or strangle the other man *before* he does the same to you.) Never to stray from each other's company, even by day. Walk with purpose, never appear undecided or lost. The quartermaster told them the fruit is good. But too much will give you the shits.

Isaac prepared plans to reduce the profile of the Zeelander. Under his instruction Benjamin scampered about the ship with a measuring stick, making notes. Isaac was determined to discard all but essential weight above the waterline. The greatest challenge to stability and speed was the towering aftcastle. Gilded carvings on the stern were simply unproductive weight. Angels, mermaids, dolphins, winged lions, eagles and serpents, no matter how pleasingly decorative, all had to go. This was a fighting ship not a floating cathedral. Even the faces carved into the knight's heads, he regarded as an unnecessary frivolity. Another forty pounds saved. Dutch puritanism was infectious. Even the figurehead came into his calculations. But an acid glance from the Admiral informed him this was indeed a step too far. A woman uncovering her body has the effect of calming angry oceans. Some superstitions were beyond the ambition of even his scientific mind to challenge. He reached a compromise with the Admiral, half the stern decoration would go. The remainder removed, hollowed out and replaced.

Isaac and Benjamin sat side-by-side in the main crosstrees. Their backs to the fierce sun. Their feet dangling over the dazzling turquoise sea twinkling a hundred feet below. The ship's boy huffing up the ratlines disturbed their black mood.

'Oh, there you are. His grace's compliments, you will join him in the great cabin.'

Crips was waiting by the big double doors, taking in the sun:

'Oh, there you are. Mind him,' he said, stepping over the slumbering form of the Admiral's Dyak bodyguard. He make a shushing gesture — like, let sleeping dogs lie.

1624

The Admiral turned from a window. The town's battlements gleamed white across an expanse of glistening ultramarine water. He looked surprised:

'Oh, there you are,' he said. His long white robes moved like a bridal train as he seated himself behind his great gilded desk:

'Sit yourselves down,' he said, nodding to a pair of oak chairs.

At the delicate rattle of porcelain, Isaac glanced into the anteroom. Sheng was busying himself with the tea things. A salt breeze ruffled the Admiral's long white hair. What little was visible beneath a loosely constructed turban.

Reis Mourad emerged from the shadows, attired like an Ottoman potentate.

'Our friend has some news,' said the Admiral.

Reis Mourad spoke in the softest of registers, it was like the fabric of the ship resonated to his voice. Isaac felt a sympathetic vibration through the oak seat of his chair. Sheng served tea. Reis Mourad announced he'd brokered the sale of the captured vessel. Sold its arms and cargo to a French Corsair of their mutual acquaintance. He glanced at the Admiral, smiling.

'Pleased to inform ye,' said the Admiral, 'ye're included in the ship's good fortune. Agreed it with Mister Crips. You will each receive one sixteenth of a share.'

Isaac and Benjamin stumbled over each other to express their gratitude.

'Nothing less than ye deserve,' huffed the Admiral.

Believing the interview over, the brothers went to stand.

'Ah, but wait,' said Reis Mourad, almost sub audibly. Isaac and Benjamin sank back into their seats. 'Word from one of my people in Cadiz. Reports of a striking, tall, fair-haired woman in chains at the quayside. Freshly arrived from the low countries. Property of the Duke of Medina, sailing aboard a vessel bound for Cuba.'

The brothers sat stunned, processing this unexpected information. Crips cleared his throat loudly.

'No name?' said Isaac eventually.

'Something Biblical, all they know,' said Reis Mourad. 'Rumour had it she was a Jew.'

'Good news eh,' said Shoenmaeker.

Isaac was leaning on the ship's rail, lost in the bitter-sweet news. He looked up, squinting in the bright sunshine: 'Sorry, good news?'

'Your share.'

The brothers had forgotten all about that, swamped as they were by unfamiliar emotions. It was gratifying the ship's company acknowledged their small contribution. But one sixteenth of a one hundredth share seemed like a token at best.

'Oh yes, that.'

'Have you any idea of the sums involved?' said Shoenmaeker.

A week later saw the crew filing into the fo'c'sle. Crips sitting in the shadows, stacks of gold and silver glinting on a desk before him. Suddenly the brothers possessed, if not a fortune, certainly the foundations for one.

Given the report from Cadiz was accurate, Esther was alive. But she's soon to be more out of reach than ever – an ocean between them. The Lord gave, and the Lord hath taken away; blessed be the name of the Lord. Faced with this cosmic joke, Benjamin had fallen into a dark pit of despair. Isaac attempted to raise his spirits, although he was equally tormented. The Lord wouldn't create this challenge, he argued, without providing the means to meet it.

The crew were celebrating that night. Isaac persuaded his brother to join him on this late-night excursion to the fleshpots of Salé. Forbidden fruit eaten. Drink, drunk, hashish and opium smoked, fights fought and forgotten. And, for a brief, blissful moment, so was the plight of their beloved sister. Events spiralled in the direction these things go. The brothers' last memory of the Corsair Republic was staggering down an unlit street. Three young women hanging on their arms. Intent, it seemed, on showing the newly enriched pair a good time.

1624

TWENTY-TWO — *the Dutch cure*

Isaac's eyes opened. From swirling darkness, a superabundance of light. From unconsciousness, a superabundance of sensation — without context, without meaning. Scrunching his lids reduced the intensity of light, but not the feelings. Raising his head caused his universe to explode. After a pause, he tested his vision again — tentatively this time.

He took in a long, deep breath. The fetid stench of human waste assaulted his sinuses, dry-retching, eyes watering, nose streaming. The copper of blood, the acid of bile clagging his mouth. His tongue, bloated like some half-tide flotsam, choked his throat. Attempting to swallow triggered a jolt of agony but produced no moisture. His right side was numb, like a slab of meat. Rotating onto his back, the feeling returned in aching pulses, as did jumbled memories. Flashes of pretty faces, generous red lips, huge kohl blacked eyes, firm pointed breasts. The hot, moist musk of woman. Then there was choking, and a wall of pain, beyond which his thoughts couldn't penetrate.

He made to rub his crusted eyes. Rusty iron manacles bit into his wrists. He shook his head like a wet dog. The swirling fog clouding his vision dissipated explosively — focus abruptly returned. Filthy bodies crammed around him. Faces he didn't recognise, eyes glazed. Struggling to rise against the press of bodies, he glimpsed Benjamin, head lolling, unconscious in a pool of vomit, mucus bubbling from his nostrils. He too chained, wrist and ankle. *What had they done to merit such treatment? Yes, what hadn't they done?* His shoulders rose and fell in a dry parody of laughter.

Cold planking beneath him. An urgent, tilted motion. Hissing waves, the groaning of tortured timbers. Gulls crying their perpetual lament for the souls of lost sailors. His first thought, they were back aboard the Zeelander. Punished for their many misdemeanours. But the conversion work was half-complete; she wasn't seaworthy. And that suffocating, gagging stench. He wriggled towards his brother, between bodies tangled like eels on a fishmonger's stall. Chains jerked him to a stop; he tried swivelling to reach him with a foot: 'Benjamin, wake up.'

A tanned face like a badly shaved monkey looked down on him, dried saliva on cracked lips, sleep in the corners of rheumy eyes.

'He'll be all right lad, jus' leave 'im be.'

The monkey had a name — Alwin Jurksen. He hailed from Volderdam. Returning, he said, from the Spice Islands. His ship fell foul Barbary Pirates. His crewmates' families paid ransoms, but his couldn't raise the scratch. Or, more likely, didn't care to have him returned. So he became the property of a Turk. Isaac learned they were aboard an English Guineaman bound for the slave markets of Jamaica. They represented the most recent purchases, which proved a hollow blessing. Others had been aboard for a month or more, suffering the heat, the filth and close confinement. Over the days, Isaac learned more. Kidnapped, yes, but the why and the how of it went unanswered. They should shoulder some blame, drunk and incapable in a pirate republic. Lured from the company of shipmates by the promise of sex. They couldn't claim there hadn't been warnings. There they were, crammed with eight strangers in this cramped compartment. Dutch and English for the most part and one Swede, with a couple of uncommunicatives of indeterminate origin. Prisoners of war, criminals, debtors, the unransomed victims of Pirates — they all had stories. One poor fellow was tending sheep on the outskirts of Bideford when he snatched. After a year in the galleys, his back succumbed to the strain. So back to the slave market for him. What future torment awaited him, he wasn't sure.

Isaac noticed Benjamin's neck was naked. 'Did they take Esther's charm?' he hissed.

'No,' said Benjamin.

'Where is it?'

Benjamin looked embarrassed. 'Don't ask,' he said, and was thereafter silent on the subject.

Some captives derived comfort from telling their stories, eyes clouded with tears and regret. Others guarded their past jealously, as though sharing may diminish its value. Isaac and Benjamin came to learn the ways of a slave ship and to recognise members of the crew. And they weren't a well starred assembly. At times it was difficult to know who to feel more sorry for, the captives or the captors. Working a slaver was the least popular job at sea, for a reason. Slaver crews comprised the dregs of the ports. If whalers were the warriors of the waves, slavers were surely the night soil men. No self-respecting sailor would sign aboard a slaver. These were not self-respecting sailors.

1624

The ship owner and nominal captain was one Charles Geoffrey Wellesford. He was the bastard progeny of some minor aristocrat or claimed to be. He'd learned the slaving trade as a surgeon, grading captors' in terms of value, deciding which lived and should suffer commercial death. Painfully thin and with a wracking cough, he gave every impression of being a terminal consumptive. The voyage of the African Prince was his first independent venture. A sure route to a fortune. That is, if events proceeded as anticipated. He rarely appeared on deck. Sick or drunk, whatever reason, doubtful it was shame.

In Wellesford's absence, the first mate, Elias Fosberry, oversaw the day-to-day conduct of the vessel. Then there was Gideon Budock, the boatswain, keeping himself to himself. His face bore the livid marks of the initial stages of syphilis, tremors betraying symptoms of the mercury cure. Hendrig Aadrens was perfectly qualified for his task as slave master. A weasely creature in both attitude and appearance, indifferent to the suffering of others. A parsimonious bean-counter apportioning food like it came directly from his profit-and-loss ledger.

Edmond Poundstock was a Westcountryman with the brawn and demeanour of a farm labourer. The role of pilot became his when a more suitable candidate failed to materialise. His mantra: 'Keep going west, how hard can that be?' Elias Fosberry, the first mate, was the only true sailor amongst them. Drummed out of the English Navy for suspected sodomy. Fond of dangling little black boys on his knee.

Henry Crabb, ordinary sailor, twice flogged on other ships for abusing female captives. On the African Prince, such infringements went unnoticed. Isaac and Benjamin and the rest of the Europeans were the property of Ismail Burakgazi, the only passenger on board, a Turkish trader. An overdressed fat fuck in a fez. The white captives' welfare was the responsibility of Hasan Kilik, Burakgazi's catamite factotum.

Unusually, a crew of just eighteen held dominion over four-hundred captives. Many times fewer than was prudent or usual for a slaver. Fifty would be barely sufficient. Whether this was a factor of greed or inexperience, the brothers never ascertained. The overseers trod a fine line — needing to maintain brutal discipline, without being lethally harsh. No matter how well-armed, eighteen men couldn't stem an insurrection of four-hundred slaves. Adult males, deemed the greatest threat, remained in chains. Women were less of a danger. They were caged-off from the men, spending the voyage unmanacled. Children were in separate quarters. In the daytime, they had the run of the decks.

Netting surrounded the ship to frustrate captives, preferring death to a lifetime of servitude.

Sustenance consisted of rice and beans and tepid water. At first there were yams and peppers, but fresh food was soon exhausted. In the second month, the purple blotches of scurvy began to appear in crew and prisoner alike. Apart from segregation, white captives received no appreciably better treatment. They were, however, allowed to wash on deck in relative privacy. Isaac and Benjamin concealed their circumcisions. You could never tell what reaction these might provoke. Jews, everyone's favourite scapegoat.

The brothers began their ordeal watchful of opportunities for liberty. But forty days into the middle passage exhausted all such potential, even in private fantasy. Malnutrition, dehydration and monotony took their inevitable toll. In the daily scrabble for food and water, you found out who your friends were. Nothing more certain, there were no friends on the African Prince. Plans for escape drifted into irrelevance. Escape to where? Or mutiny? Take over a ship mid-Atlantic with four-hundred hostile African warriors to pacify and feed, and no willing crew?

Arriving at last, the brothers were the most well-nourished. As the weeks passed, they descended to the same abject state as the rest. Ribs poking through their skin, their only remaining currency, their unity of purpose. The past was all but forgotten. The future a curdled collision of dread and wishful thinking. Their reality was the narrow corridor of the present. Their immediate environment became the entire world. There was always a spiteful squabble for prime positions by the porthole. The squabble revisited every time they returned from exercise. There was a piss bucket, which doubled as a puke bucket, which doubled as a shit bucket, if you couldn't wait to squat over the beak head grating. Personal hygiene restricted to the dubious pleasures of the tow rag. Bloody flux was endemic, the decks swum in filthy discharge, slopping backwards and forwards with the movement of the seaway.

Through all this, the brothers clung on. The choice was stark. Live this squalid existence or scramble over the netting. Become a willing meal for opportunist sharks. Days stretched into weeks, weeks to months. Boredom and helplessness spawned lassitude as the brothers drifted ever further into the toxic realms of self-pity.

Survival in such conditions required cooperation. Titus Dobel, a wizened old sailor from Bristol, winked at Benjamin. He opened his palm, revealing his treasure, a rusty ship's nail the size of his index finger.

'My way out of here,' he said, slyly: 'Help me get an edge on it and you can have it after me.'

They took turns grinding it against ever finer surfaces. After two weeks, Benjamin held it to the light — it was getting there. It struck him that Dobel hadn't thought this through. If he intended to attack a guard, what about their shackles?

But what else did he have to occupy himself? Benjamin and Dobel worked the iron together, short abbreviated soundless movements. Passing it one to the other when muscle trembled, and ligaments ached. From time-to-time Benjamin would ask:

'Say we finish it Titus, what then?'

'Escape,' he'd say, tapping the side of his nose. Then he'd be off on some rambling story of his youth.

Another week saw the top inch of the nail formed into a crude blade. Benjamin drew it down his arm, mowing off a strip of hair. Dobel snatched it from his hand, his eyes dancing with delight. He thrust the nail deep into his neck and dragged it across to his windpipe. The carotid artery burst, spurting like a fire hose. A fountain of blood erupted from his scrawny neck. As he toppled forward, he dropped the nail into Benjamin's open hand. No one could ever say Titus Dobel wasn't a man of his word.

'Taken the Dutch cure,' someone said.

Benjamin flung the blade away. Horrified, he screamed for help. The other prisoners took up the call, stamping the floor and banging the walls. Into this mayhem stepped a thoroughly irritated Hasan Kilik, whip in hand. His eyes bugged out at the sight of Dobel spouting blood. He began lashing the baying captives with his whip. Ismail Burakgazi waddled in with a pair of pistols, restoring calm, cursing his factotum. The prisoners were Kilik's responsibility. His negligence had cost a tenth of his master's projected profit. Slave master, Hendrig Aadrens, arrived next with a cabin boy and dragged Dobel's corpse away. Minutes later, there was the all-to-familiar splash — further sustenance for the trailing sharks.

The next day during exercise, they passed Kilik's naked body roped to the ratlines, his back flayed raw. The cat hung next to him, dripping blood and fragments of flesh. Aadrens strolled past, ejecting a stream of tobacco juice over his raw wounds. Hearing the man whimper, he chuckled to himself. Sharing the joke with the white captives, smiling slyly as they cheered. This incident, and others like it, provided rare relief from the tedium of the middle passage.

1624

It wasn't long before the brothers slipped back into the leaden trance that is the fruit of boredom. It was Benjamin who eventually released them. Or rather, it was Esther. Beautiful Esther. Lost Esther. His dreams about Esther. As they lay in their own filth, Benjamin whispered of fragrant enchanted gardens. Of incense-bearing trees, verdant green meadows, and lush forests. Of Esther hand-in-hand with a tall naked shadow bedecked with glistening jewels. She was smiling, mouthing words he said he didn't comprehend, more likely couldn't express.

In the darkness, Isaac saw the light flood back into Benjamin's eyes. Hope was returning, towing confidence in its wake. Thereafter, they sought opportunities to ingratiate themselves with the overworked crew. Benjamin noted the African Prince was steering a far from direct or consistent course. At this rate, neither slave nor persecutor would make it to their destination. As time passed and the heat increased, negro captives began to die. White captives began to die. As did one of the crew. Benjamin began to suspect the navigator was incompetent. He shared this thought with Isaac. Could this be something they could leverage?

It was a noonday exercise period. Benjamin approached Edmund Poundstock as he was taking a sight. The idiot was sighting along the wrong end of the cross-staff. Benjamin corrected him and received a thorough kicking for his insolence. Rough hands dragged back to confinement, bleeding and semiconscious. Next day the first mate hammered out the iron wedge in Benjamin's manacles and ushered him back on deck.

'D'you know how to use these things, or were you gobbing off?'

He pointed at an array of navigation instruments arranged in a jumbled pile.

'May I?' said Benjamin, picking through the tools of the navigator's trade. 'So what have we here? Cross-staff, quadrant, astrolabe, sandglass, nocturnal, traverse board. Before the "interruption" to my career I was a pilot's apprentice aboard a three-decker.'

He burst into the great navigator Van den Broucke's zodiac mnemonic to the tune of the hymn, 'Wilt Heden Nu Treden.'

'You first see Andromeda's belt rising in the sky, pursued by Cetus the Whale, followed by the ear of Aries the ram da de da, de da...' He broke off.

'May I see your compass?' he said.

They conducted him up to the middle deck. The instrument was in a box on a shelf above the whip staff. Resting beside it was a pistol. Benjamin reached for it. Unforgiving fists clubbed him to the deck.

'Wait, wait, w-w-wait,' he pleaded, as boots kicked the breath out of him. 'Move that pistol, w-watch the compass bearing.'

As the pistol moved, the compass needle shifted fifteen degrees further north:

'Satan's bones,' bellowed Poundstock.

'Looks like you've got yourself a job,' said Fosberry.

'We'll keep this amongst ourselves. Right?' said Poundstock.

'You want me to navigate I'll need to concentrate,' said Benjamin. 'And I'll need my brother's help. You'll have to get us out of that privy, and we'll need decent rations. In return I'll guarantee we can shave at least twenty days off the passage.'

Benjamin and Isaac moved to a sail store where they slept in hammocks, instead of on bare boards. Each night, their shackles snapped on. Time passed, their captors ceased replacing them. When the wind increased, the crew found themselves critically shorthanded. Benjamin and Isaac regularly took to the ratlines, treading the foot ropes alongside the skeleton crew. And when equipment failed, Isaac's skills as a shipwright became evident. Over time, they insinuated themselves into positions of trust. Their food rations increased; even allowed rum. They smuggled food into other prisoners. Thieved ships' biscuits for the African children. They found themselves crew side of the barricado when the Africans exercised. The ship was operating efficiently for the first time, as they romped towards Jamaica.

But then events took a turn for the worse. The absentee captain became irrationally fearful of a water shortage. Regardless that it had rained three days, replenishing their water stores to capacity. He ordered the crew to institute rationing, accelerating the death toll. Which in turn appeared to justify rationing. Following this warped logic, he ordered the crew to throw healthy Africans overboard. Discarding a proportion now, he explained, would save the bulk of the cargo dying of thirst later. And drowned Negros were an insurable loss. Death by thirst or illness was 'natural spoilage' and thus unrecoverable.

Slaves shackled in pairs came on deck ten at a time to wash with buckets of seawater. Forced at gunpoint to dance to the point of exhaustion. Much to the hilarity of the crew. Captives judged fit went back to the increasingly filth-strewn hold. Their weaker brothers casually tossed screaming overboard. Crew members not involved in this murder, protecting their shipmates with cocked muskets. It was another two months before they sighted land. Isaac and Benjamin had watched helplessly as women and children met their fate of in this manner.

Rape was commonplace on slavers. Women arriving pregnant at the slave markets being a windfall bonus. But with this sparse a crew, they avoided potential flashpoints like rape.

Benjamin had just taken the evening star sight. He was below plotting the ship's position on the chart. Isaac, now thoroughly integrated into the crew, was taking the night air. He heard a muffled scream from the women's compartment. The cage door was swinging open. Isaac crept below. He found Noah Pascoe, the slave master's assistant, taking his pleasure with one of the women, as the others cowered against the bulkhead. She was fighting back, passive submission being the norm. Through the intervening grating, skeletally wide-eyed men watched helplessly from their filth-strewn slatted shelves. Isaac slipped silently behind the rapist, blinded by rage. He wrapped a forearm around Pascoe's neck and squeezed. The man struggled. Isaac increased the pressure. There was a dull snap; the attacker's legs carried on kicking, but there was no mind behind them. Panting, Isaac dropped the body. It tumbled from his grip like a discarded marionette. He slumped beside it. What had he done? He flinched as a firm hand gripped his shoulder. The would-be victim's face jolted him back to awareness. Footsteps overhead. He went to speak. She put a hand to his mouth. The footsteps passed.

The woman pointed below, nudged the corpse with her bare foot. First one, then another of the male captives, began their chant. Soon the whole below deck population was hammering chains, banging the ledges that passed for beds. Isaac and the woman dragged the corpse deep into the hold. They opened a hatch to the bilge and dropped his body into the swirling water. He could rot down there to his heart's content. Who would notice a little extra stink? Isaac's victim lay on his back staring up, eyes wide, mouth open, like he was about to say something, but had lost the thread of the conversation. The wind gusted, the ship groaned and heeled a little further to port and Noah Pascoe floated away towards the stern, arms flapping in a last farewell. Isaac replaced the boards. Then he sank down on his knees, trembling. The woman draped herself around him like a warm black comforter. Isaac rose slowly, stiffly, taking her with him. Three hundred pairs of eyes had witnessed murder. Three hundred voices sang on into the night.

'Hangbè,' she said, taking his hand.

'Isaac,' he said, squeezing gently.

He glimpsed her on deck the next day. Tall, lean, square-shouldered, head shaved, a sleek slice of midnight naked in the noonday sun. He avoided her eyes, or was she avoiding his? The crew searched the ship for Pascoe, finding no sign, but a hat and a half-finished bottle of rum on the poop, they concluded the obvious, he'd gone overboard. Afterall the man was a notorious drunk, weren't they all. Their share of the profit had just increased, every cloud, right? Pascoe's shipmates didn't mourn him for long. Thereafter the slavers became ever more reliant on the brothers.

Benjamin received a summons from the captain. Wellesford's cabin stank of vomit and gin, his stale unwashed body and a faint scent of death. The man lay half-dressed, half out of his hammock, half-drunk.

'So where are we?'

'Four-hundred and thirty miles west of Jamaica sir.'

'So, what, four days?'

'I'd say so.'

'Good, now get out.'

'Sir.'

Isaac got word to Hangbè. That night the slaves thudding dirge once more echoed through the ship. Isaac followed their rhythm as he hammered the wedges from the shackles of the European prisoners. The crew being mostly drunk were unprepared for insurrection. With just a watch of six on deck the prisoners overpowered them with ease. Wellesford barricaded his door. This proved little obstacle for the escaped prisoners. They skewered him screaming in his bed on the end of a boarding pike. Burakgazi and his catamite suffered disembowelment and shortly thereafter became supper for the sharks. Other slavers met a variety of ingeniously horrific ends. The question of the black captives arose. To the brothers' horror, rather than free them, the escapee's consensus was to leave the African's chained and continue to Port Royal to sell them. They'd all be rich. Isaac and Benjamin were the only opposing voices. Gratitude for their freedom forgotten, they narrowly escaped pitching overboard. It was Benjamin's navigation skills saved their skins.

Isaac meanwhile had discovered the armoury. He loaded and hid four pistols and two muskets in the rope locker, spoiling the remaining powder with water. Another week passed. No more negros overboard, the mutineers, of course, having no claim on insurance. They were initially suspicious of the brothers, but this faded over time. Benjamin predicted a land sighting within two days. Thirty-six hours later they passed between Barbuda and Antigua. In just a week they'd be dropping anchor at Port Royal. They set about conditioning the captives. Extra rations of food. Longer time on deck. More exercise. Healthier the cargo, better the price. Each man represented thirty-five guineas in good health. The mutineers' plan was to assume the identities of the murdered crew, auction the Africans in the slave markets, and return home, each upwards of a thousand pounds richer. Not a bad turn of fate for penniless kidnap victims.

Two days out from Jamaica the mutineers located the rum supply and they fell to celebrating the dual aspect of this unexpected twist of fate, freedom and fortune. Steering became neglected; the ship turned to windward and locked firmly in irons. Sheets hung loose; canvas flapped uselessly. No cause for concern, there was sea room aplenty. And anyway they were beyond caring. The evening started well enough. Singing and dancing and gambling. They dragged African women on deck for their lascivious entertainment. Quarrels broke out, over women, over the equity of shares, over cards, over dice. This debauch continued for a day and a half. Slaves went unwatered and unfed. On the pretext of selecting a woman, Isaac went below. He handed Hangbè a hammer miming the use of it. Then he and Benjamin armed themselves from the rope locker. The slow rhythmic slave chant began reverberating around the ship once more. An hour later three dozen freed Africans maddened by thirst burst out of the hold. They tore into the mutineers in a frenzy of vengeance, killing some and capturing others.

Isaac and Benjamin found themselves cornered. They backed up the companionway to the poop deck, pistols cocked, reluctant to use them. Hangbè forced her way through the blood crazed mob.

The brothers negotiated the release of Boaz Hocklin and four more. Skyler Hurst an English sailor, Sem Smitt the surviving ship's boy, Daan de Vlaeming a Dutch sailor who had initially sided with the brothers, and Gustav Evertson a Swedish sailor. Someone needed to sail the ship. The remainder of the scoundrels met their God courtesy of a frenzy of hammerhead sharks, amid jeering in *Hausa, Yoruba, Igbo, Akan, Ngomba and Fulah.*

1624

TWENTY-THREE — *Andromeda*

The Zeelander was mid-Atlantic, two days out from the Azores. The Admiral had taken Isaac's advice and razored down the ship. In so doing he had sacrificed his stateroom. Less topweight produced a much lighter and more stable craft. Which, in turn, sailed closer to the wind. It didn't accord with the Admiral's traditional aesthetic. But, in the event, he preferred the motion — lower in the ship he slept better. It also brought him in closer proximity to the men. He didn't mind that either. A general should always be close to those under his command. No chance of overfamiliarity, so unchallengeable was his adamantine authority. Hanging a sailing master did tend to do something for a master's reputation. What chance would lesser ranks stand?

The armour was out again. The ship's ironworker had made a poor job of tapping out the dents. But it was still highly decorative. And, as its scars would testify, highly effective. By way of compensation Sheng had located a freshly starched ruff. These were still fashionable in the United Provinces. Most especially since the hated Philip of Spain had recently banned them.

You meet a ship in these waters, automatically run out your guns. That or you make a run for it. No matter the ship seems friendly, you don't take chances. This especially applies if the ship out guns you and is flying the black. With Isaac's modifications they could easily outrun or out manoeuvre her. But retreat was not in the Admiral's nature. He called a conference and out came the charcoal and model ships again. They would pull ahead, then bare off to larboard. Feign rigging problems, dropping back parallel with their pursuer. This would surrender the tactical advantage of weather gage. But their guns'd be able to deliver a devastating broadside. And the other ship's ordinance would be pointing uselessly downwards.

So this they did. The gun crews poised, fuses in hand. But the order never came. The other ship lowered it s ensign, hoisting the yellow and blue of Sweden. The Admiral reciprocated. Lowered the Portuguese flag and raised orange, white and blue. They sailed like this in parallel.

A longboat left the Swedish ship, arriving with an invitation. The Zeelander didn't close its gunports. The Swedish ship didn't open hers. The message, if we harm your representative, feel free to blow us out the water. The Swedish boatswain took the Admiral's hand, helping him aboard the longboat. The effort Sheng put into the Admiral's hair wasted. Wind and sea spray saw to that. But the rest of his appearance was no less impressive. As he clambered aboard, the glint of gold engraved armour flashed all the way back to the Zeelander.

Schoenmaecker never cared for armour at sea, the reason being obvious. But, judging from the marks on the Admiral's breastplate, it had likely as not saved his life several times. Perhaps he should get some. The Admiral was nimble for a septuagenarian wearing armour. Once aboard the boatswain passed him his rapier. He returned it to its sling and flattened his tangled hair. The Admiral had left instructions. If they attempt to hold him hostage, sink the Swedish ship without hesitation. Schoenmaecker could see Matamata on the Zeelander's rail and returned his wave, feeling proud. Had anyone ever a better friend? But no new clothes for him. Just a brace of pistols which he surrendered once aboard.

A figure appeared from the shadow of the poop deck. It took Schoenmaecker a second or two to realise it was a woman. Especially so, given the sexual ambiguity of their admiral. She was wearing a black doublet with slashed sleeves, breeches, yellow hose and rolled back leather boots. Her hair was the same in colour and length as that of the Admiral. There was a silver and gold rapier on her hip. Were the Admiral surprised he hid it well, taking her proffered hand and bowing low.

'Lieutenant Admiral Count Jochem Bartholomeuz Van Den Hamel Count of Asterfoort and Spakenfoort, Knight of the Holy Order of Saint Botolph, Captain General of the Zeelander and your humble servant madame.'

She responded with a gracious court bow.

'And I am the Grevinna Ingela Olofsdotter Gathenhielm, Captain General of the Andromeda. Your servant sir.'

Schoenmaecker gawped. Was it only he who saw it? It was like they were siblings. Soon to be incestuous siblings to judge by the look on the Admiral's face. She unclipped her rapier and handed it to her boatswain. The Admiral did the same, handing his to Schoenmaecker.

'Would you care for some refreshment sir.' said the Lady Captain.

'That would be very kind Madame.'

They went below. Schoenmaecker sat on the fo'c'sle with his opposite number, a huge blonde bear of a man. But that was okay,

1624

Schoenmaecker knew how to deal with bears. He had one of his own back onboard. They shared a plate of bread and cheese and a flagon of beer.

'Karlsson,' said Karlsson.

'Schoenmaecker,' said Schoenmaecker.

'Nice seamanship, Dutchman.'

'Nice cheese, Swede.'

'Fuck you.'

'Fuck you back.'

'So what are you doing out here?'

'Like they tell me anything,' said Schoenmaecker. 'Looking for Spanish treasure ships I hope, anything Catholic comes our way. You?'

'Letters of mark from Gustavus Adolphus. Locate and ransom or otherwise liberate Swedish subjects from slavers. That's all I can say. Can say this though. The Missus comes across any Spanish ship Christ help 'em. She comes across a slaver, not even Christ will be able to help 'em. Her family fell foul of Barbary slavers. Lives in hope she might find 'em. Finish your beer.'

Karlsson reached for a tall stone bottle and charged their tin mugs. Schoenmaecker sniffed the contents, blanching — akvavit; Christ help him too.

'To kind seas,' said Schoenmaecker, raising his drink.

'And nice cheese,' said Karlsson.

1624

TWENTY-FOUR — *Hourglass Shoal*

The great cabin had been repurposed. Benjamin had set up a trestle table, across which he'd spread charts and navigation equipment. Isaac noticed he was once more wearing Esther's golden pendant. The consumptive Wellesford's bed and baggage went overboard along with his mutilated remains.

Dozens of bare feet thumped overhead. Freed captives were rampaging about the ship. African voices, a babel of languages. Nameless items smashed in misdirected fury. The last mindless shriek of a dying mutineer.

Sails slapped about, drawing and backing purposelessly. The vessel yawed across the wind, gaining and losing momentum, sliding sideways, going nowhere.

'We need to get underway,' said Isaac. 'These seas swarm with Spanish warships, and privateers of every colour. We haven't enough men to crew a single cannon. And if we encounter hostiles I'd like to do so under more equal terms.'

Benjamin shuddered: 'Add to our misery,' he said, 'couple of old hands are saying we're in for a storm. Classic signs of a hurricane. Wind's veered to a sou' westerly, the swell's steadily increasing in height and frequency. All we need is... Damn me, is that rain?'

The brothers rushed on deck. As they stood there a light downfall became a monsoon.

Benjamin looked to the darkening heavens: 'This is not looking at all good. You and me and five hands to do the work of fifty.'

'So, we reduce sail,' said Isaac: 'Strip her down to something we stand half a chance of managing. Reef early, ride it out under bare poles if we must.'

The brothers exchanged a glance. Isaac shook his head in a parody of despair — brave words. Brighter side, the cold downpour had calmed the roaming bands of Africans. Some sought shelter, some stood, arms outstretched, heads back, mouths open, laughing. The brothers returned to the cabin, shaking off the rain.

'So, how long before it hits,' said Isaac.
'Could be up to three days, our luck, less.' said Benjamin.
'We'll cover a long distance in three days.'
'We'll cover a lot less in two.'
'Especially short handed,' said Isaac.
'So, big brother,' said Benjamin, 'you have a plan?'
'Rather hoping *you* might.'

Hangbè entered the cabin naked, black as pitch and glistening with a sheen of water. Isaac had only ever seen her in partial darkness. A disembodied voice. He was unprepared for the full impact of her daylight presence. Light became lighter, dark became darker. Such enhanced contrast overspilled into emotions and decisions. Square of shoulder, long of limb, she moved with a leopard's economy and efficiency — for even the slightest movement a clearly defined purpose. Isaac imagined her an African princess. The doting daughter of a fierce tribal chieftain from an ancient noble lineage. Or, he speculated, she was a priestess, a wise woman, a cruel officiant of revolting cannibalistic rites. He shuddered. Something within him, he'd best not acknowledge, rather hoped for the latter.

Two men entered behind her. One of them had to bend to pass through the door.

'The big fellow is Khamisi. The skinny one is Xaawo.' Her heavily accented Portuguese was deep, resonant, almost masculine. 'There are many peoples amongst the captives. These men speak for the two majority tribes. You talk. I'll interpret.'

Isaac, deeply in the thrall of Eros, deftly diverted attention to Benjamin.

'Begin with our position brother,' he said, eyes locked on Hangbè.

Benjamin glanced up at her: 'Will they understand charts?'

'My men will understand charts.'

Isaac opened a window, suffering the rain for the benefit of light and ventilation. Benjamin directed them to the table. He unrolled a chart and drew a charcoal 'X' about fifty miles south of Puerto Rico.

'We are here. We are going there, for sale in the slave markets.' He pointed to Jamaica, drawing a line from their position to Port Royal. 'We intend to divert here. He drew a heavy line from the 'X' through the broad channel between Puerto Rico and Hispaniola. 'Enemy,' he said, stabbing Puerto Rico, 'Not so enemy,' he said, stabbing Hispaniola.

'That true?' said Isaac, leaning over his shoulder.

'It's what I get from the men. They say the Spanish have withdrawn their forces to a city south of the island. The north coast and interior are open country. Escaped convicts and freed slaves, freebooters like us, occupy most of this land.'

Isaac looked to Hangbè. 'This next will be difficult. Tell them big winds are coming. Waves so high they could swallow this ship. They must not liberate any more captives. Not,' he said with great emphasis. 'All those already freed can feed, water, and clean those who remain chained. But do not release them. And when the wind comes we must lock everyone below. Nail down the hatches.'

Two-hundred terrified men on deck. The seas would wash them overboard in minutes. But stored below, twenty tons of human ballast could be the difference between floundering and survival. They were no longer people; they were factors in weight distribution.

Hangbè translated their reaction. 'They won't agree. They ask why they should trust white people?'

'Tell them to forget the colour of our skin. Weren't we captives just like them?' Isaac jerked down his sleeve, revealing a livid crescent moon and star burned deep into his shoulder. 'Wasn't it us that freed them? They have a simple choice, trust us and live — or don't and drown. Two days, three at most will take us into the lee of this island.' He pointed out the north shore of Hispaniola. 'This will shelter us from the worst of the weather. We will either discover a secure anchorage and ride out the storm or beach the ship and walk ashore. Then they can decide their next move, with or without our advice. But first they must clear the decks.'

'Our men will show them how to work the pumps,' said Benjamin, 'They'll need to be going continuously, if we are to survive.'

Isaac turned to Hangbè. 'Tell them we'll take ten men. The youngest and fittest. Best way, we'll have three days to make sailors of 'em.'

Before Khamisi and Xaawo retreated to ponder their options. Isaac turned to Hangbè. 'Tell them to take what they need from here,' Benjamin opened a sea chest packed with pistols and swords.

Benjamin, as navigator, was the ship's most vital asset. He naturally deferred to his elder brother. Isaac in turn looked to Hangbè and her men to control the Africans. So Isaac and Hangbè emerged de facto captains of the African Prince.

Plundering the slaver's sea chests outfitted Hangbè with breeches and boots, shirt and doublet. Add a sword sash and a cross-belt bearing a brace of pistols and she was every inch the pirate queen. The effect on the Africans was remarkable. Simmering rebellion cooled to awed compliance.

Alone, Benjamin and Isaac took stock of their skeleton crew, starting with the cabin boy. Something about him was wrong. His proportions weren't right for what claimed to be a thirteen-year-old. You'd think Shem Smitt had shrunk in the wash. Save there was little evidence of washing. That or he'd stepped into this world from a fairy realm, save for the stink. He didn't show the least sign of grieving for his fellow ship's boy, close though they'd seemed. Wounds close fast when you're young and seen as much as him.

Then there was Skyler Hurst whose naming could well have been oracular. That or deep, dark confinement had fulminated an irresistible desire for its opposite. If you needed Skyler, you just had to look skywards. There he'd be, closest he could get to the heavens — up in the royals, blonde pigtail waving proudly in the wind, like an Admiral's pennant, eyes glazed with bliss, grin as wide as the sea of Cortez. This was a man so defined by his location, he hardly required further description.

Boas Hocklin was a big man emptied, like a wine sack all drunk out. Skin hung loose about his sallow face; jowls wobbled when he talked. And what he talked about in the main was a particular type of food. This had been so during his confinement. But since his release the true scale of his obsession became clear. Spaniards were the ones who had hollowed him. Now he had one single overriding ambition, he wanted to eat a Spaniard. Spit roast at best. Worst way, he said, he'd even eat one raw.

Daan De Vlaeming was from the Free Provinces. He had those stubby, abbreviated features, cornflower eyes and sandy colouring outlanders associate with Netherlanders. He put Isaac in mind of Luuk, Neeltje's gentleman caller. Giving De Vlaeming orders was like towing a barge. Tough work getting him motivated. But once he was going in the right direction, you'd have trouble stopping him. He gave the impression of having an inner compass. The role of helmsman was ideally suited to his steady unwavering nature.

Bring to mind Scandinavians and you picture hearty Viking raiders — blue of eye, blond of hair. Warriors, plunderers, rapists and priest killers. Yet Gustav Evertson was of no great stature, dark of complexion and mood. Not the sort of berserker would come at you mindlessly swinging an axe. Evertson was a thinker of thoughts — a plotter. Not that he would be averse to a little raping and priest killing, or the accumulation of treasure. It's just he'd would go about it in an entirely different way.

After the mayhem, the decks were eerily quiet. The crew mustered on deck. Khamisi arrived with ten young Africans.

'Gentlemen, your apprentices,' said Isaac. 'At best you have a day and a half to teach them the ropes, make topmen of them.'

'Mister De Vlaeming,' said Benjamin, 'to the helm. I will require a course nor' nor' west if you please.'

The sails snapped and flogged petulantly as the ship wore away from the weather. The rain-sodden canvas filled, taking up the strain, the shrouds creaked, and everything changed. The African Prince became transformed. One minute an old nag grazing aimlessly in a field, next a racehorse taking the jumps. Soon her bow wave was churning the sea white, a delta foaming to infinity from their stern. He became aware again of the rhythmic clatter of the pumps. Their steady, clank-gush-clank, as they gulped water from the bilge, provided the rhythm to Isaac's thoughts.

Needles of sea spray stung his eyes. With one hand gripping the rail, he dragged the other across his face to clear his vision. Licking the salt from his lips, he followed a pod of humpbacks on the starboard quarter. Their mountainous backs rising and falling in an effortless aquatic ballet. Bursts of vapour rose high in the air, white against the darkening waves. The pungent odour of part-digested krill drifted over the decks. One of them breached closer than the rest. As it rolled in the hull's turbulence Isaac fancied he glimpsed an eye. It felt significant, like a greeting — or a warning. Then the leviathan spouted and submerged, leaving its sleek lesser cousins skylarking in the bow wave, clicking and chirruping.

Isaac felt vindicated in his controversial interpretation of ship design. Given a chance he'd apply the same principals to this vessel. Razor the superstructure down — reduce windage. Slice it off like a maritime *brit millah*. The day of the galleon was passing. With so much superfluous height to the aft castle, the African Prince was weathercocking, making furious work for De Vlaeming on the whip staff. She was handling like a drunken sow. Picturing how one would get a sow drunk, indeed what one's motivation to do so might be, made Isaac smile.

By the late afternoon, the African youths seemed thoroughly at ease aloft. Scampering up the ratlines, treading the footropes to the furthest extent of the yards. By the evening they had mastered reefing, and it had become a game for them. Playing chase in the topgallants, peering up at Skyler Hurst, their new hero, standing in the royal crosstrees. Boaz Hocklin slithered down the ratlines. He clambered up the companionway to the poop deck. Isaac, lost in thought, became aware of him leaning on the rail to his left.

'Wait till it blows proper, then we'll see,' said Hocklin, 'then we'll see.' There was an idiot grin on his not-such-an-idiot face. 'But give me another week with 'em and they'll be the best sailors on the ship.'

'Adonai grant us that week,' muttered Isaac.

As Benjamin watched the sky rapidly darkened to the southeast. A single lightning bolt sizzled into the sea. As dusk fell the sun appeared to stutter as it slipped beneath the horizon. All visual distinction between sea and sky disappeared. Like Gerrit Dou priming a canvas in tones of grey. Preparatory to painting what? A picture of lost souls clinging to wreckage swallowed by a maelstrom, or victorious triumph over the vicissitudes of Neptune. The drizzle let up, like the strengthening winds had blown the air dry. Hocklin left the poop deck to join Skyler Hurst in chiding the playful 'apprentices.'

Benjamin joined Isaac at the aft rail, mesmerised by the fast-arriving hurricane. Beneath them the rudder churned the sea to white foam. This seemed the place to be when contemplating an uncertain future. This ship seemed emblematic of the human paradox — riding a sliver of present awareness, future before their bows, past to their stern.

'We know something's coming,' said Benjamin: 'We just don't know what, or how severe.'

'De Vlaeming was talking of an *orkaan*,' said Isaac, 'but isn't it too early in the year?'

'And if that's the case, let's hope it tracks north of Puerto Rico. Or we might as well say our goodbyes now.'

'It's the classic choice,' said Isaac, 'stay as far out to sea as possible, or seek a haven. If we had a full crew and well found ship I'd be counselling heading to open water. Ride this bastard out. Let it do its worst.'

'But that's clearly not the case,' said Benjamin, 'We've made the right decision. The only decision. Run for the lee of Hispaniola. Follow close to land as prudence allows. See if we can't make it into the Bay of Samaná. Seek an anchorage there.'

'Even if we have to beach the beast at least we won't drown.' said Isaac.

'Hopefully, won't drown,' corrected Benjamin.

'So, far as I can see,' said Isaac, 'there's one overwhelming obstacle. Hourglass Reef. It's covered by deep water by our standards, twenty-five fathoms at least. But the seabed shoals dramatically, rising from unfathomable depths. And this kicks up huge waves in even moderate conditions. We're a big heavy ship, with a following wind we'll have massive momentum. We should be able to punch through. And it won't last so long. That's if we hit the hourglass slap in the middle.'

The wind howled through the shrouds by the time they were mid-channel, the Isla de Mona a misty shape to their starboard. Further to the north was a tiny island, companioned with Mona like the earth to the sun.

They were running on half-reefed courses, the full lanteen mizzen and a single jib. Yet still they were sailing too fast. Overtaking the wave train. Leaping across troughs, smashing into the wall of the oncoming seas. Waves were breaking over the deck as the bows dug in. African sailors washed the length of the deck, crashed into the aft castle. It seemed like fun until one of them went overboard. It came as a shock, not least to him, when Boaz Hocklin grabbed a rope and leapt into the roiling sea after him. They pulled them in half-drowned barely maintaining a grip on the rope.

'Get below. All off you,' screamed Isaac. 'We'll call when we need you.'

'We've got to reduce speed,' bellowed Benjamin, 'or we'll lose helm control.'

'Take Collings and Smitt. Rig up a drogue. Wrap a couple of dozen round shot in and old mainsail and cast it off on forty fathoms of stout line tied off on the sternpost — see what that does.'

When the drogue bit, there was a jolt, the ship creaked and shuddered, torn between opposing forces.

'Seems to be working,' Benjamin reported, 'Daan reckons she's lighter on the helm, less skittish.'

Another wave rolled over them, submerging the deck. Then up she came like a cormorant diving for fish.

Isaac cocked an ear:

'Can you hear anything?'

'No?'

'That's what's worrying me. I'm going below.'

The strain on the ship had opened planks. De Vlaeming and his African boys were busy with caulking irons pounding in hemp. The water was slopping up to the slave deck. The pumps were idle. Isaac didn't need telling the intake had blocked. He waded past the terrified Africans and dived down, releasing the bilge hatch. He rose, took a breath then plunged through the hatch into the turbulent bilge. And there he encountered Noah Pascoe once more, intent on revenge. Face bleached white, eyes bulging, his left arm jammed into the canvas hose of the pump. Isaac gasped, sucking fouled water into sore lungs. Bursting to the surface he vomited brine. Hangbè arrived, frantic. They dived together into the churning water. Between them they dragged Pascoe's corpse free and floated it through the bilge hatch. The pumps began again and the water level stabilised.

A flash from the top mainmast — the crack of gunfire. Skyler Hurst waving, pointing a pistol dead ahead. He came scrambling down. What he'd seen had motivated even he to head for the illusory safety of the deck. Isaac was the next to see them. The overfalls of Hourglass Shoal rose before them like a cliff face. Now he'd some impression of what the Pharaoh experienced when the Reed Sea closed in over him and his army. Chaotic white water came rushing at them from every direction. The ship rose and fell from mountainous peaks to bottomless troughs. More seams burst, water poured in, the pumps couldn't hope to keep pace. Yet the wind powered them through. The weight of the water flooding in, added to their momentum. Two hours later they burst through the worst of it into less chaotic water. The wind strength reduced, and the wave train re-established it's orderly flow.

If the reef had been dangerous, the brothers knew there was much worse to come. They needed to turn the ship to the west. Run the risk of uncharted sandbars, broadside on to the wind and waves. They needed to survive at least two hours in this precarious point of sail before they were in the wind shadow of the land.

Now came the true test. They must coordinate the realignment of the sails. Turn from a dead run to a beam reach. They could see the coast of Hispaniola now. Isaac checked with Benjamin then gave the order. Even the carthorse that was Daan de Vlaeming with the strength multiplier of the whip staff had trouble. The braces repositioned the sails. And nothing happened, they ploughed along on the same course.

Isaac rushed to the middle deck where De Vlaeming was struggling to force the whip staff hard over.

He looked to Benjamin and shook beads of sweat from his brow.

'The whip staff only moves the tiller fifteen degrees. Not enough against this wind.'

Isaac clapped De Vlaeming on the shoulder. 'Daan, were going to rig blocks to the tiller arm. Then you can dismantle the whip staff. We need to give it at least fifty degrees of rudder. You with me?'

'With you, Captain.'

'Captain, eh?' Benjamin raised his eyebrows, smiling.

1624

Isaac didn't notice.

Twenty minutes later the blocks were ready.

Isaac gave the order, 'Haul away starboard.'

The tiller began to bend as they hauled on the ropes. Then the rudder came round with a rush of churning water. The ship began to heel alarmingly. Isaac clambered onto the middle deck. The lee rail was completely under water, the coast of Hispaniola was coming up fast, he could hear the breakers.

'Bear away twenty degrees.' he bellowed down the hatch. He heard Benjamin relaying the command. The rail rose above the water line, and as they continued into the bay, the wind began to ease. As they pressed ever further into the Bay of Samaná the swell died down, the waves ceased to break, the ship sailed on an even keel. The boy on the lead line called out the depth.

Twenty hours later at six fathoms they dropped anchor. The Africans released from captivity, found themselves in what must have appeared to be paradise. The next day it was calm enough to go to shore.

TWENTY-FIVE — *the devil's arse*

Well-oiled wood creaked as Captain General Álvaro de Güímar leaned back in his chair. He sucked deeply on his long clay pipe. Another cloud passed through the white bush of his waxed moustache, rising to join its fellows stratifying below the nicotine-stained ceiling of the Great Room. Before him paced Ferdinand Ramirez, the pilot, the top third of his head obscured by smoke swirling like clouds about a mountaintop.

'Humour me Senior Ramirez,' said de Güímar. 'Explain again why we find ourselves becalmed in the Horse Latitudes.'

Ramirez sighed: 'The storm. We couldn't hold course. Forced to run before the wind, and then there was...'

'Now here's the bit that fascinates me,' said de Güímar: 'That was a week ago. Why did we continue sailing south, what was it you saw, purple salamanders playing in the rigging, or was it pink frigging fairies?'

'*Corpo santo*, your Grace sure sign of...'

'*Huracán?* Now correct me if I'm wrong Mister Ramirez doesn't that involve a superabundance of wind? And yet here we sit, every square inch of canvas we possess hanging from the high heavens to dragging in the sea and yet we move not.'

'But we are safe, your Grace. I have successfully navigated away from the Huracán's path...'

'And from the path of every other bloody wind,' de Güímar dabbed his bald pate with a lace-edged kerchief: 'And here we sit and roast. Huracán, bloody huracán I'd kiss the devil's arse for a huracán, hell I'd let him bugger me for a bastard breeze.'

'We need to have patience your Grace. We'll pick up the trades soon, there's really no need to fret.'

'Fret, *fret* say you. Fret about this. If we don't get a move on soon I'll have you strapped bare-arsed across m' best cannon and set the sergeant-at-arms at you with a cat.'

'But your Grace, I can hardly be held responsible for capricious acts of providence.'

'Act of providence, capriciousness? I'll hold you responsible for anything I damned well please. I'll hold you responsible for my cat farting if I so choose. But that would involve wind, something that you claim is beyond your remit, you poxy little weasel. Now get on and produce me some wind or you'll feel my boot up your arse. Go on, sod off.'

'Idiot,' he said when the pilot had gone. He turned to Aal like he'd just remembered she was there and shook his head. She raised her eyebrows and tutted, refilling his wine glass. He squeezed her arse on the way to the *seat of ease* out on the gallery. He squatted, breeches round his ankles, looking dolefully at the sky — a chain of clouds overhead stretched from the easterly to the westerly horizon, taunting him.

'Christ girl, even my bowels have come to a standstill.'

1624

TWENTY-SIX — *Any chance of some gravy*

The door to the sail store opened abruptly. Light flooded the passageway. Aal held up a lamp, peering into the darkness. She caught sight of a small deathly pale face.

'Oi you, wait your turn. Plenty to go round,' said Aal. Then she saw the man's Franciscan habit. 'You're on the wrong deck young man.' She glanced down at her bare breasts: 'Unless you've come for some of this.' She giggled, jiggling them seductively.

The friar stared, mesmerised. Then his face crumpled; she thought he was going to cry. Shrugging, she said: 'Suit yourself,' and went back to pleasuring her soldier.

Frantically crossing himself, the friar scurried away. Bursting onto the starlit deck, he took deep breaths as though the chilly night air might cleanse his tainted soul. He leant exhausted on the rail like he'd just run a race, his tonsure reflecting the moonlight back to its source. Clasping his hands, knuckles showing white, he prayed for release from the Satanic temptations bubbling up from his groin.

The following night he was back again — moth to a flame. But more circumspect this time. Eyes wide, young hands trembling, spirit battling carnality in a mess of contradictory of impulses. He tiptoed up like a thief and listened silently to the doings within, desperately stilling his breath. Light percolated through the ill-fitting door. The sounds, the smells, the sights seeped through a crack in the shrunken planking. His hand, of its own volition, reached inside his coarsely woven habit and began working his throbbing manhood. Eyes screwing shut, knees shuddering, his free hand grabbed his mouth stifling a moan of release. His universe erupted into bursts of fiery ecstasy and heavenly visions. And then it was gone. Immediately guilt and horror flooded the vacuum. He shuddered, opening his eyes.

Esther had appeared as from nowhere, staring at him aghast. She screamed and dropped her tray of food. Aal rushed out, catching the friar frozen in the light of her lantern. His feet seemed nailed to the spot, his hand dripping spilled seed.

'Witches,' he screamed, 'witches,' and rushed away, clattering through the darkness.

Father Rodrigo de Segeda waddled into the luxurious Great Cabin, followed by Tomás de Güímar, the Captain General's senior lieutenant and nephew. Seating himself before the Captain General's equally impressive desk Father Rodrigo smiled pleasantly. His jowls jiggled like half risen dough overspilling the proving bowl. His pinprick-eyes darted to Tomás like a heron spotting a fish. The Captain General took the hint.

'Tomás, if you wouldn't mind checking on our current chart position with Senior Ramirez...'

'But we haven't moved in a fortnight,' he protested, then he caught on. 'Oh, right.'

The young lieutenant rolled his eyes and, red faced, bowed his way out of the room.

'Wine Father?' said the Captain General. The friar's over-ripe strawberry nose, ample testimony to a man unafraid of pulling a cork.

'Later perhaps. But first I wish to report a matter of the utmost gravity pertaining to the safety of this vessel, both temporal and spiritual. I believe there are women aboard sent to disrupt our mission of rooting out heresy in New Spain. They have been offering carnal temptation to my young friars...'

The Captain General couldn't believe what he was hearing:

'Do you seriously wish to report this Father. Do you really want to bring this to my door? I have discipline to maintain. Matters such as this will sow the seeds of discord in the company. Isn't it bad enough we're stuck, unmoving out here, drifting around on this bloody barge?'

'That's another thing,' the friar blustered on, 'the crew are openly saying that two women have bewitched the wind. That they possess powers to curtail this voyage and impede our mission to cleanse the church of Mexico. That, simply put, these women are controlling the weather — in league with the devil.'

'You clearly are not a man of the world Father. I'll try to break this to you gently. *All* women are in league with the devil.'

'Our Lady?' said the friar.

The Captain General shook his head, turning away to glare out the window. You don't debate with these pricks.

'Saint Agnes, Benedicta, Catherine, Dulcissima, Eanfleda, Florentina...' continued the friar.

There followed a litany of female saints, in alphabetical order, would you believe?

Christ, he'd a good mind to kick the fat fucker's arse. But where to aim? Difficult to tell where the arse ended, and the man began. Christ the man was all arse.

With difficulty, the Captain General suppressed a chuckle.

'This might as well be a blasted fireship,' said the Captain General, when the the fat friar had finally waddled off.

'Don't know how you got yourself talked into this, uncle. This must be the most incendiary payload any ship has ever carried.'

'The cards I was dealt.'

'I'm in awe of your philosophical attitude.'

'No, literally "the cards I was dealt." *L'hombre*, I was convinced it was a good hand. Medina said he'd forgive my gambling debts if I took on this one last voyage. Should have known better.'

The Captain General confined his recklessness to the card table. In all other matters he was an each-way bet man. A man of solid build, and character. An aura of unquestionable moral authority clothed him like armour. His nephew was his greatest admirer. His being so often away from home, the Captain General's wife had yet to form an opinion. The boy, his nephew, was in his late twenties, fresh of face, with luxuriant natural curls falling past his shoulders, a single strand of platted lovelock falling on his left breast. His unspoken function, to bridge the gap between the Captain General and the ship's company — the Ares to his uncle's Zeus.

He shook his head, shuddering: 'A hundred horny soldiers, Tomás. A hundred-and-fifty superstitious sailors. And half-a-hundred women. But they couldn't be ordinary women could they? No, *conversos, moriscos,* and no doubt a proportion of secret Huguenots to boot. Forced transportees condemned to breed with the colonists. All that wailing and moaning. Supposed to stop our soldiers fornicating with the natives. Then there's the other lot. The Holy Fathers. God's own extortionists. Going out there to enforce the iron will of the money-grubbing Holy See. Thievery and bloody terror. Anyway, no matter, the pious pricks'll all fall foul of the pox in a six-month. All they do is eat, shit, moan and buggering up my Sundays with their endless masses. Christ Tomás, stop crossing yourself, they can't hear me. And don't you ever forget this. On this boat, I'm God All-bloody-mighty. Don't ever make me prove it.'

'Then there's the horses,' said his nephew.

'Yes, the horses.'

'Six big muscular pure-bred Andalusian stallions.'

'And one mare.'

'And she comes into season.'

'Thought those big beasts were going to kick a hole in the side of the ship. If they hadn't have calmed down I'd've sent for the master-at-arms and we'd've had fresh meat all the way across.

'Oh, and there's our bloody pilot. Couldn't find his arse with both hands let alone a fly spec of an island across five-thousand miles of ocean.'

'And those two trouble-making pretties under the orlop deck.' said Tomás.

The Captain General leaned out of the window. There was not a breath of air. The sea was a sheet of turquoise glass.

'Only bright light,' he said, 'in this great steaming pile of ordure if you ask me. I can see why Medina wants them for himself. Prize fruit. Let's hope this voyage doesn't spoil them. Christ's wounds. I feel like Pontius Pilate. What is it about those girls. Aal seems to act as Esther's handmaiden. And no doubt she was from a noble household — got a bearing to her. Beautiful in their own ways. Aal, earthy and attainable. Esther, above it all. They're like Mary Magdalene and the Madonna.'

'Aal is very "friendly" with the soldiers,' observed Tomás. 'They treat her like she's some sort of mascot. Got four or five of them on the go from what I hear. They're very protective of her. Their officers say as far as morale goes, she's the difference between a few mild complaints and a full-blown bastard riot. And Esther, she's got something, have you seen her with those stallions, she's all that's keeping them from tearing the place up. This bloody trial goes ahead, there'll be trouble — mark these words.'

'The sailors on the other hand,' said the Captain General, 'haven't had the pleasure of the girl's charms. Abject state of those fellows I can see why. They're as superstitious as those idiot monks. They've got it rattling about in their empty heads the women are a curse. That we'll be stuck here forever 'cos of them. I've had a delegation of the morons. Tugging their sodding forelocks. They'd throw all fifty of the poor bitches overboard if I let 'em. Given the choice I'd sooner do the same for those holier than thou monks. Closely followed by our idiot pilot. But you're right, of course. This ship's a tinderbox. I'm God's representative on this vessel, not that bunch of mumbling friars. What would God do?'

'Everything that's necessary to get his ship safely to port, regardless of his personal inclinations,' said his nephew.

'We'll make a captain of you yet, Tomás.'

1624

Later, in the darkness of the priest's candle-lit quarters:

'Father Rodrigo, will you confess me?'

'Of course my son.'

'Bless me Father, for I have sinned. It has been ten days since my last confession...'

The ritual preparatory to confession complete, the young friar blurted out his sins. Father **Rodrigo de Segeda** listened impatiently...

'So you stumbled upon this... er, event.'

'Yes, Father.'

'And lust came upon you.'

'Yes, Father.'

'And you... you...'

'Yes, Father,' he sobbed, 'I did, for my sins...'

The young Franciscan cringed in the shadows lean and sunless like an underfed snake.

'Venal, my son. You fell into this temptation through no fault of your own. Your soul was briefly in mortal jeopardy. But by demonstrating contrition, and making a sincere confession, that danger, you will be relieved, has now passed.'

'Thank you Father,' more tears.

'And now, by His very word I absolve you of all participation in sin committed in thought, in word, and in deed, in the name of...'

'Now we must report this matter to the Captain General directly.'

'But Father...'

'No, no we cannot keep silent. The Devil resides in silence. We must not tolerate fornication. Ungodly acts cannot go unpunished. "For the harlot is a deep pit, and the foreign woman a narrow well; she lies in wait like a robber and increases the number of the faithless." We owe it to every other fellow on this ship that this sinful contagion does not spread any further.'

'But Father...'

The court convened.

'My name is Esther Amsalem. My Hebrew name is Cohen. As a Jew this Christian court has no authority over me.'

They weren't expecting that. And certainly not expecting her opening address delivered in faultless Hebrew. The Inquisitors had enough knowledge of the language to recognise it as such, but their comprehension was less than perfect.

'The accused will please speak in the language of the court.'

'Nomen mihi est Esther Rachael Amsalem. Meum nomen hebraicum est Cohen. Quia talis haec curia Catholica in me nullam iurisdictionem habet.'

Now they were confused. A woman fluent in Latin?

'The common tongue if you please.'

'Which common tongue?'

'Spanish.'

'But I thought you said... never mind.'

She repeated her statement in faultless Castilian Spanish.

'Can you prove this?' said the fat Dominican.

'I'm the victim of abduction. There's no documents, no witnesses who can speak for me. I'm a Jewess of a noble priestly tribe, daughter of a learned Rabbi and make no secret of it. And would practice my faith openly had I recourse to our Holy books. I'd willingly submit to examination on any articles of my faith.'

'You are a criminal, a spy for the heretic Six Provinces. It was the merciful grace of the Duke of Medina which saved you from the hangman's noose.'

'*Miraculous* grace, if you please, your worship.'

'That's as may be. Nevertheless by your various criminal misdeeds you have become the legal property of the Duke of Medina.'

'The *Jewish* property if your worship pleases.'

The inquisitors went into a long huddle on their dais and came back with: 'We will leave this matter in obeyance. Next case.'

'If it pleased your worship,' said Esther, 'I represent Aal le Draginier.'

'As her attorney?'

'Yes, if it please your worship.'

The court sat, as far as the shipboard limitations allowed, with all the pomp of a typical Auto-da-Fé.

A pair of Inquisitors, in this case a representative each of the Dominican and Franciscan Orders, a *fiscal* (prosecutor), an *alguacil* (bailiff/torturer - Rodrigo Hamández), a *notario de secuestros* (to inventory the accused's property) a *Notario del Secreto* (notary of secrets), keeping the record. And an *Escribano General,* managing proceedings. And a couple of *Familiare,* hangers on.

The officials occupied the middle deck, looking down from under an awning on the accused standing in the burning sun in a makeshift dock on the lower deck, guarded by Hamández. The fiscal read out the charges: 'On this twenty-sixth day of September in the year of Our Lord sixteen-twenty-four it is hereby charged that you, Aal le Draginier, did engage in...

1624

The day before the trial Father Rodrigo de Segeda had waddled into the Great Room, slamming his letter of authority, complete with the papal seal, on the Captain General's desk. *That was his second strike*, noted the Captain General, should there be a third... Well, ships can be dangerous places. Especially for insolent overweight monks.

'I note,' he said, perusing the document, 'this license is valid for the diocese of Mexico. He glanced over his shoulder to his nephew, 'Now tell me Tomás where are we?'

'Not Mexico, Captain General.'

'Father Rodrigo, it is plain to me you have no authority here. However, because we are all devout Catholics and, for the general discipline of this ship and the satisfaction of the men under my command, I will allow some limited examination of these women.'

The Captain General despaired. Things were getting completely out of hand. He remembered the words of his sainted mother — *'Never trust a fucking priest.'*

There was open antipathy between soldiers and sailors. It wouldn't take much of a spark to ignite this tinderbox. Despite Esther's relentlessly logical argument, the court convicted Aals of fornication. To make matters more incendiary, were that even possible, a soldiers stated he'd forced her and therefore she was blameless. The court sentenced him to hang, passing him to the secular authority to carry out the sentence. While the Captain General had no objection to hanging if it served to maintain discipline, he did object if it was likely to achieve the opposite. He commuted the death sentence to a token whipping. This earned him little sympathy from the soldiers. But his esteem amongst sailors improved.

This left the fate of Aal in the balance. There were the more serious accusations of witchcraft to answer. The fiscal read out the charges:

'On this twenty-sixth day of September in the year of Our Lord sixteen-twenty-four it is charged that you, Aal de Dragoner, did cause the wind to cease to blow by impious and satanic conjuration...'

The Friar and Captain General had previously discussed this matter.

'A conviction's all very well, Father. But if you're thinking of having a fire on my ship you can think again. No, no. Not even a small one.'

The Friar stormed out.

Mind you don't trip over your arse you fat fuck. The Friar turned and glared at him. Which confirmed the Captain General's long-held suspicion that the arseholes can read your thoughts. *And whilst you are*

1624

at it, why don't you...

It was coming on for noon, the heat was intense. In the interests of enhanced compliance the Alguacil left Aal tied on deck, subject to the baking sun and freezing night, forbidding her the benefit of food and drink. The ship's complement dispersed for the afternoon siesta. Soldiers took shifts ensuring Aal remained unmolested.

After supper Esther petitioned to visit her. She kissed Aal on the mouth, passing slices of chicken she'd stuffed in her cheeks. Aal gobbled them up greedily.

'Any chance of some gravy,' she said.

The trial convened in the late afternoon of the next day when the sun was weakening. Aal looked surprisingly well. The Alguacil suspected soldiers had seen to her comforts overnight. His keen sense of self-preservation tempered any thoughts of accusing them.

Esther argued on Aal's behalf before the court until the early evening. She produced reams of Biblical precedent, responding to counter arguments from the fiscal and the inquisitors. The core of her defence rested on whether it was possible to conjure wind to cease to blow, with or without satanic cooperation. She kept her killer quotation till last.

All the miracles, she pointed out, in both the Old and New Testament were performed by God, or his representatives on earth. She cited the Book of Job 1:12.

'The LORD said to Satan, "Very well, all that he has is in your power; only do not stretch out your hand against him!" So Satan went out from the presence of the LORD.'

Which, she said, proved that Satan needed to make a request of the Lord when he touched Job's family. Satan had no agency over nature until the Lord empowered him to act.

'So,' said Esther, 'we're forced to the inescapable conclusion that either the accused did not conjure the wind not to blow, or she did it with the full cooperation of Almighty God. Which, by definition, makes her a saint.'

It was getting on for dusk, lamps flickered in the still air, the moon rose over the horizon. It was obvious that Esther was winning the reasoned argument. But, of course, you can't reason with the unreasonable. Especially if they happen to be irredeemably corrupt.

The Captain General winked at Esther. She called her star witness. Ramirez the pilot shuffled shame-faced before the court. He proceeded to offer scientific evidence as to what meteorological conditions caused the doldrums exist to in these latitudes, and how the storm had blown

1624

them excessively southwards and his prognostications regarding St Elmo's fire and the seasonal processions of Hurricanes — Galileo would have had a more receptive audience.

Aal had been patiently silent all this time. But the pressure had been building inside. She let out a despairing scream, and the moon turned blood red, and the wind began to howl.

TWENTY-SEVEN — *scattered by tyrants*

The river was at full spate and congested with craft of all sizes. The Rabbi was glad he'd chosen to arrive by land. His carriage trundled through the shipyard gates entering a different world, where they speak a different tongue. The language of wood, iron, canvas, rope, and pitch. Of stop waters, hanging knees, sister keelsons, sheerstrakes, futtocks, garboards, dead eyes, trenails, and winter cut wood.

A dozen men stumbled by, legs buckling, red faced, carrying a lower main mast, like irritable daemons preparing to batter their way out of hell. Oxen hauled carts of planking from mill to ship. Four vessels were under construction; skeletons of various configurations were fleshing out in finest Baltic oak. The Rabbi was conducting his puritan friend and fellow syndicate member, Govert Terborch, on a tour of the facility.

'How's the new mill working for you?' said Terborch.

'No more waiting for planking, no more complaining about disparities in thicknesses or quality of timber. Overcharged? Thing of the past. Licensing the patent. Best investment advice ever received.'

'Whose idea was that?'

'Isaac's.'

'Have you any news.'

'None, that's damned nearly my whole family gone. Benjamin seeking Esther, Isaac seeking Benjamin.'

'And now it's you joining the list,' said Terborch.

'Perhaps.'

The Rabbi sniffed; they'd stopped by the mill: 'The dust.' he said, wiping his damp eyes: 'Hey, come see for yourself.'

As they climbed the steps to the dark mill floor another huge oak log, dragged by wind power, progressed up the ramp from the sea where it had been pickling for the last year. Four banks of saws, eight blades each were steadily ripping their way through what had once graced a forest. Massive wooden cogwheels rotated, saw arms rose and fell. The building throbbed as though alive. Dust motes danced in shafts of sunlight; the heady tannin of oak perfumed the air. The wind picked up; saws began cutting faster, yard an hour at least, as the blades relentlessly tore through the logs.

Sawdust crusted their broad-brimmed hats by the time they re-emerged into sunlight, the rotating sails of the mill casting giant shadows over the yard.

And there she was, the Rachael. Elegant, fast and tough with a hidden sting. Double-planked both above and below the waterline, gunports invisible to all but the closest scrutiny. She was on a slope, supported by a forest of props, bows pointing impatiently at the water. Scaffolded ramps ran up either side of her. The painters and gilders were clearing away their things. She was unadorned, relative to the standard of her day. But her lines spoke for her. The masts lay, fully rigged, by her side. The yard foreman, Menno Blaeu, joined them. A boy followed behind carrying a tray with a bottle and glasses.

'Masts'll be going up today,' said Blaeu: 'Sailmaker's delivering tomorrow. Nothing like the smell of fresh canvas.' He passed out brimming wine glasses.

'To the Rachael, your honours.'

Half-finishing his glass, he passed it to the boy, ruffling his hair.

'Drink up lad, this is a day for great celebration.'

Heavy brocade curtains covered the single window. There was an open fireplace, embers glowing through grey ash. A single oil lamp afforded limited illumination. The chamber was dark; their clothes were dark, save for their wide white collars. At a glance they could be mistaken for disembodied heads served on silver salvers. Half-a-dozen John the Baptists in black broad-brimmed hats. On a table draped Low Countries style, with a fine Persian carpet, rested a cradle-mounted terrestrial globe. Those assembled were poring over the western hemisphere with particular attention to the Caribbean and East Coast of North America.

'No, no. Don't misunderstand me,' said Rabbi Abraham Amsalem. 'I hope all here will agree with me, we are grateful to the Six Provinces and will forever owe loyalty to the House of Orange-Nassau. They have provided a haven for us, and I hope they feel we have amply repaid their hospitality.'

'Nevertheless,' said Rabbi Jakob Gómez, 'we do live under certain Christian restrictions. These we accept and honour because we are but sojourners.'

'Our nation has been scattered by tyrants over much of the globe.' said Rabbi Moshe Diego Picco. 'Is it not written that the Moshiach will not appear until Hebrew populations spread over the *complete* globe? And now the Americas open before us. You might think that would make our task the greater.'

'But' said Rabbi Nehemiah Lopez Abbas, 'to date we have only counted the tribes of Judah and Benjamin. The other Hebrew tribes, lest we forget: Reuben, Simeon, Dan, Naphtali, Gad, Asher, Issachar, Zebulun, Manasseh, and Ephraim, were not entirely erased. A Hebrew tribe exists in farthest Cathay I understand. And now there is word of other tribes discovered in North America. Rabbi Eliezer states: "Just like a day is followed by darkness, and the light later returns, so too, although it will become dark for the ten tribes, God will ultimately take them out of their darkness.".'

'Our Protestant hosts,' said Rabbi Abraham, 'share our passion for the coming of the Moshiach and therefore our desire for Hebrews to inhabit the farthest reaches of this planet. We have received permission to cross the *Sambation* and mount an expedition into the interior of New Netherland from Fort Nassau to contact the North American tribes in peace and friendship to ascertain if they are, as I believe, and as our Ashkenazi cousins put it *Die Roite Yiddelech*.'

'L'Shana Haba'ah B'Yerushalayim,' said Rabbi Jakob Gómez. 'Next year in Jerusalem.'

'On whatever continent that may turn out to be,' said someone.

Rabbi Nathaniel Amsalem lost count of the times he'd paced the length of the long gallery. He'd arrived in the early afternoon. Since then the watery sun had dipped beneath the horizon. Torches had been lit. Sconces illuminated the endless gardens. Carriages came and went. The Rabbi waited patiently.

It had been two weeks since he had requested an audience. Initially Frederick Henry had appeared interested. But the war, the war. The unequal battle against the world's greatest empire. It required every ounce of his attention. The Rabbi had outlined the theological motivation in their correspondence. The scope and ambition of his proposed mission. An artful combining of Jewish ministry and seaborne privateering. The latter contrived to secure the Prince's patronage. But, truth be out, the Rabbi was burning to strike another blow against his family's tormentors — the avowed enemies of both the United Provinces and the Hebrew Nation.

'So,' said the Prince, 'you've been wearing out my carpet again. Off again seeking the lost tribes, eh? This is indeed a worthy enterprise. And we wish your expedition good fortune. But' said the Prince, 'forgive our

1624

bluntness old friend, you're too old to be roaming about the seven seas gathering up lost Hebrews. This will be the last time I'll sanction such an expedition. We value your wisdom and intelligence too much. So, like a modern-day Moses you're forbidden to enter Canaan.

'You may treat any Spanish and Portuguese vessels you encounter as legitimate prizes. French ships, well that's up to you. Grey area. But leave English shipping strictly alone, and they'll do the same to you, hopefully. Anyway, we've spoken with their ambassador, best we can do. This war is bleeding us dry. We will expect you to return with your hold bulging with Spanish silver. And, through the reverse alchemy of commerce, we'll return it to Philip transmuted into iron shot. So, here's what you came for. We have signed and appended our seal. Go with God. Locate your people, bring me my silver.'

A fine drizzle was falling as the Rabbi's carriage pulled up in the forecourt. He left the marble halls shielding a letter of marque under his cloak. Smiling, he stepped aboard. Their prince, their Joshua, fighting a war, the duration and scope of which, the world had never seen. Not Nebuchadnezzar the Great, nor the hated Romans, not even Genghis Khan had fought such a conflict. The horses picked up speed. Noordeinde Palace faded behind him in the mist.

1624

TWENTY-EIGHT — *a flash of steel*

The bay rang to the clanging of hammers, of chains shattered, of freedom restored. They released African captives in batches. Allowing them to become accustomed to the change in their situation, before releasing more, forestalling a potential riot.

Twenty-five fathoms of anchor cable flaked out on deck. Landfall was imminent. It had to be. The ship was sinking.

They were in Samaná Bay, running west, close to the coast, sheltered from the weather. The deck had ceased to roll, the bows no longer pitched. Isaac was reacting to a phantom swell, anticipating waves that no longer disturbed their passage. Such sluggish stability was disorienting after three months tossed about at sea. He closed his eyes, willing the nausea to subside. The symptoms persisted; this was going to take time.

Benjamin had located a tattered chart of Hispaniola. Identified a sheltered cove on the south coast thirty leagues in. By the time they arrived there was barely enough wind to shiver the canvas. She carried every scrap of sail she possessed. Despite continuous pumping, water had long since risen above the bilge, and was now lapping the lower decks.

The Africans crowded the rail. Men, women, children. Noisily excited, leaping exuberantly about the rigging. Several fell or dived overboard and swam to the beach. They danced and whooped on the glistening white sand. Did they believe they were back in Africa? Did they believe this was home? Isaac didn't relish breaking the news.

Benjamin ordered two longboats lowered. They began towing the African Prince stern first into the narrow entrance of the cove. Two dozen sweat-slick backs bent to the oars. The rhythm of their efforts joined the clanging of shattering irons, and the rattling gush of the pumps. The Englishman, Boaz Hocklin, in the larboard boat added the melody:

> '*All those with us the walrus throats*

Must be men with beards'

The Dutchman, Daan de Vlaeming, in the starboard boat returned the next verse:

'Al die de dood en de duivel niet duchten
Moeten mannen met baarden zijn'

It was coming on for dusk. Unfamiliar noises rose from the dense forests bordering the beach. Flutterings, screechings, a disarming high-pitched shriek. Isaac was leaning on the poop deck rail. The nightshade figure of Hangbè joined him — shoulder to shoulder. Isaac shivered as static arced between them like St Elmo's fire. He turned, picking out Benjamin on the bowsprit. He was leaning precariously over the crystal void, one hand grasping a shroud, scanning the seabed. The boy, Shem Smitt was swinging the lead, chanting out the depth in a sing song voice.

'By the mark five. By the deep four, mark three, mark...'

Benjamin dropped his hand.

'Mister Evertson,' Isaac yelled, 'let her go.'

The anchor plunged. Crushed coral clouded the water. But neither wind nor tide were enough to cause the rode to pay out. The oarsmen strained but couldn't generate momentum against the drag of the heavy cable. Isaac looked to the masthead pennant, there was a faint flutter.

'Mister Hurst,' he yelled, 'we shall back the mizzen'

Skyler Hurst raced aft. His young African trainees scampered with him, eager to do his bidding. As the yard swung lazily across, the canvas gathered what little wind there was. The ship began moving ponderously astern. Eventually the full length of cable was looping from the bow. With a grinding shudder the anchor dragged and dug in. Colourful fragments of pulverised coral floated past the hull.

Isaac yelled over the rail. 'Mister de Vlaeming. Take a line to those trees if you will.'

Benjamin heaved a heavy cable off the stern to splash in the water. De Vlaeming collected it, and his crew rowed him to the beach. They secured it to a stand of stout mangroves. Gustav Evertson organised Africans at the capstan to tension the cable. Moored fore and aft, the ship couldn't swing to wind or tide. No danger of beaching or grounding on the reef as it swung.

Benjamin joined Isaac on the poop deck. They watched as Hurst oversaw the furling of the mizzen.

'Won't withstand heavy winds,' he said, 'but the arrangement'll do for now.'

Night fell like an axe blade; a cloud of fruit bats briefly darkened the sky. Drink was taken. Isaac set a two-man watch, and they retired for the night.

Light flooded down the companionway. Isaac rubbed the sleep from his eyes as he clambered clumsily on deck. Benjamin was deep in his hammock, and his dreams. They moored in a bay within a bay. Columns of white limestone like fortresses rose out of an improbably blue sea. Lush green undergrowth overtopped their edges. Trees crested their summit like triumphant mountaineers.

Benjamin appeared on deck yawning and picked his way across a deck carpeted by recumbent black bodies. None had wished to revisit their former quarters. Who could blame them? He found Isaac and Hangbè sitting on the middle deck. Fierce unreadable Hangbè. The brothers' authority, their lives were now in her hands. At sea they'd sway over two hundred African captives. With landfall, the prisoners freed, everything changed.

'Morning brother,' said Isaac, passing him a stone bottle. Benjamin took a slug — the refreshing astringency of juniper. He rinsed his mouth, spitting over the side. He took another gulp, swallowing this time.

Palm trees dotted beaches of purest white sand, sparkling like crushed diamonds. Isaac and Hangbè joined him leaning on the rail. Beneath the glass-clear surface of the sea, all was colour and activity. Purple ribbed fan coral; orange brain coral, swaying anemones, veridian sea grass. Everywhere tiny fish darted. Flashes of yellow and blue and red like capricious jewels. A nursing sperm whale and her calf passed by the mouth of their cove, stately and majestic. A dense blanket of forest covered the land from the lowest valley to the highest mountain. Mangroves stood poised on tangled toes, as though about to invade the sea.

Egrets and frigate birds, gulls, and herons — all familiar. But there were others of strange configuration and colour: vibrant greens and reds and purples and blues and fiery orange. They took these colours into the air, like church windows illuminated by sacred light, smashed and cast to the wind. Everywhere was ablaze with colour, so unlike the begrudging, muddy, shit-stained pallet of the Low Countries. This was nature exuberantly demonstrating its ultimate potential. Life without limits, bursting, unfettered.

Breakfast consisted of rice, half-cooked beans and ship's biscuit softened in gin. A scattering of mocha-skinned Taíno natives materialised on the distant beach — women with babies on their hips, staring at the ship wide eyed. Glossy back hair like horse manes framed intricately tattooed faces. Isaac and Benjamin rowed out to them in the jollyboat. Hocklin and de Vlaeming covered them from the side deck with muskets. The women retreated into the forest like frightened sparrows.

Isaac discovered trade goods in the captain's trunk. He laid out a selection on the beach. Murano glass beads for the women. Fresh minted ship's knives for the men. Isaac glimpsed something in the forest. The glint of an eye, or the tip of a spear? He nudged Benjamin. They backed slowly, warily away. They weren't stupid. By the time they'd returned to the ship their gifts had disappeared. Mothers replaced girls — beckoning, giggling, promising pleasure.

Still not stupid.

An hour later their generosity was reciprocated: game birds, dried meats, fruit, freshly caught fish. Breakfast was looking up.

Isaac's background, if not necessarily his inclination, was a collision of Protestant and Jewish fundamentalism. Hangbè unclothed, had Isaac pondering the paradox of nakedness. Wasn't a woman's worth measured by what she revealed and what she concealed. Or was that a dishonest game of tease, a rule inconsistently applied, a code imperfectly understood. If a woman's body is freely available to any eye, surely that's a currency irredeemably debased. He shrugged away the thought. The perfection of Hangbè's physique was her gold standard — the absence of shame, her currency. Even so, he was relieved that she'd enthusiastically embraced European clothing. Albeit men's clothing. Not through modesty, he knew, but novelty and utility.

Next day they exchanged more gifts with the Taíno. Hangbè and Isaac felt safe to go ashore. There'd been no courtship. No flirty interludes, no hints, no gradual blossoming. A collision of souls in darkness, consummated with murder. No one, least of all them, had even remarked on it.

They explored cool, mysterious caves in the limestone cliffs. Discarding clothes, they bathed under waterfalls, laughed, tumbled. Splashing playfully, they giggled their way out of the water. Holding hands, collapsing naked on the shore, bundling clothes as a pillow. They lay on their backs panting. Water beaded off them, as they stared at the flawless blue heavens through a canopy of palm fronds.

Hangbè's breathing became urgent. Isaac turned towards her. She rolled on her side facing him, expressionless, unreadable. Rising to her knees, she straddled his body with her long silk-smooth legs. Eyes locked on his, she eased him into her, teasingly little by little until she fully engulfed him. He grabbed her hips, thrust deep, greedy for sensation.

A flash of steel.
A knife at his throat.
A sharp pain.
She rode him groaning, eyes rolling back, grinding her hips into his. As she came, she cut.
He gasped.
Pleasure overwhelmed him, obliterating thought. His mind flashed to Genesis. His sacrificial namesake.

'The fire and wood are here, but where is the lamb for the burnt offering?'

This Isaac, this time, a willing sacrifice.

Hangbè's eyes filled with tears. She nuzzled his neck and suckled the wound like a hungry infant. Sliding off him, she pressed herself to his side, one leg entwining his.

He stared up into the forest canopy, eyes vacant. A tiny green lizard scuttled along a branch. A drop of dew fell on his face. He had but one thought — she should have cut deeper. If that was what had given rise to such pleasure, she should have cut deeper.

Small perfect breasts crushed into his side. He enfolded her in his arms. Would it always be like this? Giggling came from somewhere behind them. He reluctantly opened his eyes. Taíno girls, perfect in their nakedness, were shyly peering from the forest. Would they remember this strange coupling in years to come? Would they tell others, immortalise this moment in legend?

He struggled to his elbows. Hangbè rolled languidly away and stretched like a great cat. Branches twitched, the gigglers disappeared, he felt his throat. The bleeding had almost stopped. Their eyes met. The unspoken question.

'The knife?' said Isaac.

'No man may touch me,' Hangbè said, 'save with my consent.'

'But, between us, really — the knife?'

'Women can be fickle,' she said.

Everyone mostly slept on deck, a dark tangled puzzle of bodies. In the open air the cloying fragrance of the forest mitigated the stench rising from the slave hold. Nightmares periodically disturbed the calm. Nocturnal cries of anguish and despair.

Small wonder the Taíno were suspicious — the ship stank like a slaver, was a slaver in all but intention. On that first night half the Africans disappeared into the forest, and were never seen again. Could be they viewed this as the natural option. Returning to Africa was never going to be a possibility. That or they thought this *was* Africa. Same latitude, same climate. They were young, and adaptable. Warriors in their own land. But those brands marked them as slaves. And should they encounter European colonists, that could still be their fate. This was better. A fresh start in Eden. If they'd survived a slave ship, they could survive in paradise.

For those who remained aboard there were important matters to address. What to do next and, not least, the matter of leadership. But these decisions were needs deferred. The ship was sinking. They manned the pumps continuously. Clank gush, clank gush, like a failing heart. They urgently needed to beach the vessel. Assess the state of the hull. Address whatever damage they found before the African Prince sank irretrievably. It was past time to careen the hull. Isaac told Hangbè, she told Khamisi and Xaawo, and thus the message reached the hundred or so Africans remaining.

The tidal range in Samaná Bay is minimal — half a fathom at best. Smitt rowed the jolly boat about the inlet as Benjamin noted soundings. There was an ideal spot, a deep channel parallel to a prominent sandbar.

Hangbè identified a defensible peninsular of beach, dotted with palms. They emptied the ship of powder and muskets. Anything else immersion might adversely affect, then set up camp on the sand — kindled a fire, speared fish, boiled rice.

On the next high tide they towed the ship over the sandbar. The sea was at least a fathom above the ship's marks by the time the keel settled. They shifted ballast causing it to lean as the sea retreated. Taking lines from the masthead to trees they hauled her over with block and tackle. The shrouds hummed with tension; the mastheads bent alarmingly. But everything held and soon she lay on her flank like a bitch about to whelp.

Inside the ship the lower decks had submerged. As the sea washed in and out the slave-stench began to abate. They floated a charcoal brazier on a raft inside, brimstone heaped on the embers. Rats scuttled down anchor cables, ahead of the toxic vapours. Hatches sealed, the fumigation lasted two days. At the end of this interval the ship stank like hell, but at least it didn't stink like shit.

A week went by, and the sulphurous fumes began to dissipate, and the rats were considering a return. Africans were set to scrubbing and scraping — inside as well as out.

The hull had become encrusted with limpets, barnacles, muscles. Long lengths of seagrass trailed in the tide. Such extensive fouling brought a welcome windfall. Arms aching, work over for the day, the molluscs became a welcome treat — bundled in seaweed and broiled over embers. Isaac and Benjamin had per force abandoned a kosher diet. But they drew the line at a scavenged seafood feast.

By noon, the next day the surface of the hull was ready for inspection. Below the waterline they discovered a sacrificial layer of planking — no expense spared in this vessel's construction. Even so, marine organisms had taken a heavy toll on its timbers. Isaac spiked the wood seeking soft areas, hunting the dreaded Teredo Worm. *Teredo navalis* — forget Leviathan, these are the true terror of the seas. Sunk more ships than all the warships ever launched and all the storms that raged from the beginning of time.

As outer planking needed removal, the filth trapped inside the hull gushed out through blown seams. Pascoe didn't go unremembered. They hoicked the rapist Pascoe out of the bilge, dumping him in the mangroves. Some words were said, many of which were not pleasant. No grave, they left him to the crabs — he'd be gone soon enough. Work on the hull progressed apace.

'Found one here,' said Shem Smitt, a grey worm looping through his fingers: 'Must be two feet long, think I'll keep it as a pet.'

'They're good eating,' said Boaz Hocklin, 'they taste a bit like clam.'

'Really?' Smitt took a bite, the creature thrashed about his face.

'No, no, stop.' said Hocklin: 'Cook it, you need to cook the sodding thing first.'

'Still,' said Smitt, wiping ooze from his chin, 'not bad though, if a bit...' he smacked his lips, searching for the appropriate descriptor, 'woody.'

The infested timbers needed plugging or replacement. Lesser infected areas were charred to kill larvae and form a toughened barrier to further proliferation. Iron riveted buckets of pitch and brimstone bubbled over fires to seal the hull's wounds.

They toiled for a week — hacking back, recaulking, replacing, sealing. On the next high tide they rolled the ship over to address the other side. Another week and the last nail hammered home, the last lick of pitch applied. Pumping now relegated to an infrequent chore — no more the frantic battle to stay afloat. With the ballast rebalanced the ship was ready for righting. In the morning they would tow the ship off the sandbar into deep water.

But what then?

On the beach by torchlight they addressed this pressing question. Leadership was central to the debate. In the extremis of the voyage Isaac became de facto captain. But they would never have arrived at their destination without his younger brother's navigational skill. That he'd murdered the last captain, was not his least qualification. The Europeans voted for Isaac to continue in the role. They agreed he'd done a decent job so far – sense of authority, yet a light hand on the tiller, good organiser.

Despite mass desertions, the African outnumbered Europeans ten to one. In a contest of force, no matter how many muskets at the sailors' command, numbers would surely prevail. Not exactly democracy, but democracy of sorts.

It was Isaac who'd been instrumental in releasing the captives. It was Benjamin who had delivered them to a safe landfall. Would they understand this? And if they did, would they care?

These were fierce young men. Food, sanitation and freedom had quickly restored body and spirit. They were angry, resentful, confused, needful of a focus for their frustration. Tension was building, squabbles were breaking out. Providentially, events would soon occur which would provide a positive outlet for their aggression.

They could not remain where they were. Supplies would run out. They couldn't rely on Taíno generosity forever. Most importantly the island was a Spanish possession. The enemy would discover them, the bay entrap them. The European sailors yearned for civilisation, or their soiled versions of same. The Africans for a place to settle. Of all people Jews understood this impulse. The African diaspora was just beginning, that of the tribe of Judah had been three-thousand years in the telling. Was the Caribbean big enough to accommodate everyone's ambitions?

Isaac and Benjamin were impatient for action — to find their lost sister. Isaac explained their mission to Hangbè in these terms: the great persecutor of their tribe had unjustly condemned Esther to slavery. Hangbè understood about tribes, about persecution and about slavery. She also understood about destiny. Action and consequences were everything. And if nature didn't present acceptable options then you created your own. She persuaded the Africans to cast their lot with the ship, under Isaac's leadership.

Next morning preparations were under way to right the hull. Isaac ordered Skyler Hurst to the clifftop as lookout. An hour into his watch he scrambled back down to the beach, breathless.

'Ship. Ship just entered the bay,' he panted: 'Looks Spanish.'

Isaac turned to Benjamin, then to Hangbè. Would it be possible to be any more vulnerable? They doused the fires, took what weapons they could, and scattered into the forest.

The Spanish ship had anchored half-a-league offshore. As they watched from the mangroves two longboats launched and soldiers climbed aboard. The boats pulled past their position and beached a league further along the bay. Laying on its side, shielded by the forest-covered cliffs, the African Prince went unnoticed. Armoured and helmeted Spanish soldiers shouldered muskets and filed into the forest. Two sailors remained behind to guard the boats. The soldiers returned three hours later dragging wailing Taíno natives in chains, rowing them back to their ship.
'Slavers,' said Gustav Evertson, unnecessarily.
Night fell. The next day the Spaniards followed the same routine. The longboats pulled away from the ship and beached further down the coast. The soldiers entered the forest. Two sailors stayed with the boats. The soldiers returned dragging more struggling Taíno. The two sailors minding the boats turned and drew pistols, killing the foremost soldiers. Benjamin and the three other Europeans appeared from the forest and opened fire with muskets. Africans swarmed the survivors dispatching them with boarding axes.

Isaac and some fifty Africans swam out before daybreak, supported and hidden by branches of forest flotsam. They reached the Spanish ship and clung to the hull until the Spanish raiding party departed. When the boats were beyond recall they swarmed over the rail and overwhelmed the remaining crew. They discovered gold and silver coinage in the captain's great room — profitable business this slaving.
A Spanish officer sprang from the shadows and slashed at Isaac, cutting him across the face. Half-blinded by blood Isaac blundered into an oil lamp setting the cabin ablaze. The officer lunged for the death blow. But then his eyes lost focus, he dropped his rapier and slumped forwards with an axe buried in his head. A naked figure appeared behind him, silhouetted in the doorway. Isaac had refused to allow Hangbè to accompany him on this mission. Lucky for him, she cared little for such orders.
The flames were out of control. They freed the Taíno captives and escaped in the ship's remaining longboat. By the time they reached the shore the slaver was burning to the waterline.
The Africans unshackled the captives, who retreated into the interior. Returning with his party to the African Prince, Isaac became aware of a soft rustling in the forest. He turned to find the beach thick

with Taíno. Women with soft skin and diamond hard souls. Men lean and sharp as their spears, swift as their arrows. There was a low ululation expressing what, appreciation, bewilderment?

As Dawn broke the African Prince sailed out of Samaná Bay, past the masts of the burned-out Spanish slaver, into a freshening trade wind. The first rays of sun activated a bout of philosophical musing. *Everything that could be, would be. Everything that would be, was.* He'd picked that up from who knows where. Or it was of his own composition. Whatever its origins, it summed up his philosophy. Control is illusory, set your objectives, sit back and enjoy the ride.

He'd learned a universal truth of human nature. Or just his own nature. Eyes can become inured to beauty if it reveals itself in too much abundance. If it's too gaudy. If it displays itself wantonly. Eve, at the dawn of time had discovered the same thing. Too much paradise can be hell. They left the Taíno in peace with no confidence others would do the same.

A vague unstructured plan was forming. Link with the Corsairs of Hispaniola. Ever aware of their ultimate objective — to locate and rescue their beloved sister. If this meant cooperating with pirates, so be it.

1624

TWENTY-NINE — *genuflection*

Seabirds overhead. They must be closing with the coast. Then came the soft silhouettes of the camel hump hills of the interior. Soon the tip of the lighthouse came into view. Finally the twin forts at the entrance to Havana. They weaved through the multitude of ships clustering about the bay, like bees at a hive entrance eager to unload pollen.

The wind had been strengthening all morning. It was coming in gusts, swirling around the headland funnelled down from the high country beyond. Windward standing rigging was straining hard, and the running rigging vibrated with the enormous energy captured by the sails. Timbers groaned as the Grace de Deux grudgingly leaned with the wind. The flat water beyond the entrance looked welcoming. The defence boom did not.

Havana, a favourite target for sea raiders, had suffered numerous attacks. Lessons hard learned, but learned they were. Moro Castle to the east of the entrance was, indeed, impressive. This harbour was where the treasure fleet, *the Flota de Indias* assembled before charging en mass across the Atlantic. There was safety in numbers. Corsairs would follow like wolves trailing buffalo, looking to pick off stragglers. As soon as the hurricane danger had passed they'd be running the gauntlet for Cadiz laden with gold and silver with which to prosecute the war against the Protestants.

This close to shore the waves were shorter and steeper. Whitecaps blown off their peaks made the sea look like a snowdrift. The first mate ordered men aloft. Soon they sailed under spritsail, forecourse, foretopsail, main topsail and mizzen. The pressure reduced; the vessel relaxed. As the helmsman rounded up to the wind the canvas fluttered losing its urgency. Decks levelled out; the ship slowed to a steady, stately progress. Sails began to thrash, yards swung erratically. The anchor dropped, dragged and bit as the ship swung head to wind. Sailors swarmed the rigging, stowing the square sails, leaving her masts bare save a reefed lanteen mizzen, like a fig leaf to cover her nakedness. All

1624

became quiet save the wind hissing through the rigging and the rushing of the waves.

A pair of friars burst on deck and retched over the windward rail. They retreated below, covered in vomit. Would they never learn? Crew and soldiers crowded the deck elated at the prospect of shore leave. Monks also, for much less carnal reasons. The captain appeared on deck in his finest shoreside outfit, a gold chased rapier by his side, with his valet fussing about him. Flanking him were his officers likewise dressed for court. Soldiers mustered like a slovenly parade.

The voyage had not been kind to Father Rodrigo de Segeda. Nature had answered his fervent prayers for wind. The captain could not remember a rougher passage. Tormented by seasickness, the Inquisitor's jowls bagged like an empty wine sack. His habit hung loose. His tonsure and cheeks stubbled over. Eyes red-rimmed and vacant. His gait a stumbling shuffle. His companion, the stick thin Franciscan, had faired not much better. They stood at the rail staring at the distant land with longing. A service of thanksgiving delegated to a fellow Dominican. Monks wailed theatrically in the background. Many of the assembled crossed themselves absently. But no one took any real notice.

A galley pulled up to their lee and the harbourmaster clambered aboard. Signal flags flew. Sails unfurled. The capstan manned, the anchor weighed. The chain barrier lowered, and the pilot guided the ship through the fortified entrance. Falling under the wind-shadow of the harbour the ship slowed. Sailors swarmed the rigging furling sails. Lines taken to the shore and the ship warped into a berth alongside the wharf by black slaves whipped around a huge shore-based capstan.

The friars shoved a passage through the throng queuing to disembark and were the first ashore. Father Rodrigo's sandal caught on the hem, his habit causing him to stumble to his knees. This gesture, instantly aped by his cowled confederates and there followed a flurry of genuflection and kissing of the ground. Onlookers felt obliged to follow suit. The gesture swept the town like a contagion. Soon church bells were tolling in a spontaneous fever of piety.

Esther and Aal didn't share the festive mood.

Aal fanned her face: 'Least we won't freeze to death.'

'Yes, but we might cook,' said Esther, nodding towards the monks: 'If they have any say in the matter.'

'That skinny one's got a thing about us,' said Aal: 'He keeps staring in our direction. Him and his fat mate.'

Esther shuddered, despite the heat. So much unfinished business.

'So what next?' said Aal, scanning the harbour crowd: 'Is someone

1624

coming to get us, drag us off to some fresh hell?'

'Don't worry about the priests. D'you think the Duke shipped us out here just to have us rubbed out by those pricks. Don't think so. We represent an investment. Hand picked, that's us. His nibs wouldn't be happy if whilst he's stuck up to his tits in Brebantine mud to know someone's interfering with his choice lady stock. Christ, there must be benefits to enslavement, to being someone's property. You want to protect your investments, right?'

Aal eyed the two dozen women doomed for sale to Cuban colonists as companions, servants, field workers, whores or wives. Whilst they waited for a summons Aal played a cruel game, allotting each to a category.

'Whore, definately. Labourer that one, who'd want to dip that? Childbearing hips, that one's a breeder...'

Esther didn't join in. Throughout the voyage they'd had separate quarters from the general rabble. Nevertheless, Esther didn't feel comfortable mocking their fate.

'Me,' said Aal, 'I'm going to get me a rich patron. Army officer, maybe. Then I'll get him to buy you from the Duke. An' we'll all live together in some big mansion overlooking the bay, with servants an' slaves of our own, 'an rooms full of fine dresses, an' we'd tumble all day an' all night long. An' when he went away to war we'd miss 'im, but we'd still tumble all day an' all night, right?'

She gave Esther a big nudge in the ribs. Esther wiped away a tear, hoping it went unnoticed. She slipped an arm round Aal's waist and gave her a warm squeeze.

'No, no, you're wrong. My father is going to sail in with an armada. He'll pound those forts to rubble. Hang all those monks, burn this wretched place to the ground killing as many Spaniards as he can catch. And when they do that girl, make sure you stick with me. Then you'll have the choice of my two handsome brothers.'

'Sad to say,' said Aal, 'mine is the most likely outcome. And I hold out bugger-all hope for that.'

'Or we could escape, give them the slip,' said Esther, serious now.

'And then what?' said Aal. 'Go where? This place ain't like Amsterdam, can't exactly loose yourself in this pox hole. Or what, blunder into that forest? How far would we get, they'd set the dogs on us. Track us down, and you know what happens to runaway slaves. And if by some bloody miracle we did evade 'em, we'd starve to death, or get ourselves eaten by wild animals. Christ knows what hideous beasts live around these parts.

'We could get another ship, stowaway,' said Esther.

'Skillet into fire,' said Aal: 'Least here we'd be working on our backs in feather beds, not breaking our backs down some copper mine. Have you seen the way those monks are looking at us.'

It's the definition of not good when your only comfort is suicide. Esther smiled weakly back at her friend, but there was always that.

'But let's see what turns up,' said Aal, 'you never know. Never second guess fate. Or him upstairs, know what I mean. What are the chances my young lieutenant buys my contract. Maybe he'll buy yours too. You can be my hand maid, give me baths, wash my tits, do my hair, dress me up all posh. Or he'd buy you as a present for his old dad.'

'Or he could never give you a second thought and jump the next bit of tail comes along,' said Esther.

'You think I haven't considered that? You're right, some men think tail is tail — don't matter what it's attached to. And sometimes it's difficult to disagree with them. 'Cos, let's face it, cock's all cock to me, right?'

Aal reached out for Esthers hand.

'Cock's all cock to me,' she sang in a whisper, tapping the toes of her clogs, executing a shuffling dance: 'Cock's all cock to me, cock's all cock to me... Gotta keep your spirits up, come on... cock's all cock to me.'

She beamed as her lieutenant approached through the throng. When she saw what he was carrying, the smile dropped from her face.

'Sorry ladies, orders. Gotta put the bracelets on.'

He conducted them down the gangplank. A crowd swamped the wharf. Folk with nothing better to do crowded the ship, hungry for a glimpse of fresh meat.

'Hope we get time to fluff ourselves up a bit. Get a bit of sleep afore the sons of whores have at us,' said Aal. Esther's eyes were watering. Aal reached across, brushed her cheek with the back of her hand. 'Don't let 'em see you cry. Don't give 'em the satisfaction.' Esther blanked her expression. Was this the toughest thing she'd had to do? She flashed back to her "execution" — no, not hardly. She stared straight ahead, avoided eye contact, endured the abuse with calm dignity. She'd returned from the dead. God had a purpose for her. And this wasn't it.

Fresh from the aseptic cleanliness of the sea, the sour cloying stench of human habitation came as an unwelcome shock. Esther felt her gorge rise. A sharp yank on her chains from Aal jolted her back to impassivity.

A wall of Dominican friars blocked their path. The skinny masturbator and his now deflated confessor pushed through the ranks.

'These're with us.' said Father Rodrigo, grabbing Aal's shoulder.

'Forgive me father,' said the Lieutenant, 'these are the property of his excellency the Duke Francisco de Medina Carranza. It is my duty to deliver them to His Grace's estate.'

Father Rodrigo held up his hand. 'We are all the property of the Almighty my son, and I am His representative in Cuba. You will relinquish them to our charge on pain of excommunication.'

'But the Duke...'

'Which would you prefer, to risk the displeasure of an earthly authority some seven thousand miles across the ocean or be condemned to suffer eternally in lakes of fire?'

The lieutenant's colour drained.

'We're screwed,' said Aal.

'I am so looking forward to continuing our debate,' said Father Rodrigo, eyes injecting venom into Esther. The skinny friar went to speak, but a glance at Aal's breasts and his blushes got the better of him.

Guards bundled Esther and Aal through the jostling, jeering, spitting mob gathered in the colonnaded city square. Their route took them past a smouldering corpses chained to stakes, and into where the Inquisition was headquartered, shivering with the screams of its victims.

1624

THIRTY — *give fire*

The ship was heeling to a steady south westerly with a regular and predictable motion. Hispaniola, with its lush green coastline, passed to windward, an unchanging backdrop. Regardless the sails were filling, you'd think they were motionless. Yet the triangular wake, and the dolphins riding the bow wave spoke of satisfactory progress. Six knots by the last count.

Light flooded through the windows of the great cabin casting lively patterns on the captain's table. A soft sea breeze counteracted the oppressive mid-day heat. Isaac and Benjamin were in light linen shirts. Hangbè had taken to wearing a thin cotton smock and breeches. She'd discovered a fine rapier in the deceased captain's sea chest and was wearing it slung on a thick leather belt. Khamisi and Xaawo were naked save for loincloths. The rest of the Africans were enjoying their freedom outside. Within the cabin the appointment of officers was under discussion.

Isaac smothered a yawn. He wasn't bored, but exhausted.

'You can't organise everything,' said Benjamin: 'You have to delegate.'

'As I see it,' said Isaac, sighing, 'there are four areas urgently need covering. Gunnery, musketry, ship-craft, and supplies. For cannon master I'd suggest we look no further than Elijah Brankfleet.'

'And Skyler Hurst is the best topman we have,' said Benjamin: 'He's young, but he's worked wonders with his "apprentices." We should try him out for sailing master. He's practically doing the job anyway.'

'Khamisi, knows muskets,' said Hangbè, 'he's fought wars.'

'What about Boaz Hocklin for quartermaster,' said Benjamin, 'he used to be a bookkeeper.'

'Also a convicted embezzler,' said Isaac.

'What better qualification?' said Benjamin.

It was getting on for twilight by the time Isaac had assembled the candidates in the great cabin. The land breeze was counteracting the trades and progress had dropped to three knots. Isaac took stock of the lamplit gathering.

Elijah Brankfleet bore an expression of perpetual surprise. As though, like his namesake, fiery miracles might sprout from his fingers at any moment. With his explosion of black hair, eyebrows half blasted away, he seemed ever poised for a backward leap. Brankfleet, the diffident master of thunder, a tremulous god amongst men. A life dedicated to mediating the most violent forces of nature. One hand stuffed in his jacket. One eye a raging mass of ticks. One stocking round his ankle. And a pigtail hanging down his back like a fuse begging to be lit.

Those that take to the sea do so because they are of a different temperament to the mass of humanity. Or they take to the sea and become so. What sets them apart from the common clod? Surely, it's the constant proximity to the primal forces that shape our world. On land wind can be destructive. But it won't make the ground beneath your feet pile up into mountains, won't make it fall down and crush you. And it won't suck you beneath it and spit you out dead — well rarely.

If Brankfleet was an imp of fire, then Skyler Hurst was a sprite of air. Skyler Hurst, the savant of the mastheads. They had seen him coax movement from the half-hearted wheezes of Zephyrus. And harness the awesome power of Boreas' storms, inspiring his crew by heroic example.

Boaz Hocklin, in contrast to the pair, was a landsman. A man of numbers, of counting. Enumeration was his obsession - the numbers of things. Counting provided a measure of control in a universe sorely lacking in numerical order. He'd found his ideal occupation in the counting houses of the City. Life had ticked along with mechanical precision, joyful if dull. But a light-fingered manager diverted blame for his embezzlement to a lowly articled clerk. And thus was Boaz Hocklin ignomised. Locked in the Clink Prison sentenced to transportation. Counting soothed him through his many months of tribulation. Days in incarceration two-thousand-and-one. Nails in the door three-hundred and twenty-six. Bricks in his cell walls one-thousand five-hundred and fifty-two. Slabs in the floor two-hundred and fifty-three. Paces to the ship two-thousand-three-hundred and forty-one. Links in his chains one-hundred and twenty-six. Now, days since liberation fifty-two. He accepted Isaac's job offer with a tear in his eye for those six words, forty-two characters.

'Khamisi,' said Hangbè, 'was my father's bodyguard. He and Xaawo were captured when the Portuguese overwhelmed our kingdom. He fought bravely and he knows European weapons. I have seen him load and fire a musket five times a minute.'

Khamisi nodded enthusiastically. Xaawo slapped him on the back, beaming.

'Mister Brankfleet,' shouted Isaac, 'we understand you served under Lieutenant Admiral Swartzenhont.'

'Sorry, pardon, yes, yes, under Old Black Dog, oh aye,' yelled Brankfleet, 'ran the fleet as he did his pub, orderly. I'd just come up from powder monkey to junior gunner. We engaged the Spanish off Gibraltar, chased 'em all the way back to Cadiz. Lost half me hand in that action.'

'Do you think you'll have a problem training crews if you don't speak their language?'

Brankfleet cupped an ear. 'I said,' repeated Isaac. 'Training crews if you don't speak their language.'

Brankfleet held up his right hand, sans two digits. 'They hadn't mopped the gun out proper. When I pricked the powder the bastard went off. The spike flew out the touchhole caught me fingers. Didn't let it stop me though — carried on. Put on a charge 'cos me blood damped the powder. That's that bastard Black Dog for you.'

Isaac and Benjamin shared a glance. 'Language won't be any more of a problem with the Africans than with us, bastard's stone deaf.'

'I heard that.'

'It's a miracle,' said Benjamin, reeling back, 'he's cured.'

Isaac shook his head, suppressing a smile. *Change of subject.* 'If we are going to survive, let alone make our fortunes privateering in these waters we'll need gun crews. We'll also need sailors who know what they are doing. And everyone will need fight, there'll be training. We only have a hundred and twenty bodies to choose from. The majority have no experience, but they seem to learn fast. Cannon, musketry, and ship handling will each take forty men. Drill them to within an inch of their sodding lives. I said, Mister Brankfleet, drill them. Drill them.'

'Mister Hocklin,' said Isaac, 'This ship is in sore need of resupply. We need clothing for our crew, food, water. Powder and shot we have aplenty. and there are over three-hundred muskets in the armoury. I can only believe they were for trade. The only way to survive is to trade or to raid. This is a Spanish island. Raiding is our only realistic option. And if we happen to come across any of the glittery stuff on the way, I'm sure no one here will object.

'With the newly cleaned hull and a fair wind we could be in Tortuga in thirty days, or less. You have that time to train your men. My hope is you'll instil a high degree of competence in your brigades. And by the time we make landfall we'll have a fighting force. Right now a white flag will be of more use to us than the black.'

The African Prince was running along the north coast of Hispaniola towards the pirate haven of Tortuga. At five miles out to sea they were clear of the reefs, mottling the turquoise coastal waters. A strip of white sand formed a boundary between the sea and the mangroves, between blue and green. Rich veridian forest rose mile after mile to the uplands of the interior. A line of light cloud kissed the skyline, and all was again blue. Benjamin was sitting astride the skysail yard hugging the mast. Ninety feet below, the ship jostled business-like through the waves. On a comfortable broad reach she was making at least seven knots. Sea foamed at the bows; a creamy wake streamed off their stern.

Beneath his swaying perch, soldiers tiny as toys stood poised in brigades. Guns, ropes and muskets. A longboat rigged with a square sail bobbed alongside; an order barked, casting it adrift. This had been their daily routine for the last three weeks. Twenty minutes passed, the longboat all but disappeared in their wake. Another order, and the ship exploded into activity. Benjamin clambered down to the topmast crow's nest to better observe the action. Skyler's men rushed to the braces. Brankfleet's gunners separated, six to a cannon. The helmsman gybed the ship hard a starboard and the yards swung across. He held the rudder over, tacking to a reciprocal course, bringing the ship to a close reach.

The deck rumbled as the gun crews ran the cannon out. The longboat came back into view. Passing it they blasted a rolling broadside, shredding its sail. The helmsman ran on for ten minutes and turned onto a broad reach. As they overtook the longboat the larboard guns thundered in their turn. The last gun held back. Khamisi and Xaawo levered the barrel. Brankfleet squinted along its length before wedging the elevation with the coin.

'Stand by to give fire,' he bellowed.

Blowing on the match to a bright glow he applied the linstock to the cannon. A plume of fire hissed from the vent, catching the main charge. The iron beast roared and recoiled on its heavy carriage. Smoke enveloped the gunners. And two hundred yards away whirling chain-shot neatly nipped off the top of the longboat's mast. Like a stage magician Brankfleet appeared through the smoke and took an elaborate bow.

But the show wasn't over. At Skyler's command the sheets slackened, the sails spilled wind and the ship lost way. Khamisi barked an order. Musketeers filed on deck forming into three rows. Firing in volleys, they peppered the sail, and what remained of the longboat's mast tumbled down.

That done, every crew member grabbed boarding pikes and axes. Xaawo led them rushing to the rail screaming for blood.

Benjamin skipped down the ratlines and joined Isaac on the quarterdeck. The crew reclaimed the longboat. And the helm, having completed the figure of eight, proceeded on their original course. Hangbè on the main deck, leaning on a boarding pike, looked up, her even teeth glinting brilliant white as she smiled.

'Maybe now we're worthy of the black,' said Benjamin.

'Sail ho,' yelled Skyler.

1624

THIRTY-ONE — *el tiburón*

Were they spotted? They didn't know. Had their artillery exercises given them away? They didn't know. They held back just below the horizon like a bashful bride nervous of meeting the groom. Were they ready to join the party?

'We get any closer, they'll see us,' said Isaac: 'Then we're committed. Kill or be killed.'

'What if they're friendly?' said Benjamin.

'Then we are not,' said Hangbè: 'Whatever they've got, we want it.'

'Everyone in these waters feels the same way as us,' said Brankfleet.

'She's right,' said Isaac, 'we're running short of everything.'

'Wind's picking up,' said Skyler, 'Our hull is clean. Chances are we'll be faster — attack or retreat.'

'And our men are fresh trained,' said Brankfleet.

'Trained, but untried,' said Isaac.

'As are we all,' said Benjamin.

'Not all of us, young man,' said their gunnery master.

Skyler's men danced about the rigging like circus acrobats, piling on every ounce of canvas. The excitement was palpable. The ship throbbed with it. The wind had risen; white caps on waves. They were heeling hard; waves were crashing over the bows. Clouds tore themselves away from the landmass, scudding across the clear blue sky. Salt spray was drenching the crew. It was mid afternoon; they were catching up fast. The ships were a league-and-a-half apart. Isaac's heart began beating faster. He raised his battered spyglass. The hated saw-toothed saltire of Spain was flying proudly in the wind. So far there was no sign that the Spanish had any awareness of their presence.

Then came the sound of distant thunder, and clouds of smoke drifted across the sea. Now Isaac knew why the Spaniards hadn't seen them — there attention was elsewhere. A single-masted sloop was doing its best to evade her. Cannons were roaring, the sea was pluming around her like a transient forest of frost-white poplars. The top section of mast damaged; the rig was swaying. Undamaged such a sleek vessel would easily outpace that man-of-war. This was the Spanish having fun; this was gunnery practice for them; his was the *banderilla* before the *descabellar*. Isaac passed the telescope to Brankfleet.

'She's a hundred guns to our twenty,' said Brankfleet: 'A broadside from that monster and we'd be matchwood.'

'Is there anything we can do?' said Isaac.

'Take them up the arse,' said Brankfleet. 'See what they do then.' He turned to Skyler: 'Mister Hurst would you be so good as to hove to whilst my crews load. Then, with your permission Mister Isaac, get us to within a quarter of a league of that bastard's stern. Spill the wind, level us off to give me as steady a platform as you can...'

Skyler looked to Isaac who nodded. Brankfleet took his twelve best gunners to the fo'c'sle deck and uncovered the long slim bow-chasers. Only six pounders, but their range was prodigious. Within three minutes they were both loaded. Brankfleet signalled Skyler to get back underway. Skyler barked orders. Braces eased, the ship ceased to heel. Sails providing just enough way for the helmsman to maintain steerage. The larboard bow chaser fired. A plume of white water erupted twenty yards behind the Spanish stern. The enemy seemed too engaged in shooting fish in a barrel to notice a distant cannon shot. The second shot sent a ball through the gallery, punching a hole in the wall of the great cabin. The crew frantically worked to reload. The next shot smashed through the Spaniard's middle deck. A hurricane of oak splinters made a porcupine of the helmsman. The fourth ball smashed into a rudder pintle.

Braces re-tensioned, the African Prince picked up speed overhauling the Spaniards. At the last second before smashing into their stern Isaac steered the ship hard to starboard. Brankfleet released a rolling broadside. As they arced away from the Spanish ship, there came a roar from behind, and the great cabin windows blew out. Another explosion and the mizzen yard flew from the mast crashing to the deck. The enemy gunners were doing fine work with their stern chasers. Another ball fell short, sending up a rush of water. By the time they arrived back in range of the Spanish ship, Brankfleet had elevated the larboard guns. He unleashed a devastating broadside. Chain shot brought down the Spanish mizzen, shredding sails and rigging. The Spaniard was temporarily dead in the water but remained prodigiously dangerous. Nothing in the African Prince's armoury could penetrate that hull. And should they come within range of a Spanish broadside the end would be swift, and certain.

Isaac backed the ship away to a safe distance from the Spanish stern chasers. A surprise attack had descended into frustrating stalemate. Through the smoke clouds billowing from the galleon, the sloop had slipped away. Night fell, Isaac gathered the officers in the wrecked great cabin to plan their next move. They opened the last of the stale wine, setting the cabin reeking with vinegar. A lone maggot crawled from the last of the Taíno supplied meat.

They were reminiscing about extravagant meals gone by. Fantasising about meals to come. Bemoaning their grumbling bellies when the cabin door burst open.

'Keep your seats. Messieurs, madame.'

He was a big man. Extravagantly dressed. His blouse pouched over a broad belt with an elaborate silver buckle. Hanging from it a scallop-hilted sword. But that was not what drew everyone's attention. It was the pair of double-barrelled pistols he was waving languidly in their direction.

'And you are?' said Isaac.

A long strand of back hair dared stray from the cascade of same flowing across the intruder's shoulders. He brushed it away with a flick of his head.

'I?' he said, 'I?' with the air of someone stung by an insult: 'I am Alphonse du Lac. And you will please accompany me.'

Maintaining eye-contact Hangbè's hand edged towards a table knife. *'Mademoiselle, non je t'en prie,'* he barked.

'You're not Spanish are you?' said Isaac.

Du Lac's dark deep-set eyes widened. He tossed his head with the air of another insult received and parried and didn't dignify the question with an answer. Instead, waving his pistols, he herded those assembled onto the moonlit deck. The evening watch were bound and gagged and looking very much the worse for the experience. Alongside was the sloop, its crew milling around securing mooring ropes. Isaac glanced at the hatches; the sleeping Africans slept battened below.

Their captor called a boy to him and whispered in his ear. *'Apportez-moi six bouteilles de mon meilleur vin, et une grande quantité de fromage, dépêchez-vous c'est une urgence.'*

He turned to his captives: 'As you can see your position is hopeless. Please return to your "feast".'

With that he ushered them back inside. As they reseated he joined them at the head of the table. Two boys came in, each struggling with the weight of a basket. Du Lac placed the pistols on the table. Bending over one of the baskets, he began riffling through straw packing. Straightening up he found Hangbè pointing his pistols at him. Unfazed he proceeded to uncork a bottle.

'Come, come. Pass me your glasses.'

And, like automata, they did. The room was immediately suffused with the heady aroma of summer fruits. The other boy began loading the table with cheeses of every variety, and great slabs of fresh bread.

'Santé messieurs, mademoiselle.'

Mouths open, they met his toast with raised glasses. All except Hangbè whose hands were beginning to shake with the weight of the pistols. Du Lac filled a glass and passed it across to her.

'Buvez chérie, ils ne sont pas chargés.'

She looked to Isaac.

'He say's they're not loaded.'

Skyler took a gulp of wine and made a dive for the cheese. Hangbè, pointed a pistol out the window; she pulled the trigger, there was a hollow click.

'Now,' said du Lac, 'what are you doing in my waters?'

'Er, saving your worthless skin,' said Benjamin, wiping wine from his chin, 'you ungrateful son of a...'

Those last words drowned out by du Lac's laughter.

Isaac introduced his officers. Benjamin, his brother and pilot; Brankfleet, gun master; Hurst, sailing master; Khamisi, muskets. Hangbè — how to introduce Hangbè?

'Hangbè and I share the captaincy,' he heard himself say. His crew didn't so much as raise an eyebrow, this shared role assumed.

Du Lac stood, taking her extended hand. Making lingering eye contact, his lips grazed her fingers. Her eyes, in turn, flicked to Isaac. She smiled, accepting du Lac's courtliness as her due. The room became quiet, or so it seemed to Isaac. Benjamin coughed, breaking the tension.

'So,' said Isaac, raising a glass, 'welcome aboard the African Prince.'

Gulping their wine, they settled down to enjoying the unexpected feast. Another bottle opened. Du Lac explained he had been feeling out the Spanish ship's defences. But he'd underestimated their gun's range and their gunners' ability.

'They got lucky,' was how he framed it. Chain shot had damaged the mast, nullifying their speed advantage hampering manoeuvrability.

'They were toying with us when you came along. You must have given them the shock of their lives. So, why did you...?'

1624

'Attack them? said Isaac: 'They're Spanish, do I need a reason?'

'How go things for the United Provinces my friend?'

'Nearly a year since we left,' said Isaac: 'But they've been fighting for independence for fifty-six years. What can have changed?'

'Maybe we'll lose Breda,' said Benjamin, thoughts flashing back to Esther, 'but we'll get her back, just a matter of time.'

Between all the small talk lurked the threat of the Spanish man-of-war not a league and a half distant. Wounded, but recovering fast.

'My mast will be repaired soon,' said du Lac: 'We'll be ready to depart by first light. And your vessel seems serviceable. Save for a little added ventilation.' He nodded towards a splintered void left by Spanish iron.

'So what do we do between now and then?' said Isaac.

'We could make a break for it,' said du Lac. 'Different directions, they couldn't catch us. Probably wouldn't bother trying. Much too concerned with catching Taíno to work to death in their mines.'

'Or we could...' began Benjamin, interrupted by Hangbè.

'Do mischief,' she said.

A grizzled face appeared at the doorway. Du Lac's longboat had returned from reconnoitring.

'The Spanish are close to completing the repairs y'lordships.'

Soon it would be sunrise. Spanish carpenters were repacking their tools, apprentices were sweeping up wood shavings. Spanish smiths were dowsing the forge. Their helmsman was testing the rudder repairs. Their captain was snoring in his bed, arm round a cabin boy.

'Fuego fuego,' screamed the lookout.

'Barcos de fuego,' screamed the officer of the watch.

A dozen flaming wind-blown nightmares were approaching from the south. Blazing stars lighting the black void of night. The Spanish launched open boats to intercept them. Crew members hung over the railings with boathooks, in readiness to fend off. Others rushed to fetch water to damp down the decks and dowse fires. Officers charged about bellowing orders. By the time they realised these 'fire ships' were just flaming barrels with makeshift sails it was too late. In their panic no one had heard the grapnels catch on the opposite rail. No one had seen black bodies sneaking up behind them — until it was too late.

They corralled the prisoners on a deck stained with blood. The first rays of the sun were teasing the horizon. Newly captured Taíno had rowed back to shore. Hangbè had attempted to limit the slaughter. But the slaughter had been great. Du Lac offered places in his crew to any who would defect — and a few did. Boats lowered, the Spanish crammed aboard, those for whom there was no room clung to the sides or struck out for the beach.

Someone yelled, *'Tiburón.'*

A swimmer screamed and thrashed. Then disappeared beneath the waves. He bobbed up in a fountain of scarlet which dissipated as did his screams. A sleek grey shape broke the surface with a limb in its maw. It wasn't long before triangular fins encircled the swimmers. Those clinging onto the boats frantically scrabbled to climb aboard. One boat overturned; the sea began churning with terrified swimmers. The survivors clambered up the beach, into a blizzard of Taíno arrows.

THIRTY-TWO — *we gather together*

Cut, thrust, parry, lunge, riposte. The clash of steel rang out across the waves. Back and forth across the deck they went. The Grevinna seemed to be holding her own. But hard pressed though he may have seemed at times, the Admiral gave the impression of not giving it his all. After five or so minutes, the Admiral's gilded and blued blade slipped through the basket guard of the Grevinna's weapon. Brushing her blade aside with his gloved left hand, he twisted his sword, forcing the Grevinna's hilt from her grip, sending her weapon skittering across the deck.

They froze, locked together:

'Il n'y a pas de rose...' said the Admiral, blanching.

'...sans épines,' said the Grevinna, teasing the blade of her secret stiletto in a newly made wound in the Admiral's thigh.

Time passed slowly as the Andromeda and Zeelander sailed in tandem across the wide ocean.

The Rabbi bowed in rhythm to the scansion of the text. A blue striped prayer shawl covered his head. Spectacles perching on the end of his nose were all that dispelled the appearance of a Biblical prophet. He followed the words meticulously with a yad, a silver pointer. His harsh voice taking on a melodious lilting quality as he chanted his way through the Hebrew.

An enraptured congregation mumbled along with him, following the reading in battered prayer books. Each member was rocking with their Rabbi like metronomes perversely set to different metres. The reader finished the *parashah* with a sigh. Bowing over the text for a silent beat, he laid aside the yad and rolled together the parchment scroll. Lifting his shawl from his head he adjusted his skull cap, blinking with eyes newly returned from visions of higher worlds. Removing his spectacles, he pinched the bridge of his nose, regarded the audience as though surprised to see them.

The cabin was full. Congregants spilled out onto the open deck. This

1624

Shabbat's sermon was from the Book of Esther, stirring unwelcome memories. It told of a Jewish beauty becoming consort to Xerxes, the idolatrous king of Persia. Of her courtier uncle, Mordecai. Of how she saved her people from extinction. Of how she exacted terrible vengeance on the murderous viceroy Haman and his people.

'Not a single mention of God,' said the Rabbi, 'no divine intervention anywhere in this book. It would seem Esther saved the Hebrews by her courage and sacrifice, unaided. Some authorities question why is this book so revered? Why is *Purim*, which celebrates Esther's triumph, such an important Hebrew festival? The answer is as simple, as it is profound. The Book of Esther is one of our holy books precisely *because* God receives no mention. The ancient writers so assumed God's hand in these affairs they didn't see the point in stating the obvious.'

As he wound up the sermon a tear crept out from the corner of his eye. There'd been no royal betrothal for his Esther.

From outside, a cry: 'Sail hoy.'

All eyes turned to the door. Some made to leave. The Rabbi glanced out the window. There were still a couple of hours remaining to sundown and the end of the sabbath.

'Stay, stay.' He flapped his hands in a gesture of calm: 'The Goyim will take care of this. They'll have their rest day tomorrow and then you'll be running the show. Now let us turn to page...'

There was a rumble as of distant thunder. The congregation froze; the Rabbi cocked his ear. A couple of seconds later he heard the unmistakable whine of an approaching cannon ball.

'Down, down,' he screamed.

Barging his way out of the crowded room, he collided with Pastor Terbrugghen, his quartermaster. The sea geysered up off the larboard bow, showering them with water.

'Lucky miss,' said the Rabbi, brushing droplets from his vestments.

'Not sure it was luck,' said the Pastor, wrinkling his weathered brow.

They exchanged a meaning-laden glance. The Rabbi bellowed to the helmsman:

'Larboard, hard over.'

The sailing master rushed on deck shouting orders. Hands raced to the braces, wearing the yards. The vessel heeled hard as it pointed closer to the wind, increasing speed.

'Spaniards?' said the Rabbi.

'Whatever, we'll outrun the fuckers,' muttered the Pastor.

The Rabbi tutted — profanity, it's still Shabbat after all. But yes, they would outrun them; few could outpace the Rachael.

Another flash, another peal of thunder, the whistle of a cannon ball. Water again pluming up at their bows. The Pastor brought a glass to his eye.

'Christ in heaven Rabbi. There's another one.'

Caught in a pincer movement. Now the only hope was their hidden cannon, and small hope it was against such superior firepower.

The Rachael hove to. Going nowhere. Sails balancing the wind. The Rabbi stood arm-in-arm with the Pastor, glaring at the eighty-gunner coming up on their stern. The Rabbi was looking over the Pastor's shoulder at the equally intimidating vessel riding the swell by their bows. Those captains knew their business, maintaining position precisely in the blind spot of the Rachael's guns. Did they even know they had guns? Maybe this formation was a practiced tactic.

'We're dead, Rabbi,' said the Pastor.

'I'm sorry, but I for one refuse to die on Shabbat,' said the Rabbi.

The Pastor nodded to the sun grazing the western horizon: 'Hold them off for an hour and you can die in peace Abraham.'

With just twenty cannons, hopelessly outmatched. Nevertheless their gunners stood by, ordnance primed to open fire should the opportunity present itself. A surprise attack was a forlorn hope. But a forlorn hope was better than no hope at all. The quartermaster was passing out muskets; the Christian sailors' plain dark clothing contrasting with the prayer shawls of the Jews, flying in the wind.

Both flanking ships were flying the black.

Time passes slowly when you're anticipating a death blow.

'What the hell are they waiting for?' said the Rabbi.

The Pastor shrugged. 'Excellent sermon, by the way.'

'One of my better, I thought,' said the Rabbi, spitting a ball down the barrel of his musket, and tamping it home.

Another hour passed. The Pastor paced the fo'c'sle. The Rabbi was slumped dejectedly on the poop deck, gazing unfocused at the ship to their stern. Between them eighty men were crouching or sprawled on the main deck nursing muskets and all manner of edged weaponry. Someone began to sing *L'kha dodi*, others joined him.

'Come out my Beloved, the Bride to meet; The inner light of Shabbat, let us greet.'

'What are they trying to do, bore us to death?' yelled the Rabbi.

Someone laughed; the black humour proved contagious. The Pastor wiped tears from his eyes. The singing had become competitive, the Dutch Protestants took their turn:

'We gather together to ask the Lord's blessing; He chastens and hastens His will to make known. The wicked oppressing now cease from distressing. Sing praises to His Name; He forgets not His own.'

And the Hebrews sung on:

'Jerusalem, sanctuary of God the celestial King and temporal capital of human kings, rise up from the midst of destruction and ruin. Enough of your sitting in a valley of tears; God's great mercy awaits you...'

'Something's happening,' shouted the Pastor, pointing forward.

The singing petered out; the Rabbi turned to the vessel haunting their stern. Something indeed was happening. A longboat lowered, the crew rowed across the intervening seaway. He climbed on the rail, steadying himself on the mizzen shrouds. Squinting ahead he made out a similar action played out on the other ship.

So far, the cannons had remained silent. There were no blood-slick decks, no agonised screams, no spars crashing down, no shipboard infernos — so far. The Rabbi absently fingered the edge of his sword like a *shochet* preparing for slaughter. He left his vantage point in the shrouds and met the Pastor mid-deck. Anticipation of imminent hostility was shifting towards naked curiosity. The Pastor met his gaze. No words, just an exchange of raised eyebrows.

This was beginning to feel like a negotiated surrender. The Rabbi knew his quartermaster. He didn't need to solicit the Pastor's advice. Front it out. Imitate the puffer fish. Small, but difficult to swallow, not to mention poisonous. So, come on, try and take us. You'll lose men and all you'll have are scraps. But why start a fight before you've heard their terms, he'd counsel. Were we talking about some sort of tribute? Now that they could discuss. Beyond that it was death before dishonour. He shuddered at the thought of enslavement. Trust in God. Surely He won't permit our mission to end here. Let's see if they have the stomach for a fight.

The day was on the last of the ebb. Low clouds populated the horizon, teasing the last of the warmth from the dying sun. Darkening skies signalled the withdrawal of the Shabbat 'bride.' In the morning, the Christian Sabbath would be welcomed in. Between times, what hell might ensue?

Longboats approached either side of the Rachael. The more protracted this drama the less threatening it seemed. The Pastor ordered ladders lowered. He and the Rabbi stood by to greet the twin delegation.

1624

Oarsmen withdrew their sweeps. Longboats bumped against the hull, rising and falling on the long Atlantic swell. Two unarmed crew members from each ship clambered aboard. The Rachael's musketeers lowered their weapons. Their synchronised actions spoke of choreographed precision. The Rabbi and the first mate remained impassive, backed by eighty heavily armed men. Were it not for that, and the two warships blocking their escape, the situation may have seemed innocuous, even friendly. They might be anticipating a productive collaboration.

After a pause, the ladders jerked taut. The sailors leaned over the rail to aid their principals onto the deck. The first to appear was a tall slim grandee with flowing white hair and a black gold-inlaid cuirass. From the opposite side a woman clothed in a long black, silver embroidered dress. Her white gold-flecked hair hung in two thick plaits over her shoulders. Both arrivals sported rapiers slung from diagonal leather shoulder straps. The crowd parted as these strange visitors walked towards each other. They met in the middle of the deck, unaware of being scrutinised. The grandee bowed low. His lips brushed the woman's hand as she executed a gracious curtsy. They smiled into each other's eyes and turned to the dumbstruck spectators.

The Rabbi squeezed through the throng, followed by the Pastor.

'Welcome aboard, sir, madam. I am Abraham Amsalem master of the Rachael, and this is my second in command Erasmus Terbrugghen. To whom do I have the pleasure of —'

'I am Lieutenant Admiral Jochem Bartholomeuz Van Den Hamel, Count of Asterfoort and Spakenfoort, Knight of the Holy Order of Saint Botolph, Captain General of the Zeelander and your humble servant sir. I have pleasure in introducing Ingela Olofsdotter Gathenhielm, Captain General of the Andromeda.'

'And your reason for —'

'Tell me Rabbi, do you believe in fate?'

1624

THIRTY-THREE — *drink more*

She came from a dynasty of priestesses. Sometimes she summoned spirits; sometimes the spirits summoned her. Sex could be a trigger. Alcohol also, and hashish and dance and rhythmic drumming. A cunning combination of same and even the most fickle of spirits would reliably appear. She was of the tribe of Fon. Prominent in the all-woman regiment they called the Dahomey Amazons.

Increasingly their tribal leaders were making their wealth from dealing in slaves. Supplying traders operating out of the port of Ouidah in the Bight of Benin. Soon they had so depleted neighbouring kingdoms they resorted to selling their own men to the Arab traders. Short of males to defend their borders they recruited an amazon army, in which Hangbè rose to general. She opposed this inhumane and counter-productive trade, which had become the mainstay of the kingdom's economy. Her military and religious status allowed her to voice this unpopular opinion. Or so she thought. One dark night enemies captured and sold her. She found herself on the African Prince, doomed to slavery in the New World.

'Returning is not a possibility,' she said. 'I am in need of a new home.'

Isaac explained about his family's expulsion from the Iberian Peninsular. Itself a place of exile. The Hebrew's four-thousand-year history of expulsions, persecutions and enslavement. About how the twelve tribes had dwindled to one. About how many of their number had found refuge in the Low Countries. And about the Free Provinces' war to gain political independence and religious freedom.

But, whilst grateful for the protection of the House of Orange, Holland was not their home. And so their ancestral story continued — a perpetual quest for a homeland. Somewhere the nation of Judah could permanently settle in peace.

'You should join us,' he said. 'Maybe we'll discover it together. A land flowing with milk and honey. But first Benjamin and I need to find our sister.'

Hangbè gave that some thought, then came back with:

'Do you possess anything that was hers? Or just something she'd touched?'

'This kerchief was a gift from her.'

He untied it from his neck. She tore off a narrow strip.

'We'll talk again tomorrow,' she said.

Next evening Isaac found Hangbè poring over a chart of the Caribbean laid out on a table in the great cabin. He was carrying the bottle of brandy she'd requested.

'Swallow this,' she said, producing something that looked like a musket ball. 'And the spirits will tell us where she is.'

Isaac's mind spun through a cascade of objections. Some religious, some secular, some psychological, but mostly because he hated swallowing pills. In the end his desire to rescue his sister overrode any scepticism. If his chances of finding her improved by a millionth of a percent, it would be worth it. And a false hope is better than no hope. He popped the pill in his mouth and chugged it back with a big mouthful of brandy, coughing and spluttering as it burned its way down.

'Drink more,' she said, tipping the bottle.

Isaac gulped again. His head began to spin. He staggered backwards just in time to avoid a burst of flame. Hangbè, blew another aerosol of brandy over the oil lamp. Another cloud of flame erupted leaving Isaac's eyes dazzled. The cabin was clagged with the sweet smell of Cognac. Recovering his balance, he said:

'What was in that pill?'

'Oh a few things.'

'What things?'

'Herbs, the ashes of that kerchief, burned, ground down, some of my shit, some of your semen, a Spaniard's blood, and —'

Isaac's stomach violently spasmed. He vomited over the chart table. Hangbè seemed unsympathetic. She pushed him away and he crouched, leaning against the wall, holding his belly as the retching continued. She picked over the charts, moving the bile and food particles with her fingers until she located what she was seeking. Without looking up she beckoned him to her side:

'Isaac, over here, quick.'

He did his best to straighten up, gut sore, wiping his mouth, shivering.

'Look, look,' she said, excitedly.

His nose was dribbling vomit, he strained to focus through watering eyes. The charts were awash with the contents of his stomach. And there was the black pill floating in a stream of mucus over Havana bay. He watched entranced as it headed through the slime towards the city's harbour.

'What was really in that pill?' he said.

She raised her eyebrows. He vomited again; she danced away to avoid the splashes.

THIRTY-FOUR — the Turtle

From the deck of the *Nuestra Señora de la Visitación* Isaac watched the African Prince shoulder her way through the long swell. She was half-a-league behind them on their larboard quarter, under the command of Skyler Hurst. The coast of Hispaniola was a hazy mirage to the south. A warm wind running south of east filled the *Visitación's* canvas, pushing them along at a steady six knots. The carpenters were taking a mid-day break. Cooling off in the shadow of the sails amidst their tools and pine-scented wood shavings. They'd made substantial progress repairing the shattered spars and cannon-shot timbers.

Brankfleet was pacing the gundecks taking stock of the ordinance, like a sultan lasciviously appraising new additions to his harem. The brothers sprawled out with Hangbè on the middle deck, feet on the rail, wearing just their breeches. Isaac took prideful note that Benjamin's body had lost all traces of boyish scrawn, muscles flexing with the motion of the ship. Boy to man in so short a span of time. Wine bottles littered a barrel top, serving as an informal table. They watched as Du Lac waved away his sloop; sleek and seakindly, a single slender mast supporting a huge fore and aft main. As she fell out of their wind shadow the canvas filled and the sloop drew ahead of them.

'Du Lac doesn't want to cause panic in Cayenne Harbour,' said Isaac. 'Spanish man-of-war comes over the horizon, what're they going to think, or do?'

They fell to discussing the strange collection of cargo in the hold.

'Wood,' said Hangbè, 'Wood?'

'Ah, but not just any wood,' said Isaac, 'Lignum Sanctum.'

Hangbè and Benjamin looked blank. Du Luc clambered up the companionway in time to catch the topic.

'Wood for your blocks,' he chuckled, 'cure for your cocks.'

'A tincture of the stuff cures the "French" disease,' muttered Isaac. 'Or so they say.'

Movement in the masthead. A voice yelling, *'Land ho.'*

Half-an-hour passed; the hump of the turtle's back rose slowly over the horizon. The sloop would precede them by a couple of hours.

'Welcome,' said Du Lac, 'to our island sanctuary.'

A distillery abutted the rear of Gedding's Inn. The sickly-sweet smell of crushed sugarcane wafted through the back door. It joined the sour astringency of ardent spirits leaking from the barrels behind them. They in turn combined with the earthy stench of unwashed bodies, tobacco smoke and seared meat. The brothers' party was sitting by an open window. Inrushes of air freighted with salt and iodine arrived from the nearby harbour. These distinct odour streams immiscibly collided. Human stench and nature's balm swirling around them like saline and fresh water at the mouth of a river estuary.

Friends met, enemies too, in alcoholic truce, under the watchful eye of a landlord of brutal stature. Payment was on an informal honour system. Some paid too much, some not at all. Money was not in short supply in Cayenne. Drink was bitter ale, spiced grog or undiluted overproof rum.

In common with all such bearpits Gedding's served as a community hub. A place for boasting boasts, planning plans and plotting ingenious plots. And where, inevitably the occasional assassination took place. Du Lac bellowed their food order over the noise of the exotic crowd. The bill-of-fare was simple: beef and yams charred over an open fire. Tomorrow it might be something else. Wild hog or blacktip reef shark. Around the table they contemplated the dark combustible liquid glaring back at them from their pewter mugs.

'Don't look at it, don't think about it, just knock it back' said Du Lac. 'The world will look different on the other side.' Draining his mug in three mighty swallows, he slammed it hard on the table. With an epileptic shudder his body tensed, eyes glazing. A far away look overtook him. Shaking his head like a dog in the rain, seemed to restore his vision. 'First one's always the worst.'

His guests shared apprehensive glances. Hangbè closed her eyes and drained her cup in one long swallow. Isaac and Benjamin copied her reckless example. The liquid hit their stomachs like blazing comets crashing to earth. Alien spectra flooded their vision. And, yes, the world did indeed look different — very different.

Eyes streaming, Benjamin found himself fixating on the cook. An obese fallen angel grimly tormenting the flesh of unrepentant sinners. Stripped to the waist, sweat spluttering, he blasphemously commanded a huge blazing griddle. Sperm whales and harpooneers engaged in mutual slaughter across the vastness of his chest. False gods and daemons rampaged around his torso contesting with Catholic saints and martyrs. Snakes entwining his arms enjoyed vile congress with terrified virgins; barbaric alphabets carved deep into his fire-reddened face spoke of obscure, ungodly heresies.

Men and women of every creed and colour swirled about them in disharmonious commune. A constant stream of patrons strode in and staggered out. They greeted, gambled, ate, drank and occasionally fought, with little account kept of praise or insult.

Hangbè had developed a theatrically androgyne persona. She'd gleefully plundered the *Visitación* officers' wardrobes. The resultant sexually ambiguous fashion explosion was attracting admiring glances. The one-armed potman passed by for a closer look on the excuse of replenishing their cups. Two plump mulatto women lingered long after they'd delivered food to their table. Bleeding slabs of seared meat heaped high on a pewter platter, whole roast yams and plantain baked in their skins wrapped in huge banana leaves.

'So,' said Du Lac, responding to an unvoiced question. 'The Spanish think they just name a place to own it. They're desperately overstretched in these parts. Clinging to Hispaniola by their fingertips. It was to their stupidity we owe our position in Tortuga. Once this was simply a lost outpost populated by a few marooned Frenchmen. They peacefully eked out a subsistence hunting feral cattle and hogs. Drying the meat over boucans, native style, curing the hides. Trading with passing ships. Harming no one. However their presence offended the Spanish. They tried driving them out, but each time they simply sought refuge in the forest. So one day the Dons sent lancers to slaughter their cattle — the legendary regiment of cow killers. Facing starvation the population paddled off in their dugout canoes to prey on passing shipping. And over the years they became very proficient at it, trading up to raiding in larger vessels. The rest...' he gestured to the packed room. 'When the Spanish come again, they'll be facing this lot.'

Benjamin, was growing impatient with the history lesson: 'Who can we ask about ship arrivals at Havana?'

'Ask me, I'm as good as anyone,' said Du Lac. 'There will be dozens of them, more every day as we approach the end of hurricane season. Treasure ships are mustering in the harbour. Spanish war ships preparing to escort them to Cadiz. One more new arrival would simply go unnoticed.'

A shadow darkened their table. They looked up. A man, a big man, full beard and piercing deep-set eyes was leering at Hangbè.

'Whose is she? How much do you want for her?' he said to Du Lac.

Isaac jumped in, 'Not for sale.'

'What about for one night?' the man persisted.

Isaac glared up at him, his face losing pallor.

'An hour then,' the man chuckled, tossing a handful of silver coins amidst the half-eaten food.

'You've got to let me have her, I've paid for her now.'

Isaac was on his feet reaching for his sword. The man hesitated, grinned at Du Lac, and walked away cursing, leaving his money amidst the left-over food.

'Mad Henri Du Sores,' said Du Lac, uncocking his pistol and laying it next to his plate like an essential component of a silver service. 'Not the best person to have as an enemy. Tell you about him later.'

Du Lac, not himself welcome on Spanish soil, nevertheless knew people of influence in Havana — the comings and goings of merchant shipping being of keen interest to a Boucaneer. He dispatched spies on the brothers' behalf, to glean news of Esther.

Days passed, hot and humid, with no word. In their frustration Isaac and Benjamin sought solace in drink and low company and pointlessly sniping at one another. With their share of the Spanish prize they were now rich men. But they would give all they owned to liberate their sister. Eventually, at Hangbè's stern insistence, they ceased bickering and began constructing a plan.

'If only we could...'

Wild boar graced the menu at Gedding's. Three bristled heads stared mournfully at the griddle, where the cook was lugubriously basting their torsos.

'Look man,' Isaac said to Du Lac, 'it's simple. You distract the Spanish from the sea, and we'll sneak in from landward. Easy as that.'

'Sure, easy as that,' said Du Lac, yawning.

He hadn't been his ebullient self of late. Drinking irritably on his own. Pacing the foreshore, scanning the horizon through his spyglass. Isaac and Benjamin had been attempting to promote the virtues of their scheme for the last hour to this disinterested audience. Tortugans, Du Lac explained, in a flat monotone, having just rid themselves of the Dons for the third time in a decade, had little appetite for poking the beast.

And human nature being what it was, the Tortugan factions which collaborated to liberate them from the yolk of the Spanish Empire had begun turning on each other. The French majority against the English, both against the Welsh. A powerful enemy, a disunited population — not a great combination for raiding the strongest defended port of the most powerful empire the world had ever seen.

Hangbè went to forward a counter argument, 'But...' she said, and petered out, like she'd just read the room and saw no merit in voicing her opinion. Slumping back down in her seat, she drifted off in her mind. She'd been looking for a local smith to forge her a weapon from her homeland. European swords were all very well, but nothing in her experience beat a *hunga munga*.

The mulatto girls arrived carrying steaming slabs of pork, smelling disconcertingly of burned hair. Merchant ships had arrived that afternoon drawing patrons away, the bar was quieter than normal. Taking advantage of the lull the girls sat down and helped themselves to wine. Their cheery presence lifted the mood. Isaac was pleased to see Benjamin smiling. Hangbè, one hand on Isaac's knee, beamed a grin and playfully punched Du Lac on the shoulder. He shook his head, reluctantly amused.

Mad Henri Du Sores appeared through the barbeque smoke. He was rolling drunk and heading for Hangbè. Isaac barred his way, sword drawn. Du Lac leapt between them.

'What business is it of yours?' bellowed Du Sores, blasting garlic laden breath into Du Lac's face. 'You and that pox-riddled, peg-legged matelot bastard Kraft have butted into my business once too often.'

'An insult to Cornelius is an insult to me,' said Du Lac, eyes burning like short cut fuses: 'Clear the floor,' he demanded, 'give us some space.' Chairs toppled, as patrons retreated.

Du Sores unleashed a looping sword cut which Du Lac effortlessly parried. Roaring, Du Sores hacked again —

A deafening gunshot. Plaster fell from the ceiling. The room turned towards the sound. Silhouetted in the doorframe was an imposing one-legged figure. Tucking his smoking pistol back into his belt he strode unevenly towards Du Sores.

Not in the best of moods.

1624

THIRTY-FIVE — *the promise*

In the gloomy corridor outside the cell the slight figure of Friar Ignatius was balancing on a wine cask, his face pressed against a spyhole. Feeling a tug at his sleeve, he flicked the hand away irritably, without interrupting his vigil.

'Brother you must come away,' came an insistent voice behind him.

'Shush.' came the reply. But the tugging persisted. The Franciscan, whirled round red-faced, jerking his sleeve away.

'Oh it's you González, he hissed: 'Can't you see I'm busy. Go about your business. Shoo...'

'But Brother...'

'But nothing González. Someone has to watch. What if they commit some unspeakable act? What if some imp should appear and suckle? What if some daemon should jump through a trapdoor from hell and have foul congress with them? Do you think that should go unrecorded?'

'Whilst I greatly admire your strength Ignatius, just how long can your soul resist such temptation? How long can you observe these heretical females without risking your soul's corruption?'

'I am fully prepared to watch for as long as it takes,' said Friar Ignatius. 'And yes Bother González, even at the risk of my immortal soul. Let no one say, I failed in my spiritual duty.'

He glanced beatifically heavenwards. Friar González shuffled off down the dark corridor muttering to himself. Friar Ignatius' hand slipped back beneath his robe, gratified to find his member just as rigid as he'd left it.

Two naked tear-streaked figures clung together, barely visible in the shadows. Unspeakable acts played through the distorted field of the young friar's onanistic imagination.

At his moment of release, a long-drawn-out animal cry echoed down the cold stone corridors.

Esther opened her eyes. Nothing. She stifled a scream. The walls could

1624

have been ten inches or ten thousand miles away. Were it not for the cold floor beneath her she could be floating in a void of nothingness. Were it not for Aal's breathing she could be alone. She longed to be back in dreamless oblivion. But her eyes wouldn't stay closed.

A sliver of light appeared on the dirt floor to begin its daily journey across the cell, intensifying the darkness, illuminating a galaxy of dust motes. She reached out and the light slipped through her fingers like skeins of brilliant silk — a moment treasured daily. Soon the chains would hold her back and it would dance beyond her reach.

Lord of light save me from this darkness.

Everyday, this tiny emissary from the world outside would describe a pathway through the shadows, marking the minutes of the day. The temperature of the cell would be stifling by the time it was midway through its course. Then a slit would open in the door. Slops would be shoved through — mouldy bread, a few beans, maybe some putrid meat — repellent at first, but now a welcome relief from the crushing monotony.

Lord of Life save me from this tedium.

By the time this luminous visitor reached the opposite wall it would have faded. Cold and darkness would take its place. Once they had kept count, tallied the days. One day they forgot. Then they listened out for the church bells on Sundays, tallied the weeks. Then one day they forgot. And now time was lost in time.

Pulling Aal closer she gently stroked the matted hair from her all but invisible face. Aal, her rock, was beyond despair, beyond fatalism. Aal had given too much. Or Esther had taken too much from her.

'There, there,' whispered Esther, 'there, there.'

Aal shuddered and clung to her. It was Esther's turn to be the rock. Her tribe's four-thousand-year history had been an endless story of genocide, survival and triumph. Why would the cycle stop now? She would survive, her God was with her. And if she didn't survive, her God was with her. Where Aal had given up hope, Esther was simply exercising patience. Something would happen —

A long-drawn-out animal cry rent the air. The Inquisitors were starting early today. Aal's eyes blinked open.

'Promise you won't let me suffer,' whispered Aal, blinking up at her.

'Yes, I promise,' said Esther.

'Will you do it today?'

'Not today, but soon, I promise.'

1624

THIRTY-SIX — *tangerine skies*

Kraft stood in the doorway, gun smoking. Chatter petered out, all eyes instantly on him. He took two steps into the inn. Standing amongst mortal men his size became evident. He lumbered past Du Sores, himself of no inconsiderable scale, as though the man was invisible, eyes locked on those of Du Lac. As he passed, Du Sorres rocked, staggering to retain his footing as though disturbed by a powerful gravitational field.

'Come here my love,' said Kraft, embracing Du Lac. 'Were you making trouble with poor Alphonse again?'

Isaac blinked. Looking past the reunited couple he caught Du Sores sneaking out the back door.

'Gentlemen,' announced Du Lac, breaking away from his partner with some difficulty, 'It is my pleasure to introduce Captain Cornelius Kraft of the Unicorn.'

Isaac, Benjamin and Hangbè were barely visible amongst a densely packed crowd, gathered at the dockside. Four new arrivals were riding at anchor on the luminous turquoise sea. Amongst them the battle-scarred Unicorn. Longboats lowered and began pulling towards them.

'Being pounded by a Spanish eighty gunner,' said Kraft, standing arm-in-arm with Du Lac. 'Couldn't work out why it didn't finish us off till I spied those fellows coming over the horizon,' he gestured at the rest of the fleet.

The longboat bows kicked up spray as they approached. It was midtide; they came alongside the kelp-draped steps of the dock. Isaac peered over the heads of the gathering crowd. His attention fell on an imperious figure seated behind the oarsmen. A black broad-brimmed hat cast deep shadow over a craggy face, shrouded in a bushy, grey flecked beard. Over an extravagantly embroidered scarlet doublet hung a leather, silver-buckled baldric. And from this depended a basket-hilted mortuary sword and a brace of pistols. A large horn-hilted dagger protruded from a sash about his substantial waist. Velvet, gold-fringed breaches met thigh length riding boots. As was fashionable these rolled back revealing vivid yellow kid-leather linings.

There was something familiar about the profile of the ship from which this king of buccaneers disembarked. There was something familiar about the man as well.

'Father?'

The landlord's wife was moving from table to crowded table lighting oil lamps. Isaac left Benjamin ordering more beer, mesmerised by her swaying tits. He stumbled into the street to relieve himself, weaving through the last of the homeward bound dock labourers. Making his way unsteadily to the harbour's edge, he prepared to empty his bladder into the water. Lost in non-specific thought, he started when a figure appeared beside him. Du Luc reached out a steadying hand to prevent him toppling into the water.

'Ah yes,' he said, liberating his member from his breeches, 'that's the other reason I came out here.'

Their streams merged as the breeze took them tinkling into the harbour below. Du Lac wiped his hands on his doublet. Then he seated himself on a packing case and sucked hard and successfully to re-vivify the embers in a fire-blackened pipe. Isaac perched to windward, avoiding thick clouds of sweet smoke. Below, in the gentle swell, ships' tenders nudged each other as though sharing a private joke. The sky was darkening to the left, flecked with livid green, ominous like an approaching plague. On their right the horizon gleamed gold like Eldorado, mythical and forever out of reach. Through a forest of masts, the mainland of Hispaniola was losing definition – blending like an assassin into the night.

'And what was the other reason?' said Isaac.

'What?'

'The other reason?'

'Oh yes, I've heard something.'

'Heard what?' Isaac's pulse began to race.

'One of my people, newly arrived from Havana, brought word of a tall, fair-haired woman, blue eyes, amongst prisoners docked two months ago.'

Isaac leapt to his feet, seizing Du Lac's shoulders. 'What, what? And that's all?' he yelled.

'Jesu, Isaac. Nothing's confirmed. It's not much more than a rumour,' Du Lac grabbed Isaac's wrists and prised himself out of his grip. 'He didn't see her himself. The man needed to get out of there in a hurry. But he left others to make deeper enquiries. Don't fret, there'll be more news soon.'

Isaac slumped down on the packing cases trembling. Du Lac sat beside him, offering his pipe which Isaac waved away.

'And that definitely was all?' To Isaac's shame he heard the pleading in his voice. Du Lac turned to him, inhaling smoke with exaggerated patience. Their eyes met. It was a stupid question, Isaac knew it. He shook his head as though clearing a pathway for fresh thinking. His mind turned to Benjamin drinking back in the inn, oblivious of this news. Should he share it, or would it be kinder to await confirmation? Du Luc read his mind:

'He's your younger brother, but he's not a child.'

They sat in silence for the longest while. Isaac said: 'Then there's my stepfather. How long have I known that man? He's married to my bloody mother. I didn't hardly recognise him. Still don't. It's difficult to get my head round what is going on here.'

'Would have thought that was obvious my friend. The Rabbi has come to rescue his family.'

'Do we look like we need rescuing?'

Another pause.

'We all need rescuing, one time or another,' said du Lac.

'My mind's spinning,' said Isaac, 'can't seem to get my bearings. It's like my life turned to quicksand. Like everywhere I tread I seem to sink deeper. Who the hell is he? One minute the old man's the pillar of Amsterdam Jewry. Ramrod straight, butter wouldn't melt, righteous example to us all. And next time I set eyes on him... I didn't know who was most surprised, me looking at him, him looking at me. And then there's the Pastor, his quartermaster, Benjamin's fencing master...'

'Sea affects us all in different ways,' said du Lac. 'Ask yourself this: which do you prefer, the Rabbi as he was, or as you find him? Surely, this version must be more appealing to you. Least you have something in common.'

Isaac paused to think about that one. 'And then there's my brother,' he continued, 'unlike me, he's actually the Rabbi's blood. How the hell is this going to affect him? And what the hell would my mother, the Rebbetzin, think? This could send her to the madhouse, or kill her.'

Du Lac shot him a sidelong glance.

'Ever crossed your mind, she might already know, have known all along?' Isaac turned towards him, mouth agape. 'Just a thought,' said du Luc, shrugging.

Isaac recovered quickly, adroitly changing tack: 'When would he have told us? Would he ever have told us? We could've gone to our graves never knowing about his double life.'

Du Lac shook his head: 'So regard this as a fresh start. He's had a shock too. Go see him, talk it out. Want my advice?' said Du Lac. 'Go and buy your old father a drink. He'll be as confused as you.'

Arm-in-arm, they stumbled back into the inn. And there was the Rabbi. He and Benjamin gulping down rum, wearing three attractive mulatto women like fashion accessories.

A small tar-patched harbour boat bumped against the side of the African Prince. An urchin of indeterminate gender clambered aboard, handing Isaac a fold of paper sealed with a smear of black wax.

Captains Cornelius Kraft & Jean-Henri Du Lac are pleased to invite... Isaac shaded his eyes. The sun reflected mercilessly off the white stucco walls of the rambling house. It stood proud, like a challenge unanswered, atop a rocky outcrop overlooking the sea. If not fortified, the place would be easy to defend. And it would be well nigh impossible for a Spanish raiding party to approach unseen from the sea. From here the arriving guests enjoyed a clear view across the Tortuga Straits. The coast of Hispaniola rose above a heat haze with misty mountains beyond.

Were it not for the mules it would be an arduous uphill trek from the harbour in the oppressive heat. Guests travelled astride these gentle beasts led by servants bearing parasols. Isaac and Benjamin led the way. The Rabbi came next with Pastor Terbrugghen. Captain Gathenhielm was with her first mate Severin Karlsson (he of the cheese). Admiral Van Den Hamel brought Schoenmaecker, Matamata and his body servant Crips. Behind them Skyler Hurst and Elijah Brankfleet representing the African Prince. Hangbè with her Zulu honour guard of Khamisi and Xaawo brought up the rear.

Scabrous dogs of unguessable ancestry and questionable allegiance sniffed the arrivals — committing their scent to indelible memory. Servants in Moorish livery directed the guests through huge iron-studded doors. A courtyard bounded by a quadrangle of Arabesque colonnades greeted them. The tenor of the day changed. The monotonous buzz of insects gave way to birdsong. Water splashed musically from a central fountain. Foliage from exotic fruit trees dappled the light flooding down from a turquoise sky. Blue and orange butterflies took to the air from around a clear pool, as they approached. Dark skinned, white robed servants conducted them to their hosts. Du Lac and Kraft appeared adorned with all the silken splendour of Ottoman potentates.

1624

It had been almost two years since the brothers had been in the company of their father. They were only just beginning to relax. He looked the same — they didn't. Or so they thought. Benjamin was as tall as Isaac now. Their complexions, beards, build, demeanour all had radically changed. He would have passed them unrecognised in a crowd — indeed he had, but for that one word — *father*. The Rabbi had whirled on Benjamin red-faced, like he'd thought it a cruel joke. Then he saw Isaac pushing through the crowd, and his eyes overbrimmed with tears.

For this occasion (and for their father's approval more than they would care to admit) they'd attended a barber. Their hair washed, oiled and tied back. Their weathered nut-brown faces clean shaven. Not restored to their former appearance, but close enough for recognition.

Isaac and Hangbè had rarely been out of each other's company since Samaná Bay. Neither they, nor others had kept the measure, or indeed felt the urge to do so.

But then his father. Matters are complicated between fathers and sons. The old lion and the young pretender to the pride. Every son seeks to impress his father. But what impresses the son doesn't impress the father. And what impresses the father doesn't impress the son. The son tries to impress the father with what impresses him. The father doesn't understand that the son is trying to impress him. He regards his actions as wayward, perverse, threatening. What if they were not father and son and neither was trying to impress the other, what if they met as men?

'Father this is Hangbè.'

The meeting had taken place on the deck of the African Prince. Hangbè flanked by the two Zulus. No explanation of their relationship. No seeking of approval, none granted. One man introducing his woman to another, on equal terms. The Rabbi bowed over her hand, not a trace of disapproval, no patriarchal condescension.

Pastor Terbrugghen had accompanied the Rabbi. There were other scars on Benjamin's face besides the nick the Pastor had given him. The Pastor took the youth's face in his hands examining it with mock seriousness, turning it this way and that in the light. Concluding by tweaking his cheek.

The Admiral had arrived next with the Grevinna. Skyler Hurst and Elijah Brankfleet were already in the great cabin. All assembled, Isaac and Benjamin revealed their skeletal plan. This gathering was ostensibly celebrating their recent victories. But everyone knew it was a council of war in pretty wrappings. The Tortugans had no structured hierarchy, but Du Lac and Kraft clearly led opinion. And the non-Tortugans needed their support for their plan to succeed.

Aromas from the kitchen reached the dogs. Abandoning their post they sauntered into the main reception room panting expectantly. A pair of monkeys followed and began grooming them.

'Is that natural?' said Isaac.

'It's natural to them,' said Hangbè.

Servants ushered the guests through to a long hall leading off the colonnades. Tables groaned with all manner of fish and fowl, sweetmeats and savoury pastries. Flagons of wine and rum, and sweet aromatic tea supplied refreshment. There was no formal seating. Divans and cushions followed the walls - Arab style, overflowing into the courtyard. Eating was with hands; rose scented water provided for washing. Servants fluttered back and forth between guests with towels. The smell of baking following them like the ghosts of banquets to come. Bright-eyed and shrill, green parrots attacked bowls of fruit. Returning to their courtyard perches, bills dripping juice.

Du Luc and Kraft proved generous and accomplished hosts. They divided their time between entertaining guests and mercilessly chivvying the house staff. Formality was in limited supply and alcohol soon stripped away what little there was.

As afternoon moved towards dusk. Tall stories grew in scale, actions on land and sea became ever more heroic. The western sky was glowing tangerine before conversation became more substantive.

It started with a toast.

'To victory,' roared Kraft.

'Victory,' the room boomed back.

Du Lac sat on the edge of the fountain. Benjamin to his left was stuffing his face with sweet pastry. Isaac to his right was loosely nursing a bottle of spiced rum.

'All very well,' muttered Du Lac, 'but Victory is a greedy mistress.'

'Sorry?' said Benjamin.

'We've significantly increased our manpower,' said Du Lac. 'And we have the makings of a considerable fleet. But without shipping on which to prey they simply represent mouths we can't afford to feed, vessels we can't afford to maintain. The way the Spanish reorganised their treasure fleet. One protected sailing a year. And private shipping now doing the same. We might as well be farmers. What the hell can the Brothers of the Coast do now?'

1624

'Something else,' said Benjamin.

'Something else, like what?' scoffed Du Lac.

'We've a plan,' said Isaac, no more.

The following day: or it could have been the day after. Who could honestly tell? Images arose and faded in a series of frozen tableau, tormenting Isaac's poor throbbing head.

Some sights he cherished, others, not so. Into the latter category fell Cornelius Kraft and Pastor Terbrugghen, competitively comparing gnarled amputation scars. On a lighter note, the dogs yelping at an inverted tarantula, their monkey companions teasing it with lengths of straw. And Cornelius Kraft bowling half-eaten chicken carcasses down the hill with a feral pack in hot pursuit, that was an image to treasure.

Exuberantly sporadic pistol shots propelling lead skywards was all very well, but maybe the trajectory could have been less acute. Luckily, the music from the Moroccan string orchestra was unaffected by the loss of one player. Hangbè, demonstrated the lethal utility of her newly forged hunga munga, delicately slicing lemons from trees at twenty paces. Songs spontaneously erupted, just as soon fading. Cloying nostalgia for homelands to which the singers never truly desired return. And which, wouldn't have them anyway. Silken houris materialised to pleasure both male and female, dematerialising just as mysteriously. Brankfleet, black of face and ill of balance, ignited fireworks of stupendous power, and little aesthetic value. The Rabbi demonstrated a Sephardic belly dance. Schoenmaecker, his most enthusiastic pupil, gyrated his stringy frame about the semi-clad revellers.

Abandoning the pursuit to collect his breath, the Rabbi collided with the Grevinna. She, also ensnared in the thrall of Bacchus, collapsed with him onto a handy divan, displacing its occupants. Speechless with laughter, she pointed through the throng. Beyond the arches of the Moorish colonnade, the Admiral was giving fencing lessons to three eager fellows, avoiding their blade by darting coquettishly behind elegant Moorish pillars. That he was sporting what appeared to be a ball gown went entirely without comment. Regardless their three combined ages did not equal his, he was comfortably bettering them. Between bouts of laughter, the Grevinna explained:

'There's a purse of silver for the first man can lay blade on him.'

'Looks like his money's safe,' said the Rabbi.

His three youthful opponents' shirts were blossoming tiny scarlet flowers, more by the minute.

'They don't stand a chance,' said the Grevinna. 'The legendary Camillo Agrippa was His Grace's fencing tutor. Or was that the other way round?'

Memorable though these hijinks were, what everyone would most particularly remember was the Grevinna's reaction to Benjamin.

'My Lady,' said the Rabbi, in his rasping tone, 'may I present my sons. This is Isaac, my elder and this is Benjamin...'

The Grevinna graciously extended the back of her pale hand to Isaac. Then, turning to Benjamin her mouth dropped open. And it stayed that way. She pointed to Esther's amulet showing through his open doublet.

'May I see that?' she said at last.

Benjamin unclasped it from his neck, passing it to her. She received it with slender trembling fingers.

'Where did you get this?' There was ice in her voice.

'This,' said Benjamin, suddenly uncertain. 'It's our sister's. I wear it in her memory.'

The Grevinna flipped the T-shaped object over, examining the runes inscribed along its length. 'No,' she said, 'this belongs to my daughter.'

The Rabbi stepped in: 'We are given to understand it was a gift from her mother.'

'And her name was?'

'Elisabet.'

The Grevinna stumbled back as though shot, grasping the Rabbi's sleeve for support.

'Surely, this can't be.'

The gilded stern of the Visitación sparkled irritatingly bright, high above the throbbing heads of the passengers of longboats approaching through an oily turquoise sea. A profusion of golden angels and saints bestrode galleries rising in stately tiers up the aft castle. Everyone now claimed to sufficient recovery to engage in serious discourse. The captains, liars to a man, clambered up ladders and shuffled into the welcome shade of the great cabin. The Admiral, in less androgynous attire than yesterday, sat at the head of the long mahogany table. When everyone took their seat, he looked up, focusing, it seemed, with difficulty.

'A plan has been proposed,' he said quietly, sighing.

'May I?' said Isaac. Receiving a nod of assent, he rose unsteadily to his feet. 'The Spanish treasure fleet, as we all know, is gathering in Havana. Already, there's more treasure in one place than in the whole of history. And yet more arrives each day.'

Kraft closed his eyes and took a deep breath: 'And more men-of-war to protect them.' he said, scornfully. 'In case you are thinking thems is easy pickings.' A grumble went around the cabin, some got up to leave.

The Grevinna was suddenly on her feet, darting eyes impaling the malcontents. She said nothing and yet the grumbling stopped and those afoot meekly retook their seats. She nodded to Isaac to continue.

'The captains in this cabin command seven war ships,' he said. 'Andromeda, Zeelander, African Prince, Visitación, Rachael, Unicorn, and a fast sloop. There must be half-a-dozen more crews in Tortuga would join us given an appropriate incentive.'

'We propose a three-phase strategy,' said Benjamin. 'My brother and I will infiltrate Havana and create a distraction. Hangbè's men will approach from land, swelling their numbers with slaves liberated from plantations raided on the way. And whilst the Spanish focused on suppressing a rebellion, our fleet will attack from seaward.

'That's alright for you,' said Du Lac. 'Whether the raid is a success or failure you'll be free to leave these waters, abandon us to the mercy of the Spanish. We have roots on this little island, and we'll be facing the wrath of the most powerful empire the world has ever known. This land may not be much, but it's all we have. Temptation though it is for the greedy pricks, Tortugan islanders simply have no appetite to awake the Spanish giant.'

The Admiral whispered to the Grevinna, she smiled.

'In anticipation of this objection,' she said, 'the Rabbi has proposed, what we believe, could be a mutually acceptable solution.'

'One of our high holy days — Pesach, Passover,' said the Rabbi, standing. 'We rid the house of any trace of *chametz* — leaven bread. To be thorough we sell our kitchen utensils to a member of the Goyim. This on the agreement we can buy them back for the same price at the end of Passover. On a similar basis we are prepared to offer Tortugan captains one shilling for each of their ships.'

'But how would that...'

The Admiral unrolled the tricolour of the Free Provinces. Captain Gathenhielm displayed the yellow and blue battle flag of Sweden.

'We carry letters of marque,' said the Rabbi, 'from King Gustav and Prince Mauritz. We can legitimately attack any Spanish interest; indeed it is our obligation to do so.

'Not to say pleasure,' said the Grevinna Gathenhielm.

Later that week Du Lac relayed news from spies newly returned from Havana. There was a woman matching Esther's description seized by the Inquisition. Now they knew where she was. And time was short.

1624

THIRTY-SEVEN — *once upon a midnight*

They departed late afternoon. No ceremony. They just slipped away. Hangbè had demanded to go with them. For her safety's sake the brothers had refused to countenance it. Knowing that was unlikely to be the end of the matter, they had colluded to sail without notice. But there she was, waiting on the dock, hunga munga in hand. No brooking Hangbè.

Ten miles out, Hispaniola was fading from sight. As sunset the temperature dipped, and a blizzard of stars overtook them. Leave in the last of the light, arrive in the first of the light. That was the passage plan.

Wind was strong and steady from the south. This rate they'd cross the Windward Passage in twelve to fifteen hours. Two tides, give or take. Should sight Cuba soon after dawn. Their little sloop was heeling hard, the lee rail kissing the waves. Every so often the bows would drop off a big one. They'd crash into the trough of the next sending spray hissing into the air. The sloop was for speed not sea-kindliness.

'Skinny as a toothpick,' said someone.

'Won't stand her canvas,' said another well-meaning soul.

But the brothers wanted speed. And Isaac knew speed when he saw it. Benjamin stood the first watch, huddling in his sea coat against the chill. At midnight Isaac relieved him.

'Anything I should know about?'

'No. Make your best course. If anything head north of west. Don't have a lot of faith in this compass.'

With that Benjamin slipped below.

Halfway through the watch Hangbè poked her head out of the hatch. Isaac was leaning back on the coaming, leg hanging over the tiller, head nodding. Not asleep, not awake — enough awareness to maintain direction. If he strayed off course the sails would let him know. He raised a hand and cracked a smile to reassure her he wasn't sleeping. She smiled and retreated below leaving him chasing the moon's reflection across the inky sea.

1624

By the end of his watch the sun was overbrimming the eastern horizon. Hangbè looked out again. The ship was heeling hard, and she struggled to mount the companionway. Isaac eased the mainsheet, reducing the angle. When she was secure in the cockpit he hardened the sails, and the sloop took off again. The old saws were right, she was tender — but, as Isaac had predicted, extremely fast indeed.

'Who's your friend.'

Isaac blinked himself into the moment and glanced down. He'd almost forgotten the large black bird resting in the crook of his arm.

'Exhausted, poor fella.' He smiled sleepily, cracking the salt crusting his eyebrows.

'What was he doing this far out?' said Hangbè.

'Lost, or blown off course,' He shrugged.

'Or risking everything to rescue his sister from enslavement in Cuba,' she said, with a twinkle in her eye.

'Now, wouldn't that be foolish,' said Isaac, straight faced.

With the rising of the sun the gleam was returning to the bird's eyes. It shook its head, ruffling its feathers. Hours before, it had come out of nowhere, collapsing on the deck; Isaac thought it dead. But then it struggled to right itself. Wing-weary, but alive. He lashed the tiller and rushed forward to scoop it up before the next wave swept it overboard. The poor creature was forty miles from the nearest land.

Hopping from Isaac's arms it perched on the tiller, preening its flight feathers. There it stayed absorbing the warmth of the sun until Benjamin came to stand his watch. It flew past his shoulder into the cabin and began pecking scraps of bread from the tiny galley.

Isaac followed it below falling into Benjamin's still-warm bunk. He felt the sails harden, the boat leap forward — his brother pushing hard. Soon the music of the waves and the creaking of the timbers dragged him tumbling into sleep. The clouds parted; he made out their little sloop far below. Creamy phosphorescence spilled from her stern as she ploughed a bright furrow through the inky ocean. Waking midway through Benjamin's watch, he found Hangbè's musky warmth beside him.

As he clambered on deck the bird followed. Jumping onto his shoulder it fluttered its wings and took off, coming to rest in the crosstrees. It stayed there a while, craning its neck, sniffing the air, then flew away westwards.

'What makes you think we're approaching land?' said Benjamin, grinning through a yawn. Isaac smiled back. His brother's navigation, flawless as usual. But his heart was strangely heavy for the loss of his avian companion.

Land is sensed before seen. An experienced mariner would feel it through the tiller. Wind and water behave differently. They regress from a harmonious marriage to a pair of dangerously quarrelsome children. When approaching an unknown coast, mariners needs must engage all their faculties.

The day before, Isaac and Benjamin left the fleet captains strategising. They arrived at the sticky question of how to coordinate the sea and the land raids. Timing would needs be precise or the plan would catastrophically fail.

'How the hell will we know when to attack?' said Du Lac.

'There'll be a signal,' said Benjamin.

'What signal?'

'Smoke,' said Isaac, glancing at his brother. 'We're going to set the bastard place on fire.'

If the wind continued fair they could make landfall at the outskirts of Havana in five days. The plan allowed fourteen days to muster the forces for the attack. The fleet would disembark the Africans led by Khamisi and Xaawo in five days. They would begin raiding from the interior and await the signal to fall on Havana. Meanwhile the Tortugan fleet would be round the coast, ready to bombard the defences.

They felt the surf before they heard it, heard it before they saw it. As they bore away nor' nor' west to avoid the coast, the wind went abaft of them. A drop in apparent wind and reduced heel made the sloop feel slower. But soon they were surfing on a following wave train. At first it was exciting to see the coast. Dense lush forest running inland to rocky escarpments beyond. But after three days of same, monotony began setting in. Benjamin had a scrappy chart; his passage plan rudimentary at best. Seven-hundred miles west nor' west. Not that a bearing was strictly necessary. Just follow the coast, take the occasional sounding, avoid the reefs.

Boredom came to an abrupt end. A flash of light flickered through the heat haze followed by the crackle of thunder. Something whistled through the air and the sea plumed up fifty yards ahead. A fine mist of chill saltwater drifted over them. The topmast of a man-of-war rose through the mist a mile off their starboard quarter. Hangbè burst on deck. Benjamin leapt up, letting go of the tiller.

'Don't take it personally,' said Isaac, suppressing the shock. 'They probably have us as a native fishing boat. Just giving their gunners a spot of practice.'

Another cannon ball whistled towards them, this time falling short. The shots were straddling them now.

Isaac grabbed the tiller from Benjamin and shouldered him away.

'Get on the bows. Watch the reef, give me some directions.'

He heaved the helm hard a starboard. The sloop lurched towards the surf line they'd spent the last three days avoiding. As they approached a huge sea reared up and cascaded over their stern. Hangbè slid across the deck. Isaac grabbed her arm and dragged her back.

'God's sake get below and hold on tight.'

Benjamin was clinging to the forestay, half hidden by the jib. Up close, Isaac realised the surf wasn't continuous. There were narrow swirling gaps in the foaming wall. Benjamin's left arm outstretched, pointing, he'd seen it too — a wider gap. Isaac looked behind, waiting for the next big roller to lift them. When it came, he steered hard for the break in the reef. The sails thrashed as the huge wave caught hold of them raising them up. They nearly made it across to calm water. But the coral heads caught the keel bringing them to a juddering halt with water cascading over their decks. Isaac turned; to his horror another enormous wave was rearing over them. But, instead of swamping them, it scooped them up and carried them over the reef.

They found themselves in the lee of a broken archipelago. To landward a long expanse of white sand, and dense green jungle beyond. Away from the reef the water was calmer. This stretch of inland sea was about half-a-mile wide, and deep enough for navigation. The Spanish ship prowled along outside the reef. The guns flickered again, thunder roared, and the sea plumed up ahead of them.

'They're aiming for the sails,' screamed Isaac, releasing the jib sheets. Benjamin rushed to the mast releasing the halyards. The sails came tumbling down. Another volley, more near misses. Only one thing left, they unshipped the mast.

Losing their target the cannons ceased roaring, but the warship continued to prowl.

'What if they send a shore party?' said Benjamin.

'Through that surf?'

'Can we afford to take chances?'

The brothers each manned a sweep, and Hangbè took control of the tiller. They rowed until encountering a narrow inlet. Jumping overboard they manhandled the sloop out of sight. And there they spent the rest of the day and following night. In the morning, the Spaniards were gone.

They remounted the mast using blocks rigged in the surrounding trees. By the time they'd finished it was getting on for noon. The wind was gaining strength. The first of the season's hurricanes flexing its muscles — but they needs must press on.

They made decent progress under reefed main and working jib. A series of islands linked by a reef protected them from the weather. The moon was waning, and at night they navigated by the noise of the surf and soundings. At midnight three days later the inland waterway gave out. With no option they rode the breakers into the open sea. When they'd made it through the channel, Isaac took in the last reef.

When morning broke, the winds eased enough to sail under full main. But the following night it strengthened and veered. A squall smashed into them, tearing the tiller from Benjamin's hand. The boom crashed across the cockpit and once more they were plunging into the surf as it surged towards the land. Breaking waves caught the sloop amidships, tumbling them over. With the crack of a cannon shot, the mast snapped, propelling them into the midnight sea. Isaac burst to the surface gasping, retching seawater. Benjamin clung to the remnants of the mast, blood washing down his face, his hand extended to him. Hangbè was nowhere.

One of Isaac's sea boots was missing, he kicked off it's pair and struggled out of his coat. The moon reflected off the upturned hull rolling at the mercy of the waves. The sails waved beneath the surface threatening to envelop him like a pair of sea wraiths. He caught a trailing halyard and frantically pulled himself to the sloop — still no Hangbè. On a desperate impulse he dived beneath the hull. There, in the darkness he felt her body floating in a pocket of trapped air. Dragging her out of the hull they surfaced in the churning sea. He slapped her hard across the face, she gasped and opened her eyes. A mighty breaker tumbled the sloop over them, and he plummeted into a dark and dreamless realm.

Isaac struggled to open his eyes. There was blinding white sand as far as he could see, seabirds screeched overhead. His mouth felt gritty, his lips crusted with salt, water lapped his feet. Bleached shells fringed the tide line. Some grew spiney feet and scuttled sideways towards the safety of the sea.

Isaac stared at his hands as though he struggled to associate them with the rest of his body. The skin was white and corrugated like an ill-fitting glove. His neck ached as he turned his head. Memories of the shipwreck flooded back. He screwed up his eyes the better to focus. What of his brother and Hangbè, last seen disappearing beneath the waves? He blinked and shook his head. Focus returning, he caught a glimpse of

1624

Benjamin sitting on his haunches, head in hands. Hangbè was on her feet and walking. She appeared unsteady at first but gaining in strength and purpose.

An arrow hissed into the sand between them. Out of the forest emerged a cluster of Taíno warriors. Hangbè carried on walking with as much regard for the arrows as she would mosquitoes. The wreck of their 'toothpick' was laying shattered on its side. She crawled into the remnants of the cabin, emerging with a cluster of metalic objects glinting in the sun. Orange spots of rust had bloomed overnight. She tore a strip from her linen sleeve, wiped them away and took a couple of practice swings. With an unearthly howl, she sent a hunga munga arcing through the air. It embedded in a palm trunk six inches above the heads of the Indians. They stared in awe at its complex multi-bladed form. Most considered the musket the most terrifying weapon they'd yet encountered. Many that day would revise that opinion. When they looked back, Hangbè was flexing her arm, readying another.

A burly black man in ragged European dress pushed through the Taíno ranks. He tugged the hunga munga free and sent it flying back towards Hangbè. She didn't flinch, didn't move, simply hefted another into the air. It intercepted the incoming missile knocking it uselessly to the ground. With a grunt, her long muscles rippling, she sent her remaining weapon whirling. The panic-stricken aggressor fled for the forest, throwing himself behind a fallen tree. With a hollow thunk the hunga munga embedded inches away from his head. But there was something even more concerning. Hangbè had collected the other two and was striding purposefully towards him. Each example featured a different configuration of lethally sharp disks, axe blades, scythes and daggers. Another figure of African appearance pushed through the Indians. He held up a hand and addressed Hangbè. She looked puzzled and shook her head, replying in a different language. Four more attempts and they arrived at a common tongue.

More distant flashes of light and rumbles of thunder came across the sea. Now there was not one but an armada of ships cresting the horizon. It was time to vacate the beach.

1624

THIRTY-EIGHT — *chase me*

The fleet were making way. Their mission's success relied on a timely arrival at Havana undetected. But then they heard the rumble of gunfire. And no true Brother of the Coast could resist the siren call of cannon. In others' conflict there's potential profit — and easy pickings too. Let the bastards fight it out, then snatch the prize from the weakened victor.

The sloop returned from scouting ahead.

The captain reported to the flagship. 'Spanish man-of-war lobbing cannon balls at some little fishing boat.'

'Could it be, d'y think...?' said the Admiral General.

'Couldn't tell.'

A week earlier in Tortuga, Kraft had presented the false flag strategy to the Tortugan captains. They in turn sought the opinion of their crews. As a result the fleet's number swelled by five goodly warships. And shortly after, sailmaker's apprentices found themselves pressed into stitching Swedish and Dutch ensigns.

Twelve captains gathered round a table in the great cabin of the Visitación. They'd invited their lieutenants and first mates to witness for their crews. Those who couldn't fit into the cabin spilled out onto the middle deck. There were liberal quantities of grog dispensed — the ship's company was in a festive mood.

Cornelius Kraft stood and stamped his narwal tooth leg, gavelling the room to order.

'We have a fleet!' he roared, raising a glass.

'A fleet!' the room boomed back.

'We have a mission!' Kraft bellowed.

'A mission!' returned the room in unison.

'We have a fleet, and we have a mission!' said Kraft.

'A fleet and a mission!' the room roared back.

'And yet we have no leader.' Kraft looked suddenly downcast.

'No leader,' repeated the room, reflecting this abrupt change of mood.

'What would a mission be without a leader?' shouted Kraft, slamming the flat of his hand on the table. 'A disaster, that's what.' He wiped theatrical tears from his eyes. 'Accordingly, we balloted you good captains.'

He reached into his doublet producing a wax-sealed envelope.

Turning to the Admiral: 'Your grace, would you do us the honour of announcing the name.'

The Admiral started. He had been paying scant attention to the proceedings. His gaze melting into that of his incestuous sister-in-arms Ingela Olofsdotter Gathenhielm.

'Sorry, me?' he blinked and cleared his throat. 'Well, of course.'

He stood, turning to face the room, his slim figure taller than the tallest man present. He received the envelope with the appropriate level of solemnity. Cracking the seal and opening it he screwed up his eyes, holding the content to the extent of his arms. Crips produced his master's spectacles. The Admiral examined the document again, staggering back a step. The parchment, emblazoned with half-a-dozen lines of cursive script and columns of signatures, fluttered to the table.

'No,' he muttered, 'Surely not.'

'That was the decision,' said Du Luc, firmly.

'No,' said the Admiral, 'a younger man, surely. One of your own...'

'Unanimous Your Grace.'

'I'm so very flattered,' said the Admiral, 'but...'

'What are your orders Your Grace?'

'Orders, Mister Crips?'

'Should we attack the Spanish man-of-war or pass by Your Grace.'

'It's my custom never to engage in fleet business before m' mornin' shave. Wouldn't be seemly, would it now?'

Holding up the hem of his nightshirt, he wafted back to his cabin. His mind was spinning between the covert imperatives of the mission and his yearning to do battle. In lesser men, dithering implied weakness. This wasn't weakness. So compelling were the options, it took a strong man to resist rushing to judgement. Outwardly he was oblivious to the dilemma, whilst Crips shaved him, and Sheng primped his hair. Internally he was struggling like Samson between the pillars of Dagon, flexing his herculean intellect.

Without warning he was on his feet, face half-covered in lather, Crips' razor nicking his cheek, shaving bowl flying across the cabin.

'Mister Crips, summon m' first mate if ye will.'

When Schoenmaecker arrived the Admiral was relaxing in his chair and Mr Crips was powdering his cheeks.

'Message to the Bear Cub and Titan,' said the Admiral General. 'Make all speed to the Bay of Cadiz. That Spaniard slips past us, they'll know what to do. Now beat to quarters. Off you go now. Quickly, there's a good man.'

Crips held the mirror as the Admiral inspected his appearance.

'Touch more rouge perhaps, d'y think Mister Crips?'

Switching attention to the keeper of his wardrobe, he said: 'Now Mister Sheng, prepare my armour if ye will.'

The Admiral scooped out the last of the yolk from his soft-boiled egg. Crips, having already removed the top from the second, deftly swapped it for the empty shell. Then he left the cabin to replenish the hot buttered toast. Sheng, ever the opportunist, dabbed his master's mouth with an immaculate linen napkin. The Admiral didn't appear to notice.

Shaved, bravely bearing Crips' newly inflicted duelling scar, he was sitting across a gleaming mahogany table from his second in command. Cornelius Kraft licked his lips, happily anticipating the stick-to-your-ribs stew congealing in the mess. Between mouthfuls of soft-boiled egg, the Admiral sipped straw-coloured Hock from green Venetian glass.

'Bear Cub and Titan — they got off, did they?'

'First light, Your Grace.'

'Then we've twelve vessels at our disposal.'

'If you count the sloop, Your Grace.'

'Well, let's not. So that leaves us eleven mid-sized fighting ships.'

'But nothing that matches the firepower of the Spaniard,' said Kraft.

'Ordinarily I'd give the bastard a wide berth Mister Kraft. But we daren't leave such a powerful vessel at our backs.'

'So, we attack in formation, overwhelm them.'

'Ah, yes, but how much damage would we sustain? No, can't risk it.'

'Then...?'

'Choose one ship, that's all I'll put in jeopardy. The rest will hold back. When the Spanish have worn themselves out blowing that ship to matchwood, then the rest will swoop in.'

'A forlorn hope then,' said Kraft, 'Du Lac and I will take the Unicorn, and —

'Oh no, you won't be going. Just du Luc.'

'Sorry?'

'You're the sub-commander of the fleet. Can't be risking you.'

'But Du Luc and me, we've signed articles, we always go into action together, we're bonded to it.'

'On this occasion sir, you won't. You're a commander now. You must learn to treat your officers with as little compassion as you would a chess piece — no matter what your relationship. One ship blasted to pieces, so what. We'll finish the Spaniard when he's finished with them. Victory at least cost is all that matters.'

Kraft was aghast. Where is the kindly old eccentric he'd so recently dragooned into office?

'Now get some breakfast,' said the Admiral. He took a long draught of his Hock, swilling it round his mouth, rinsing his teeth before swallowing. Kraft stormed to the door. The Admiral shouted after him, 'So select another captain for the forlorn hope and send them to me.'

An hour later Captain Ingela Olofsdotter Gathenhielm reported to the Admiral's stateroom.

'Mister Kraft said you wished to see me my love.'

'Did he? Must have been a misunderstanding. But always a pleasure. Have you had breakfast?'

'How dare you sir?'

'How dare I what, Your Grace?' said Cornelius Kraft.

'You know how dare you what, sir.'

'Forgive me Your Grace, I fail to see what —?'

The Admiral rose to his feet, glaring down on a man half his height and twice his breadth. There came a knock at the cabin door, raised voices from without. It went unanswered as the two men smouldered: eyes locked.

'Hanged men for less,' hissed the Admiral through clenched teeth.

'Hang me, you'd better cut two lengths of rope. My men'll see you swing shortly after.'

'Don't be so bloody sure.'

The door burst open sending Crips sprawling on the Admiral's best Persian carpet. The Rabbi filled the doorframe.

'I've an idea,' he said, taking in the frozen tableau. 'Sorry, am I interrupting something?'

When the Rabbi left the great cabin, the long mahogany table was strewn with charts and the protagonists were alone once more.

'I'm not a man to hold a grudge, Mister Kraft.'

'Such is your reputation, Your Grace.'

'And you...?'

They were located approximately hundred-and-fifty miles east of

Havana. They had the Spanish man-of-war trapped in what amounted to a twenty-mile-deep inland sea, sheltered from the Straits of Florida by a series of low-lying islands. In mitigation the wind had been a favourably steady south-westerly for the last three days. And the Spanish were in what they regarded as home waters. Still no excuse to find themselves so constrained to manoeuvre. None of this however, formed any part of the Rabbi's strategy.

Dense black smoke from the cannons drifted across their vision, high on the poop deck. The Spanish captain and his lieutenant scanned the beach. They could just make out the wreckage of the little sloop.

'That's no dug out, no fishing boat.'

'Smugglers, you think, or spies?'

Then came distant cannon fire from the north.

'What the —?'

They span round. Breasting the horizon was a merchant ship — Dutch at a guess. Behind it, chasing it, a two-deck galleon — a Burgundian cross flying from the mizzen. More cannon fire, bow chasers blazing, seas billowing up around the fleeing merchantman. The Spanish crew rushed to the rail, cheering the galleon on like spectators around a bear pit.

'Gunners,' yelled the lieutenant, 'to your stations.'

'Fire as she bears,' said the captain, 'just slow her down, cut away her masts. Mind you don't hit our ship.'

The Rachael was close-hauled on a larboard tack. She was heeling hard as the Rabbi drove her as close to the wind as he could. The Spaniard was between them and the shore. He could see their guns rolling out. Behind him came the Admiral's Visitación cannons roaring. Sea spraying up all around them, far too close for comfort. Then the Spanish opened fire. Chain shot whirled overhead, severing the Rachael's rigging, ripping sails, smashing masts. Debris clattered to the decks all around the Rabbi. A block swung across and cracked his head, but he was on his feet in seconds, bellowing orders.

'Larboard your helm. Lively now. Hard over.'

What remained of the Rachael bore away, dragging shattered spars and trailing sails. showing the Spaniard their battered stern, propelled now by the strong following wind. The Visitación made as if to chase her, cheered on by the Spanish gathered around their smoking spent guns. As she breasted the Spanish ship Visitación ran up her true colours. Then she let rip a rolling broadside from all three gundecks pounding deep

1624

into the bowels of the enemy.

Oak splinters like javelins, like arrows, like darts shot in every direction, impaling all in their paths. Fires broke out. Powder exploded. Oil ignited and flames flashed across the gundecks. Burning men threw themselves over the side to quench in the sea. The Visitación's demi-falcons raked the poop deck with grape shot exploding officers into red mist. Volleys of musket fire sent sailors tumbling from the rigging crashing to their deaths on deck or in sea.

Birds erupting from the forest circled overhead. By the time the echo of the cannons had returned from the surrounding hills it was all over. The Visitación glided serenely away through the billowing clouds of grey smoke. The pirate crew stood at the rail in silent awe of the enormous destruction they had so recently wrought. For a while all was quiet. Then the screams of the wounded and dying, began rending the air.

Aboard the crippled Rachael the Rabbi forced the helm hard over. More by momentum than by wind through shot-blasted rigging, she gracefully completed a full circle. They arrived back at the stricken Spaniard. The Rabbi was on the rail at the head of a mixed European and Moorish boarding party, poised to leap aboard. The ships collided with a dull thud and the shriek of tortured timbers. Grapnels locked the two vessels together. The Rachael's men screamed bloodthirsty war cries, as they swarmed up and onto the Spanish blood-slick decks. The Rabbi hesitated amidst the carnage, believing victory complete. Then Spanish marines came pouring from below decks, easily outnumbering the boarders. The result could have gone either way.

The Rachael's crew was being severely pressed. A dull thump reverberated through the ship. The Visitación had docked on the far side of the Rachael. Her crew swarmed across her decks to join the fight. Cornelius Kraft located the Rabbi, who was wielding a sword in one hand, axe in the other, back-to-back with the Pastor. There they stood amidst the fallen bodies of their enemies — Philistines smitten hip and thigh.

Kraft yelled to them. Only by swift reflexes did he avoid running through by a man of God in the thrall of blood lust.

'It's over Rabbi, we've won.'

Through the fire and smoke of battle, the sun glinted on a tall figure in black gold-chased armour. The Admiral bestrode the deck like a willowy colossus, engaging the enemy with a mischievous grin. Do as I say, not do as I do.

The action successfully concluded, the question of prisoners arose.

1624

'What's to be done with them?' said Kraft, 'sink the ship, yes. But release the prisoners, never. They could walk to Havana in a week.'

The Admiral sighed. 'Can't have that can we — give the order.'

'I won't be a party to such butchery,' said the Rabbi, blocking Kraft's passage to the doorway, 'not when there's no need for it.'

'What the hell do you suggest then?' said Kraft, 'Let them go?'

'Yes, but first.'

'What?'

'The soles of their feet.'

'Sorry?'

'Brand them.'

1624

THIRTY-NINE — *hidden redoubt*

The surf exploded; they froze. Round shot hurtled towards them. It bounced through their ranks, hissed across the beach and cut a swathe through the trees. A man caught in its path disintegrated above the waist. A pair of naked legs topped by half a torso tottered backwards a couple of paces, fountaining blood, collapsing with a thud to the ground.

Trance broken, Isaac span round. Benjamin and Hangbè were still standing. Way out to sea there was the Spanish man-of-war. Cannon smoke drifted from horizon to horizon, peppered with muzzle flashes. Someone fired a musket back in a futile gesture of defiance. Isaac glanced at Hangbè, then joined the frantic stampede for the cover of the trees. Once away from the beach the runners coalesced into a more coherent group. Another ball crashed a destructive path through the undergrowth. But its energy depleted before it reached them. They slowed to a trot, listening to the muffled reports of naval ordinance far out to sea. Falling into a breathless, panting walk, Benjamin turned to Isaac. He gave him a look, like: what was all that about? Surely Havana can't know who we are? All that went unvoiced, acknowledged only by a raised eyebrow. They came to an isolated clearing. The sun was breaking through the tree canopy, dappling the forest floor.

Ahead were half-a-dozen dugout canoes. But for that, the river snaking green before might be an overgrown jungle path. The party waded into the river and piled aboard the boats, their muskets above their heads. There was no discussion, no comment, no invitation, or other accommodation. Isaac, Benjamin and Hangbè had merged into the group as though shuffled into a deck of cards. Looking around Isaac noted one reason they'd integrated so easily. Native Taíno, tattooed and lithe. Muscular Africans. Escaped slaves of every race and nationality. Barely a word exchanged, save the most cursory of commands. This had all the signs of an experienced war band.

Benjamin turned to Isaac and Hangbè: 'How could they have known about us?'

'Don't flatter yourself you're their target,' said the leader. 'The Spanish will do anything to wipe us out, and those like us, return us to the workforce. Make examples of us so others don't try to follow our example. We'd been tracking the ship. Thinking they were going to send in a landing party. They'd raided some way down the coast. Snatched a score of our men.'

Cannon fire continued to rumble. Isaac and the leader shook their heads — silent acknowledgement that neither version explained events.

A white woman, naked to the waist, her back scarred by repeated flogging, sat in the prow like a figurehead. Next to her was a rotting pig carcass. Hangbè gave the leader a look, cocking her head like a spaniel hearing a woodcock.

'Cocodrilo,' was all he said, as though that one word represented the complete answer. Silent gesture, and abbreviated dog-Spanish, seemed to be their lingua Franca.

The boats pushed off from the shore one-by-one cutting the water with spear shaped paddles. The emerald surface of the river parted before them, swirling in their wake. Fecund decay clung in air, so humid the foliage appeared to sweat. They followed the river deep inland like following the twisting and turning tracks of an anaconda. Ahead the river broadened and split into a myriad of tributaries. Light made more frequent breaches of the canopy as the forest thinned. The leader whispered something and thumped his paddle against the side of the boat. The woman in the prow began chanting.

'Come to me my children, come to me.'

Dragon eyes broke the green slime surface. With a sub-audible rumble rippling the water, a long ridged back rubbed along the length of the dugout, rocking it to one side. Hangbè's eyes showed white in her darkly shadowed face, her knuckles gripped the side of the canoe. This was all too familiar to her. The woman in the prow reached into a bucket and tossed a hunk of rancid meat overboard. The river foamed white as the monsters fought over the tidbit.

'Our guard dogs,' said the leader, with a grim smile.

Beyond the forest were patches of cultivated ground. They hauled the canoes onto the riverbank and sent a boy ahead to announce their arrival.

'Follow us exactly, do not stray from the path, even by an inch.'

Isaac looked quizzical.

'Pit falls, poisoned stakes,' said the leader. 'If the Spanish slave catchers attack in force, all this will simply slow them down. But that could be all we'd need to get away. We're no match in open battle — just need time to flee and set up somewhere else. We've only been here for a year, following the last raid. Just established themselves again, starting to cultivate the land once more. Our numbers are swelling with escapees. Africans from the plantations. Taíno from the mines. French prisoners of war. English maroons. So many mouths to feed, but how could we refuse them. We call them *palenques* — these hidden redoubts. Most are out east, anything from a dozen to a couple of hundred strong, we're about the furthest west.'

Isaac, Benjamin and the leader of the rebels were sitting in the shade of a palm thatched hut. They were drinking coconut water and rum. Isaac had heard the leader referred to as El Río. He didn't know whether that was a name or an honorific. There had been no introductions. He thought it was time. Hangbè was off somewhere. Isaac didn't know how much she had told the leader about their status. He made a formal introduction in Spanish:

'Isaac Amsalem. This is my brother Benjamin. We are of the tribe of Judah, displaced from its homeland and sold into bondage two thousand years ago. And recently again displaced. This time by the Spanish who we war against, with our Northern European allies. We are exploring new worlds in which the tribe could settle. We are also seeking to liberate our kidnapped sister.'

That would do, keep it simple — the enemy of my enemy.

'And may we enquire as to your name?' said Benjamin.

The leader let out a long sigh. The cane chair creaked as he eased his long limbs into a more comfortable position. He gave them a soft, ironic glance.

'There are a few of your people in Havana, I understand. Or their forebears. You must understand I was young when taken.' He spoke with the occasional stutter, which did nothing to lessen the impact of his words. 'My given name lost to me when slavers raided our village, slaughtering the parents who were trying to protect me. I w-w- was known by a slave name. Something Spanish. I do not care to refer to that again; that part of me is dead. Since my escape I refuse to ever repeat it. For a long-time people looked at me strangely and referred to me behind my back as the nameless one — which I didn't mind so much. But as I rose in prominence here, they began to refer to me as *Jefe* which offended me. No, offend is the wrong word, upset is better. If you've been enslaved you should never call someone boss again. No one has the right to be someone else's master, slave or not. But I learned some people take comfort in such things. They enjoy my command because they were born with a weak will. That, or the strength of will stolen from them, or beaten out of them.

'But names are important. How can something b-b-be, without a name? I felt obliged to choose one for myself. But where to start? Enslaved young. Used by many men for all manner of terrible things. But when I contracted smallpox I lost my attraction to men. I grew ugly in their eyes. Who else can say they are grateful to disease. Recovering. Put to work with the grown men. They called me Pox Face. You must be strong in this world. Strong or cunning. If the gods bless you with either, you must protect the weak. I wasn't strong to begin with, but I grew in strength. I wasn't cunning to begin with, but I grew in cunning.

'My despised owners called me one thing, and my fellow slaves called me something else. In my head I was neither. One day I came across an overseer beating a woman in a cane field. Maybe because she refused to lay with him. Or she lay with him and didn't please him, or because he didn't please her, or just because he liked beating women. I didn't have any particular affection for the woman. Nor did I dislike her for that matter. And if I did either of those things I don't think it would have made any difference one way or the other. I was having a bad day. On another day I might have walked on by, like I had on many s-s-shameful occasions before. But something made my blood rise. And I killed him. Stabbing him in the eyes with a sharpened sugar cane. The most painful way my fertile imagination could devise.

'The woman and I escaped together into the forest hunted by dogs. The crocodiles took the dogs, and a couple of the slave catchers got badly mauled. But we swam through them without being troubled. You met the woman. She was feeding our guard dogs. Remember her. Not much to look at, but then look at me. So here we live. There are greaters and lessers in our number, that's inevitable. They look to me to lead them. But all our w-w-wealth is communal. And should they want another leader, that would be fine by me, long as he is a strong man with a good heart. Someday we should all live in harmony like this.

'The only name I remembered was that of a river near where they snatched me. A great wide brown swollen r-r-river. Couldn't remember my own name. But I could remember the name of that river — the Kaduna. So that is what I chose to be known by, all I could remember of the land of my ancestors. I call myself Kaduna. But my people, call me El Río.'

'Our tribe should know you as Moses,' said Benjamin.

'We didn't expect to meet you,' said Isaac. 'We expect nothing from you. Nor have we the right to do so. But fate put our salvation in your hands, and maybe yours in ours.'

1624

Isaac looked to Benjamin, who nodded reassurance. Then Isaac outlined the plan to sack Havana. He told of the fleet, of the army of freed African slaves, of the signal which would trigger the attack. That there were six days before they needed to be in Havana. Six days to save their sister. And he made them an offer. Join the attack and each man woman and child of the palenques would get passage to Tortuga and freedom from Spanish despotism.

FORTY — *gently my love*

They heard it before it came into view. Turning a corner in the warren of dark passages, there it was, lights leaking into the dark overhung streets. Music — notes from a guitar or mandolin skipping over the croaking drone of a dulzaina. And singing. Singing like every voice was following the same tune, but with widely divergent lyrics and languages. Weaving through the music came raucous waves of drunken voices. Shouting, squabbling, boasting, singing, melding into one ear-jarring cacophony. And through it all, the clatter of crockery and the sizzle of cooking. Universal drinking commotion at its most extreme.

And then there was the smell. So pungent it competed with the miasma wafting up from the gutters — intensifying with every pace of their approach. Rancid wine and cheap tobacco overlaid the crematoria stench of broiling meat. Closer still they could discern the reek of stale bodies and cheap scent. Sailors were sailors, and soldiers were soldiers, and whores were whores, and there seemed to be an abundance of all. They spilled into the street to piss, or vomit, or purchase or sell a few minutes passion with creatures that dealt in that most debased of commodities.

Benjamin was first at the entrance. Isaac held him back, poking his head through the open door. Riding on a wave of nostalgia came optimism, quite unexpected. He found himself slapping his brother on the back for no reason. Benjamin turned and smiled uncertainly. Isaac just shrugged and pressed on through the entrance. One customer, who'd had the good manners to empty his bladder outside, ambled past distractedly organising his breeches. He tripped on the foot-worn doorstep, barging into Isaac's back, sending him staggering into the tangled mass of drunks he'd been intending to avoid. Isaac mouthed apologies, shaking his head as though to clear his thinking, he grinned at the irony of his situation. Despite the proximity of the enemy, he felt a warm sensation stirring deep inside. He liked taverns. But for the difference in language and temperature this could be Amsterdam. This could be home. It could pass for The Monkey House or The Magpie. Taverns were taverns — especially so when the fleet was in town. And a fleet with such a rich cargo had never previously taken to the seas. Gold and silver to support the bankrupt Bourbon monarchy. Money to fund the Catholic wars against the Protestants. He eased himself round in the press of bodies. Craning his neck, he glanced over the heads of the drinkers for a reassuring glimpse of Benjamin. There was his brother by the door, suffering the persistent attentions of a pair of professional ladies. They had agreed there was no advantage in both risking discovery. Isaac squeezed towards the serving area, suffering elbows and coarse drunken threats.

He caught the arm of a young woman staggering through the crowd laden with armfuls of empty jugs.

'The landlord,' he hissed. 'Senior Mendez, where is he.'

'Out back my love, but he'll be busy.'

'Tell him,' he dropped his voice. 'Tell him I've come from *The River*, from *El Rio.*'

Biting her lip, her eyes flitted around nervously. After a brief hesitation she retreated through a bead curtain. There was a piercing scream and the smashing of crockery. A man protesting, bloodcurdling threats, a woman's high-pitched squeal. Voices screaming over each other. Isaac turned away from the crowd. Customers were beginning to take notice. This certainly wasn't the clandestine contact Isaac was expecting to achieve. Taking a deep breath, he dived through the curtain.

The man Isaac took to be Mendez had a fat girl pinned against the wall. The object of his affections was nails deep in his buttocks with one hand, holding her skirts up with the other. As Mendez disengaged there was a slurping, sucking sound like a bilge pump at the top of its cycle. Tucking his manhood into his breeches he turned to Isaac. The woman retained her pose, skirt up above her waist. She winked at Isaac lasciviously, making no effort to regain her modesty. The pot girl fled back to the bar in tears. Mendez stuffed some coins in the fat girl's hand and shoved her out of the room.

'Daughters,' he said, 'All like to think their father's are pure as priests.' He wiped his hand on his apron and held it out. 'The River you say...?'

'Sorry,' Isaac, avoided the proffered hand, looking confused, '...and which one's your daughter?'

Regardless the promise of salvation offered to the Hebrew community of Havana, Isaac and Benjamin weren't to meet the Brotherhood of Secret

Jews face-to-face. Mendez, the libidinous innkeeper, maintained oblique contact — hosting shrouded meetings in the back room of his inn.

'The arrival of the Inquisition,' said Mendez, 'changed everything.'

It seemed that Cuba's delicate framework of pragmatic relationships could no longer be relied on. The twin worms of fear and avarice were nibbling at the Jewish community. Friends were scheming against friends. Merchants were laying plans to eliminate rivals, whilst structuring defences to protect themselves from predation. Dormant enemies were sharpening their stilettos. Only the arrogant and addled-headed believed their position to be beyond contestation. Greed and fear walked the streets of Havana smiling at their neighbours, inwardly plotting their demise. Everyone was, or thought themselves to be, under hostile scrutiny.

'Call him Jesús,' said Mendez, 'that's not his name. I have given him half the agreed fee. He's a rich man now. Soon he'll be even richer, I'm giving him the tavern.

'What are *you* going to do?' said Isaac.

'Of course, you haven't been told,' said Mendez, 'we'll also be leaving with the flotilla.'

'This "Jesús," what about him?'

'He's a soldier. Unfettered access to the castle. Be able to get you in. Course, how you get there and make your escape is down to you.'

'How far can we trust him? What if he sells us out?' said Benjamin.

'Unlikely. We have his family. And, anyway, he's one of us. If Jesús lets you down, believe me, crucifixion will be the least of his worries.'

'He's free access to Moro Castle. That's where they're keeping the women.'

'Women?' said Isaac.

'Yes, women. Seems your Esther's got herself a playmate.'

Isaac bit his lip and walked away.

'And I suppose they're inseparable?' said Benjamin.

'That being the nature of chains. As for the other, no idea.' said Mendez, waiting for Isaac to return from pacing a circuit of the room. 'So you remember the deal, right? Every property marked with a white cross is to be unmolested.'

'Yes,' said Isaac, 'we'll get that message back. But you must understand, this is not a full-scale invasion. All we seek is to create confusion, so that our comrades can clip a sliver from Philip's coin, and we can save our sister.'

1624

Hangbè was squatting on the veranda of a plantation owner's mansion. The man himself was noisily suffering the unwelcome attentions of his former slaves. 'So why don't we march on Havana?' said Zedawo. 'Our men are thirsting for blood?'

'Numbers,' said Hangbè, 'numbers and timing.'

'But we have enough men now,' protested Zedawo.

Indeed, blazing through the countryside liberating slaves they had accumulated ten times their original number. They may equal, even exceed those garrisoned at Havana.

Hangbè sighed. She'd been a soldier since childhood and risen to command the left flank of the king's army. She knew even for a surprise attack on defended positions you needed overwhelming numbers, maybe ten times more than they currently had. She was under no illusions, they were merely a distraction, not an invading force. Superior Spanish professionalism and weaponry would soon push them back, surprise or no. Her men would eventually suffer defeat and slaughter. This offended her professionalism. She had yet to lose a battle. It was the fleet were going to do the real damage. Nip in and plunder a ship or two, like a wolf whilst the shepherd's looking the other way. Unless. Unless they switch roles and become the defenders.

'Zedawo, gather the officers...'

The last plantation they had raided was twenty miles east of Havana. And they were yet undetected. A runner had arrived from Isaac, something about protected houses. But she had decided to alter the plan. She wasn't going to Havana; Havana would be coming to her. If they could tempt the Spanish to attack their fortified position the numerical advantage switched to her. If they were sufficiently well entrenched it would take all the Havana garrison to defeat them. Their only weakness would be rations — how long they could hold out given their limited food supplies. Fortification and foraging were now the biggest priorities. She'd dispatch a raiding party to Havana. Instruct them to act out a rampaging rag-tag of escaped slaves. Draw the Spanish from their fortifications — a few at first, murder them as they came. Soon they would send more, and they would bring cannon. Which they would capture and turn on the enemy. When she decided she'd sufficiently depleted the garrison, then Isaac could signal the fleet. But first she needed to contact the brothers to let them know of her altered plans.

Isaac was asleep in a storeroom behind the Tavern. He woke with a start. A slender-fingered hand clamped over his mouth. Hangbè's voice:

'Wake gently, my love.

1624

FORTY-ONE — *grey faces*

The night was molasses black. The stars close enough to reach out and grab your share. Taverns were doing good business. Noisy patrons and bright lamplight were bursting into the street like comet tails. As one, the revellers turned and squinted into the night. Hooves were pounding the road. Crashing towards them came four hellish steeds, blazing fire, a single ghostly rider at their head, smouldering clothes trailing smoke. Past wide-eyed drinkers, they galloped down to the harbour. Leaping from the edge they disappeared into the midnight sea. Airborne embers were all that marked their passing. Then came a ground-trembling explosion deep in the city and a ball of orange fire mushroomed into the sky, turning *noche* into *día*.

They observed the distillery for two days, checking comings and goings, noting routines. This was to be their lighthouse, their signal to the fleet — attack now. One watchman on the front, two at the back, a couple on nightshift tending the steaming stills. The stables were unguarded. The yard gate not locked. But the stable doors wouldn't open. Benjamin climbed on one of the parked drays, then clambered up a rope hanging from the hoist. Once through the loading hatch and he was in the hayloft. It had been his idea, and the plan was simple. Torch the place. Thousands of gallons of high proof alcohol. They'd see the blaze from the moon.

Arms outstretched, he felt his way across bales of hay to the ladder and down to the floor of the stables. The warm comforting equine musk felt at odds with his mission. Mules whinnied at his passing, shuffling in their stalls. Isaac had mapped the layout a couple of days before, posing as a buyer for one of the merchants. With only moonlight to guide him Benjamin felt his way through the straw. He caught the feint outline of a door leaking pale yellow light. Ear pressed to the wood: slow syrupy bubbling, the occasional wheeze of steam, nothing more. He ventured a peek. Only shadows cast by embers warming huge cauldrons. The sickly sweetness of fermenting sugar filled his nostrils. Someone should be tending these vessels day and night. He picked up voices coming from a side room. Jovial good-natured banter — the glow of oil lamps. The delinquent workers, playing cards. One of the watchmen put down his cards and shone a lamp outside. Benjamin crouched perfectly still, and the player returned to the game — *probablemente ratas.*

Sneaking through the shadows he arrived at the gleaming copper stills, hissing irritably down curlicued condensing tubes. His feet hit a hollow spot and he knew he had come upon the trap door to the cellar. Sliding aside the bolt, he found the ladder leading down to a cool space the size of which he could only guess. The atmosphere was heady with alcohol. Striking flint on steel, each spark illuminated endless rows of barrels. Blowing an ember to flame he ignited a rum-soaked rag. Then he opened a barrel tap and the stream of high proof liquid burst into blue flame. As he scrambled for the exit a curtain of fire rose behind him. Retreating through the stables he heard the panicked screams of the night staff. A hurricane blast of heat burst through the door. A guard tumbled out wreathed in flame and rolled in the straw. The stables erupted into an inferno.

Then over the stalls he glimpsed those terrified grey faces, the soft velvet of their muzzles, the whites of long-lashed, heart-melting eyes, and he knew he couldn't leave them to a such a fate.

FORTY-TWO — *Blacktail Spit*

They'd anchored as close to Havana as they dared. The blistering sun and the prospect of a battle was making crews edgy. The Zeelander's masts were the highest in the fleet, lookouts raced aloft. The Admiral couldn't risk their presence discovered — any vessel within sight they'd sink or capture. Victims of this policy so far were four fishing boats. The fleet's sloop overtook and herded them back.

The Admiral may be ruthless, but not cruel. The little boats jostled the stern like goslings behind their mother. Once over their fear the fishermen settled down to make the most of the experience. Thus far they'd spent their short captivity sheltered under an awning on the lower deck. This inconvenience sweetened by the promise of a gold piece. And in the meantime they received decent rations, and as much rum as they could swill. Some were lolling in the shade staring drunkenly into space. Some spent their time more productively, mending nets. A few even joined a ship's work party. At that moment they were swabbing decks, keeping the planks from splitting. Working in a row abreast they mopped in metronomic unison.

'Give us a tune Mister Shoenmaeker,' yelled a crew member.

'D'you know Blacktail Spit?' chimed another, with an English accent.

'Know it,' said Shoenmaeker, 'it almost fuckin' killed me.' He took a seat on the rail, clearing his throat. A gravelly bass baritone rumbled up from a herring cask chest.

Wind over tide on Blacktail Spit
No one knows what to do about it
Sit on your arse and get battered to shit
Wind over tide on Blacktail Spit

'Come on boys, I'll have you joining in the chorus, if you please.'

Wanna get home to my dog and my wife

1624

But the sea's trying to suck out my life
Lord alone knows the reason for it
Wind over tide on Blacktail Spit

Can't feel my fingers, can't feel my toes
Last time I looked I'd still got my nose
Can't see through the spume, not even a bit
Wind over tide on Blacktail Spit

Just keep heading towards the east
You'll be sure to beat this beast
Hold tight to the tiller and never you quit
Wind over tide on Blacktail Spit

Wind over tide on Blacktail Spit
No one knows what to do about it
Sit on your arse and get battered to shit
Wind over tide on Blacktail Spit

The Rabbi swigged from a dusty brown bottle. Sucking over-proof rum through his front teeth, he drew alcohol vapour deep into his lungs, relishing the sweet burn. He slid the bottle back, scouring a groove in the surface of the fine Honduras mahogany.

'So, thirteenth day,' he said, sprawling boneless in his chair, 'and still nothing's sodding happened.'

'We agreed fourteen,' said the Pastor, taking a long swallow, leaning forward, elbows on the table, tonguing the fiery liquid around his gums. 'You must have faith in your boys.'

The Rabbi shook his head with a violence that suggested the banishment of dark thoughts. He squinted through the twilight at the forested shoreline a quarter of a mile distant. He turned back to the Pastor, refocusing his attention on matters nagging at him.

'Can't anchor this close to Cuba much longer, Spanish will see us eventually — they'll send out a couple of men-of-war, then we're well and truly done for. Look at us, trapped against this heathen shore.'

'We can't be seen from Havana,' said the Pastor, 'and the Admiral's sent longboats ashore, this area's deserted — nothing but mangroves and crocodiles.'

'For now, Erasmus,' said the Rabbi, leaning forward and snatching the bottle back, 'deserted for now — for fucking now.'

The offshore breeze passed through the window ruffling the Rabbi's luxuriant beard. The Pastor made a move to retain the bottle, forgetting he was sans one hand.

'It's early tonight,' he said, yawning and wrinkling his nose. Soothed by this welcome respite from the relentless heat his eyelids drooped despite his agitation. He brought the bottle to his lips and took another long draught. Have faith in his boys, have faith in the Lord. For a while he drifted between worlds. Eyelids fluttering, he woke to the bottle eased from his grip. Doing nothing about it.

A calloused, tattooed hand shook his shoulder. He blinked. His eyes flashed open. The brawl-flattened face of the bosun, lips moving, voice lost in the rata-tat-tat of drums beating to quarters.

'Quarters? Quarters! What, who?'

'Mister Terbrugghen, sir,' yelled the Boatswain. 'Says would you care to join him on the quarter deck, if you feel so minded.'

The Rabbi jerked himself to his feet, clambering up the companionway four tenths sober. 'What the hell, Erasmus!'

The Pastor smiled smugly and passed him a spyglass. Two hours ago they'd enjoyed a spectacular sunset. And now there was another. If anything, even more impressively bright. As they watched, the orange loom on the horizon birthed a ball of fire, slowly rising to the heavens.

'What did your boys say they were going to do?' said the Pastor.

'Exactly this,' said the Rabbi.

His shoulders rose high with an inbreath then collapsed, with a long audible sigh. Beaming pride he slapped the Pastor on the back. The offshore breeze was strengthening, reliable as ever. The ship had come alive. Barefooted topmen were swarming the rigging, canvas was cracking in the freshening wind as gaskets released. The boatswain bellowed orders; the drummer maintained his urgent rhythm.

'Belay that bastard racket,' yelled the Pastor, holding his head.

Across the fleet the other ships were likewise engaged. The capstan creaked as a dozen men leaned to the task of hauling two-hundred yards of saturated hemp cable, thick as a man's forearm. The anchor broke free, the braces hauled in, the Rachael began to make way. Eager to escape the shallows like a greyhound released from a leash. The fishing boats cast off with their golden gratuity. Two of the younger Spanish fishermen petitioned to join the Rachael's crew, eschewed their golden dollar, signed articles, and found themselves under the boatswain's tutelage.

Aboard the Zeelander Elijah Brankfleet mustered his African gunners who fell to readying three decks of cannon.

1624

FORTY-THREE — *sugar sweet*

The sky graduated from a soft cornflower at the horizon to a deep ultramarine overhead. Small clouds swept by, trailing feint whisps of vapour. Their dispersal as regular as pattern stamped on fabric. Even at this early hour there was sun blazing through. Cloud shadows raced across a low landscape, running over distant mountains resembling misshapen dumplings.

They avoided the red dirt trackway. Instead, they picked their way through the stunted trees that ranged along its edge. Every so often they glimpsed soldiers through the branches. The defeated troops straggling back to Havana in twos or threes, blooded and bandaged — a piteous sight. Isaac glanced at Hangbè, catching a hint of a smile. Pity was not the first emotion which came to mind.

The latest detachment from Havana marched in the opposite direction. Isaac and Hangbè crept closer to the road to gauge their strength. As they passed each other the wounded soldiers begged for water. The incoming troops didn't break formation. A couple of soldiers tossed the wounded their personal canteens. Officers screamed abuse at these acts of compassion.

The Spanish were now taking the insurrection seriously. Lash-goaded oxen were straining to pull massive pieces of field artillery. Mules laden with muskets and supplies were trudging nose-to-tail. There must have been three full companies of troops armed with swords and polearms. They marched in heavy buff jackets and crested helmets in sweltering unison. Their captain in a fine suit of half-armour rode a white stallion at their head, and three dozen prancing lancers followed behind. The artillery was slowing the formation. They were making steady if laborious progress.

It was around ten miles to the plantation. Once the troops had passed, Isaac and Hangbè broke out of the forest and took to the open farmland. They arrived at the boundary of the estate in a couple of hours. The dirt beneath their feet had turned from red to yellow. Approaching cautiously up the driveway they discovered it strewn with Spanish bodies. Hangbè ululated a greeting signal. The two Zulus rustled out of the forest of tinder-dry cane, saluting Hangbè as a returning general. The unattended windmill continued to turn the grinding stones. The overboiled molasses cauldrons tanged the air bittersweet. Musket rounds peppered the stucco walls of the owner's mansion. Women attended to injured defenders.

'How many?' said Hangbè.

'Ten dead, fifteen wounded, nine of which are able to continue.'

'And Spanish?'

'Sixty dead. Didn't count the wounded. There's still a few lying around.' A distant scream of agony and there was one less. 'We did as you said. Fired our muskets from the house. They sneaked up thinking they'd trapped us. But we weren't there. Just a few men bravely offering themselves as targets. They fired a volley. Whilst they were reloading we came out of the cane fields. Attacked on both flanks.'

'You've resisted what, two waves?' said Hangbè, 'and the strategy worked each time.'

Isaac interrupted: 'Well now's the time to retreat. In about two hours you'll be facing four hundred of the Governor's own troops. We won't fool them again.'

'Or...' said Hangbè.

The Spanish detachment finally arrived. Their captain ordered skirmishers ahead to reconnoitre. Their comrades' decapitated heads lined the road. Each impaled on a swaying stalk of sugarcane. *Out of the strong came forth sweetness.* A corporal reported the area deserted. A few dead blacks was all. The main body of troops marched through the avenue of flyblown heads. They halted in front of the eerily quiet mansion. A detachment scoured the vicinity whilst the main battlegroup stood easy in formation.

A fusillade of gunfire erupted from the cane fields. Several soldiers dropped. The captain didn't think twice. He led his lancers on a wild charge through the towering rows of sugarcane. The infantrymen, burning to avenge their brothers, broke rank and plunged in after them. The crop grew denser. Soon they disappeared into the twilight world of overhanging cane, slashing about mindlessly seeking a target for their fury.

Hangbè gave the signal. Torches. A gust of wind and the fields transformed into a candy-sweet inferno. The intense heat sucked in more air. Soon there was a firestorm, whirlwinds dancing over the fields.

1624

Towering clouds of black smoke darkened the sky, smudging the face of the sun. *Pillar of fire by night.* Soon the mansion and refinery were ablaze. Windmill arms rotating in wild arcs of fire. As they walked away there were dull explosions. Dead men's powder flasks exploding.

1624

FORTY-FOUR — *saraband for the damned*

Father Rodrigo de Segeda arranged a lavish banquet. Such was his custom when establishing a new mission. Tease out vulnerabilities, weaknesses, profitable opportunities under the cloak of conviviality. Who would betray whom for the promise of advancement? Those he could bend, those he could break. Those who would sell out their neighbour to save their own skin. Absorb what jewels of intelligence the bottle enticed out of them. Even the closest lipped Don could unknowingly condemn his favourite child in drunken jest. His suite at Morro Castle was not entirely to taste. But it did provide an adequate venue to entertain thirty or so. So, guests selected, invitations distributed.

The notorious seal — the olive branch, the sword. Summoned to attend the Tribunal of the Holy Office of the Inquisition. Many a heart almost failed. One or two did it was rumoured. Reading the contents with trembling hands pulses gradually slowed to a less threatening rate. Simply a social invitation — a privilege, an honour. Regardless of that optimistic rationalisation, lawyers received urgent visits. Invitees feeling a pressing urge to put their affairs in order — and many sought refuge in their country estates. News of the event swept the city. But soon it became apparent only the cream of Havana society received invitations. Now the event took on a less malign aspect. And, inevitably, it became the subject of boasting — of status.

The Inquisitor occupied the head of a horseshoe-shaped table. He began by intoning prayers of thanksgiving in a voice so hoarse and high-pitched it'd embarrass a eunuch. For the manifold blessings endowed by Mother Church, the merciful mission of the Inquisition, saving poor Catholics from mortal error, protecting the Papacy from the soul-staining predations of heretics...

Rodrigo Hamández, the Inquisition Bailiff, he of the pincers and rack, slouched at de Segeda's right hand. Bereft of hair. Luxuriant of beard. Pockmarked and scarred. Hands protruding from a black, silver-piped doublet, like knotted oak roots. Eyes with the dull grey compassion of musket balls. Taking it all in. Commenting little.

Friar Lorenzo, the Inquisition Secretary, stiff and slim was at the Inquisitor's left. He wore the robes of the Dominican, but his short-cropped black hair showed no evidence of tonsure. Eyes were wide and humourless like a Roman mosaic. If the Bailiff was de Segeda's cudgel, the Secretary was his poisoned stiletto.

Dominicans and Franciscans of various ages rubbed shoulders with lay invitees and their consorts — plantation managers, mine owners, slave brokers, shippers, government administrators. But no Governor. Not he. Powerful enough to resist the Inquisitor's summons. Excused himself claiming pressure of work. No matter. Could be he'd live to regret this discourtesy.

Outside, bats flittered past arched windows overlooking the harbour and moonlit sea beyond. The lights of treasure-laden ships at anchor twinkled in the blackness of the bay. Inside, thick beeswax candles dripping in smoke-blackened sconces offered clandestine, ambiguous illumination. Shadows, blacker on black danced on the walls.

Food and wine arrived in tumultuous waves. In the brief intervals between courses guests scrambled to present gifts. Then came the inevitably obsequious welcoming addresses. Each guest competing with the previous in its density of florid praise.

'Your Holy presence elevates our humble colony to a state of heavenly grace, fit for Christ to tread...'

'We bless you, Your Grace for honouring our poor city with your Holy presence. And for courageously contesting with Satan to purge the sinful few from our population, and cleanse us of the foul taint of heresy...'

Friar Lorenzo hovered over his notebook like a hungry heron, pecking away with his quill. Who presented what, and what sentiments they expressed.

The mountainous Father Rodrigo beckoned Lorenzo closer to him, whispering. The secretary straightened in his seat and raised a finger. Two nuns materialising from the shadows, collided in their eagerness to attend. Following a brief tussle a young noviciate with a pretty, if wan face, presented her delicate ear to his lips. Conversations amongst guests petered out. Soon the room was waiting developments in tense silence. The pretty noviciate shuffled to the chamber door. Opening it a crack, she clapped her hands. Half-a-dozen musicians filed in carrying their instruments like soldiers into battle. Soon a jaunty saraband began to reverberate around the halls. Father Rodrigo wiped the chicken fat from his mouth and raised his hands in a drooling benediction.

'Dance my children, dance,' he said, glaring around his guests, encouragingly.

Enjoyment smeared on their faces with very thin paint they complied. All dignity surrendered in the cause of self preservation to this gluttonous representative of Our Lord on earth.

A surprise entertainment arrived at the peak of the feasting. Inquisition retainers entered, carrying a stand chained to which were three monkeys. Cream fur about their tiny shoulder contrasted with the rich brown of their body. Nervous, fidgety movement, wide intelligent eyes, deep wells of knowing innocence.

On their handler's command the biggest set about raping the smallest. Going at it with brutal enthusiasm. Its victim screaming piteously – pain, pleasure, who knew the minds of raped monkeys? A third monkey began furiously masturbating, glittering eyes darting self-consciously about the room.

De Segeda roared with laughter. Flesh rippled from his bulging cheeks to his sagging rolls of neck fat. Tears streamed down his face. After a nervous hesitation, the room followed his lead.

But then his face fell. Guests became abruptly silent, his eyes bulged. With the roar of surf erupting from a sea cave, the contents of his stomach gushed onto the table. He surveyed the steaming mess as if perplexed. Running his tongue round his mouth, he spat out chunks of half-digested food. Snatching the Bailiff's goblet, he rinsed his mouth, swallowed three massive gulps, and spurted the excess onto the carpeted floor.

Guests sat transfixed, desperate to know how to react, eyes following his every move. Every subtlety of expression. Holding their breath, they braced themselves in anticipation of further episodes of Holy uncouthness.

The fornicating primates recaptured his attention.

'Capuchins. Capuchins, you say?' He bellowed with laughter, and the room roared back to rowdy life. 'Yes, yes, I can see the resemblance now,' he said, releasing a low, growling burp from deep in his fundament. 'How long did it take you to teach them?'

'Not long at all Your Grace,' said the scrawny Levantine trainer. 'They took to it like, well like —'

'Like fucking Capuchins,' interrupted de Segeda, racked with uncontrollable laughter, once more gasping for breath. 'I'll take one.

Christ's wounds, I'll take them all,' he spluttered. 'Name your price.'

He glanced down at the table as though seeing it for the first time. Lukewarm vomit splattered over his food. Dripping down onto his lap in viscous strands. With a casual sweep of his arm he sent the whole noisome mess crashing to the floor.

Nuns rushed to clear the shattered crockery. The beef bones, the part-consumed chicken, the islands of regurgitated peacock pie in a sea of bile. Young novitiate monks jostled for the privilege of attending to His Grace. Mopping his face, replenishing the contents of his goblet. Oblivious of all this frenetic activity De Segeda leaned across and nudged the Secretary:

'Wait till they see this performance in Rome. Capuchins, be-bastard-damned. Sanctimonious po-faced bastards. Pope's own Holy pricks.'

He burst into another shoulder-heaving spasm of laughter. But then a huge gulp from his goblet coincided with a sudden bout of hiccups. Wine jetted from his nostrils. His breath stopped; his cheeks bulged; his complexion darkened. Hamández leaned across and pounded him on the back. An enormous sneeze projected a fine scarlet aerosol into the air. Then with a quizzical expression he rolled his prodigious weight over onto one buttock. The room waited in anticipation. In almost complete silence he noisily expelled a pungent and endless stream of wind, sending the women's fans fluttered like angry butterflies.

'Better?' said the Bailiff, leaning away, with a napkin to his nose.

'So much,' said de Segada, releasing two more in a higher register.

The monkeys were by now breathless. Slowing like underwound automata. He beckoned their handler to him. Grabbing his wrist in plump beringed fingers, he squeezed a coin into the Levantine's grubby palm.

'You're a genius,' he said, waving the man away.

The handler backed out of the room with his exhausted performers.

'What's next?' spluttered de Segada, saliva dribbling from his chin.

Friar Lorenzo unfolded a note passed down the table from a giggling merchant's wife. He leaned across and muttered into the Inquisitor's ear. He in turn whispered to the Bailiff. A knotted fist crashed down on the table; briefly levitating cutlery. The raucous babble petered out. The Inquisitor raised his bloated hands in a double benediction:

'A request,' he wheezed, 'A request is received. A request from the ladies.'

Women tittered in anticipation, hiding their blushes behind fans. De Segada smiled. This request was by no means unusual.

1624

The Inquisitor led a torchlight procession of inebriated wives through the castle's dungeons, flanked by two *carcereiros*. They trudged through endless dank and musty corridors lined with oak doors. After what seemed like an age they arrived at the *cámara de interrogatorios*. The object of the women's fascination. Opening the double doors, they found themselves in a tall fan vaulted room. Three nuns stripped to the waist were scrubbing the floor. They looked up as the guests tumbled in and hurried to cover themselves. Embers glowed faint and ominous in the ashes of a brazier. The Bailiff conducted the women around the chamber.

With most of the instruments lining the walls the utility was starkly obvious. There were others, however, which required further elucidation.

'And this. What is this?' said the women's ringleader, a wealthy merchant's wife. Ebony-haired, eyes wine bright — the expression of someone for whom opportunity rarely passed unnoticed.

'We call it the horse,' said the Bailiff, chuckling.

'Show me how it works,' she demanded.

'No m'lady, I really couldn't.'

'Oh, show me,' she pouted, 'please...'

'Well, if you insist, the legs go either side of —'

'No. On me. Do it on me.'

She hitched up her skirts. And with feigned reluctance, the Bailiff helped her astride the triangular wooden block. Squealing women egged her noisily on as she play-patted the imaginary steed between her legs.

'Doesn't feel too bad,' she complained, wriggling to adjust her position. 'Bit uncomfortable, maybe.'

'Ah m'lady, but then weights are attached to the ankles and soon.'

He placed his hands on her barely covered thighs and applied downward pressure.

'Oooo, yes, see what you mean,' she began squirming.

'After a while it starts to cut into the —'

'Enough, get me off.'

As she clambered from the steed, women surged forward, lifting their skirts, scrabbling to take her place astride this instrument of torment.

'Me, I want a go.'

'No, me, get me up there.'

'My turn —'

'But I was closest.'

'I was fastest.'

Not satisfied with riding the 'horse' they insisted on exploring other exotic devices. Their fascination for the macabre insatiable. Revelling in

1624

this rare and privileged insight into the torturer's art. Finally, having exhausted their curiosity, the topic abruptly changed:

'So, where do you keep the prisoners?'

'Yes, yes, the prisoners.'

'Can we see them?'

'Please, please —'

'Yes, can we see them, can we see them.'

The Bailiff looked to the Inquisitor who had slumped wearily onto a vacant rack. He sighed: 'Oh, let the *carcereiros* take them. Help me back upstairs if you will.'

1624

FORTY-FIVE — *sacrifice*

Esther's eyes fluttered open. Internal darkness flowed into external darkness, challenging her to tell them apart. The cascade of nightmare images stuttered for a moment, then continued unabated. Same on innumerable wakings, horrors reaching back into perspective like opposing mirrors. Lately they were growing in strength as her malnourished body weakened. A writhing rat's nest of crimson memories, fears and forebodings.

The last words of the hangman:

'Step gently my love, can't have you breaking your neck. You've one last dance left in you my little beauty.'

The kaleidoscopic explosion of light as the rope bit.

But he'd been wrong, there were plenty of dances left in her.

The cut of the lash.

Dreams of great seas. Of vile monsters lurking beneath. Of worse monsters lurking above, bestriding the decks of vast ships.

She saw herself led to a place of slaughter — bound, compliant. Or, at least, reconciled. Knowing her end would be productive — the martyr's consolation. A solemn crowd parting, dark shadowy featureless faces, making the way open to her doom.

The Passover table. And Aal was there — guest of honour. Esther felt herself hovering, formless like Elijah, invisible yet present. She saw an empty place she knew was set for her. *Charoset* untouched. Salt water. Bitter herbs. The Rabbi was at the table head, blessing the wine, his movement treacle slow. Tallit masking his face. Voice through his beard, deep, resonant, otherworldly. All her relatives were there too. Both the living and dead. Isaac and Benjamin silently raising overtopped glasses to her shade. Her Nordic birthmother, clothes steaming, freshly arrived from Valhalla. Choleric complexioned, following the service in the Haggadah, blue lips silently articulating the Hebrew. The dark-haired stepmother scowled like she disapproved of this inconvenient resurrection. The Matchmaker opposite, plotting where they could profitably discard her.

Why is this day different to all other days?

Then she glimpsed the kindly face of Joseph, her true father. Joseph, white-faced, throat gaping, grave dust on his shoulders like dandruff. Joseph the suicide. Joseph the informer, the deserter. What worth was she, so carelessly left behind? The tablecloth beneath his chin, stained with vermilion splashes. Blood darting through the weave, the warp and the weft, the up and the down, the in and the out of things.

Death of the firstborn.

Esther slowly returned to lucid consciousness. Dreams overlaying her reality, crawling over her mind like lice, like flies, like maggots. Fading now to translucency, as her eyes regained focus. Finally disappearing like dust motes into darkness.

On this day, the beam of light was weaker. It came skulking along the wall like it was ashamed to find itself in such squalid conditions. Esther followed it in a listless, disinterested way. Each brick touched by its wan illumination represented an increment of agonising monotony. The court had pronounced sentence — she knew their fate, wouldn't be long now. But when? That was part of the torture. By the time the dull fragment of daylight reached its zenith, it had all but faded to invisibility. For once the noonday temperature had been bearable. The sky was overcast — a minor, but welcome blessing.

Blinking, she fumbled for Aal. Fingertips finding her sleeping face was cold and drenched in sweat. She shook her, gently at first. No response. Harder. The hoarse rattle of shallow breath. Panic rising:

'Aal, wake up. Don't play games.'

No response — was she dying? Were this the case, should she allow her to drift away? A kindness, perhaps.

Footsteps, a hint of light beneath the cell door. She yelled, feeling selfish for disrupting her friend's route to peace. But she needed her. No response from the guards. The footfall faded. The light dimmed. She rolled back to Aal, uniting their body warmth; their sum was always greater than their parts.

She held her tight all night. Her arms were cramping as the first rays of the sun crested their tiny, barred window. Aal still hadn't woken. Esther screamed for the guards until her voice became to a sore blood-flecked whisper. Finally footsteps approached. She crawled to the entrance. The door opened. Their usual guards, and one other; coarse hands dragged her upright.

She stood, head bowed, gazing up through trembling lashes,

swaying, weakened legs aching. Hamandez the Inquisition Bailiff was louring over her. A figure she recognised and feared. He'd said he wanted to be her friend. To help her. She'd rejected his advances on numerous occasions. He'd come close to raping her. But he wanted her soul as well as her body. One, he'd said, was no good without the other. She must come to him willingly. Until then there was nothing he could do for them.

The guards brought candles, jamming them into waxy niches. They hung about shuffling their feet until the Bailiff dismissed them. His voice gravelly coarse. When the door thudded behind them he addressed her. His words followed on from their previous encounter, as though the last month had not passed:

'It could be a year before you come to trial. Even then my influence could delay procedures further. And then who knows, this whole matter could disappear? These things happen — *have* happened.

'In the meantime your food could improve as could these conditions. Who knows your friend may even survive. It's a holy wonder what the native's boiled bark can achieve.'

All this was in his gift, he'd said. Did she realise that? And he wanted so little in return. So little. All he required was in her gift to give. Would she continue to refuse him, and let her friend die? He'd be sure to leave her corpse there to keep her company as it corrupted. A gift for a gift. Was it so much to ask?

Her resistance collapsed. Such a little thing, he was right. She had seen Aal perform similar acts. And she had benefitted from Aal's sacrifice as if it had been some trivial thing. And perhaps it was. And perhaps it wasn't. She'd know soon enough. It now fell to her to shoulder the burden of survival. To do that which was unconscionable, but necessary.

An undertaking given, a bargain struck.

A native wise woman shuffled into their cell. Foul-smelling potions trickled down Aal's unresponsive throat.

Pale as a waning moon, Aal opened her famine-widened eyes, blinked, then slitted them. She locked gaze with Esther and nodded to the door. Then Esther too picked up the sound, letting out a short involuntary gasp. The distant march of booted feet, getting closer. A flickering light under the sill, getting brighter. Keys rattled in the lock. Muffled voices through the heavy oak. Hinges creaking, the door opening.

The usual guards — the fat one with the hare lip, the thin one with the facial tick. Two stunted native women shuffled in behind them. They were hauling overtopped pails, slopping water on the flagstones, towels over shoulders. One balanced a cloth bundle on her head, tied with fibrous string. The fat jailer wobbled over, positioning stuttering oil lamps. The thin one unlocked their shackles. Closer to Aal his nose wrinkled.

'Get out of those rags puta, it's bath time,' he said, with a grimace.

'What's this in aid of,' croaked Aal, rubbing her wrists, 'our stink finally get too much for you?'

The soldiers sniggered to themselves, exchanging glances.

'What?' demanded Aal.

'Could be someone wants blondie looking her best,' said the thin one, winking at his mate.

The guards left the cell grinning lasciviously, locking the door behind them. Esther and Aal were alone with the Black Madonna of the Bucket and the Brown Madonna of the Towels. Relieved of the weight of irons Esther's arms floated into the air. Fascinated, she let them drift above her head like a bird testing its wings. Then darkly suppressed thoughts flooded in, filling her limbs with lead.

Aal, eyes wide: 'What have you done?' She thought she knew the answer and began to sob. 'Why?' Of course, she knew the answer, but continued sobbing.

Esther shrugged and shook her head. It would be wonderful to feel clean again. Later, it felt like several hours later, impossible to tell at night. They were sitting on mounds of fresh, sweet-smelling straw in clean floor-length shifts. They remained unchained. Esther was holding Aal, arms wrapped round her, salt rivulets on her friend's cheeks. The food had become bearable, even appetising. Their water no longer stank of piss.

They came for her later that day; wary, almost respectful. Knocking. What guard knocks on a cell door? They led her through endless corridors to an upper level. Another door, another knock.

The Bailiff's quarters were not lavish, neither were they Spartan. Sparsely spaced candles provided scant illumination. Esther's mind was numb. A victim led to the scaffold. Knowing their fate. Disbelieving its imminence despite the prickling of the rope about their neck. She knew that feeling well.

The guards slunk out of the room. The door thudded closed. Without their support her legs struggled to hold her upright. She swayed, concentrating hard to maintain balance. Alone with him, her chest rising and falling. Hearing her own breath, and in the congealing silence becoming aware of his. Of his eyes examining her under overhung brows. He was a far from handsome man. In the full blossom of his youth, she doubted he looked any better. Tall lean, angular. At least thirty years her senior. He came towards her, loosening his breeches. A blade glittered in the flickering light reminding her of something. Something buried deep. He cut the shoulder loops of her shift and the light fabric drifted to the ground. Tiny eyes glittered in his grizzled face; a grin flickered across cruel scarred lips.

He pushed her, gently. She staggered back half a pace. Her eyes locked on his. Manhood protruding now, he chuckled and pushed her again. Push stagger, push stagger, until her calves met the edge of the curtained bed. She tumbled on her back onto the sheets. Sleeping on stone and straw for months, the softness took her breath away.

She heard herself sobbing. Was this what it was like to be with a man. Or just this man. She knew no comparison, save the gentle caresses of Neeltje and Aal. Her first time with a man. Blood darted through the weave – the warp and the weft, the up and the down, the in and the out.

Death of the firstborn.

Two weeks passed, near as she could tell, since his last summons. Some part of her might even be longing for another summons from her torturer. Anything to break this endless tedium. That first time she returned to the cell, trembling, almost fitting with shock. She had no framework for such an experience. But boredom. Anything was better than its crushing weight.

Aal continued to recover. They were clean. It was the same cell. But it was cleaner. They had exercise periods, could even roam the corridors. Bedding, food, clothes.

She heard footsteps, her breath quickened. Her mind flashed to his rough, tree root hands tormenting her. His glittering deep-set merciless eyes. His ravaged oak-bark body. Entering her, like a siege captain battering his way into a fortress. The guilt at her body's innocent reaction. The pain. There is perverse pleasure in accepting punishment for something you believe you deserve. And she was glad for once she was able to do something for Aal. Protect her with the sacrifice of her dignity. But there was something more.

Their treatment continued to improve as did the food. And they no longer wore chains, yet he hadn't sent for her. Had she done something wrong, didn't she please him anymore? Then one night, the rattle of keys, the blinding blaze of lanterns. His voice. Women's giggles. A stab of jealousy, jealousy? He was her abuser, but he was her's. The women sounded drunk. Slurred, whispered feminine exchanges. The voices of the jailers. The jangle of coin. A woman's face peering through the grating.

A fold of paper fluttered through the slot in the door.
Your brothers are coming. Be ready.

Days passed. He came for her, breaking the deathly monotony, easing her ache for punishment. Then one-night footsteps approached their cell. This wasn't his brutally confident footfall. These feet were surreptitious, hesitant, like a poacher approaching forbidden traps. Sensing danger, she and Aal clung together. The lock rattled, keys jangled, two hooded figures opened their door. Friars Ignatius and González crept inside.

'On our way to confession,' said Ignatius, slyly.

'But we rather lacked something to confess,' said González.

Esther and Aal parted, scrambling to the darkest corners of the cell. The monks went to pursue Esther; beautiful, flaxen haired blue eyed, angelic Esther. But then they heard Aal's voice and turned boggle eyed.

'You wanted something to confess boys,' she said.

She was laying splay legged, dress pulled up past her breasts. They turned and fell on her.

But it was Esther who screamed.

A face at the door.
A ghost.
Isaac?

1624

FORTY-SIX — *repairs*

Most of the the Rachael's damage was above deck. Carpenters, sailmakers, riggers, and iron workers converged from across the fleet. Half-a-dozen nationalities united by the language of their craft. Four longboat crews towed the cannon-blasted Spanish ship and lashed it alongside the Rachael. Craftsmen swarmed over it like leafcutter ants, stripping it of everything that repairs necessitated. This took just three days, working shifts through the night as the donor vessel slipped progressively lower in the water. On the third day she was untethered and drifted towards the shore to settle on a reef, decks awash.

The Rachael was seaworthy once more. Seaworthy and significantly better armed. Twenty gleaming bronze cannons now graced her upper deck, protruding through freshly installed gunports. Elijah Brankfleet appropriated the Spanish powder and ammunition. Having tested its potency, he ordered it distributed around the fleet. The remaining Spanish cannon replaced the ballast in the Zeelander. No use for now, but their time to bark would come. The Admiral tasked his pilot with collecting the ship's charts and log. Brankfleet travelled ship-to-ship conferring with master gunners, and interrogating those crewmembers acquainted with Havana's defences. Distance and trajectory formed the basis of heated debate. Eventually Brankfleet calculated an optimum elevation and reported his satisfaction to the Admiral.

The Pastor was testing a new weapon by torchlight. A steel, fleece-lined gauntlet strapped to his forearm. A broad flexible double-edged blade of some thirty inches extending from it. With a small buckler in his good left hand he whirled in circles, slicing the air. The blacksmiths stood by, taking notes.

The Rabbi approached cautiously. The Pastor came to a halt, catching his breath. 'What do you think? It's called a Pata. Something I heard of in Hindustan. The Mogul bodyguards use them. Without a hand I have no wrist action; this thing doesn't require wrists — works better without 'em. We've made one small improvement, watch this...'

He took a key and detached the blade, replacing it with one shorter and broader of serpentine profile.

'We have already developed half-a-dozen variations. And they don't just have to be swords; could be axes, cleavers, spearpoints, there's even a pistol option I've got the smith working on.'

He unstrapped the device with his left hand, releasing his stump. He flexed his arm and rolled his shoulders. The Rabbi's attention wandered. The crews had been on high alert all day. A fog of black smoke was drifting across the countryside. It wasn't from the direction of Havana, nevertheless it jangled nerves. Cane burning — maybe.

'Look lively now.' Skyler Hurst was urgently pacing through the gundeck, tipping men out of hammocks. 'Hands off those one-legged octopuses you sons of Onan.'

He assembled both watches of topmen on the starlit deck.

'Time you earned your rations boys. Get aloft, get aloft my nightshade beauties. Every stitch of canvas she can bear. Skysails, Royals, topgallants, topsails, courses. Get studding sails on the blasted lot of 'em.'

As gaskets released and sails dropped, the moon eclipsed by acres of flogging canvas. The glistening shapes of topmen clung aloft like black pearls on a wedding dress. A dozen groaning Africans worked the capstan, there was a jolt as the anchor broke free. The ship moved backwards with the tide, and the shore approached with horrifying rapidity.

'Come you all down,' cried Skyler, now halfway up the main mast ratlines. 'Man the braces now. Heave away for old Skyler boy. Sharply now. That hulk Zeelander is making way already. Have you bastards no sodding pride?'

The ship retreated a few more cables. Then the sails drew hard, and the rigging strained. Windward shrouds bar taut, the leeward slack. The rudder bit hard, turning the ship towards the open sea as the wind came abaft the beam. The African Prince gently healed, crashing through the waves in playful pursuit of her sisters on into the night.

The fleet was underway. Picking up speed. Thirteen ships. Straining canvas horizon-to-horizon. Skyler's first engagement in Skyler's first command. Excited, yes. Nervous, yes. Daunted, no. Overwhelmed, no. Sniffing, he realised he was crying. He released his grip on the rail to brush away a tear. A gust snatched at the mainsail. Caught out, he began to stagger. A huge hand clamped on his shoulder, steadying him. Petrus Stoffel the giant first mate had come from nowhere. Staring fixedly in the same direction, his one good eye watering.

The Visitación, the Admiral's flagship, was in the lead. Six ships either side fanning out like a flight of geese. Skyler's African Prince was the last-but-one feather in the southern wingtip. To his larboard was the sloop Johanas D. To his starboard the Titan, the Bear Cub, the Unicorn, then the Andromeda. To the Visitación's starboard was the Zeelander, the Rachael, the Lady Amelia, the Anne of Bute, the Hiram of Tyre, and the Inishowen. Seven hundred and fifty cannons between them. An earthquake on the move.

1624

FORTY-SEVEN — *sea of shoes*

Skyler stubbed his toe on the doorsill. Grimaced and stifled a yelp. He hoped no one noticed — unlikely. Thirteen pairs of eyes. Thirteen captains of which Skyler was by far the most junior. They sat around the gleaming mahogany table of the great cabin. Admiral Jochem Bartholomeuz Van Den Hamel was at the head, having adopted the Visitación as his flagship. A forty-gun, two-decker. It was not appreciably larger than the Zeelander. But it had the attraction of the palatial great cabin the Admiral had sorely missed. His straight white hair hung loose. It flowed past the square shoulders of a black velvet robe. High collar. Epaulettes. Glinting silver thread embroidery in a foliated Moorish pattern.

Behind him, hands resting lightly on the back of his baroque gilded chair, the Grevinna Ingela Olofsdotter Gathenhielm. Not much short of six foot in her sea-boots. She rivalled even the Admiral for physical presence. Her attire was in every respect masculine. No man with eyes in his head and functioning gonads would mistake her for such. A pair of ebony-handled pistols rode high on her hips, a military rapier of German design slung low on a cross belt over a white linen shirt. Her gold-flecked white hair hung in two loose plats over her shoulders. The Admiral cleared his throat gently, taking in each of the assembled from beneath straggling black eyebrows through sea mist eyes. Murmured conversations drifted away like smoke on the wind.

'Chentlemen,' said the Grevinna, her English diamond facetted. 'Your admiral will acquaint you with the disposition of our forces. But before he does so, we should agree the division of spoils. I have drawn up articles as per the *Jugements de la mer, Rôles d'Oléron.*'

Blank looks.

'*Vonesse van Damme,*' said a Dutchman.

Fewer blank looks.

'*Little Red Book of Bristol,*' chimed in a Westcountryman.

'Ah.' Now they got it.

'In accordance with *the Rolls* the Admiral shall be responsible to the captains here gathered for a fair distribution. Each captain including myself will receive one full share, and the Admiral will receive one and a half shares. Should a dispute occur between us the majority will prevail. And should this fail, the Admiral will be the final arbiter. Each captain shall be responsible to their crew for the fair allocation of funds as per the articles signed upon joining the individual vessel. Similarly, should a dispute occur within your crew, and which is not resolved, your ship's quartermaster will decide.

'Are we all in agreement with this proposition? Good. You will now make your mark.'

'Mister Crips, if you will,' said the Admiral.

The articles passed around from master to master. Crips followed with a quill and an ornate silver-capped cut-glass ink bottle, spectra dancing wherever it went. Finally, dusting the parchment with sand, he handed it inky fingered to the Grevinna, now seated at the right of the Admiral. Sheng leaned across and poured a generous deposit of black wax at the foot. The Grevinna stamped it with the Admiral's brass Van Den Hamel seal.

'So it is recorded,' said the Admiral. 'So it will be.'

As he stood, his terriers jumped from his lap, startling thems as didn't know him. He stretched his long lean arms. Rolled his neck, bones popping. Eyes followed as, without uttering a word, he wandered to the door, shielding his eyes as if taken by surprise by the caustic sunlight.

'Gentlemen,' said Crips to the assembly, 'if'y'd care to join his excellency on the quarterdeck.'

They shuffled out. Again Skyler's shoe caught the threshold. He looked down. The sole of his starboard shoe had come loose. Flapping like a hound's tongue after a long chase. Shuffling like an ice skater, he made a note to have his sailmaker to throw a stitch into them when he got back to the African Prince.

The Admiral's voice, reedy, penetrating: 'Mister Sheng. Shoes, if y'would. Lively now.'

Skyler's face burned. Sheng shuffled inside leaving smudges on an elaborate chalk map which covered the entire deck on which they stood.

'Gentlemen, you are obstructing the coastline,' said the Admiral, herding the ship's masters like sheep. 'If y' move back to the rail ye'll be better able to appreciate the scheme of things.' He took a boarding pike from the rack at the mizzen. He hefted it as though assessing it's weight and balance. 'This gentleman is us,' he stabbed at a pile of shoes. 'And this is the coast of Cuba, and this Havana Bay. And here you can see

1624

Havana, with the Spanish treasure fleet crammed in its guts.' Sheng trotted up an cast shoes into the chalk delineated harbour. 'Ships assembled from Cartagena, Porto Bello, Panama, Veracruz, Maracaibo, Caracas, Campeche. And here's its escort of men-of-war waiting for the end of the hurricane season to make for Cadiz. The entire year's supply of New World booty concentrated in one place. Safe, they think, behind a chain boom strung between two castles.

'Gold and silver gentlemen. Gold and silver looted from the Americas to enable a corrupt and crumbling Habsburg Empire to prosecute a war against the House of Orange-Nassau and the United Provinces and all good free-thinking Protestant peoples. Well I'm here to tell you *this is not* what we are here for.'

Stunned silence, broken by howls of protest.

'Sorry, what...?'

'What the hell are we doing here then...'

'What d'you think we're all risking our lives for...'

The Grevinna took a half pace forward, slim fingers teasing the hilt of her rapier. Jugah Tawi Koroh's eyes glinted from the shadows.

The Admiral didn't react. Lucky for someone. The Rabbi walked across the Bay of Havana and took a position in the chalk forest to the east of the city, standing shoulder-to-shoulder with the Admiral.

'No, that is not our target,' he said. 'Use your bloody heads. We have thirteen ships, not a bloody armada. What us? Take on prime men-of-war of the Spanish Navy? Three deckers, hundred gunners, two-and-a-half dozen of 'em. You'd better pray they don't lower that boom and come out and give battle. Now listen to your Admiral. Watch him earn that extra half share.'

The Admiral picked up the thread of his discourse like he was addressing a class of particularly dull children.

'The treasure fleet isn't the only treasure in Havana. The rivers of Cuba run yellow with gold. Rio Buey, Rio Biamo, Rio Ocha, etcetera. And there are dozens of open cast mines across the country. The Sun Mine at Bayamo, the San Jose Mine at Santa Clara. Mines at Gamaguey, Holguin. Two year's output of Cuban dust and bullion is in the warehouses in Havana ready to be loaded onto those ships. We are not going to take our loot from the sea, but from the land.'

'Why didn't you tell us sooner? Why keep us in the dark?' said someone.

The Rabbi shook his head. Most of the assembled got it. For the sake of the few who didn't he explained:

'That lop-jawed shit breech Philip has spies everywhere. An

incautious whisper and they'd hurry all that Cuban gold safely aboard a three-deck galleon. And hide that behind battery of warships. This way even if we're betrayed, they'll be thinking, we're attempting to plunder the fleet whilst it's bottled up in the Harbour. They'd prepare a warm reception for us, but that wouldn't interfere with our core objective.'

The Rabbi took a step back ceding the floor to the master tactician. The Admiral's knee length Spanish boots were now bestriding the mountainous jungle-clad interior, north-east of Havana. Sheng stood behind him with another armful of footwear. Silver-woven curl-toed Moroccan slippers, native rattan sandals, soft leather seaman's shoes, laced up ladies' suede pumps, wooden clogs. Rope soles, leather soles, worn and new examples of the cordwainers' art, from the exotic to the mundane.

'Prior to our action, under cover of darkness, Mister Bird will take the Johanas D and set up a bridgehead on the coast west of the city. Mister Crips, if y'would.' Crips took a shoe from Sheng and placed it in the appropriate position on the chalk map. 'Noon, when the sea breeze establishes, our first squadron will take up position. That's (he consulted a paper passed to him by the Grevinna) the *Unicorn* under Mister Kraft, the African Prince under the shoe-impoverished Mister Hurst, the *Bear Cub* under Mister Kneebone, the *Lady Amelia* under Mister Coeymans, the *Rachael* under Rabbi Abraham, and the *Titan* under Mister Dobel. They will pass in file within two hundred yards of the fortifications and discharge their guns at a ten-degree elevation into the packed harbour. Mister Crips if you please...'

Crips lined up six shoes by the entrance to the harbour. 'By the time the gunners on the castle battlements have depressed their pieces,' said the Admiral, 'our first squadron will have passed by in a cloud of smoke.

'The Spanish won't have time to wonder where they have gone, because they will be dealing with our second squadron consisting of, the *Anne of Bute* under Mister Rogers, the *Hiram* under Mister Budock, the *Inishowen* under Mister O'Driscoll, the *Andromeda* under Mister Karlsson, and the *Visitación* under Mister Shoenmaeker, pounding the city battlement from a mile offshore. More shoes Mister Crips, look lively man.' Crips carefully placed six shoes in a line further out to sea. 'I will be aboard the Visitación as will the Grevinna, who acts as my deputy, with Mister Schoenmaecker as master. Should I become *hors de combat* you will take your direction from her.

'Following their attack, our first squadron will proceed along the coast and link up with the Johanas B and begin landing troops equipped with oxen and sleds.' Crips moved the appropriate footwear. 'They will drag artillery pieces to the city and gold on their return.'

'So that's what those bastard cows is doin' in our holds,' said Blaze Kneebone.

'The Spanish will be fighting an army of rebel slaves to the east,' said the Admiral, 'ravaging their precious sugar plantations, whilst at the same time dealing with a fire raging through the city. Soon our flotilla will be battering them from the sea. Now whilst their forces concentrate elsewhere we will advance on a third front and punch straight through to their bullion warehouses.'

He stabbed down with his steel tipped pike into the heart of the chalk city. He left it swaying there, taking a step back:

'D'ye know.' He said, 'I'm not sure they'll even notice. And if they do, their focus will still be on protecting the treasure fleet. If that leaves Havana intact they may even think the gold warehouse is a sacrifice worth making.'

The Grevinna scanned the room, eyes the colour of polar ice:

'Questions?' she said.

Cornelius Kraft proud master of the Unicorn took a pace forward:

'How can you be certain after all this effort and sacrifice the gold will be there?'

'*Conversos,*' said the Rabbi, 'Jewish Catholic converts, acting as my intelligencers.'

'Been with Spain till now, what's made them switch loyalties?'

'The arrival of the Inquisition,' said the Rabbi. 'They'll be exposed as secret Jews, which indeed they are. Their assets will be confiscated, and they'll be burned in the city square. Happened all over Spain and Portugal. They know it'll happen here.'

'But can a turncoat ever be trusted?'

'No need for trust, they're coming with us. They'll be lighting beacons to guide the Johanas D. And waiting on the beach desperate to embark.'

'So, when do we go?' said Lisagh O'Driscoll.

'Now,' said the Admiral. He hesitated, then added: 'And Mister Skyler, for heaven's sake pick yourself out a decent pair of shoes.'

There were other priorities besides gold, allowed for in the Admiral's planning: the Grevinna's mission to liberate Swedish slaves and granddaughter. And the Rabbi saving his children. Glistening, steely priorities with which all the gold in the Americas couldn't compete.

1624

FORTY-EIGHT — *kindling*

Havana squatted on the coastal plain like a whore taking a shit. Her sphincter constricted by a fort on either side, a chain slung between them. Chaotic rat-runs of streets spread out from a central square. Lumpen half-born mountains overlooked the city like they resented this unnatural intrusion.

Greasy smuts descended on the crowd gathered to witness burnings. A thin spiral of smoke corkscrewed heavenwards. Eventually it would join the dark pall above the distillery on the outskirts of town. A three-tiered platform provided a clear view for the Inquisition officials clutching their crosses. Presiding in stern pomp, from under its canopy was the elephantine figure of Father de Segada. Glancing around from his position of eminence, he noticed the absence of the bailiff, Hamandez. No matter, it had been a good night.

Balconies beneath the terracotta tiled rooves surrounding the square had been rented out to the highest bidders. Those of lower rank, or lesser purse forsook the shade of the porticos, mingling with the peasants for a better view. Children perched on the shoulders of their parents. Vendors sold snacks and souvenirs. Urchins splashed in the shallow pool surrounding the central fountain. Yellow-coated guards sweated as they slouched in formation three deep, lest things get out of hand, as these events had the habit of doing. It wasn't unknown for sympathisers to disrupt the order of these solemn proceedings. Or smuggle prisoners a knife, with which to cheat the flames. A late coming grandee alighted from a coach-and-four. His entourage ascending the platform to shuffle into the row beneath the priests. Black slaves loitered mid-errand. Dogs sniffed the air. Fire had already done its work once. The victim had ceased thrashing; the screams had come to a gurgling stop. Flames crept over flesh, popping and crackling like suckling pigs. Hair gone. Features melted. Eye sockets blackened tunnels, open portals to hell. Crowds drifted across to the six empty stakes piled with wood and the promise ever more delicious spectacle.

1624

The drummers beat their drums. The master at arms called for silence. The crowd noise reduced to expectant murmurs. The Secretary of the Inquisition cleared his throat. He read the charges concocted against the next two victims. The recalcitrant Jewess, Esther Amsalem. The blasphemous witch Aal De Dragoner. Being obdurate in their heresy, neither were granted the mercy of strangulation. They would burn alive in this world, as a foretaste of the everlasting lakes of fire awaiting them in the next. The secretary droned on reading the charges against other unfortunates doomed to the fires that day — those too impecunious to buy forgiveness, or too rich to avoid the avarice of the inquisitors. Executioners led the chained prisoners into the square astride mangy donkeys. Each victim wore the tall white conical hat, the *capirote,* the symbol of penitence. The crowd surged about them jeering and spitting. Soldiers did an imperfect job of preventing assaults.

Hoods covered the faces of these condemned. Gags rendered them speechless lest their satanic heresy infect onlookers by glance or word. And no chance of them begging Christ's mercy in their dying minutes, earning them the merciful garrotte. Members of the audience joined executioners stacking bundles of wood around the trembling bodies. Fires were lit. Kindling crackled. Flames burst forth.

Wailing Franciscan monks burst through the crowd. Water slopping over the tops of buckets as they forced their way past the cordon of confused soldiers. Dousing the screaming heretics, they frantically kicking away the flaming faggots. They dragged Friar Ignatius and Brother González from the pyre blackened and scorched but still alive. Few minutes later they would have cooked to a turn. Jesús' parting joke had been discovered.

There was a rumble of thunder out to sea. And iron shot began descending from the heavens.

FORTY-NINE — *the Black Parrot*

The fleet had been assembling in Havana for going on a month. Ships arriving every day. Shop keepers and landlords were gleefully hiking up their prices. Locals complaining it felt like an invasion. Harbour master pulling out his hair. Anchored galleons crowded the bay. Merchant ships, bulk carriers, their bellies bulging with exotic produce converging from all points of the Spanish Americas. Rare species of timber, coffee, tobacco, sugar, spices. Taking advantage of the protection afforded by the men-of-war escorting the treasure fleet.

Ship's long boats and pinnaces, ferrymen constantly coming and going. Seamen drunk on the way out, insensible on their return. Merchants' boats supplying provender for the officers and crews. Chandlers shipping materials for ship maintenance. The Admiral's launch; on the way to his lunch with the Governor. There were not that many on board. Just resentful skeleton crews maintaining the ships vital functions. Marines guarding the strongrooms. Sailors on punishment duty or waiting impatiently rotation, swabbing decks to keep them tight, checking rigging, double stitching sails to withstand the rigors of the Atlantic crossing, seizing frayed shrouds, slavering on tallow. Watching what their mates were up to in town from the topgallant cross trees. Sitting around in the shade, swapping the exploits of their last shore leave — tales of drink, of women, of epic fights.

The city had been one great *carnavales* — the bullfights, the parades. As though the feast days of St. John, St. Peter, St. Christine, St. Anne and St. James the Apostle all rolled out end-to-end. But it wasn't without crisis. that distillery going up in flames sent the price of spirits sky high. The city stunk of burning. Smuts were falling like black snow. This tragedy couldn't have come at a worse time. Celebrating for a month, sailors were now broke, drunk and irritable. Squabbles were breaking out between locals and crews. On one hand merchant class Havanans enjoyed the bounty these visitors brought with them. On the other they were getting to resent these turbulent interlopers. Now the influx of money had slowed, tempers were fraying on both sides. The Inquisition was in town setting neighbour on neighbour. That was proving a welcome distraction. But there was no denying the fleet had thoroughly worn out its welcome.

Matias Suárez was second mate on a sleek little carrack. He'd one of those deceptive faces. Some might mistake him for young and inexperienced. Yet he comported himself as though he'd seen his fare share of this world — its good and its evil. Sorry would be the sailor of high or low degree who mistook his easy manner for naivety. His gait had a rhythm falling just shy of a swagger. More indicative of a seaman newly ashore than of alcohol or hubris.

He'd just woven his way through the harbour-front crowds from the *Piña de Oro*. Drink prices were low there. But so was the quality, and the company stank. His knuckles stung in the breeze as he strode along. Anyway, the grub was much better at the *Loro Negro*. Least that was the prevailing opinion. When he arrived at the sign of the Black Parrot they were doing a brisk lunch-time trade. He spied a table of junior officers from his convoy and pushed his way through to join them. The *Nuestra Senora* their vessel — big-bellied merchantman. Just ten guns. Slow and virtually defenceless. Some of the drinkers were onetime shipmates. Looked like they'd taken more rum than he. No matter. He'd catch up soon enough.

'*Hey chicos, largo tiempo sin vernos.*'

He chuckled inwardly at his joke — hadn't seen them for all of two hours. Not since he'd jumped that *señorita* with the tiny tits and long legs. The one who turned out to be both very professional and very married. Looking to make a little pin money she'd said. Husband didn't approve — *puta madre.* Obviously, an act. Probably an act. Either way her old man's untimely intervention mid-coitus earned the man a split lip, and he a sore hand. Fair exchange when you think about it.

He grabbed a rustic chair. Set it so his back was to the wall. Unobstructed view of the *Canal de Entrada*. Just in case that little prick fancied his chances again. More likely he'd turn up with a few mates. Looked like the sort. At that thought, he eased his *papá's* old bollock dagger in its scabbard.

'Always carry that thing do you, eh Suárez?'

'Always. Never know when I might need to cut a throat.'

Unusually the day was overcast, like the weather had aligned with his mood. Every now and then the sun'd poke its sharp beak through the fine cloak of smokey cloud which was currently ranging from horizon-to-horizon. Cooler air made a pleasant change though. Pity about the smell of burning. He was confident the cloud cover would fade off by mid-afternoon. Thereafter they'd be roasting again. Enjoy the shade while you can, he told himself. But that pall of black smoke would still be hanging over the city. It was at its densest where dwellings petered out into fields, fading away as agriculture met the forest.

'See the fucker's still burning.'
'Crying shame.'
'Don't bear thinking about.'
'Dangerous business is distilling.'
'Anyone hurt?'
'If you call dead hurt, yes.'
'Hear about the mules?'
'Charged right out of the flames they did.'
'Ridden by the devil himself.'
'So they say.'
'Flew straight through the gates of hell.'
'Or jumped in the harbour.'
'So which was it?'
'Depends on who you ask.'
'Old Nick himself, off his face on overproof rum.'

'Let's hear it for the Devil's donkeys,' one of them yelled, raising a tankard. The table eagerly followed his lead.

'Devil's donkeys,' they chorused, knocking back their rum and smashing down their empty tankards.

'Devil's donkeys,' roared the room. 'Devil's-sodding-donkey's.'

At that point, an exceptionally well-proportioned mullato girl sashayed through the excitement, escaping molestation with success borne of long practice. Voluminous curls, long blue dress. One eye. Calico bandana serving as a patch. Jagged scar the length of her otherwise unblemished coffee-bean face. She came to rest by Matias's left elbow, delivering a tarnished tankard. He looked up, smiling his dark smile.

'That clean?' he said.

She spat into its grimy depths. Wiping the rim of the mug with the hem of her apron, she set it back before him.

'It is now.' She said. 'You eating Señor, or what?' She passed him a grubby hand-scrawled menu. 'That's todays' she said.

Mindful of his shore-leave-depleted purse, he ordered a plate of egg and potato tortilla. She bobbed, turned and took a pace away. He called her back.

'What the hell,' he said, changing his order to *lomo alto de ternera*.

Best the house had to offer.

'Very rare, if you please *cariño*.'

This was the kind of grub you dream about when faced with the shipboard alternative — weevil-riddled biscuit and rancid salt pork, half-boiled beans if you're lucky. She took his money. Bobbed another curtsy. The sway of her hips not unappreciated, as she navigated her way between the crowded tables to melt into the shadows of the smokey kitchen.

She returned with his change. He said keep it. She thanked him and lingered provocatively. Chuckling, he pulled her onto his knee. The table applauded — always good value was Matias. He offered her a drink; she shook her head. He insisted and forced his tankard to her mouth. They locked eyes. She spat a large gob into his rum, leaving saliva dribbling down her chin. Without breaking eye contact he drained the tankard then kissed her hard on her scarred mouth. She struggled from his grasp in mock indignation, giggling her way back to the kitchen.

When the ribaldry abated Matias leaned back in his chair, shoulders resting on the rough stucco wall. One of his mates leaned across and refilled his tankard, making a hawking sound, deep in his throat.

'Would Señor take his rum with or without spittle on this occasion?' Matias let it pass and relaxed into absently observing the street market through the lashes of half-closed eyes. With no particular focus his gaze drifted to Morro Castle high up on the other side of the canal. Sailor's gossip swirled around him as he followed the massive chain boom strung across the harbour entrance. The aroma of searing meat drifted towards him, setting his gums tingling with anticipation.

He was the first of his table to glimpse the line of topsails drifting into view from behind the forested headland. They were a league to the east of the battlements. Squares of taut canvas approaching with the menacing inevitability of a shark's dorsal fin. What's so remarkable about sails? Ships enter the harbour daily. The horizontal tricolour of the Free Provinces, however, was a serious cause for concern.

There came a rumble as of distant thunder. Round shot began hailing down deep into the harbour. Plumes of water jetted up. The mainmast of a galleon crumpled. Dockyard buildings on the far side of the city collapsed.

Hostia puta. Matias rushed into the street.

'*Jesucristo, cuidado.*'

Passers-by scattered for shelter. His mates took off for the *Nuestra Senora,* Jesu knows what they thought they could do. A huge round shot smashed into the pavement and bowled past. So close the draught spun him round. He froze swaying, bleached complexion, eyes wide. He patted his torso, fingers exploring under his ribs. Cannons don't have to hit you to kill you. Wind-of-ball. Not a mark on you. Walk a couple of paces, hit the deck, dead as yesterdays breakfast. Organs rearranged, guts turned to mush, heart stopped. He took a tentative step, and then another. Amid the rain of iron, a smile bisected his face. His giblets felt like they were in their appropriate places.

The attacking ship drifted across the entrance in a haze of smoke. Its great guns blasting, one by one. The castle gunners, taken unawares, gave no immediate response. Yet another ship came into view. This time the battlement guns erupted. But their shots merely ripped into the topmasts, shredding sails, clipping off spars. Doing no real damage. Plumes of water rose far out to sea where their shot passed through. The guns set high in anticipation of a more distant enemy. These marauding ships were not aiming for the castle. Their shot flew high over the battlements, landing a mile or more beyond. Smashing into the anchored fleet, and the crowded city beyond. Soon clouds of smoke obscured the castle and drifted across the canal. He pictured what might be occurring up there. Gun crews desperately adjusting the elevation of their pieces. Loading, firing, loading firing, to no great effect. At best just shearing off the upper rigging.

He flattened himself against the wall as two score, crested-helmeted musketeers clattered past him. Their officer formed them up at the sea wall. Three rows deep they began blasting lead at the ships as they passed. Topmen fell from rigging. Officers collapsed on deck.

The ship's lower battery fired this time. Round shot ploughed through the soldier's ranks smashing them like toys. Bouncing high, one massive ball ripped a path of destruction through the market stalls. Oranges spun into the air. Poultry stalls erupted in a storm of blood and feathers, pottery smashed, wagons smashed, horses bolted.

Matias stood mesmerised as an iron ball skipped across the surface of the harbour like a pebble over a pond, smashing through a pinnace and embedding itself into the dockside wall. Six enemy ships thus passed, pounding shot-after-shot over his head. The last two suffered more grievous damage. Some bright spark in the garrison had ordered light field artillery rolled onto the foreshore. They blasted the last of the marauding ships with grape shot at point blank range. Matias rushed to the sea wall. He watched stunned, as the final battered stern ghosted into a bank of smoke, and the last shore gun fired. And then nothing, like a pregnant pause in a heated conversation.

1624

Silence.

Ears ringing.

Relative silence.

Questions ricocheted about his shocked mind. *Mierda*, was that it? What had this achieved other than wanton destruction? No landing parties. No invasion. Soon our men-of-war would be out in the open sea. They'd chase down those Dutch pricks. Then we'd see.

Crews were manning the capstans, warping huge war ships towards the harbour entrance, aided now by a following wind. The mighty Asunción, triple decked, hundred gunner was even now approaching the entrance, towering high above buildings lining the street.

Yellow flashes far out to sea. Faint puffs of smoke. Another line of ships. A mile or more out this time. The familiar sonic rumble. Once again they were under bombardment. Iron balls whistled through the air. A section of battlement high on Morro Castle exploded. Great chunks of masonry tumbled into the sea. Cannon clattered over the parapet.

More lights twinkled in the distance. Yet more iron rained down. The Asunción fell victim to this relentless hail. Whip staff smashed, it turned awkwardly. Its mainmast fell, crashing into the street crushing house roofs, canvas and shrouds dragging along the cobbles. Fires broke out aboard. There was a dull explosion deep in its gut, as the magazine caught. Water gushed up through its gundecks. Soon only its aft castle and masts were above the surface of the canal. The fleet was securely bottled up, with one of its own as a cork.

Castle gunners would now be sweating to re-elevate their ordinance. This was more like the trajectory they'd trained for. Cannons continued this brutal exchange until dusk. Another ship caught fire in the harbour. An explosion far out to sea. The artillery duel continued with ferocious intensity for the remainder of the day. When they finally lost the light, batteries ceased to exchange fire. The mysterious fleet faded into the night.

FIFTY — *the butcher's tally*

'Mister Jensson at the door, Your Grace,' announced Crips.

Jansson wasn't a man to relish delivering unwelcome news. Not that he was a coward, far from it. He'd just simply suffered the curse of a sensitive nature, which didn't sit well with his Viking blood. He left the great cabin of Visitación with shoulders slumped. His apprentices greeted him and received clips round the ears for the indolent useless waste of flesh that they were. The look of desolation on the Admiral's face had fair crushed his heart. And someone but Jansson had to suffer.

'With no chance of careening Your Grace,' he'd said, 'she's going down.'

Words stuck in his mouth. The look on the Admiral's face fair broke his heart. The pride of his fleet had suffered catastrophic impact below the waterline. Stove in two of her mighty planks, snapped one of her timbers like a rotten carrot. He'd done all he could. Draped canvas on the outside, braced her from the inside, the pumps were working constantly, but that was only staving off the inevitable. To save her he'd need to beach her. And that wasn't going to happen.

The Admiral called for Shoenmaeker.

'Transport all my gear back to the Zeelander. Strip everything of value or utility off her. I'll give you an hour. Pack the hold with powder. Douse the decks with oil.'

'You're not, are you?'

'Assemble a skeleton crew,' said the Grevinna.

'Volunteers,' added the Admiral, a tear making stately progress down his cheek. 'Ask for volunteers.'

With nightfall the artillery duel petered out. After a while, Havana's residents came out of hiding. Tears wept. Fires fought. Injured tended. Dead carted away. On the sea wall a bemused and increasingly angry crowd fermented in their bitterness. Unable to rebuke the unknown enemy on the horizon they screamed abuse at the soldiers who'd failed to protect them. Matias found himself caught up in their movement like a fish in the sway of seagrass. Troops were massing on the beaches. Far as the eye could see in either direction more platoons were arriving. Positioning field artillery. Erecting barriers. Embedding rows of sharpened stakes. Pikemen. Musketeers. Grenadiers. Ranged in straggling formation along the shores. Officers barking orders. Bonfires flaring, hissing at the water's edge, illuminating the sand dunes.

Something was happening at sea.

Out of the darkness a lone ship materialised. A spiderweb of rigging silhouetted in the moonlight. Full sail. Heading towards them. The crowd went silent as cannons blasted out from both forts. As it came closer the field artillery on the beaches opened fire. White plumes of seawater billowed up in the darkness around the vessel. Round shot began hitting home. Debris flew from the fo'c'sle.

The shore batteries roared again. A blaze of light from the battlements, clouds of acrid smoke drifting down. The ship's mizzen sagged. Men were darting in the shadows of the deck; soldiers opened fire. Musket balls peppered the ship. A yellow light blossomed in the stern. Soon the whole aft deck was on fire. Flames climbing like salamanders up the rigging. Sails caught. The whole vessel became enveloped in a massive fireball. And it was heading straight for the harbour entrance.

Something occurred to Matias. And he recollected experiencing the same feeling just once before. Second mate on an old Caravel. Undercrewed. Beating through a five-day storm in Biscay. Sixteen-hour watches. Exhaustion. Isolation. Hunger. Cold. Pitch black, blinded by sleet. In his mind he saw the entrance to Santander laid out like a chart beneath his feet. Like streets he could walk down. He knew with unsupported certainty which way to steer. He never forgot that transcendent moment of unblemished clarity.

Same today. Later years he described this as a mechanical whirring followed by a dull metallic clunk. Like a mighty cathedral clock preparing to chime the hour. Somewhere deep in the maze of his mind, lightning arced, connections occurred. The random nature of the attack suddenly made complete sense. He stared at the faces in the crowd like puppets pressing around him. At the toy soldiers manning the sand barricades. At the officers bellowing orders in their comically theatrical uniforms. He felt unchallengeably superior. Godlike. A giant observing a chess game played out by blindfolded imbeciles. Did no one else recognise what was occurring here, what all this signified?

There was a sudden gust. The fire ship accelerated and flared brighter. Wasn't it obvious? He turned and pushed his way out of the sweating, tight-packed masses. As he broke free the blazing ship smashed into the harbour boom. Flaring sails wafted into the air. Burning spars hissed into the sea.

He shoved his way through the crowd, picking up pace. There were two reasons for this haste.

First was the explosion he knew was about to occur. A few more paces and the ground shook. Cracks zig-zagged through the mortar of the harbour wall. He stepped hastily aside as a chimney tumbled into the street, followed by a shower of roof tiles. The chain barrier blasted apart. Matias considered the very real possibility his ears would never work again. He looked back at where he had been standing. Huge chunks of flaming ship's timbers rained down like hell fire on the bystanders. The fractured remains of the burning hulk trailing smoke floated into the crowded harbour propelled by a flood tide. Terrified bystanders ran about mindlessly. Matias shook his head and strode away from this mayhem, ears ringing, slipping into the dark side streets.

His second reason was simple. He knew with great confidence what had motivated the attack. This was not an invader softening up a target. It was all too obvious for a genuine attack. Again he found himself bestriding a vast chart — information flooding in, like water through a stove-in hull. This bombardment had been an ingeniously choreographed distraction. The soldiers could scan the sea long as they liked; raiders would not be swarming up the beaches in longboats.

No, they were already in the city. And, what's more, he knew where and why.

FIFTY-ONE — *the falconet*

'The Bear Cub's had it. Scuttle the bitch. Disperse the crew over the surviving ships. I'll be back in a minute.'

Such were the last words of Captain Cornelius Kraft. He took to his bunk for a quick restorative nap and never awoke. They discovered a musket ball had entered below his heart, passed through his left lung and exited two inches below his scapula.

Alphonse du Lac collapsed, beyond consolation. On the Black Bear Blaise Kneebone fell victim to the last shot of the engagement. Fourth in seniority, young Skyler Hurst found himself thrust into the role of squadron commander.

The squadron gathered at the mouth of the Rio Almendares, close to the shore as they dared. The buffalo swam ashore, led by longboats. Sleds floated through the surf. Sleds rather than carts, for a good reason. Little there to break. Easy to store onboard. Nothing complicated to assemble. They could float the damned things ashore. Sleds had disadvantages, of course, or the wheel wouldn't have superseded it. The most obvious being friction. To compensate they'd brought teams of massively muscled oxen and planned to take an off-road route through the tobacco fields. Crushed crops, someone posited, would act as a lubricant. They took a ship's cannon and powder to blast access. At first the sleds seemed to work. Hard going, nevertheless.

But a demi-culverin was an over ambitious choice. The sweet jasmine aroma of crushed tobacco followed them as they trudged. But a misstep sent the barrel toppling into a deep ditch. And there it lay, and no amount of effort could lift it back onto the sled. So, they cut it free and proceeded on their way. They'd have to hope powder alone would be enough to blast into to the warehouse.

Skyler hung back, checking the map. The storehouse should be just round the next corner.

Ahead of them in the narrow, overhung and otherwise dark street stood a figure illuminated by a pair of lanterns on either side of the path. In his belt a pair of big saddle pistols kept company with a wicked looking bollock dagger. But that was not the most threatening aspect of his appearance. No, that honour fell to a bronze falconet set on iron-rimmed wheels, mouth modelled after a hound's maw, pointing directly at them. They reined back the oxen, and the party came to a ragged halt. Skyler folded his map as he walked. The man in the shadows ahead was leaning on the carriage wheel of his cannon, close by the touch hole, a smouldering linstock cradled in his arms. No one could accuse Matias Suárez of lacking initiative. Or guts.

Skyler walked uncertainly to the fore of the oxen.

'You the capitán?' said Matias.

'I am,' said Skyler, doffing his cap theatrically.

'You look awfully young.'

'There's a reason for that,' said Skyler.

'Which is?'

'I am awfully young.'

'But you're still the capitán?'

'That I am. What's in your pretty little cannon. Grape?'

'And a few chains, bit of everything really.'

'You're not... with the garrison?'

'First mate of the *Nuestra Señora*, your lads just sunk her,' he lied.

'Please accept my apologies,' said Skyler. 'We could use a smart fellow like you.'

'Good,' said Matias, 'I was rather hoping we could be friends.'

The falconet was indeed a work of art. Engraved along the five feet of its slim barrel were intricate depictions of birds of prey and hunting scenes. They'd turned it round, hitched the wheel hubs to an ox, and hauled it before the huge double gates of an anonymous and substantial looking stone warehouse. Matias had previously revealed he had appropriated his bronze 'pet' from the governor's residence in the confusion of the bombardment. Manhauled it there himself. In response to disbelieving looks, he explained it was mostly down hill.

One of the gunners in the crew hoicked out as much of the grape as he could, then rammed home a one pound round shot wadded with moist sacking. The carriage leapt backwards as the ball punched out the entire lock mechanism. But the doors remained stubbornly closed. Troops could be heard mustering within. Challenges issued, orders bellowed, trumpets blared. Matias reloaded the falconet, and the next blast took out one of the hinges. The remains of the door hung on by it's one remaining attachment. Creaking, it slowly sagged, but did not fall. A volley of musket fire burst through a gap. A couple of Skyler's raiders received injury. Skyler's men hastily reloaded the mini cannon with a double charge. The touch hole fizzed, the carriage leapt back, and the barrel blasted a wicked assortment of grape, disintegrating the damaged gate. Screams came from within. Men shouting *rendición.* Urged on by Skyler, his men axed through the remaining hinges and what remained of the doors collapsed inwards. Wounded Spanish soldiers scattered about the inner courtyard. Those whole-of-limb abandoned the fight and surrendered.

Their sleds were loaded to capacity with bullion. Men stuffed their pockets, but they couldn't carry it all. They scattered excess gold through the streets about the warehouse as a distraction to potential pursuers. Matias liberated a donkey, packing panniers with all the beast could carry and hid his hoard out of town. He agreed to join Skyler in Tortuga when he got a chance. But secretly his heart was set against the high seas now. He'd had his fill of adventure. Nice little inn would do for him.

'Take what you like mate,' said Skyler, 'we can't carry it all.' *What an invitation.*

Next morning Matais strolled back to the Loro Negro Inn, finding it in ruins. Smoke drifting up from what once was a kitchen. The future Señora Matais Suárez sat dazed in the rubble like a discarded rag doll, surveying the carnage with her one good eye.

'*Hijo de puta, eres tú,*' she moaned, without looking up.

FIFTY-TWO — *Frœyja and Óðr*

Severin Karlsson tongued beads of salt spray from his stubble. The crossing from the Andromeda had been wetter than anticipated. Short choppy seas: the oarsmen couldn't find their rhythm. He removed his headgear as he strode across the Zeelander's deck. Two plaits the colour of summer wheatfields tumbled past his shoulders. He stared at the cap; it wasn't his cap. It was a common sailor's cap. He'd served the Grevinna eight years, yet her summons still reduced him to a hopeless imbecile. It wasn't fear, but it wasn't something so far removed. The Grevinna, the vengeful Frœyja of the seas. Kind mother, cruel seducer, rampaging Valkyrie, cunning witch. And now she'd met the Admiral, her mighty Óðr. Her power must surely be boundless. Facing the great cabin, he took a moment to calm himself, to check the rest of his attire. Was he at least wearing the correct breeches? Crips' and Sheng's voices echoed in the vestibule. They were vying for the privilege of serving the great man his tea. He'd taken to his bed with a headache in the company of his dogs. The door opened and Crips admitted Karlsson.

Karlsson found the Mistress of the Fjords alone. The day had been stifling. The wind was strengthening. Perhaps foreshadowing something more intense. Tropical skies were less easy to read than those of his ice-bound homeland. Whatever may develop, its cooling effect was more than welcome. He found her by the gallery window, her loose silver hair teased by the breeze. Havana was aglow across the darkening seas. Smoke wreathed the stubby mountains, misting the sickle moon beyond. She didn't turn, speaking as though they were in mid-conversation. Like he'd missed the beginning of her declamation through inattention.

'There are galleys in that filthy port,' she said, turning now. Her eyes flashed like lightning across a glacier. A glow of perspiration on a fair brow, crossed with filaments of grief.

'They'll be bound to have some of our boys working their cursed oars. *Bland mördarna, förskingrare, sodomiter och andra fattiga olyckliga.* My soul bleeds to think of my poor granddaughter. And Anders could be there, Severin. He could in that harbour chained in one of their galleys. Vain hope, yes I know. We will free those slaves in Anders name. Burn the Spanish *stinker båtar*. Under normal circumstances you know I would lead a raid myself. But now I have responsibility to this fleet. A duty to my admiral. Will you take my place Severin, *med ditt starka vikingahjärta?* Will you be my right hand. Will you be my sword of vengeance Severin, say you will.'

'You do me great honour My Lady,' he said, lowering his head, the better to hide a tear.

'Take who you wish from the Andromeda's crew,' said the Grevinna. 'Butcher the overseers without mercy. Do murder to them all, any who seek to impede you. Free the slaves without exception. Bring our boys here, help the rest go whichever way they wish. But the slave masters, no mercy, *absolut ingen nåd...*'

Karlsson, hesitated before speaking, at first unsure she'd finished.

'There are two members of His Grace's crew,' he said, 'who wish to join us. They suffered together on a Spanish galley; they'll need their vengeance too. Will you request the Admiral release his sailing master and boatswain?'

'Of course. If you don't hear to the contrary, consider it done.'

'My Lady.' He turned to leave, trembling, infected with her passion. She grabbed his arm. He started, her sacred touch.

'My little Anders, Severin. Write his name in blood. In blood, d'you hear me. *Skriv hans namn i blod.*'

'*I blod och smärta,*' said Karlsson.

Karlsson selected six men from the Andromeda, their best fighters, murderers all. Schoenmaecker and Matamata took leave from their fleet duties.

Austin Bird welcomed them aboard his little sloop. Karlsson was surprised to find the Rabbi and the Pastor below, closed-mouthed, on a private mission of their own. The sloop cast off from the Zeelander. The wind strengthened promising a fast passage. They reefed along the way, lee rail dipping beneath the waves. In less than three hours the battered masts of the squadron appeared, silhouetted above the tree line. They dropped anchor, finding the disembarkation well under way.

1624

FIFTY-THREE — *is that your daemon?*

The Rabbi had warned him there'd be moments like this. Isaac never fully appreciated what he'd meant. Like having an intellectual appreciation of a slap in the mouth. But never having first hand experience. Now the lesson was blindingly obvious. He and Benjamin had arrived at that point where planning collided with reality, in all its perverse and random unpredictability. They'd *planned* to steal a boat. Row across to Morro Castle, link up with Jesús, free Esther, return the way they'd come, rendezvous with the fleet. Simple. Nothing complicated in that.

They stood at the dock. So where was the boat they were going to steal? In his head Isaac had pictured a line of smart rowing gigs all moored up neatly at the harbour wall, from which he'd take his pick. Any day of the week they were there. Dozens of them, painters tied to iron mooring rings, tugging like tethered puppies. But this was not just any day. Today it was raining iron. Since the bombardment began there'd been a frenzied scramble to return to their ships. To his relief there was one tender remaining. He wandered nonchalantly towards it. It was a long heavy clinker-built monstrosity. What had once been smart white paint, now cracked and flaking, laminations of previous colours underneath. Must be eighteen feet long, some kind of gig. Three thwarts, intended for six oarsmen. Only two pairs of thole pins remained intact. Which was not a problem because there was only two of them. What was a problem was the water in the boat hiding under a surface of algae and weed, and the leather bailing bucket upon which toxic white fungus had made its home.

They stared at it for the longest time.

'I'd rather swim,' muttered Hangbè, shaking her head, backing away disdainfully.

No doubt in Isaac's mind, she could. And he wasn't sure they should trust their lives and their mission to this wooden death trap. Optimistically the water in the boat was below that of the sea surrounding it. Benjamin scooped his hand under the surface scum and tasted it. Isaac and Hangbè exchanged a look. Benjamin spat, smiling weakly.

'Rainwater,' he said. 'She'll be as tight as a drum.' Reaching for the bucket, he began bailing.

Six oars, three of which hadn't rotted beyond utility, tucked under the thwarts. There was also a mast, wrapped round by a surprisingly serviceable sail, stained a mottled cutch-amber. When the water level reduced enough, Isaac tapped the garboard planking. Seemed solid enough, few spots where it rang dull. But beggars and choosers, right? The sail will be no use on the way out, save it for their return — they re-stowed it.

Hangbè stripped off her clothes, for ease of swimming — such was her confidence in this craft. She stowed them on the stern thwart. If the water got that high, clothed or otherwise, they'd be swimming. Hangbè naked was not an unusual sight for the brothers, but it didn't instil confidence. A mule swam past them and clambered up the foreshore, shaking water off like a dog, tail like a burned fuse. With an imperious toss of its head, it very wisely took the road out of town.

She positioned herself at the stern, ready with the steering oar. Isaac shoved off and clambered aboard, joining Benjamin on the central thwart. It gave a warning creak and then snapped. Hangbè roared with laughter. They scrambled up wet of arse, moving to the forward thwart which creaked, but held. Once on the water they lost sight of Morro Castle behind the host of anchored galleons. The overlapping hull planking creaked ominously as they strained at the sweeps. A couple of hundred yards out, the water began creeping up through the bottom boards.

Isaac looked to Benjamin: 'Wanna taste it?' he said.

Hangbè sniggered, tossing Benjamin the bucket.

There was relief when they fell under the shadow of the nearest galleon. No one had challenged them, so far. They described a course through the shadows, ship-to-ship. Soon they would have to make a break across the exposed open water of the channel. The moment of maximal danger. But then, over the creaking of the oars, came an all too familiar sound. A faintly distant whistle, building to a deafening banshee howl. Another and then another. Soon too many to differentiate, as iron round shot came ripping through the pitch-black fabric of the sky. Stars breaking from their moorings in some raging heavenly tempest, crashing angrily to earth. Seawater plumed up all around, water cascaded down on them. The densely packed galleon fleet, through which they weaved, began taking hits. Giant timbers crashed into the sea. Masts toppled, tearing rigging from the decks. Crewmen screamed, officers bellowed orders, bells rung out, drums beat out the alarm. Fires broke out illuminating a scene of waterborne mayhem. Their fragile boat rocked alarmingly; waves slopped over the gunwales. The bombardment had clearly begun. Hangbè shook her head and bailed stoically. Heads down, the boys rowed on.

Round shot continued to fall. Isaac was secretly doubting the success of this reckless crossing. But then, as abruptly as the bombardment had begun, it ceased; returning fire petered out. Ships were burning, floating infernos reflected in the surface of these darkly confined waters. Longboat crews were desperately bending their backs to tow damaged vessels to shallow water. Harbourside buildings mirrored the conflagration at sea. Fires ignited by the bombardment reached through the smoke to link with their incendiary kin blazing fiercely around the distillery. By the time Hangbè had steered their little tender into open water a thick blanket of acrid smoke obscured the moon.

Passing the last anchored merchantman the wind picked up. Waves began slapping dangerously high on the gunwales. Isaac and Benjamin increased their stroke rate. Seas were piling up before them. Waves were coming from all directions, pitching them about. The water was up to their calves and the boat was wallowing dangerously. After what seemed like an age they began benefiting from the lee of the castle, and soon they'd entered calmer waters. In sight of the shore, they let their momentum take them. The keel grated reassuringly on the gravel bottom. Landfall was a rocky foreshore at the foot of Castle Moro. Panting, exhausted, but relieved, they dragged the boat ashore behind a natural rock promontory.

The brothers left Hangbè bailing sulkily in the shadows. They took a narrow foot-worn path which intersected a long, paved slope. Two hundred yards ahead of them was a squat arched doorway hung with heavy iron-bound oak doors. The air stank of cannon smoke, drifting from the battlements to hang in stratified layers over the water.

Once again that all too familiar banshee whistle. Masonry exploded high above. Screams followed the thunder of returning fire. The ground reverberated with the deafening bark of cannons. The artillery duel had recommenced. *What if the noise drowned out some crucial signal from Jesús, his voice or some secret knock?* They moved closer to the door, flattening themselves against the cool stone walls.

'You sure this is the place?' hissed Benjamin.

'Have faith,' said Isaac.

1624

'You sure this is the right time?'

'There was no specific time. After dark was all we agreed.'

'Can we trust him, what if this is a trap? Maybe he sold us out?'

'Didn't seem like the sort.'

'Maybe he forgot?'

'Now you're sounding desperate.'

'Just saying.'

'I can't speak to his memory. All's said and done he's one of us. That and he came highly recommended by people who have a lot to lose by aiding us. Try to have some faith little brother.'

'Don't know how you can be so calm.'

'Want to know the secret?'

'Well?'

'I'm not.'

'Not what?'

'Calm.'

'Oh.'

The castle door creaked open. Isaac glanced across to his brother, a dagger glinted in his hand. Jesús face. Look of concern. Knives, the least of his worries. He beckoned, and they slipped through the gap into the cool interior. The door closed behind them with a dull whisper that seemed to reverberate around the vast stone edifice.

'With me,' he said, like they needed the telling. He held an oil lantern; wick low, offering minimal light. Their guide knew precisely where he was going. Benjamin's insecurities echoed around Isaac's head as he followed close behind. What if this was a trap? What if this was betrayal, what if?

Jesús was wearing the uniform of a castle guard, yellow breeches, green doublet, crested steel helmet. They passed a row of doors with barred windows inset into the thick oak.

Voices ahead.

The soft glow of candlelight.

Women, giggling, half-a-dozen tiny footfalls, click, clack.

The occasional barely discernible word, meaningless out of context.

The light and voices faded up a winding stone staircase.

'My master's wife,' Jesús whispered, 'The Donna Carmelita.'

'But why...'

'All in the plan...'

As they waited two figures approached. A single oil lamp. Shadows forming grotesque shapes up the walls and across the ceiling. The rattle of keys. The creak of a door. Men's voices in hushed tones. A whimper, muffled screams, cut short. They burst into Esther's cell, clubbing Friar Ignatius and Brother González insensible. Esther squinted in Isaac's direction, face deathly pale in the flickering lamplight.

'Is that you?'

Jesús hung back, keeping company with the now insensible monks.

'Arrangements to make, bribes to pay,' he said, 'threats to issue. The Brotherhood is arranging a little surprise for those poxy priests. Keep going, the door will be ahead of you. I'll meet you outside.'

Esther caught his sleeve and whispered in his ear.

Thick crudely moulded candles illuminated the cold passage. Generation upon dripping generation set in irregular stone recesses. The chill mossy dampness in the air reminded them they were below sea level. Trudging up worn stone steps the walls became progressively less saturated. The temperature, less bone-numbingly chill. Four flights up they arrived in a corridor lit by sweet-smelling candles in ornate sconces. The austere decor not out of keeping with the servant's quarters in some lesser baronial palace. Aal looked about her in wonder. Esther, who was only too familiar with this location, shuddered uncontrollably.

The Bailiff's lair was just a little further. Aal opened her mouth to speak. Jesús signalled quiet. Esther's eyes widened like a tortured animal; it took all her strength to continue. Jesús trod lightly as he approached an arched door. He blew out the candles either side, reducing the corridor to a riot of ill-defined shadows. Again Esther found herself shuddering; fear, and something else. Something eager, something impatient. She bit down hard on her lip tasting coppery blood. Trembling she reached out for Aal's chill hand. Esther and Aal flattened against the wall on either side of the entrance to the Bailiff's quarters. The muffled sound of snoring came from within.

Jesús smashed his fist on the door:

'Captain Hamández sir,' he yelled.

He banged on the oak panel once more.

The Bailiff's sleep roughened voice bellowed out: 'What?'

'Sir, there's something up with the prisoners.'

The same irritable voice:

'Well deal with it why don't you. I'm trying to get some sleep.'

'But sir, the head jailer asked for you. Must be serious. Wouldn't dare wake you otherwise.'

Noises from within; closer this time.

'This better be good,' came a gravelly rumble.

At the sound of a bolt retracting Jesús threw all his weight against the door. It flew open, it's iron studs smashing into the bailiff's stubbled face. As he staggered back, Jesús shoved past the recoiling door, clubbing him in the face with the butt of his pistol – once twice, three times, marching into the room as the Bailiff staggered further, and further back with each successive blow. On the third impact he dropped to his knees. And there he remained, swaying, eyes staring straight ahead, with a perplexed expression fixed on a barely conscious face. Jesús stuffed a cloth into his unresisting mouth, securing it with a gag. Turning to Esther he slipped a slim double-edged dagger into her hand.

'You'll be wanting this.' he said. 'I'll be outside, don't take too long.'

Ten minutes of muted shrieking later the door opened. Aal burst out and vomited in the corridor, the door slamming behind her. More time passed. The sounds reached a crescendo, softening to mere murmurs. Finally Esther's blood splattered face peered into the corridor, locking eyes with Jesús. Over her shoulder he caught a glimpse of a candle-lit room newly decorated with offal and body parts, some of which were still moving. The Bailiff, kneeling, opened as if by an impatient child. Entrails still attached somewhere inside his carcass draped around the room like seasonal decorations. His mouth lolled open, sans tongue. The puzzled expression persisted, eyes flicking left to right. Was he grudgingly perhaps admiring the quiet efficiency of this flamboyant exhibition of the torturer's art?

Jesús found himself amazed by Esther's productivity. He chivvied them from the blood-soaked chamber, conducting them through a maze of passageways to where their rescuers waited impatiently in the shadows of the beach.

'You took your time,' chided Isaac.

Esther walked past him to the boat. 'Hello little brother,' she said, smiling sweetly at Benjamin. 'How much you've changed.'

They made it to the boat. Jesús had wisely decided to join them. Quite apart from his recent actions, with the arrival of the Inquisition every converso family in Havana was under threat. The wind was favourable and strengthening. They mounted the mast and pushed off from the shore. As the patched brown sail filled, they shipped the oars, sailing across the inky waters.

The rendezvous point was a mile, or two from where the city petered out into plantations, and plantations into scrub. The distillery fire was spreading fast. Further fires were breaking out close to their objective. Within half-a-mile of the shore, they could see galleys ablaze and all

1624

manner of murder occurring.

The crack of gunfire. Musket balls whistled overhead, puckering the sail. A Spanish galley, must have ten men rowing, was powering towards them.

'Where's Hangbè?' said Isaac.

He caught a ripple in the water. A black shape in the path of the Spaniards. He slipped into the water. He clung for a moment to the gunwale:

'We'll catch up when we can, look after them Benjamin.'

With that he was gone.

The Spanish vessel powered towards Isaac, oars kicking up white water; just in time, he dived beneath the thrashing oars. Hangbè's lythe form leapt from the darkness, like a breaching Dolphin. She grabbed the helmsman, dragging him overboard, and beneath the waves. Startled soldiers spun round firing pistols into the dark. Hangbè broke the surface using the helmsman as a shield. The vessel rocked precariously, as Isaac clambered over the gunwale behind them. He dragged two soldiers tumbling into the sea, slashing at throats with his long knife. Hangbè now appeared on board; her strange weapon hacking from victim-to-victim. As the last two Spaniards toppled overboard, she turned frantically to the oarsmen, expecting attack, but found them lolling disinterestedly, chained to their sweeps.

They drifted alongside the gig, now swamped and barely afloat. Benjamin and Jesús helped Esther and Aal transfer to the galley.

'Keep pulling my friends,' urged Hangbè, 'and soon you'll all be free.'

The slaves rowed urgently to the distant shore.

1624

FIFTY-FOUR — *whistling a happy tune*

The beachhead was a monotonal picture of lively industry. The sun had softened, lost its fire, the great brazen orb was descending below the horizon. The crews of the five great ships of the first squadron were busy unloading and repairing. A longboat towed the sleds. Others, heaped with weaponry, men and equipment, plied back and forth between ship and shore. Carpenters were at the masts tearing down damaged spars, hauling up fresh timber: lashing, hammering, nailing. Riggers were ripping down damaged cordage, tightening stays.

Men goaded oxen through the surf onto a white sand beach, fringed with palms, forest beyond, hills beyond that. Released from gravity, luxuriating in the cooling water, the huge oxen appeared reluctant to make landfall. Lookouts amongst the palm trees cresting the dunes, shouldered muskets. Groups of men were coalescing on the beach. Jansson was grateful for the cooling breeze, for the surf splashing over their bows. Six men pulling hard to keep the craft aligned in the foam of the tumbling waves. Helmsman hauling on the sweep, as they surfed out of the breakers and onto the fine sugar sand. Janssen, caught sight of Skyler's fair hair amongst a group of grizzled hands. Supervising disembarkation, he was. Pointing, giving instructions, being obeyed. Men rushing from the huddle to carry out his commands. Jansson approached, trailing footprints in the saturated sand. Skyler broke off when he saw him.

'Welcome friend. How goes it?' said Skyler. Face of a boy; a man very much in control of events. Jensen outlined his mission.

'You'll find the galley docks about two leagues west sou' west.' Skyler nodded towards the hills. 'Scouts say they're in the bay, about half a league south of the city. There are paths to follow. When you get closer, follow your nose.'

Jansson returned to his men. They'd already dragged the longboat above the tide line. The boatswain was handing out muskets. Each man carried his preferred close-combat weapon, edged or blunt force. Some had bits of scavenged armour. A couple wore Spanish crested helms, a parody of proud Conquistadores. Matamata, his scarified, tattooed face daubed in war paint, was taking practice swings with a wooden club edged with shark's teeth. Striking terrifying poses.

'West sou' west,' said Janssen. 'Maybe an hour's march.' Matamata grunted a response in his native tongue. Shoenmaeker slapped him on his broad back: 'Soon my friend,' he said, grimly, 'soon.'

The going was tougher than expected. Hills to circumvent, paths dividing or petering out, steps to re-tread, undergrowth to hack their way through. Jansson relied on his seaman's instincts and the occasional glance at the stars. Skyler had been correct, in the final approach there was no problem locating the galleys — a blind man could have accomplished it with ease. Indeed, someone muttered, too deeper breath might render you blind. Even the city slum dweller, the sailor confined to the least commodious fo'c'sle, the prisoner-of-war chained in a mildewed prison hulk, anyone inured to the reek of close-packed human habitation, the miasma pervading a Spanish galley would come as a profound shock.

Breaking through the edge of the forest they sighted their prey. Thin moonlight filtered through a snot of clouds. Four of the beasts, moored side by side, in a harbour the colour of curdled milk. There was cold fury in rescuer's ranks, becoming more combustible as they crept closer. These captives exuding this stink could be countrymen, shipmates, brothers of the oceans — *but for the grace of God.*

Matamata took the first sentry. As his Samoan war club ripped through the Spaniard's neck, he went to scream his war cry. Schoenmaecker leapt onto his back, clamping his hand across his mouth just in time. But the fragile cord of restraint had already frayed through, and the raiders rampaged through the Spanish encampment regardless of danger, exacting murder and mayhem and torture and justice.

Jansson burst in on their commandant. The overdressed pig was ripping off chunks of greasy chicken, stuffing his fat mouth in sight of starving slaves. He didn't kill him but trussed him up. This was not an act of mercy. Shoenmaeker's blacksmiths hammered the pins from the prisoners' shackles. Tears of gratitude turned to anger when they caught sight of the commandant. Jansson shoved him into their midst and the Chicken-ripper was himself torn to pieces.

Sights onboard would melt the most flinty of hearts. Each vessel, two rows of hairless skeletal heads, scarred by brutally enforced shavings. Eyes bereft of hope staring out from hollow, red-rimmed sockets. Bodies barely recognisable as human, hunched in their own filth. Shoulders

1624

puckered like a crocodile's back by repeated lashings. Hands swollen and calloused, wrists raw from the manacles attaching them to the oars. Ragged remnants of clothing jumping with fleas, crawling with lice. Insects wriggling in the accumulated filth beneath their benches. Clouds of flies buzzed overhead — the human station, rendered coequal by abuse.

He and Matamata had liberated galley slaves before. And for Jansson it was the ultimate mission of his voyage — his mistress's obsession, her life's work. And now the Spanish had her granddaughter.

There were a dozen Nordics amongst the slaves of which four were Swedes. Also ten English, four French, nineteen Moroccans, sixteen Flemish, twenty Africans, eleven Spanish and sixty-one native Taíno. Jansson kept meticulous record.

The Taíno raided their tormentor's supplies and took to their native forest. The rest, shuffling on atrophied legs, followed their rescuers. Schoenmaecker and Matamata put the galleys to the torch. Jansson's last act was to leave a message — *död åt alla slavvårdare.* He planted the Swedish flag into the ground, wiping his bloody hands on his breeches. The Grevinna would be proud. As he strolled along, he began whistling a happy tune, picked up from who knows where. Snatches of verses came to him, something about 'Blacktail Spit.'

Catchy little ditty.

1624

FIFTY-FIVE — *shooting sparks*

The slaves pulled at the oars. Mechanically, unerringly; anything but perfection long since lashed out of them. But then one rower mistimed, his oar clattering between the thole pins. He cringed, head spinning round, shooting a fearful glance over his shoulder with the expectation of the whip. He froze, shivering. But the pain didn't come, he collapsed over his oar, shoulders shaking. Then picked up the rhythm once more pulling in perfect unison with the others. Moro Castle dissolved into a cardboard silhouette behind them. Flashes from the battlements, periodically reminding them of its three-dimensional form. The wind had veered eastwards, swirling around the damaged fleet.

Looking north, Benjamin took no little pride in his first foray into arson. The landward side of the city was offering up a pall of black smoke. He could make out the fire's genesis from halfway across the harbour — its glow illuminating the night.

Ahead of them, where they planned to beach the boat, more fires had broken out. As they approached ever closer, they could see half-a-dozen hot spots, spreading, growing, merging. Soon they were but bright halos in dense banks of smoke enveloping the boat. Disoriented in the darkness, eyes stinging with the fumes, they found themselves making landfall downstream of their initial objective. Cutting through the smoke blanket, they faced a raging inferno. What once were docks, were now a collapsing twisted charred framework. What once were slave galleys were now hissing, spitting blazing hulks, fighting an uneven battle with the waves. The intensity of the light was dazzling in the darkness, the roar of the wind-driven flames deafening.

The galley's keel grated on gravel. They ground to a gentle halt. Yet the slaves continued to pull. Oars kicking up sand and mud. 'Stop, stop, stop rowing,' yelled Isaac. 'Benjamin stop them.'

His brother jumped into their midst, sliding in filth. He attempted to stay their arms, yet still they pulled, looking up at him with hollow eyes, uncomprehending.

1624

'Para, para, para de remar...' yelled Jesús.

They immediately ceased to pull. Benjamin and Jesús jumped overboard, up to their knees in cool water. Relieved of their weight the boat lifted from the seabed. Splashing, muscles straining, gasping with the effort, they began dragging it closer to the grassy bank. Isaac and Hangbè helped Esther and Aal over the gunwale, wading ashore with them. The oarsmen, as one, looked over their shoulders blinking at Jesús plaintively, like sleepwalkers rudely awakened. Isaac leapt from the boat leaving them chained to the sweeps. Not a word was raised in protest. They were part of the boat, and boats don't complain.

There was a scream. Aal had been impassive, even when musket balls buzzed past her head. But she was quiet no longer. Hangbè's hand clamped over her mouth. They stood in the water, like statues. Hangbè naked between them, her other arm supporting Esther. Before them, a nightmare vision. Like a triptych Isaac had once seen. That mad painter from the Brabant, Jheronimus van Aken. Every variation of horror that could be visited on the human form was displayed before them. A field of bloody murder, illuminated by the fires of Hades. Mostly dead, yet some who should be dead still moved. The smell of charred wood and charred flesh overwhelmed them. Isaac's mouth watered reflexively. Then he discovered what was roasting. Spanish bodies half in, half out of fires. Crackling, bubbling like suckling pigs, grease running out of them. Smoke and flames rising like burnt offerings. Whirlwinds of fire shot sparks to the heavens.

Isaac took hold of Aal lifting her up to the riverbank. Feeling her breasts crush against him, his body reacted as men's bodies do. Despite the death-saturated surroundings, sexual chemistry triumphs overall. He imbibed her essence, became momentarily engulfed in her. This creature he knew could be an elixir or a poison. Wasn't it Paracelsus who'd said that these extremes could coexist? He left her trembling on the bank and went back for his sister. He took her in his arms, again an autonomic reaction and just as powerful. But this time it was the blending of similarities. Two bottles of the same vintage poured into one glass.

Jesús, the secret Jew, guided the party through the mayhem. Some victims clung onto life. Perhaps wishing they had the courage to release their grip. Which would be the most cruel act, Isaac thought, to leave them, or finish them off? In the end practicality was the decision maker. Mercy took time. They hurried on despite the pleadings. Bodies were strewn as far as the light of the fires permitted them to see. The cause of death and manner of mutilation was too varied to register. A breastplate over a fire glowing red. The flesh within sizzling and popping like a joint of beef. Torsos swaying inverted from trees, their limbs arranged in grotesque displays beneath. Impaled, disembowelled, ripped apart. Some playfully reformed in a spiteful parody of human anatomy. A leg from this man an arm from that. Bodies, limbs, organs strewn for them to trip over. Blood turning the thirsty ground into a sticky muddy obstacle. And so, they blundered their way through this carnival of the dead – through this hellscape.

Isaac hesitated, looked back the way they'd come. He tugged an axe from the chest of a corpse. Disappeared back through the smoke. Benjamin didn't need telling what he was about. Back aboard the galley Isaac hacked the manacles from the oars. The galley slaves assembled on the bank, confused, uncertain. The last of their number unchained, they stumbled mindlessly after their liberator. Catching up the main party, they formed the rear-guard of their stumbling procession.

The last sight was the most horrific. A headless, seated figure. It was supporting, or supported by, a staff. The yellow and blue of the Swedish flag fluttered from it in the breeze. Mounted on the top, the distorted head of the standard bearer. Eyes bulging, mouth open, drooling blood like a pig's head on a butcher's counter.

As they made it further away from the flames, darkness progressively swallowed them. There was no discernible path. Jesús seemed to be guiding them just north of west, as much as the terrain allowed. Neither brother could afford for emotion to overwhelm them. There'd be time enough for that later. When the task was complete; when they could say Esther was truly safe, when they were aboard a ship clear of Spanish waters. Nevertheless, a sense of achievement burned deep inside, fuelling them. They followed ditches. Blundered through undergrowth. A nicotine-stained nail paring of a moon offering little illumination. The odd cloud drifting across reducing that small blessing. Even with eyes now accustomed to the dark this was tortuously heavy going. There needs be an urgency to their progress. They needed to link with the squadron. With the rest of those fleeing this Spanish hell. The burning galleys would inevitably attract attention from the city. More soldiers would surely come.

They passed through a dense forest and onto an open plain where they intercepted a red dirt path. Jesús pointed east. This must have been what he'd been searching for. Hangbè and Benjamin supported Esther and Aal, their weakened legs dragging. Isaac brought up the rear leading the slaves, chains rattling. In the distance far behind they saw lights twinkling, swaying. On the open plain there would be nowhere to hide.

1624

Too far to retreat to the forest. So they ran. They stumbled, they scrambled, they hobbled, they did the best they could. There were more trees up ahead, cover in which to hide. If they could only make it. But now they can hear them, the soldiers. The rhythmic rattle of infantry at double time. The clatter of armour; boots in rhythm. Dogs. Horses. Closer by the second. Upon them, almost. Aal stumbled. Isaac threw himself on her, rolling them into a shallow ditch.

Orders barked:

'Fuego, fuego, dispara a los perros.'

The crack of musket fire; soldiers rushed past where Isaac and Aal hid. Slaves fell — dying, still chained. The rest ran on, gasping, crying. Mindless. Defenceless. Ready to collapse. To give in. End the running, to turn. If not to go down fighting, at least to face their enemy. And now there were men ahead of them blocking the escape into the forest. They found themselves surrounded, herded into a trap. Isaac could see one figure in front, dozens assembled behind. So, despite all their efforts, despite all their travels, they had lost at the final moment. Trapped. Helpless, Isaac watched Benjamin clutching Esther's hand, stagger to a despairing, breathless stop. Dropping to their knees, lungs bursting, they collapsed in a tangle onto the dirt of this cursed plain.

The man in the shadows ahead was leaning on the carriage wheel of his cannon, close by the touch hole, a smouldering linstock cradled in his arms. The falconet erupted. Grape blasted a path through the Spanish troops, followed by a devastating volley of musket fire from the forest. A wave of frenzied slaves and Tortugan buccaneers rushed from behind the smoking artillery piece. A tidal wave of hate smashed into the Spanish lines. Soon the few survivors were fleeing into the dark, harried by their own dogs, trampled by their own horses.

FIFTY-SIX — *adios á Cuba*

The sound of battle raging behind them. Jesús led the party through dark forests, around steep escarpments, and across moonlit plains. The crisp iodine aroma of the shoreline grew stronger with each pace. From the summit of the last hill they glimpsed the dark ocean stretching into infinity. A swarm of fireflies flickered on the shore. Out to sea mighty ships rose and fell like giant cormorants on the swell.

Gravity impelled their exhausted bodies the last half-mile, down a sharp incline. Passing through sparse stands of palm trees they crested the dunes, gasping for breath. The tide was out; white caps danced out to sea. Waves rolled in; surf broke noisily along an endless stretch of white sand beach.

They paused, flooded with relief, taking in the scene. No one spoke. Chest heaving, Benjamin glanced down at his hand. Esther's delicate fingers intertwining his. He turned to her, she to him. They looked away embarrassed, as though unsure what their expressions should convey. Disbelief perhaps. Or gratitude, maybe, to a higher power.

'Oi. Who the hell are you?' came a suspicious voice from the darkness. A dozen shadowy figures stepped out of a stand of palm trees; the sound of muskets cocked. Benjamin recognised the speaker:

'Petrus, it's me. Ben Amsalem.'

'Christ man, we'd just about given up on you.'

'Could you send someone to Kraft. Tell him we've arrived.'

'Sorry mate, Kraft's dead.'

'What?'

'Young Skyler as was, Mister Hurst as is, 'as taken command.'

'What about Du Lac?'

Embarrassed silence — Benjamin didn't press him.

'Anyway, Skyler's, running the squadron now,' Stoffel said. 'You need Brankfleet. Skyler's made him beachhead boss.'

Benjamin scanned the frenetic scene acted out below, not seeing Brankfleet.

'If you see him before us Petrus, let him know we're here, will you. Oh, and tell him we've picked up a few strays.' He nodded back at the freed galley slaves straggling towards them through the trees.

Hands on hips, he bent at the waist, catching his breath, like this brief exchange had exhausted him.

Hangbè huddled under a woollen cloak supplied by Jesús, naked beneath. Her head nuzzled Isaac's shoulder, one arm about his waist, panting like an over exercised hound. They collapsed on the warm sand next to Benjamin and Esther. Aal leaned on Esther's knees, arms intertwining her friend's legs like a cable about a capstan. Esther smiled and stroked Aal's tousled hair. Hangbè rested her head on Isaac's shoulder, he leaned into her. They sat there propped like dominoes. Despite the rush to the beach, Isaac felt no hurry to board, content to inhabit the moment.

Esther had changed, he thought, and yet she hadn't. Different, but the same. Child to woman, but something more, something deeper had shifted. Her naïve arrogance had dissolved along with her puppy fat, revealing something adamantine beneath. Had that iron core always been there? He couldn't believe they were together again. Their dream fulfilled. A voice within was asking, was this how he imagined it would be. Time enough for such thoughts, echoed back a voice.

Look at him. Look at Isaac. After two years they must seem unfamiliar to her as well. Indeed she hadn't recognised them at first. But now was not the time to wallow in such speculation. And then he saw the puckered lash lines on her shoulder, leading down beneath her shift. Tears of rage overbrimmed his eyes.

On the ridge above, Petrus Stoffel's men patrolled the dunes, skirting the edges of the palm forest, welcoming back the stragglers from the battle. A noise: they started, raising weapons. An ox snorted from the trees, sauntering past, with wide-eyed bovine self-possession. They laughed, releasing tension, uncocking muskets.

Jesús hadn't collapsed on the sand with the brothers. He'd continued to the sea. The galley slaves had staggered after him on atrophied legs, collapsing into the surf. Waves washed over them. Sea water cleansing and rehydrating their abused bodies.

The other occupants of this beach appeared oblivious of these new arrivals. Their focus was on the boats rowing back and forth between shore and ship, riding the foaming waves. Elijah Brankfleet's Africans were busy dismounting Matias's falconet from its ornate carriage. Loading the gleaming barrel as it rested in the stern of Brankfleet's personal craft.

1624

Isaac stared soft-focused through his tears at the sights surrounding them. The tribes of Yīsrā'ēl, he thought, fleeing the wrath of Pharaoh, hesitating on the banks of the Sea of Reeds, for a sign from their Creator. In this instance, the Lord's mercy was manifesting in a less spectacular display of His might. The escapees were going over the waters this time, not trudging through them — an altogether more plausible scenario.

There they gathered. Those who were free, those who had freed themselves, and those freed by others. This rigid demarcation lost definition as they approached the crashing surf.

The converso community of Havana. Their families and retainers, fleeing the malevolent spite of the Inquisition, carrying what they could. Jews genetically predisposed to evacuate at a moments notice. Embracing the opportunity of escape to Tortuga. Anywhere that was independent of the Spanish Empire, and its anti-Semitic edicts. Anywhere that forbade the Inquisition entry. They huddled on the sand in family groups, surrounded by their scant possessions.

The dwellers of palenques, escapees and rebels. Liberated mining and plantation slaves. Women from bordellos freed from lifetimes of indignity and servitude. An admixture of colours, and religions and nationalities. Those who had so bravely and enthusiastically harried their Spanish overlords. Who had raised an army to burn their oppressor's crops. Native tribesmen dreaming of throwing off the Spanish yolk forever.

And, most tragic of all, the galley slaves. Their shaved heads luminous in the weak light of the begrudging moon. Walking ghosts. Standing hunched like hairless emaciated apes. Waiting in the waves. Allowing the balm of mother ocean to heal their sores, cleanse their bodies, free their minds.

They loaded the gold first, an unspoken and unchallengeable priority. An hour before Isaac and his party made it to the beach, an argument had erupted within the squadron's ranks. There were those who would honour their pledge to the evacuees. And there were those who declared them a superfluous liability. They had the gold securely on board, why not leave those silly twats behind? They'd served their purpose. The Spanish were bound to arrive in force soon. The complaints turned physical. Pushing, shoving, moments away from resorting to weapons. Fresh-faced Skyler, untried Skyler. A vociferous minority was bombarding him with a barrage of raucous complaint.

On hearing the commotion Du Lac emerged red-eyed from his couch of mourning to support his appointee with drawn pistols. But Skyler was a consensus leader by inclination. He was also a realist. He recognised that in certain situations one didn't have the luxury of reasoned debate. Situations where the democratic process was simply unworkable. Situations where action trumped diplomacy. This, he concluded, was just such an situation. The ringleader was nose-to-nose with him, bawling obscenities and spittle in his face. Sighing in resignation, Skyler simply walked away from what was, so obviously, doomed to be a fruitless confrontation.

Grabbing a boarding pike, he spun round, impaling the aggressor through the belly. He propelled his screaming victim across the deck on the end of a boarding pike, pinning him like a bug to the gunwale. For the avoidance of ambiguity, he pounded the spearpoint deep into the wood with the flat of a boarding axe.

'Leave him be,' he ordered, over the pathetic screams of the would-be mutineer, 'let the bastard wriggle. If he's still alive by the time I've finished m' breakfast, you may unstick him.'

It would be a long time before Skyler's leadership was ever questioned again. Certainly on the remainder of this voyage his orders were most particularly obeyed. Longboats continued to distribute passengers through the squadron; the beach was clearing rapidly.

The crackle of a musket volley. Isaac spun round. An ounce of lead buzzed past his ear to bury itself in the trunk of a palm. Spanish army reinforcements had arrived earlier than anticipated. Horses crested the dunes hauling field artillery. More soldiers teemed into sight by the second. Clattering through the palm forest. Forming up in ranks on the overlooking hill.

Brankfleet's men returned fire, crouched behind sand dunes. The last of the evacuees rushed to the longboats under a blizzard of lead. Some didn't make it, spilling their lifeblood in the surf. As the Spaniards rushed down the beach the squadron opened with the long nines, churning up the sand. Half-a-dozen startled buffalo broke from the trees, trampling through the Spaniard's ranks. The last boats prepared to embark. A Spanish officer urged on his men. Matias touched a fuse to the falconet propped on the transom of Brankfleet's longboat. It leapt into the air, blasting grape into the Spanish ranks, before toppling into the sea.

Benjamin tripped, struggled to run, limping badly. Isaac rushed back and helped him to his feet, desperately dragging him towards the last longboat. A Spanish officer let loose with a big saddle pistol. Isaac flinched, blood blossoming through his shirt. Yet he continued to struggle on. The officer raised his other pistol, taking more careful aim.

Hangbè uttered a shriek, leaping from the boat, splashing through the surf, rushing back up the beach. Her weapon left her hand with the added momentum of her sprint. The blades struck the officer full in the chest, knocking him off his feet. His pistol discharging harmlessly in the air. Between them, Hangbè and Isaac dragged Benjamin limping to the boat and hoisted him over the gunwale. Hangbè checked Isaac's wound and tutted, she'd seen worse.

Arriving at the African Prince, they found them busy raising sail. The squadron had hauled in their bow anchors. They'd swung to stern-hung kedges with the wind and outgoing tide pointing their figureheads to the open sea. No longer broadside on, their cannons ceased to pound the beach. And now they began receiving fire from the Spanish artillery. The Prince's aft castle exploded in a storm of splinters. Anchor cables groaning, bar taut. Wind shrieking through the rigging. Sunlight-bleached sails, threatening to split. On Skyler's command Brankfleet let off a stern chaser – the signal to release. Crewmen axed through anchor cables thick as a man's thigh. As the fibres parted the strengthening wind propelled the squadron out of the mouth of the river, from churning freshwater into storm tossed salt.

1624

FIFTY-SEVEN — *delicious*

The Admiral's squadron was making little way, drifting on the tide. His Grace had resisted the temptation to reunite the fleet. Strategically unwise to do so, was his opinion. Two squadrons provided more flexibility, more resilience. There was always a possibility of a threat from an unknown direction. Although from whence this would be he couldn't think. The Spanish men-of-war were all that could challenge them, and they were safely bottled up. Just because a matter was improbable, didn't mean it was impossible. But it would surely take the Spanish days, weeks to clear that obstruction. In truth he felt his position quite secure.

The Grevinna and the Admiral took supper in the great cabin. Mr Crips and Li Sheng we're competitively serving. The rules of the competition unspoken, unknown, even to the combatants. Prescience, punctiliousness and precision were the governing factors. The admiral's diminutive Dyak bodyguard, Jugah Tawl Koroh, as usual, took no part in onboard activities. His sole duty, the safety of their master. And that earned respect, even admiration. He sat cross legged on the deck by the door, human bone-handled sword laying across his tattooed thighs. Li Sheng brought him a bowl of food which he ate with his fingers.

The Grevinna and the Admiral discussed new appointments following the temporary absence of their top hands. Obadiah Hawkewind would cover as first mate of the Zeelander. Abraham loveless as boatswain. And Bengt Claësson was now acting first mate of the Andromeda.

'Your little *jäkel* on the floor over there,' said the Grevinna.
'What about him my love?'
'Don't like the way he looks at me, like he's wondering how I'll taste.'
'Oh, we've all been guilty of that from time to time.'
'And how best to cook me, slow roast or griddled.'
'Raw, I have found is best.'
'So how *do* I taste?'

'Quite delicious.'

Before the second bombardment began, the Spanish dockhands had been attempting to warp their war ships into the bay. They were mid-way through lowering the chain barrier. But when the fire ship approached they raised it again. The closest ship to the entrance was hit by round shot and sunk in flames. Two more ships snagged on it, rigging locking together, flames spreading. The fire ship then exploded, disabling all three ships. The harbour entrance at its narrowest was blocked with sunken debris. Risking more war ships with hostiles offshore would be unthinkable. The treasure fleet was safe, why risk depleting its protection further?

The Admiral was correct in his thinking. The Spanish were reluctant to risk more men-of-war. There were, however, other vessels under their command. The *patashe* and the *frigatta* amongst them, which he had overlooked. Small sailing galleys rowed by soldiers, not slaves. Fast, shallow draught and independent of wind.

On the dark deck of the Zeelander, a muffled grapnel fell with a quiet thud. It dragged across the planking seeking purchase, finally biting into the starboard rail. Another snagged the shrouds. Another, and another. Soon the deck was swarming with Spanish soldiers. The Admiral's crews, exhausted from the gruelling artillery duel, were at their rest. They were unprepared to defend against such an unexpected and ferocious boarding action. The ship's bell clanged vigorously. Crips poked his head out of the great cabin door to determine the cause. He leapt back, ashen faced, with news of the attack. The Grevinna rushed to the great cabin windows — first one side, then the other. Dozens of galleys were emerging from the dark and fastening themselves to the squadron. Spanish troops were scrambling aboard, more by the minute. Crewmen rushed to arm themselves.

The winds were strengthening, but management of the vessels was suddenly not a priority. Untended sails brought the ships up to the wind, flogging noisily over the clash of battle. Seas broke over the decks. Those off-watch raced from below to throw themselves into the fray. Pistols roared. Steel clashed on steel, sliced into flesh. Screams of anger, screams of pain. Desperate though they battled, the squadrons' crews were succumbing to sheer weight of numbers.

Cripps rushed to barricade the cabin doors, but the Grevinna stayed his hand.

'The crews need their Admiral.'

His Grace rose to his feet and reached for his mameluke, a treasured gift from Murat Reis, flicking off the scabbard. Grasping the silver-bound shagreen grip, he grimly fastened the leather strap about his wrist. The jewelled pommel and gold chased guard contrasted dramatically with the unembellished blade. Damascus steel, so many folds the acutely curved weapon was almost black. An ancient process lost to history. There was no time for armour. Its absence the Admiral regretted, more from the perspective of style than protection. The Grevinna tied back her long white gold hair. Pulled on fine black leather, pearl-studded gauntlets. She took a few practice cuts with her rapier.

Then slipped out her main gauche from the scabbard strapped to the white flesh of her thigh. A gleam came to her ice blue eyes. Like she was gazing into Valhalla and relishing the prospect of a glorious death. Li Sheng retreated to his quarters. He swept off his Mandarin cap, his pigtail springing from within like a startled mamba. Shrugging off his long gown, he stood bare chested in just breeches and rope sandals. With great solemnity he knotted a red silk sash around his waist. From a sea chest beneath his hammock he produced a heavy package. Carefully untying the red silk bindings, he reverentially opened the black cotton cloth. Inside, shining bright as a mirror, was a curved triangular blade of epic proportions — the legendary two-handed Chinese war sword. He hefted it, teasing out the long red tassel attached to the ring pommel. Testing the blade with a finger brought forth a bead of blood. Satisfied, he rolled his shoulders and rotated his head, flexing his back. Inhaling deeply, he invited the spirit of Lord Guan to possess him. Muscle rippled across his lean figure, coming alive like an awakening army. He muttered something in his heathen tongue — could have been a prayer, more likely a curse. Face as expressionless as a jade carving, he re-joined his master in the great cabin.

Contrasting with Sheng's composure, the Dyak was snarling like a feral dog, straining on the leash — taut skin trembling in a frenzy of anticipation. His short sword clamped in a hand blue with tattoos, commemorating the lives he'd taken. The diminutive Crips, bulldog-jawed, white of face, clutched a brace of duck's foot pistols.

They positioned themselves by the cabin entrance. The Admiral swept a strand of long white hair from his face and glanced down the line. Then he nodded to Crips who threw open the big double doors.

Stepping out onto the moonlit middle deck they faced the ensuing carnage. The Zeelander was awash with Spanish soldiers beating back the ill defended and unprepared crew. On seeing the Admiral's party they paused. Then there was a rush to scramble up the twin companionways.

Attack on two flanks. Easy pickings. The aristocratic old couple, their liveried servant, and two others that defied description. A goatee-bearded officer pushed through the crush of common soldiers. Li Sheng's blade arced through the air. The man took a step forward. Another step and then another, sword raised, a puzzled expression spreading across his face. Then the top of his torso detached from the lower, both tumbling to the deck in a fountain of blood. There were gasps of horror, then the Spanish rushed to the attack.

Crips pistols fired simultaneously taking out the whole front row. In a hurricane of glittering steel, the tiny Dyak set about detaching Spanish heads with astonishing rapidity. The Grevinna's rapier darted into the attacker's ranks like a sailmaker's needle. And the Admiral's mameluke sliced this way and that, liberating Spaniards from their limbs. More troops were piling up the companionway. Both sides knew with the Admiral out of play, the end would be inevitable. Similar scenes enacted throughout the squadron. Despite ferocious opposition, surprise and force of numbers was overwhelming the crew. The attackers steadily beat them back.

Brankfleet and his lightly armed gunners fought their way to one of their most mighty cannons. Holding off a ring of Spaniards with boarding pikes, they managed to load the beast. The cannon leapt back; its throat roared. Round shot arced across the sky to drop harmlessly into the dark sea a mile away. But striking the Spanish was not Brankfleet's intention. Not directly.

The muzzle flash cut through strengthening winds and darkening skies. The sound heard, albeit faintly, from the shore. Under full sail, Skyler's squadron burst out of the jungle-fringed shelter of Rio Almendares. In the distance through tempestuous seas the Admiral's squadron rolled dangerously, sails aback. Each ship tethered by smaller boats like harpooned whales. Closer to, they could pick out Spanish soldiers still swarming aboard. Battles raged across the decks, on the castles, in the rigging. Closer still, they caught the bitter crackle of small arms fire and the screams of the dying. Skyler led the charge in the African Prince. His five ships crashed into the Admiral's squadron in a chevron formation; smashing through the galleys; severing their umbilical ropes; crushing boarders between their hulls. It was Skyler's men who were now throwing grapnels. The ships slammed into each other, water gushing up between their hulls. Locked together, they spun like dance partners in a self-generated maelstrom.

Prior to the collision, Isaac charged his father with protecting Esther. The brothers hadn't come this far to lose their sister again. The outcome

1624

of this action was far from certain. Should the counterattack fail, he solemnly undertook to break off and sail the Rachael to Tortuga. With that comfort Isaac and Benjamin leapt onto the crowded blood-slick deck of the Zeelander. Benjamin flailed into the Spanish ranks with twin boarding axes, pistols in his belt, held in reserve. Isaac fired his weapon first, taking out a Spanish officer, transferring it to his left to act as a club. In his right hand a heavy short sword flashed with deadly purpose. As more of the squadron's men piled aboard, the battle began turning against the Spanish. They found themselves pushed to the rails, jumping overboard to swim for the wreckage of their galleys.

Exhausted, nursing cuts and bruises, the brothers clambered back to the Rachael. They found half-a-dozen Spanish soldiers besetting the Pastor. The Rabbi was taking his ease, casually leaning on the cabin door. His pistol was smoking, blood was dripping from his sword. The Pastor was providing a masterclass in Hindustani swordsmanship. He countered each attack, slashing adroitly with the flexible blade attached to his stump. And each time he did so there was one less combatant. The brothers joined the Rabbi in his leaning. Was the Pastor holding them at bay whilst the Rabbi reloaded, or just having fun? The remaining Spaniards had had enough. Scrambling to the rail they threw themselves into the white-capped sea.

Isaac knocked on the stateroom door, announcing himself. Hangbè answered, her signature weapon poised. Relief flooded her face. With that, his sister's last line of defence threw herself into his arms.

To be continued... (maybe)

1624

Printed in Great Britain
by Amazon